THE *Calling* OF CROWS

a paranormal historical novel

By

Julie Jones

The Calling of Crows: a paranormal historical novel

By: Julie Jones

Dedication

Take me home with you

Fold me in your arms

Let me wrap around your form

I promise to keep you warm!

To Jon Richards, my best friend and confidant, band mate and fellow songwriter, lover, life partner, and husband, with lasting and eternal love,
Forever, Julie

PROLOGUE

1864 New Albany, Indiana

Awinita shoved aside her long black hair as she scanned the surrounding establishment. She quickly twisted the straight strands into a single fat braid. She had arrived here in Indiana along with a couple hundred women and children. There had been four-hundred in the beginning, but that was a lifetime ago. Now there were half as many, maybe less. This town of New Albany was a bustling river town, and apparently their new home. For how long she did not know. She was a native of Roswell, Georgia, and she, along with all the others, had been accused of treason and forced to walk north to this land beyond the Ohio River. The townspeople stared as the threadbare women approached; The New Albany Ledger had predicted their arrival. Jealousy was plainly stamped on the faces of many of the local females who saw only competition. But there was also a ripple of compassion among the crowd that was nearly tangible. These were the quiet ones with the ability of putting themselves in another's place. Yet no one knew what to do with so many new residents, especially when they didn't even share the same allegiance. It was enough that they were poverty-stricken.

Awinita's quick mind flashed back to the beginning when they had piled into wagons at every opportunity. Occasionally on a whim, a selected few were swept atop a soldier's horse. The rest of the time they were forced to walk. Eventually they had been stuffed into trains of human cargo where infants wailed in the airless confines, and stomachs growled during the pathetically long stretches of enforced travel. Mothers wept when they could no longer produce milk. And no one was there to listen to their last breaths except for those like Awinita who held them in sorrowful silence.

Union General William Tecumseh Sherman was bent on demolishing the South. He had the mill workers arrested, and turned over to General Garrard, who immediately set fire to all three mills in the vicinity. He showed no mercy, nor compassion, but opted instead to celebrate the capture of Roswell. A ration of whiskey was distributed. The women were to set out on foot with only the clothes on their backs, and what few possessions they could carry. Half of them would be dead before they reached Indiana.

Awinita thought of all those lost along the way. Many were too weak to have made this trip from the start. They never stood a chance. No one cared there were several new mothers, still weak from childbirth. There was no sympathy for the young widows struggling to make a new life for themselves, yet alone for those who had lost entire families. They were lost souls before they even began this arduous journey. While all were hungry, many were literally starving to the point of emaciation leaving Infants in need of wet nurses. The South was ravaged by a war that had gone on for four brutal years. And this was the outcome for a large band of women and children who had done nothing more than struggle to put food on the table.

Awinita was perhaps stronger than most. She was half Native American, and had spent a number of her years with her Cherokee mother. She possessed the knowledge of the land, and was able to hide her own discomfort. Her opaque dark eyes gave nothing away. She held herself erect even when she was tired. Her high cheekbones suggested a proud heritage, and while several of the men lusted after her, they often backed down in favor of easier game. Awinita held up under the weight of travel. She quietly endured the nagging pain that twisted at her gut, often sharing her portion of rations with another in need. The other women naturally liked her, for Awinita was both kind and brave. She helped out whenever possible. She had become invaluable.

And then one day they were led into the countryside. The sun had not yet kissed the sky when they had been herded like cattle and forced to walk deep into the woods. Women sobbed as babies were torn from their arms. Children screamed for their mamas, their cries lost in the noise of gunfire. Horses snorted and stamped. Dust flew. It was hours before the sounds died down, and Awinita, like the others, found herself trussed up in the back of a wagon. Later, after days of rough travel, Awinita was dumped to the ground. The sun was in her eyes, and a circle of male faces peered down upon her. Their voices penetrated her shock as she realized what was happening. Above, a group of magpies gathered. The leader of the bunch descended upon her, its cries vicious. For the first time Awinita hid her face.

PART ONE

White Fawn

CHAPTER ONE
1970, Yountsville, Indiana

Amara lived alone on her grandfather's small farm. At one-hundred and sixty acres, it gave her a great deal of freedom. Her grandfather had purchased the land in the 1930's, and Amara couldn't remember a time when it had not been an enormous part of her life. James Asher Owens had been a strong man. A recluse, he was both friend and family to Amara, and she had lost him the winter before last. He had passed away so suddenly she had been unable to get him to the hospital. He had taken his last breath while she sat beside him, awaiting the ambulance. They told her later he had contracted pneumonia, yet he had never uttered a complaint. And now even with the constant companionship of Grim, her black shepherd, and her other two comedic house pets, she was still unused to the silence.

Sampson, who was four-years-old and the same age as Grim, was a Maine coon cat and quite large at twenty-six pounds. Solomon was a Maltese pup, and weighed only nine pounds. He was now fully grown at one year of age. Both were male, both had long white coats. Sampson's fur was adorned with soft patches of butterscotch while Solomon's was as pure as snow. Sampson and Grim had shared in the responsibility of raising Solomon. Sampson behaved like a combination of mother and big brother. He simultaneously checked on Solomon, and then included him in playtime. Grim behaved as a father figure to both the smaller animals going so far as to carry Solomon around in his mouth when he was newly born. Amara sincerely considered Grim the head of the house.

Grandfather had left her enough money to live on if she used it wisely. And he had trained her well. On her sixteenth birthday he had given her a Buick that was built to last. On her eighteenth, she had won a scholarship, and he had proudly packed her off to the college of her choice. She had elected to stay close to home. On her twenty-first birthday, he had presented her with the deed to the house and property, "Just in case", he said. He was in perfect health as far as she knew. He just wanted to secure her financial future. Everything was in order; she had only to keep up the taxes each year.

Amara lived in the house he had built. It was a sturdy home with cedar closets and linoleum floors. The walls were knotty pine making it easy to clean. Amara had her own room at the end of the hall opposite the one her mother had occupied with a small sewing niche in between. Grim slept at her side; always. Her grandfather had slept in the den down the hall on the other side of the large bath. Aside from the vast front room, there was a warm kitchen complete with dining nook, and a root cellar below the enclosed back porch. Both Sampson and Solomon slept in the kitchen.

Amara grew her own food. She had kept the immense garden she had shared with her grandfather where she raised everything in abundance. She worked hard to preserve enough for winter. She cooked and canned tomato salsa, and her own fragrant sauces. She pickled a variety of vegetables to be served as entrees. She put up jams and other fruits. And she stocked the root cellar with every possible food source including a bulk of potatoes and onions. Beets, carrots, turnips, squash, and radishes were plentiful enough to last the season.

Amara spent many an evening shelling peas, breaking bens, shucking corn, and preparing produce for the massive top-loading freezer that sat on the back porch next to the cellar door. She preferred frozen foods over canned in the winter, but the main thing was to keep a substantial quantity to eliminate worries. If she lost, or ran out of one substance, there was always another. She enjoyed creating meal packages such as fajita mixes and specialty dishes that could go from the freezer to the oven. She cooked up substantial batches of borscht and other homemade soups and stews for those cold days ahead. She made mixed vegetables in such forms as to be unique, and experimented with recipes throughout the year. She was a good cook, and an intelligent one, capable of replacing one ingredient with another at any point in time.

At summers end, Amara dried the wide selection from her herbary, storing them in a cool section of the pantry. Each jar or bundle was labeled and dated in her neat handwriting, and the variety would season pretty much anything she chose to cook. They also provided a wide range of tinctures as Amara had cultivated the art of medicinal herbs from a young age. She owned a stand at the front of the property that she stocked fresh each day. The cash from her sales supplied any groceries she could not create herself. She remained open from spring to fall and sold everything from fresh foods to baked goods. She allotted specific hours to this task unless someone wished to buy in bulk. Winter sales were by appointment only. This freed her up for all her other activities. The greenhouse took a great deal of time during the cold months when the garden was no longer producing. And the barns required constant upkeep, just as the animals needed tremendous care. Her pets were her closest companions, and she refused to cut her time with them short. They made life fun, gave it purpose. The animals and the land, they were the sources of her pleasure.

Of course, Amara had human friends too. But she was ever cautious about letting anyone too close. "One couldn't be too careful," Grandfather had warned. And Grandfather had taught her well. He was friendly enough to those who had earned it, and kept a shotgun at the ready for those who hadn't. He taught her to shoot at an early age. She had a healthy respect for firearms of any kind, and owned a revolver as well as a shotgun. She had a permit to carry and was frequently armed. Even though it was a small farm, folks knew she lived alone. Word of mouth spread like wildfire in these parts. She expected it was like that everywhere. It was necessary to be self-reliant.

Amara was now twenty-six years old, and her close friends knew her to be both calm and capable. Still, they checked on her as frequently as they felt she would allow. Not that Amara had ever tossed any of them out! No, she was the perfect hostess. They simply held her in high regard. Amara was a private person. She had chosen a life far different from the bulk of the populace. Maybe that was what they admired most about her? Even in college she had never truly fit in. She was far more serious than the other kids, and seldom attended a party of any kind. It was obvious she preferred her books to loud crowds any day. While the rest of them stayed out late and got high, Amara studied, attended Native American powwows, and explored the nearby caves and forests of her home state. She seemed intent on soaking up every scrap of history and culture that she could uncover. She was an interesting person and loyal friend, and anyone who came to know her well considered it an honor.

Amara dated sparingly. It wasn't that she lacked interest. It was just that she had more important things to do. Her friends often commented among themselves that it seemed as if she was waiting for one particular guy. All the boys followed after her, their eyes filled with unabashed fascination. After all, she was a beauty with her wealth of black curls that fell all the way to the small of her back. She had dark eyes that held a peculiar glow like she knew something no one else did. And her features were well sculpted with high cheek bones, a straight, slim nose and full wide mouth. Her lips had a habit of turning up in a perpetual smile regardless of what she was about. In short, Amara was tantalizing, all the more so because she appeared unaware of her looks. Unlike the majority of college girls of the day, Amara's poses were not practiced. She moved with a fluid grace all her own, and her expressions reflected only honest emotion.

Amara finished her morning ritual, and after caring for both Sam and Solomon, left the house at a leisurely pace. Grim tagged after her, never straying from her side. He was on guard around the clock, and was so intensely loyal that Amara never feared for her safety. Grim was already a large dog, and with his shaggy coat, he appeared even more so. He could go from playful pup to deadly guard in a fraction of a second. Amara kept her handgun tucked into the waistband of her jeans for further insurance, however, because she loved her dog so much she would never put him at risk. She knew that if they were ever attacked, he would fight to the death, and she could not bear the thought. She ran her hand down his smooth head, giving him a loving pat. Grim shot her a look of pure adoration.

They had nearly reached the machinery barn when a crow flew overhead. It called loudly, "Caw! Caw!" and the

sound reverberated in the trees. The crow flew directly at her and dropped a shiny object at her feet. Amara smiled the wide smile that turned so many heads. It was a brilliant smile, one that transformed her from a mere beauty to a goddess-like creature. The crow's bright eyes came alive as she spilled a path of seeds in her wake. The bird swooped to snatch the seeds even as Amara bent to lift the object in question. "Why, Crow!" she cried happily, "You've brought me such a beautiful coin, I shall have to make a necklace of it!" She fingered the penny, noting that it was quite old. It was, in fact, an 1864 Indian Head penny! Crow puffed out his chest, gathered the last of the seed, and with his eyes aglow, took flight once again. Woman and dog stared after the bird who had become such a faithful friend.

The machinery barn was the same size as the cattle barn. They were both painted the same creamy shade of off-white. The doors were adorned with black hardware. It looked pristine for a structure of this nature, and housed all the gardening tools from hand shovel, to rake, to plow, and everything in between. All that Amara would need to manage the small farm was kept in here, and she was capable of doing most of it herself. "Come on out, Karma!" her voice rang out. "It's me!" A rustling sound had begun in the rear of the barn, and as she glanced that way, a tiny ball of fur streaked across the vast space landing square in her arms! The ball of fur was a baby raccoon no more than a few weeks old. She had already produced the still-warm bottle of milk from the pouch she carried over her shoulder. She slid to the floor in one smooth motion, folding her legs under her as she fed the baby coon. Karma followed Amara everywhere during the daylight hours. It was only at night, or when she couldn't watch her, that she kept the baby separated from the others. When Karma was old enough to hold her own, she would set her free. But for now, she needed a protector. While Karma polished off the bottle, Amara realized she had been absently humming beneath her breath. It was a song that had been in her head all morning, but she had no idea what it was. It was so completely unfamiliar that she wondered if she had dreamed it. Amara shook her head to clear it, and climbed to her feet. She wore soft knee-high moccasins with her cut-off jeans.

The trio left the machinery barn behind with Karma chasing happily after Grim, who in spite of his great size was incredibly gentle with her. As Amara led the way to the cattle barn, the song continued to echo in her head. It was so clear she could almost make out the words. The cows had gathered beneath the window of the loft where they were lowing piteously. Though they were not particularly intelligent creatures, Amara felt sorry for them. After all, they knew nothing of life except their own basic needs, and those she cared for gladly. The cattle belonged to a farmer who paid her well to feed and keep them. He hadn't enough land for the extra dozen head. Amara didn't mind. Cows, like most animals, never forgot a kindness. And the income was worth the time spent. She liked the man well enough. He would come and help her out when things got too hectic, or she was unable to handle a task alone. And he always checked on her when a truly bad storm was brewing, making sure she was safe. The only problem she had with Tanner Lake was that lately she had noticed an increased interest in her personally.

Tanner was divorced, and had been living alone for some time now. She was content when they struck their business deal, but he'd been married then. He was her closest neighbor, and several years her senior. He had known her grandfather, and she had grown up around him. She had become comfortable with his visits. But now he was single, and she, a grown woman. And she had caught him looking at her in an entirely different manner. She was very much aware of his scrutiny, and could almost read his thoughts. Now she was careful to keep a discreet distance between them. Still, she felt uneasy.

While Amara agilely scaled the loft, allowing her mind to wander, Karma climbed alongside her. They now spoke from across a mountain of hay. Amara answered the small animal in kind. When she mimicked the coon's voice, Karma reacted with apparent glee. It was as if the tiny creature understood her every syllable. Amara was grateful she had gathered the eggs first thing that morning. It was one more job behind her, and easier to accomplish without Karma teasing the chickens. Amara didn't use very many. She was a lifelong vegetarian, cutting out meats completely except for the occasional egg. She loved cheeses and adored real butter, but used milk only for cooking. She never could stand the stuff as a beverage.

As she tossed the last bale of hay to the cattle below, she dusted off her clothes and turned toward the ladder. Grim had begun to bark. The horses stamped nervously beneath her, and Grim growled low in his throat. He barked sharply once again, and Amara gasped when she spied Tanner standing there by the ladder, blocking her descent. He looked tense, but in control, his long body coiled like a snake about to spring. He was watching her, an odd look in his eyes. She was conscious of the way that she was dressed when she saw how his eyes followed her every move. Why hadn't he called out to her? Amara straightened her spine and stood tall and lithe in the July heat. She wore a red plaid crop top with her blue jean shorts. Her moccasins were perfect for any weather and were incredibly comfortable. She had several pairs and sported a red pair of knee-highs today. Tanner cleared his throat when he realized he had been caught staring. His Adam's apple bobbed up and down, and he shifted his gaze. He mumbled an apology and the tension of the moment was broken.

Amara felt like she had awakened from a bad dream. There had been something different, something truly threatening about him today. He claimed he hadn't meant to startle her, yet he had remained deliberately still. She was keenly aware of the way her body quivered. She had a sick feeling in her gut as she tucked her hands behind her back so he wouldn't see how badly they were shaking. "I've got to go tend the horses," she murmured. When she poured dry food for the cats, a group of little faces popped out of hiding. But they didn't move. They didn't even blink. They remained perfectly still, their eyes wide. Ordinarily they would have been in the midst of things. Today was the exception. They remained silent even as Amara slid past Tanner and swiftly descended the ladder. Karma rode her shoulder, but even the baby coon was reserved. Grim met her with a protective look, and they moved as one to groom and feed the horses.

That evening after the chores were done, Amara fixed a simple meal of pinto beans and corn tortillas. She had a green salad on the side with some of her own homemade dressing, and a fresh glass of lemon water. Afterwards she washed the few dishes and put them away, and then poured herself a glass of cabernet. She had already fed Sampson and Solomon, and laughed at their antics as they romped together in the big front room. With Grim as her sole companion, Amara went outside to sit quietly in the woods behind the house. They listened to the night sounds as they enjoyed the refreshing breeze that carried across the water. Rock River, as Amara knew it, was Indiana's Sugar Creek. She preferred the old name, but didn't know why. Maybe, she thought, because even though she had no blood ties on this earth, it was what her ancestors had once called it. All of her family history came from her grandfather, and the dim memories of her mother. Whatever the reason, it was a beautiful setting and she was grateful for it.

Maybe, she thought, because even though she had no blood ties on this earth, it was what her ancestors had once called it. All of her family history came from her grandfather, and the dim memories of her mother. Whatever the reason, it was a beautiful setting and she was grateful for it.

As she breathed in the scent of honeysuckle, she noticed a shift in her awareness. There was something out here in the woods. She took a sip of the dry, red wine. She held no fear, but instead knew a wealth of curiosity. She glanced up at a slight movement, and to her astonishment, there directly ahead of her stood a perfectly poised fawn. What separated it from other fawns, and made it so utterly unique, was that this gorgeous animal was white; pure white. Amara had never seen a white fawn before. But she knew without a shadow of a doubt, this one was magical.

CHAPTER TWO

1970, Yountsville, Indiana

Amara was wading in the brook at the back of the farm. Her black hair gleamed in the stark sunlight, only it was straight rather than full of its usual curl. The stream was identical to the one she walked every day of her life. It was the surrounding woods that were different. They looked as if someone had picked up the ribbon of clear liquid and plopped it down in a new location. The wind sighed, and the waters rippled. Amara cocked her head, paying attention to the slightly altered sounds that filled her consciousness. She swerved suddenly, spearing a large fish as it shot past. The waters turned red as she stooped to pull the animal free of the arrowhead in her hand. She dropped the still-wriggling fish into her pail and turned toward shore. "I caught dinner, unitsi!" she called to the slight figure awaiting her. Her mother looked upon her with pride, only it was not her mother as she remembered her. The face looked familiar, however, and as Amara struggled with her confusion a great magpie swept down from the sky. It shrieked, and the waters roiled violently until they became a great wave that washed her mother away! Amara tried to go after her, but it was too late. Her mother was gone in a flash. Amara covered her face and wept.

Amara sat up in bed, her riotous curls tumbling freely down her back and shoulders. She wiped the tears from her lashes as Grim poked his long nose in her face. "I'm okay, Grim," she whispered, her voice husky. "It was just a dream." As she spoke she hugged the thick neck, wanting to cling to him a moment longer. She found the nightmare deeply disturbing.

Amara's memory of her mother was distant, but she knew one thing for certain. And that was the woman on shore was not the one she recalled from her faded youth. Amara's mother had died in a fatal accident when she was just a little girl. Amara remembered the horrible day when her grandfather sat her down and told her what had happened. She had gone into her shell for a good long time refusing to speak to anyone, even Grandfather. Somehow she had thought that if she kept quiet, her mother might magically reappear. But she never did, and gradually Amara came to accept that she was gone forever.

Grandfather had been patient with her. He gave her all the time in the world to come to terms with this harsh new reality. After a while she realized that Grandfather was having difficulty with his own loss. Her mother was an only child, after all, and he had raised her as a single parent. Losing Alina must have been like losing a part of his soul, she thought. Indeed her very name signified *Light* which in turn translated into *Soul*. They had been close, the two of them. And when Alina found herself with child, it was her father to whom she turned. They would raise Amara together. At least that had been the plan. Amara's own name meant *Eternal*. And she knew with moral certainty that her mother would always walk beside her in this life.

Amara was only six years old at the time of her mother's death. But she remembered watching the same news cast over and over again. It was as if she continued to watch, she might somehow make sense of her loss. But she never did. To this day she could still recite the headline of the regional newspaper: Local Woman Drowns in Ohio River. The reporter had gone on to explain that the female driver, Alina Owens, had lost control of her car. The accident had happened out on River Road. The cause of the accident was undetermined. Later, she overheard a conversation between her grandfather and an officer of the law. The officer said in a queer voice that the only thing found at the scene of the accident was a mess of black feathers at the juncture where the skid marks left the road.

"Black feathers?" her grandfather had queried.

"Yes, black feathers," replied the officer, "and lots of them. Looked like magpie feathers to me."

Alina was an antiquarian as well as a knowledgeable historian. She taught school throughout the season, spending her summers buying and selling antiques. She made numerous trips into Kentucky stopping at various towns along the way. She had an obsession with the Culbertson Mansion in New Albany, Indiana, and visited frequently just as she did many of the historical homes along the way. She knew them all, and often took young Amara with her.

The pair would delight in viewing the sights, making numerous purchases, and staying in a different motel every night. She always chose the ones with a swimming pool who served a complimentary continental breakfast. Amara loved this part of the trip! The mother-daughter team would then set up a booth in whatever promising Antique Show Alina had booked, after which they would go for a swim, later ordering room service for dinner. Amara loved to try new foods, and

Alina always seemed to know what her daughter would most enjoy. They spent the remainder of their evenings watching late movies or swapping ghost stories until Amara fell asleep.

When the show was over, Alina would pack up the remains of her booth along with any new purchases, and set out on the long journey home. There were all kinds of recreational stops along the way. They would take side trips to tour old houses, caves, and parks, and Alina would regale her daughter with stories about the Culbertson Mansion, careful to keep them interesting without terrifying the small girl. But Amara knew the place was haunted. It gave her chills at times, yet she put on a brave front. These trips were priceless to her. Besides, she sensed her mother was frightened as well. Funny how you could be both terrified and fascinated all at once!

Alina made it a habit to share detailed information on every antique she purchased so that Amara knew exactly what each item was worth. She explained how each one carried with it the vibrations and energies of its former owner. "This is called psychometry," she told the young Amara. Amara was enraptured by this new phenomenon, and the pair spent hours holding individual objects and discussing the emotions they experienced. If a piece felt uncomfortable, cloudy, or in any way negative, they cleansed it accordingly. Alina seemed to know everything! It made Amara's eyes shine with pride.

Sometimes Amara would fall in love with a particular piece of jewelry or other personal object, and Alina would declare she was the intended recipient, and therefore it must be hers. Such was the case with an antique necklace from the Victorian era. It was a perfectly shaped fire opal pendant. When it caught the sunlight, the smooth round stone came alive with brilliant color. Alina told her the stone was primarily for protection, and that it would absorb and transform negative energy. She went on to say that it would aid the development of personal strength and stamina, particularly in times of stress or grief.

As Amara was by then approaching her sixth birthday, Alina decreed this pendant to be her rightful gift. She placed the intricate chain around her daughter's neck and proudly fastened it. Amara fingered the pendant in awe as she gazed at her image in the mirror. She caught her mother's liquid gaze staring back at her, and for just a moment, felt as if she might burst into tears. But Alina flashed a bright smile, quickly dispersing her sorrow. The resemblance between mother and daughter was uncanny. Amara was truly a tiny replica of the other, and proud of it. She hoped to be exactly like her mother when she grew up. To this day Amara wore the necklace proudly. She never removed it. It was her most treasured possession.

As Amara's thoughts resurfaced in the present she heard her mother's voice whisper, *"You are Cherokee. You carry the blood of the people. You must hold yourself in high esteem."* Amara automatically straightened her shoulders. Her eyes gleamed in the morning light, and she thought of the vision of the night before. What had it meant? And why had her mother looked like someone else? In an odd way she realized she recognized the other woman, but she did not know how. She associated her with a relative, yet she had little knowledge of her ancestors. Her mother and grandfather were the only family she had ever known! And Grandfather had assured her on several occasions that they were the last of their line. There were stories of their lineage, of course, but they had been passed down vocally. There were no written records that she was aware of. Amara knew a deep sense of remorse.

Her mind skimmed back over the dream. She had been in the stream that opened into the creek. She was fishing, and proud that she had caught dinner for her mother and herself. She had the strong impression there were only the two of them, that they were alone in the world. Her lips turned down at the overwhelming odor of fish. It was so strong that she could actually taste it. She hated seafood. Absolutely despised it! She was allergic to many kinds of seafood, and somehow the thought of it made her ill. Now she wondered if there was more to her dislike than she knew. While she pondered this, she recalled how her mother was carried away in a sudden tide. The same could be said of her real mother, for Alina's car had gone off the road into the Ohio where it was pulled down river. Was this some kind of parallel where the mother in the dream drowned in a sudden tidal wave, while Alina drowned in the Ohio trapped within her own vehicle? Amara didn't know the answer to this, but she recognized that she called the woman in the dream *unitsi,* and without knowing how, Amara realized the word meant *mother.*

Another memory surfaced. Grandfather had come in from outdoors one day shortly before he took ill. He had a magpie feather clinging to him, and he hurriedly brushed it away. He carried it outside without handling it, and smudged the house immediately. Amara was familiar with the practice of smudging, and would probably have let it go without asking except that Grandfather also had several deep gouges on his arm where the skin was exposed to the sun and air.

"You were attacked, weren't you?" she cried out.

He didn't answer at first, and somehow that made it all the more ominous. Finally, seeing that his granddaughter was distraught, he admitted the truth, "Yes," he said succinctly. "Magpies carry grudges. And for some reason they do not like our family. It has always been so. You must be ever leery of them. Feed the crows, and make friends with them. They will watch out for you."

Grandfather had passed away within a week. Amara respected his request, and set out to befriend the crows. She fed them on a daily basis every morning after breakfast. But first she fed Sampson and Solomon who were busily tumbling one over the other. She let Solomon out to relieve himself, and then carried him back inside, plopping him down before his bowl. The little guy wolfed his food down while Sampson nibbled sparingly, all the while glancing at Solomon with a look that said, *"You'll be hungry later!"*

Sampson raised his regal head with a grace that displayed extreme pleasure. Solomon woofed and Sam stretched languidly. This action caused the small pup to wiggle uncontrollably. Sampson yawned as though bored, and Solomon did the puppy crawl. He stuck his little bottom in the air, and took his time arching his back like a cat. Amara couldn't help herself, she actually giggled. Grim ducked his big head as if to hide a wolfish grin. He would have succeeded too except that his bushy tail gave it away as it thumped hard against the floor. Amara laughed out loud.

Amara set her own breakfast out and turned on the kettle, after which she filled Grim's bowl with dry food. He was ever patient. Grim had the personality to put his mistress first. He was confident of Amara's love and loyalty to him, and was accepting of the antics of others. Sampson and Solomon were babies, his actions seemed to say. He was protective of them, and helped Sam watch after the tiny pup. Sam was big for a cat, but even at twenty-six pounds, he was still a member of the feline family.

Grim glanced at his mistress as he went to his bowl. She seated herself, having poured a fragrant cup of rosehip tea, and took a cautious sip. The hot liquid was delicious making her stomach growl. Hurriedly, she opened the parcel of homemade bread she had laid on the table. It was Boston Brown bread, a personal favorite. She smiled faintly as she

sniffed the combination of corn, rye, and molasses, and then took a hearty bite before opening the tub of yogurt she had made a couple days ago. It was a simple breakfast, yet healthy and filling. She liked it that way.

It took only minutes to wipe the table clean. As Grim followed her out the door, she reached out to give Sampson a loving pat, and scooped Solomon up for a close hug. Solly wriggled and kissed her nose before she deposited him at Sam's side. "Watch after each other," she ordered softly. Solomon only grinned at her, but Sampson gave a superior wink in her direction.

As woman and dog strode toward the woods, Amara scattered a trail of crumbs in their wake. Moments later the calling of crows could be heard throughout the valley. It followed her into the woods.

The eggs had been gathered, the barn work was done. The horses had been exercised, and baby Karma had been fed. Grim accompanied Amara for a quick dip in the creek while keeping a watchful eye on the tiny coon. Karma chattered happily while Amara slipped easily under the current. She kept her eye out for any activity on the opposite shore. She listened for canoes or humans on the creek or path. She knew the land like the back of her hand, and she knew how to get around stoically. Still Grim was an excellent guard, and it was good to feel safe.

She barely disturbed the stillness of the pool when she climbed out wearing nothing more than a tiny pair of hot pink panties. She slipped into her clothes incredibly fast, taking in the old abandoned mill across the way. She cast a glance at the Yountville Bridge where the local teens liked to party. Grandfather had taught her to respect the woods enough to clean up after those who littered the earth. Her mother had taught her to move silently through the brush and to swim like a fish. She had a great reverence for the wild; for the trees, shrubs, and animals. She believed she was closest to God in the woods. She felt humbled when she knelt in prayer, especially when on the mound. And she always left an offering.

Amara did not look down on others for attending church, but crowded places made her feel confined. Even in the cold of winter she sought out the woods when she spoke to God. And she spoke to God often. She knew much of the culture passed down from her Native American heritage, just as she knew that of the Caucasian part of her. She was at peace with the combination, and set her own path. Amara was an animist. She walked with the angels, and loved them dearly.

They set out for the garden at a comfortable pace. There was still much to be done before the day was over. Tomorrow was Saturday, and she always had a major sale the day before the Sabbath. Folks came from miles around for her produce and baked goods. She had loaves to prepare, and smudge sticks to bundle. Yes, tomorrow would be a busy day. But it should be a profitable one, she thought, as she padded through the warm sand gathering water reeds as she went. There were so many uses for these beautifully versatile stems! She found the garden overflowing in its abundance, and reveled in her crops for a time. She was halfway finished before she knew it, and set about loading the small wagon. She was hungry, and had left a meal cooking in the crock pot.

By now her mind was on the hearty mix of fresh veg-etables bubbling slowly in a tomato based broth. She had a wedge of baby Swiss cheese to enjoy along with it, as well as a watercress salad. Her stomach rumbled at the thought. She brushed the hair from her eyes, and squared her shoulders. The sooner she finished, the sooner she could eat. Amara realized her body was like a well-oiled machine; she took care to eat right, exercise, and get plenty of rest. Unlike most females, she knew how to shut off her mind and fall into an instant sleep. This was necessary to keep things running smoothly.

Amara added a handful of marigolds to the profusion of vegetables in the wagon, careful to leave plenty of the pungent orange flowers to repel garden insects. Her marigolds were a blessing. She glanced back over her inventory before climbing onto the small tractor which would navigate the overly laden wagon to the house. She had separated the items she had decided to keep, and now paused to carry her vegetables indoors along with the flowers and reeds. The little ones met her with enthusiasm. They romped for a few minutes before she made a game of carrying everything inside. The animals trooped along after her, leaving dusty paw prints in their wake. Tails wagged, thumped, and streaked across the porch. Karma remained with the wagon where she scurried about entertaining herself, while Amara placed the flowers in a vase, set the vegetables on the kitchen counter, and spent time with her domesticated babies. They were eager for attention, and she was equally happy to comply.

After they had calmed a bit, she returned to the wagon where she made sure Karma had plenty of food. She was a smart little thing. She was growing rapidly, and eagerly accepted the bounty Amara provided. The little coon would not need a bottle much longer. Already she was spending more and more time on her own in the woods. She was learning to fend for herself. The bottle was really just a comfort now, no longer a necessity. Amara went in to eat her lunch, and Karma called happily after her. Amara flashed a smile.

With Grim at her side, Amara spent the afternoon

stocking the mudroom behind the stall near the highway. She cleaned the produce, gently making sure to pat it dry, and locked the door behind her. She had a long evening ahead of her. She would let Karma continue to play in the woods around the house where she was able to look out for her. She kept plenty of food and water for strays. Occasionally the barn cats made it over this far, and were grateful for a bite as well. They were a lively bunch, and knew they were safe around the house and grounds.

Amara was heading back up the winding gravel road when she heard a passel of crows. They were communicating loudly when one separated from the group and flew in her direction. "Why, hello Crow!" she called brightly. Crow dove and dropped a piece of what felt like curled plastic at her feet. "Thank you, Crow!" she responded, then reached into her pocket and left a trail of seeds in her wake. She heard Crow's eager response even as she frowned at the piece of plastic. "What the heck," she muttered.

What she held in her hand was a portion of a negative. She knew this because she had taken enough photography classes for it to become a common sight. That in itself was innocent enough. Except that she rarely did photography work, and was fanatical about cleaning up as she went. Of course, one of her friends could have taken some photos at any given time. But they wouldn't have left any litter behind. No, it was the feeling she got when she handled the object that disturbed her. Her whole body quivered as queasiness washed over her. Her stomach muscles tightened at a memory of her mother demonstrating the science of psychometry. Amara reluctantly put the *gift* in her pocket for later inspection. Why did this disturb her so much? That was the question.

CHAPTER THREE

That evening, after indulging in a hearty mushroom pizza for dinner, Amara relaxed with a glass of her favorite cabernet. She sat quietly with Grim in the wooded backyard and listened to the wildlife. It was a noisy night, but a pleasant one. She kept her eye on Karma, who was busily scampering up and down a particular tree she fancied, while casting an occasional glance at the oversized picture window where Sampson could be seen avidly bathing himself. She grinned when she caught sight of Solomon hopping up and down as if to join him on the sill. Grim raised his big head and looked at her with what appeared to be parental pride, and Amara truly felt her heart skip a beat. She enjoyed these quiet moments with Grim. The sounds and scents of the woodland filled every fiber of her being, and she marveled at how anyone could ever live in town. It would be like living in a cardboard box! That thought alone literally made her cringe. Her location was such that she could be in town rather quickly when necessary, yet she had all the space in the world to call her own. Life was good in the wilds. The closest neighbor was four miles away. Not so far when needed, but definitely not close enough to be a bother. She enjoyed the solitude.

People often asked if she was lonely out here, or perhaps afraid. She thought those peculiar questions. How could she be lonely? She was perfectly capable of taking care of herself. No, she didn't scare easily, but people bothered her more than anything else in the world, and that was because they were so darned unpredictable. That was why she had studied astrology, to help her understand human nature. She loved reading psychology as well, especially Jungian psychology. Carl Jung was the most fascinating psychiatrist and psychoanalyst she had ever come across. He had founded analytical psychology. *"Who looks outside, dreams; who looks inside, awakes."* That was magnificent insight, Amara thought. The human mind was fascinating. But she never wanted to live in a closely knit group of people. She was definitely a country girl. She sighed when she finished her wine, knowing it was time to get busy. Grim sighed along with her. She laughed softly as she nimbly gained her feet. She had a lot to do this evening. Karma trilled from the top of her tree. Amara wished her a good night as she stepped inside. Grim followed suit. The big dog was fond of the baby coon.

Amara set out for the kitchen to get started on her bread baking. She sprinkled yeast in warm water and set it aside while gathering the necessary flour, oil, and salt. She was making her traditional whole wheat bread that was so loved in these parts, along with her own favorite sourdough bread. The whole wheat bread contained wheat germ, which according to Adelle Davis was the healthiest part of the wheat. The formula was sweetened with a small amount of nutritional honey. Amara had great appreciation for bees. Her recipe was an old one, and was very well received. She had found it in a rather ancient soul food cookbook. The sourdough recipe required a starter which she made from potatoes. This, she fed on a daily basis. One had to be dil-

igent, or fail altogether. But in Amara's mind, bread truly wasn't difficult to make. It simply took a little time and patience, and a lot of folks didn't have either.

As the honey wheat bread took longer to make, Amara made a double batch before starting on the other. Her loaves were on the second rise when she popped the first load of sourdough into the oven. She was grateful Grandfather had provided her with a mammoth hearth and an extra wide stove with full baking capacity so that she could work multiple loaves at once. She had brushed the tops with fresh creamery butter before loading the oven, and set the timer before punching down each loaf of wheat bread in turn. The first batch of sour dough was out of the oven when the wheat bread was on its final rise. She brushed the tops of the hot loaves once more when taking them from the oven, and loaded the second batch. Once this was accomplished, the wheat bread would be ready to bake.

Everything was running smoothly, and Amara knew a moment of satisfaction, when all of a sudden Sampson decided to jump atop the counter and lend a helping hand. She was momentarily horrified as Sam was usually so well behaved. Yet he saw an opening and took it. She scolded lightly knowing he just wanted some attention. And that's when Solomon looked up with an ornery grin. Grim glanced from one to the other, and took both little ones in hand. Amara shook her head wondering what he said to them. Well, whatever it was, it worked. They followed him to the kitchen door and settled down to watch.

Amara hid a smile and went to put on a record. She kept a small stereo in the kitchen because she was in here so much of the time. She had a jumbo unit in the front room, but many of her favorite albums were stored in the kitchen pantry. The little ones laid their heads down almost immediately. Amara dimpled when she exchanged glances with Grim who yawned widely and lowered his head. Amara decided that yawn said, *"My work here is done."* By now, the last load of bread was almost ready to come out of the oven. She could load almost twice as many wheat loaves in their neat rectangular pans as opposed to the oversized round slabs of sour dough. The kitchen smelled like a dream.

The song *Lay Lady Lay* came on the stereo, and Amara's mind skipped backward to her college days and the enormous crush she had had on her English-Lit professor. He had dark hair with long sideburns, and the most unsettling eyes she had ever seen. They were so mysterious that Amara sometimes wondered what she saw in his obviously well pumped ego. She grimaced as she recalled what a jerk he had turned out to be. The guy literally kept a scrapbook of all the college seniors he had nailed. She had come across them right after an intimate dinner when she slipped upstairs to freshen up. She had stripped down to bra and panty, and was awkward in her nervousness. The scrapbook was sitting on a nearby table beside the door. She'd had an extra glass of wine with dinner. When she bumped the corner of the table, a few loose photos fell softly to the floor. One was face up. Amara had been heartbroken at her discovery. When she recognized a fellow student, she dropped to her knees to examine the painful proof. And like a fool, turned the others over one by one. Every single picture was of a nude classmate! When Amara stood slowly to her feet, she burned with a newfound fury. The professor got a lesson he would never forget. And Amara wore a new coat of armor. The timer on the oven shrieked, gaining a remorseful look from both Grim and Solomon. She hurriedly turned it off and unloaded the oven, shaking off the memories as she did so. She was glad she had not become a part of *his* collection. But until that time, Amara had not realized the depth of her own temper.

The hour was late. Amara picked up, wiped up, and

swept up the entire kitchen while the loaves cooled. She had covered them with soft linen cloths in case Sam got any more ideas. All the dishes were washed and put away. It was time to make the sage bundles, and bag up the sprouts. These were pleasant tasks that Amara could enjoy along with a second glass of wine. She put on her favorite Beatles album, *Rubber Soul*, and poured the wine into a crystal goblet. As the bread was warm, she kept a loaf for herself and cut a thick slice. She had a round of fresh Gouda that she added to the arrangement to compliment the wine. She carried the items to the table where the sage was waiting in several neat stacks.

There was plenty of twine as well as a pair of scissors along with a box of sandwich bags, and two giant sized jars of sprouts. Amara stretched and yawned before taking her seat. Grim looked up to check on her, and both the little ones did the same. She loved her animal babies. They were the best company. She fell into the music as she took care of the sprouts. This was the simplest of chores. All she had to do was divide the alfalfa sprouts into several even bags, and then repeat the process with the mung sprouts. She accomplished this quickly enough and set them aside. She would keep them refrigerated until it was time to take them to the stall in the morning.

As she tackled the sage bundles, she put the white sage with cedar to one side of the table, and the black sage on the other side. White sage was commonly known for cleansing, and by far the most sought after. When bundled with cedar, it would remove the negative and bring in the positive. This was an unequivocal combination. Amara always sold a lot of these bundles so she made them first, wrapping each with twine before tying it off. When she had enough for the market, she left the rest for herself. She could bundle those later, so she packed the remains away in a labeled box.

She was working on the black sage bundles when she

had the eerie feeling that she was being watched. She had gotten up to put on the kettle, and play another record when all at once she stilled. She glanced at Grim and saw he was staring at the window. His coat had bristled, and a low rumble emerged from his throat. She felt the hair on the nape of her neck rise in the same instant Solomon leaped to his feet. Both dogs were barking furiously, and Sampson had disappeared altogether. Suddenly, she found herself with her revolver in hand. Funny, she didn't remember reaching for it. She turned to the window, backed to the kitchen door, allowing her gaze to sweep the front room. Her eyes fastened on the front door. She saw that it was locked, but nodded imperceptibly all the same.

She cut the sound on the stereo, flipped off the kettle, and proceeded to check all the windows as well as the back door. The house would remain silent now. There was an additional outside door that led to the cellar, but she kept it locked. She also bolted it from downstairs so that she was the only one who could use it. The trap in the floor was in the enclosed back porch. She rechecked that lock just in case. All was sound. Amara was fanatical about locks.

She returned to the kitchen table to complete the task at hand, but the festive air of the evening was ruined. She felt uptight as she finished the black sage wands. Her muscles were bunched, all traces of relaxation gone. Black sage was often burned as a prerequisite to crystal gazing, and other forms of divination. It was considered essential for serious protection, and could be hung above doors for this purpose. It was a powerful cleanser, and one she decided to put to good use tonight. She finished the wands, adding them to the others for tomorrow's sale, and carried the rest to her bedroom.

She returned to the kitchen long enough to put the kettle back on. She needed that cup of tea now. She had closed the blinds in the kitchen even though she hated the restriction it enforced. It was like being in a cave without a light. She did not like being confined. She considered doing the same in the front room, but couldn't bear the claustrophobia. She had slept outside in the past to avoid this problem. She settled for turning the lights down, and then slipped off to her room. The boys all followed in her wake. It was obvious they were not letting her out of their sight. Even Sam had come out of hiding to join the others. They all sat there in one tight little group and stared at her.

She paused long enough to wash her face and change into a short night shift. She did not, however, remove her moccasins. Now that she was more comfortable, she relaxed against the fluffy pillows on her bed. Her room was decorated in bright reds, blues, and greens, compliments of her mother's skill with a needle. She had a striped comforter and curtains to match. There were purple pillows scattered about. They were adorned with delicate bead work. The knotty pine walls were warm and mellow, and there was a thick, purple area rug to tie the room together. She kept a work tray in her room that she could place across her lap. She did this now so that she could work more comfortably. It had legs that held it firmly in place, allowing her the luxury of keeping her hot tea safely within reach while the remainder of black sage sat before her. She set to work braiding it. She had a lit pair of tapers on her dresser to set the mood. They were handmade of beeswax. The scent was sacred. She had sprinkled salt into the corners of the room as well. Her ritual was of her own design. It brought her peace. It never occurred to her that the animal babies might disturb anything. They never had. The little ones looked serious as they set up camp nearby. Grim had moved silently to her side where he kept guard. She finished the black sage, and held up her handiwork for her own inspection. She had woven the herb into intricate sachets, filling each with an assortment of salts that held a subtle hint of frankincense. She had made enough to cover each outer doorway.

She set off with Grim at her heels to hang each sachet. When she was finished, she spoke to God and her angels. She had a love of angels, and kept them close. Then she returned to her room where she had hoped things would feel calmer. But she was still tense, and the air felt constricted. She decided it was time to call in her grandfather. He would know which of their ancestors to bring in. She felt inept in that area. As she spoke to Grandfather, things began to shift. The air smelled sweeter. There was a hint of spice that had not been there before, and in that shift she caught his personal fragrance. It enveloped her, making her feel comforted. She relaxed into his hug even though she sensed the mayhem was not over. Still, she knew she wasn't alone. She had protectors. She had great faith in this.

When there was a scuffling sound at the window, her spine stiffened. For a moment it sounded like someone was trying to break the lock. She slid the shotgun out from under the bed in the same instant the glass shattered. She dove for the telephone in one smooth movement and dialed 911. An operator answered and she began to blurt that someone was breaking into her house when the line went dead. The quiet was so profound she could hear its evil cackle. And the house was swallowed by the night. The only remaining light flared from the twin candles. She doused these immediately and gave herself a second to adjust to the blackness, then sent the little ones scurrying for cover. Sam was in the lead; Solomon obeyed without pause. The dogs were well trained. She was halfway to the living room when her bedroom window exploded. She called Grim on instinct alone; he was already at her side. She raised her chin in the same moment she brought the gun to her shoulder, and stepped out into the night.

She had excellent night vision. Her friends had always

admired her keen sense of sight, and she gave thanks for this now. She swung the gun at an arc as she held her position, keeping her limbs relaxed, her feet spread. She was amazingly calm and moved as quietly as a cat. Any nervousness she had felt was gone now. She approached her window from the rear, studiously tracking her prowler. There was a crunching of gravel as if someone was one step ahead of her. She caught a blur of motion round the corner of the house. Grim bared his teeth. They gleamed in the dark of night. That sinister showing of teeth was all that was visible of the big dog. It made him look demonic, and she was grateful he was on her side. She never dropped her gaze, but remained steady and unyielding. She felt the air around her intruder stir, and knew he was contemplating a quick confrontation. She planted her feet more firmly at a forty-five degree angle. Grim was one huge muscle about to lunge, and she almost wished she had left him indoors with the others. She was afraid to risk him. But there was no time for regrets. Her senses were honed and she knew it was time to act. A shadow stepped forward. It was male, and he was armed. She racked her gun, watching as he rocked back on his heels. She stood her ground, ready to shoot. She had the advantage, and she knew it.

There was a sudden crashing in the nearby brush. All the while she had been keenly aware of another presence, but had no inkling as to what sort of energy the night might cloak. Saplings snapped in the heavy offense of an unseen force. This was no will-o'-the wisp, but a stygian phantom she sensed. It caused a frisson of excitement to skitter up and down her spine. The man was still within close proximity. She literally heard him expel his breath. He was angry, incredibly frustrated, and still intent on his game. He had to know he had lost this round. She stood stock still. There was no room for fear. Grim growled low in his throat. He would pin the man if he made another move toward her.

This was fact. It was then they heard sirens in the distance. The man turned to make his escape, and nearly collided with the anonymous creature that had trampled the woodland. He ran in the opposite direction giving Amara a chance to turn the other way at last. She heard a door slam, and a moment later an engine roared to life. It was a pickup truck, she was sure of it, an Indiana redneck.

What she witnessed next left her stunned. In the spilt second before the man disappeared she glimpsed only his broad back. But she clearly saw what he had confronted. It was a beast with tufted fur so badly matted it made the creature look demented. It had hooves, and the sort of horns that curled and snapped off with age or ill health. It held itself at an odd angle, and its eyes were unlike any she had ever observed. It was so extraordinary she found herself calling in her ancestors, and was instantly rewarded. She never broke her stance, but remained unflinching with their strength at her back. Grim remained at her side. He, however, had an odd bearing as though he truly understood what was happening, while Amara held staunchly to her faith. The intruder beat a hasty retreat and was gone before she could get his plates.

The beast turned to her, and in one mythical moment she found herself staring into the gorgeous gaze of the white fawn. How could this be? How could this chimerical creature have transformed so quickly? They locked eyes for only a fraction of a second. And in that instant Amara knew an inner peace such as she had never known existed. Just like that the animal was gone.

The county police arrived on the scene. They surrounded the farmhouse, and did a thorough search of the property. They checked the skid marks left by the interloper's vehicle, verifying that it was indeed a pickup truck. Amara answered all of their queries, repeating that she could not positively identify the man in question. She never saw his face. He kept to the shadows at all times, and never at any point spoke to her. The officer in charge asked if she had any enemies, and she answered, "None that I know of." At the detective's pointed look, she continued, "My nearest neighbor has a pickup truck. And he has been a little too friendly of late. That's all I've got," she shrugged.

They called someone to temporarily patch her damaged window, warning that she should get it fixed immediately. It was all she could do not to roll her eyes. They also said that if she wanted to press charges, she might be able to avoid paying for the window. But as they did not have a suspect, it was her responsibility for now. She gave an aggravated sigh, but agreed to meet at the station tomorrow afternoon to fill out the necessary forms. There was a lot of muttering, and she was checked out by a paramedic since there was one on the scene. He told her what she already knew. Stay warm. Get some sleep. She was in a state of shock. He offered a mild sedative, but she declined in favor of her own remedy. She wanted to keep a clear head.

CHAPTER FOUR

aybreak came much too soon, and while Amara had slept deeply, she found herself humming a now familiar tune as she went through her early morning ritual. Where had this song come from? She wondered as she stepped from the shower. And why was it haunting her? She toweled off, taking time to dry her hair before fingering through the glossy curls. She absently applied a touch of eye shadow and just a hint of blush. She didn't wear much make-up, preferring a scrubbed natural look. She pulled on a clean pair of cut-offs and a purple tee shirt before leaving the bath with Grim at her heels. He moved like a silent shadow. She fed him as she entered the kitchen, then scooped up little Solomon who was wiggling nonstop. He was still restless from the previous night. The little ones were acutely sensitive. Sampson touched his nose to hers, and she included him in a hug, feeding them all at once. She wanted to reassure them.

She fixed a quick breakfast of tea and toast, and carried it to the table. Afterwards, she packed up the sprouts, loaves, and sage wands, and set them out on the porch for the drive down to the stand. She spent some time playing ball with all three of the babies before it was time to go. They needed the normalcy as much as the recreation. So did she, she thought to herself. It would be a busy morning and a lucrative one, she hoped. When the little ones had settled down a bit, she and Grim locked up and climbed into the car.

It took twenty minutes to get the produce stand one hundred percent ready. She plumped up a pile of ripe red tomatoes, tidied a basket of sweet corn, found a spot for the sprouts beside the loaves of newly baked bread, and placed the sage wands near the register to entice buyers at the very last minute. She was good at sales strategy. People thrived on finding bargains and exciting impulse purchases. She had just put out the *OPEN* sign when the first car pulled up. A young couple climbed out, and before they could step into her booth, several other car doors slammed from somewhere nearby. There was plenty of parking on down the hill, and more on the other side of the bridge. Amara was pleased with the gathering crowd. It was only midmorning and she had sold a great deal already. There were people literally lined up for baked goods, making her grateful for her insight. She rearranged what was left of the breads, adding a couple of pies she had made as an afterthought, and then stopped to replenish the bin of cucumbers and zucchini. She overheard a woman comment, while eyeing the crisp mung sprouts, that everything for the perfect sandwich could be bought right here. She flashed a sincere smile when she handed her a complimentary sample as a thank you for her generosity. Her purchase had been a substantial one.

By the end of the morning, she had sold all of her pastries and every last smudge stick in the place. As the last few people left her stand, she heard someone whisper something about the break-in. "Poor thing," the female voice said, "It must have been terrible for her. I do hope she wasn't hurt." Amara gulped a little at that, realizing that she was still feeling emotional and a bit nervous about her upcoming visit to the police station. She would make an appearance after lunch. She put out the *CLOSED* sign and proceeded to lock up. It was already 12:20 and she wanted to spend time with the babies before she had to leave again.

Amara pulled up in front of the farm house. She stepped out from behind the wheel with Grim in her wake. Karma trilled a greeting from a nearby tree, and Amara returned her call. She beamed when the chubby young raccoon scrambled down the tree and launched herself into her waiting arms. She cradled the baby for a few moments before pulling a piece of fruit from the satchel she carried over her shoulder. Karma chattered happily as she sprang to the ground, slurping greedily on the juicy treat, and Amara slipped inside.

She glanced at the clock briefly, but was distracted. Grim was sniffing curiously at the kitchen door. It felt like it opened in slow motion. She breathed a sigh of relief to see the little ones. But Solomon was anxiously hopping up and down. He walked to her on hind legs all the while staring into her eyes; his own were enormous in his small face, and his tail was tucked. Sampson was prowling nervously, his pretty features ruffled. She frowned as she bent to hug first one, and then the other. Grim nudged her with his nose, and Amara wondered what was wrong. She decided they were still off-kilter from the events of the night before. She spoke to them gently with a smile in her voice while treating all three of them. That seemed to do the trick, but she was pensive when she ate her sandwich.

After she had eaten, she quietly closed the little ones in the kitchen, and headed for the bathroom. She brushed her teeth, pausing to splash some cold water on her face. It was hot outside, and she had to admit her nerves were shot. She ran her fingers through her hair deciding to change into fresh clothing. *Something* was off, she was sure of it. And

then it clicked into place. There was something about the clocks, something that required her attention. She hurried back down the hall to the front room, and stared at the clock. Its hands had stopped at 12:10. She gasped aloud as she retraced her steps. She did a double take at the hall clock seeing that it, too, had stopped at 12:10. Amara froze. Running her hands up and down her arms, she literally felt the blood drain from her face.

She knew a moment of utter panic when she entered the bedroom where she stopped in her tracks. Her gaze swept the window, and then traveled the perimeters of the room, taking in everything at once. She eyed the closet door, approaching it cautiously even as she scanned the bed with its colorful pillows. She took a brief inventory of every item on her night stand. At first all appeared to be in place. And then she saw it, the wind-up alarm clock that she kept beside the bed. It was lying on its side, and it had stopped at precisely 12:10! There was no way that could have been a power outage!

She was frightened as she jerked the closet door open, grateful of Grim's solid presence behind her. She reached up to pull on the light cord, and had the creepiest feeling just prior to making contact. Her fingers brushed a foreign object, and she let out a girlish squeal. It was dark in the closet, and the object was too small to identify without benefit of light. Whatever it was, she was pretty sure she had knocked it loose. She steadied herself, and pulled the cord a second time. The bulb came on. The item was dangling from a string in midair. Amara reached out a tentative hand, her expression puzzled. It was a grimy piece of film leader identical to the one Crow had given her. She didn't need to handle it to know that the negative would be just as disturbing as the first.

It occurred to her then that there was no breeze outside. Yet in spite of the stillness, she could distinctly smell the flowering trees in the back yard. The scent of dogwood combined with redbud was staggering in the small space. Silent tears coursed down her cheeks as she approached the draped window. She wondered how her legs carried her when they felt so rubbery. As her fingers closed on the bright fabric, she knew what she would find. It still came as a shock when she pulled the curtains wide. The glass was gone leaving a yawning cavity in her room! She had checked that window before leaving for the sale. It was intact then. Even the crack had been repaired. That meant her trespasser had done this today while she was right here on her very own land. Dear God! She was just down the road at the front of her property line! No one could have possibly driven up her road without her knowing!

Amara walked into the Montgomery County Sheriff's Department with an air of confidence that was completely contrived. She had stepped into a little orange sundress that clung to her curves and suited her sun bronzed skin. Tiny diamond earrings adorned her ears. She wore tan sandals on her feet, and her nails were painted. Her telephone line had been repaired and she had, of course, called and reported the break-in immediately. Although the police were again on the scene, she had an appointment to keep and forms to sign. There were still formalities to observe, and no doubt more questions to answer.

Amara was tired and wanted nothing more than a quiet day at home, including a hot soak in her claw-foot tub. She never was particularly comfortable in public places, and these were no ordinary circumstances. She fingered the fire opal she wore at the hollow of her throat. The smooth round stone sparkled in the sunlight streaming in through the open window. She had no idea how classy she appeared when she glanced first at one face, then another.

Detectives Avery and Allen were present as she knew they would be. They were County. Mike Avery was a hard nose, and very opinionated for someone so slow to act. Detective Troy Allen was kinder, softer. She didn't think he fit the profile of detective, but she liked his quiet demeanor. When a third man whose presence seemed to dominate the entire room addressed her in a calm tone, she was momentarily thrown off her game. He overpowered the other men, no contest. She felt his close scrutiny, and wished she could turn and run. Why did he affect her that way? It was as if he knew her intimately.

"I'm Sheriff Wheeler, ma'am. May I call you Amara? Or do you prefer Miss Owens?"

"Amara is fine," she replied politely.

"Please, take a seat, Amara. Would you care for a glass of water?"

"Please," she slid into the proffered seat, and reached for the paper cup he had already filled. "Thank you," her voice held a hint of the strain she was feeling. Her expression revealed nothing of her thoughts. She had expected the detectives that had been to her house, but she wasn't prepared for this commanding figure of a man! Though she was taken aback, she was more than a little grateful that the sheriff was more observant than the rest. He hadn't missed a single detail when he had sized her up. Of that, she was certain. And that was already a huge improvement over the investigative officers. Sheriff Wheeler exuded an intelligence the others lacked. She took a sip of the cool water before setting it down on the corner of his desk. He had provided a coaster.

He sat opposite her, allowing her a moment to collect

herself. As Sheriff Wheeler took in her cool composure, he seemed to recognize it for the personality trait that it was. Her poise didn't fool him. At least she didn't think so. Any female who had just discovered that someone had broken into her home would be terrified. The fact that she held it together better than most was simply a part of her demeanor, and she was fairly sure he had read her correctly.

"Done sizing me up?" he arched a brow that said she had been caught staring. She gave a slight nod, horrified by the hot color that warmed her cheeks. She never blushed!

"I'm sorry. I expected the officers who came to my house," she answered.

"Yes, I can see that," he supplied, a twinkle in his eye.

Oh, boy, she thought, she was going to have to watch out for this one! He was a bit of a ladies' man. She took another sip of water to hide her sudden attack of nerves.

"I intend to drop by this evening before I head home. If you don't mind, that is?" he made it sound like an inquiry when it truly was a statement. She figured he would do exactly as he wished. The question was a mere formality. "We have to decide what to do with you."

"Oh?" Her mouth had formed a perfect O.

"Well, you can't very well stay alone when your window is broken out." He displayed a small grin at her discomfiture. And bless her heart, she blushed a second time!

"I hadn't intended to," she fought to regain control of her senses, squaring her shoulders as she did so. "By now, my friend Gregory is already on it." Gregory was Nikki's boyfriend. And Nikki was her best friend. But Amara had no intention of explaining.

"Good to know you have a plan," the sheriff said dryly. "I'll still be stopping by before dark. My boys here," he indicated both detectives Avery and Allen, "have given me the details, but it is my job to take a look for myself." Before she could respond, he continued with a different line of questioning. "They say our boy must have come up from the creek?"

"Yes, I was at my stand all morning. No one could have taken the road without my knowing it," she replied evenly," which leaves only the creek or the corn fields. The creek would be far easier, and much more discreet."

"I agree. I have sent out a detail of men to check the banks that border your property. He could have pulled up in a canoe or kayak at any number of points along the way. Or he may have bypassed you altogether from the bridge by walking the lower route along the water. That also leaves the possible arrival from the back of your land if he entered from Camp Rotary."

"The camp is booked all summer. Someone would have seen him if he entered that way. And there are scout leaders and conservation officers as well."

"Hear that, boys?" the sheriff glanced first at Avery, and then at Allen.

"We're on it," they chorused on their way out.

"Now," the sheriff gazed directly into her eyes, "what was it about the clocks? The boys said something about them all stopping at the same time?"

Amara knew full well he had heard the entire story, but she humored him all the same. His muscled forearms bulged where he leaned against the desk. She was close enough to see each individual hair, and for some reason this made her uneasy. She reminded herself she was the victim here. "Yes, the clock in the front room, like the one in the hall, runs on electricity. That could have been a power outage," she explained. "But the one by my bed is battery operated. All three stopped at precisely 12:10." She shivered in spite of herself. The slight movement was not lost on the sheriff who leaned back in his chair taking in the full picture. He was silent just long enough for it to grate on her nerves.

"And what do you suppose that means?" he asked. The question was spoken softly enough to be construed as menacing.

"I don't know," she wet her lips as she reached for the paper cup. "I'm not sure."

"But you have some idea?"

"Am I on trial here?" she arched a brow.

At that, he relaxed his stance a bit. "No, of course not," he assured her. "It's just that people often miss the details unless they are brought to their attention. Does the time have any significance to you, for example?"

"No, none, except that I left my stand at 12:20," she almost gulped. Without asking, he refilled her empty cup, and handed it back to her. Her hand trembled when she took it from him, and he softened noticeably.

"And what do you think that means, Amara?" Their eyes locked and held.

"I think he was in my house just minutes before I arrived home," she said clearly, and then told him how nervous the little ones had behaved when she entered the kitchen.

"I think so too," was all he said. "And I think he wanted

you to know that. Are you sure you haven't overlooked any feasible suspects?" Her eyes rounded, and he repeated, "Old boyfriends, jealous girlfriends, someone from your past?"

It was late in the afternoon when Amara left the station. She stopped for takeout at her favorite deli on her way home, and selected a few salads, and a beautifully frosted cake. Nikki and Gregory would be joining her for dinner. And cooking was out of the question. She kept turning everything over in her mind that she had discussed with the sheriff. Grant, she thought. She had learned that his first name was Grant. Why hadn't she told him about the piece of film? She wondered. It was tucked safely away in her purse, wrapped in a clean tissue. She had intended to hand it over with an apology for not mentioning it sooner. But there it was, still stored away in her purse. She needed to talk to Nikki. Her friend had a good head on her shoulders, and Amara found herself in dire need of a friend.

When she arrived home, she spied Gregory's tan van with his business logo and phone number in the driveway. She caught a glimpse of him around back where he was busily restoring her bedroom window. She walked around the corner of the house and greeted him warmly. Gregory was a professional. He was not only replacing her window, he was doing so with a high quality shatterproof glass. And his plans included a floodlight that would cover the whole back yard. She was amazed at his abilities, and humbled by his generosity. She had known she could count on him no matter the cost. When she inquired about the amount, she was told not to worry about it.

"I'll give you my cost on everything, and you can pay that off in produce, or however else you like. You and Nikki can discuss it. You two always have worked well together."

She thanked him sincerely, and told him she would

have dinner whenever he was hungry. Nikki hadn't arrived yet. She worked late a lot, so Amara went inside to take care of the animals. She let the dogs out, keeping a close eye on Solomon, and then carried him back indoors, making sure he and Sam had food and water. Before she had a chance to change out of her dress, she heard Grim's warning growl from afar. Gregory had disappeared into the back of his van, and Amara could see that Grim had someone pinned in the woods bordering her creek- side property. Amara grabbed her shotgun, and without skipping a beat, went in pursuit.

CHAPTER FIVE

*T*he dude's head snapped up when she racked the shotgun. Simultaneously, Grim sat awaiting her command. The man glanced from one to the other before attempting to speak. Amara didn't see herself as she was. She and Grim made a formidable pair. The dog, made huge by his shaggy coat, looked more wolf than not. At the very least he appeared feral. And all that could be seen of her was the scowl behind the gun. Her stance was serious, and her hair was as wild as the dog's. "Who the hell are you? And what are you doing on my property?" Her golden brown eyes fairly gleamed. She had taken note of the camera over his broad, muscular shoulder, and her temper had instantly flared.

"My name is Daniel. Daniel Collins," he explained. "I got permission to come onto the grounds, and photograph whatever I found. Gregory said you wouldn't mind." When she continued to stare at him, he murmured, "You are Miss Owens, are you not?"

Amara drew herself up short. "Gregory gave you permission? He didn't mention it." She lowered the gun, took a step back, and told Grim to calm. Daniel watched the transformation. Her features softened, the eyes that had appeared almost inhuman were in reality quite stunning. Her long hair tumbled over her shoulders, and for the first time he noticed how she was dressed.

Amara watched as he assessed her. She was suddenly conscious of the little orange sundress she had chosen to wear that day. She tossed her head baring the smooth column of her throat, causing the diamond earrings to glisten in the mass of black curls. Her collar bones were prominent above the cleavage that was the perfect foil for the fire opal that adorned her chest. His eyes widened, and she took a step back, "Come Grim," was all she said. She turned and walked away. And nearly ran smack dab into the barrel chest of the man approaching from behind.

Grant caught her easily enough, and evaluated the situation through shrewd eyes. It was clear he did not like what he saw. "I'd like a moment alone with your trespasser," he muttered curtly. Amara thought to correct him, but was dismissed immediately. She felt like a recalcitrant child being admonished for her behavior. Grant somehow managed to gain the advantage, and Amara, with Grim at her side, returned to the house. She cast a quick glance back over her shoulder, and noticed that Grant was engaged in a quarrel with Daniel. Honestly, in that moment, she didn't know how she felt. Embarrassed should about cover it.

A short while later Nikki popped her head into the kitchen, finding Amara at the table with a cup of hot tea, "Penny for your thoughts?" she smiled her shy smile. Amara took in the slim lines of the beautiful blonde who looked a great deal like Julie Barnes of the Mod Squad, a role played by actress Peggy Lipton.

"Hey," she sang out, "I didn't hear you!" Grim wore a

guilty expression, and Amara couldn't help but laugh. "Some guard dog you are!" she stroked his big head, regaining his devotion.

"He's used to me," Nikki assured. "No one else could have gotten by him." That comment gained Nikki a sloppy kiss from the loyal dog. Sampson and Solomon acted on cue. They took that as an invitation to join in on the fun. The two little clowns had been quiet up until now, sensing all was not well in their world. Solomon wagged his tail furiously at the turn of events, and wiggled his way to the table, causing Sam's plume to swish furiously back and forth. The girls burst out laughing.

"Leave it to these guys to lighten the mood," Amara wiped her eyes. "God, it's good to see you!"

"What happened out there? And who is your new hero?" Nikki took a chair, and her long hair brushed the seat. It was as fine as it was long, and the kind of blonde hair that would glint in the sunlight. Her light brown eyes were penetrative. They did more for her pale good looks than blue ones ever could have.

Amara blushed, and immediately covered her face with her hands. "I don't know," she literally moaned. "You mean Sheriff Wheeler? I only met him today. I had forgotten he was going to stop by. I came home and caught that fellow, Daniel, out in my woods. Good grief, Nikki, I feel like a fool!"

"Don't," Nikki was immediately at her side. "You have been through enough, and it was really Gregory's fault for not warning you. I scolded him, you know."

Amara groaned, and fingered her thick tresses, peering up at Nikki, "I overreacted," she explained. "Grim growled, and I saw this guy in my woods with a camera, and freaked out."

"I might have done the same," Nikki reassured.

"Not you," Amara fairly pouted, "You are more logical. It was the camera that did it, and I should have taken the pieces of film to the police. Grant will be furious with me."

"Whoa! Hold on a minute," Nikki stopped her tirade. "What film? What are you talking about?'

"I haven't mentioned it to anyone yet. I was waiting to talk to you," Amara described the jagged pieces of film that Crow had given her, and went on to tell her about the one she discovered hanging in the closet. "They are negatives, but they have been butchered. It would require a microscopic lens to discern what's on them. And I honestly don't like to handle them. They feel so filthy!"

Nikki gasped, automatically taking her seat again. "That's too big to be a coincidence," she whispered. "Let me see them. I'd like to see the closet too."

The girls were just about to leave the kitchen when someone rapped on the front door. Amara was in the lead with Grim and the little ones following at her heels when the sheriff popped his head in. Grim bared his teeth, awaiting command. Solomon hopped up and down. Sampson ran and hid under the bed. Amara called, "Come in!" She looked at Nikki as if to say, "Mum's the word."

Nikki gave a faint nod and took a step back as Sheriff Grant Wheeler's massive frame filled the doorway. He immediately crossed to Amara, almost rudely ignoring the blonde. But Amara was fully aware that Wheeler hadn't missed a single characteristic of her friend's appearance. He was simply following protocol. He had been rude to her earlier, and was now making amends. "I didn't mean to be brusque with you," he said, taking Amara's hand, "But I didn't like that fellow's looks. What was he doing on your land?"

"Gregory gave him permission," she answered slowly. He wasn't fooling her one iota! She would bet her bottom dollar that Grant had already done some investigating of his own. He would have asked both men that very same question.

"I don't want him coming around here again, got it?" he looked her square in the eyes. When Amara held her tongue, he gave her a little shake. Not too much, just enough to gain a response. His sandy hair fell down over his brow, and his cheeks grew ruddy.

Amara was taken aback. She wasn't used to taking orders. Not from anyone. "I really don't anticipate seeing him again, *Sheriff*," she emphasized his title. She was pretty sure that made him angry because his cheeks gained a tad more color, and his gaze fairly seared her. "I never met him before today, and as you could see that didn't go so well."

He was smart enough to know when to back down. Amara could sense he was holding back when he added, "I only meant to warn you. That guy's a reporter. I don't trust him."

It wasn't a direct apology, but it did get her attention. "Is this true, Nikki?" she searched her friend's eyes.

"Well, yes. But he's also a good friend of Gregory's," Nikki didn't like where this conversation was going. She felt compelled to stand up for her mate. Nikki had been with Gregory ever since college and she knew him inside out. He was a good judge of people, and if he said his friend was to be trusted, she believed him. She sent the sheriff a baleful look. "Not every reporter is out for blood," she added in a brisk tone.

"All right, all right," Amara announced, "Enough! There is no point to this discussion. I don't know the man, and that is that. Should he come back around, I will watch my step," she promised Sheriff Wheeler, "But either way, I do owe him an apology for today. Now, is there anything else I can help you with?"

Sheriff Grant Wheeler did not look satisfied. He did not want Amara anywhere near the creep, or any other guy for that matter. Or so it seemed to Amara. Nevertheless, he decided to let the matter rest. He nodded, and forced a placid smile. "Just promise to call if you need anything," he said. She agreed, and the topic turned to the other issues at hand. She dutifully led the way as she showed him around, answering his official questions. The last comment he made was that he would be calling on her again soon. Nikki couldn't help it; she rolled her eyes.

Amara audibly let out her breath as she leaned against the door. She was tired, and it showed in the strain on her face. Nikki was instantly by her side, putting an arm around her, and guiding her to the kitchen table. "You sit," she ordered in a kind tone, "I'm getting you a cup of tea and we're going to eat. It's plenty late. Gregory should be wrapping things up any moment now." Amara didn't argue, and Nikki automatically set about warming the savory stew that Amara had set out to thaw. There were takeout salads from the grocery deli, she noticed; potato, bean, and Cole slaw, all of Gregory's favorites. And Amara had laid a loaf of homemade bread out to compliment the stew alongside a marvelous viand of raw fruits and veggies. Nikki nodded at her friend's expertise before slipping outside to check on Gregory. She found him wiping his hands on a rag as he finished reloading the van.

"I'll be in to wash up in a minute," he promised, aware of how exhausted Amara must be. At least she would sleep better knowing she was safe.

Nikki had fed the animals, and was setting the table when Gregory came in. He had soaped up down the hall, and now leant a hand with the meal. Amara smiled at the picture of the two of them weaving comfortably in and out around the kitchen. Gregory was as dark as Nikki was light. His great height dwarfed her, making her appear smaller than she actually was. They made the perfect picture, and Amara envied them their happiness. She told them so too because she was of a mind that people didn't say enough kind things about others these days. Nikki blushed, and Greg's eyes crinkled at the corners. Amara smiled knowingly.

"Everything looks so good!" Nikki said brightly once they were seated. "Now, no disturbing conversations for the time being," she warned. "Let's just have a relaxing meal."

"Yes, ma'am," Greg grinned. He was used to Nikki's ways, and understood she was trying to create a peaceful atmosphere for Amara.

Amara was only too happy to comply, knowing there would be time later for serious discussion. "It does look delicious, doesn't it?"

"It is," Greg said around a mouthful. "I couldn't help but notice you picked up dessert too!" he meant it as an accolade, and she knew it. Gregory didn't miss much.

"It's butter rum," Amara grinned, eyeing the layer cake, "Your favorite."

Later, Nikki helped Amara wash the dishes, and then they tidied the kitchen together, all the while carrying on an easy conversation. They avoided stressful topics by mutual consent. "You need to get to bed early tonight," Nikki suggested, and Amara nodded in agreement.

"You won't get an argument from me," she yawned behind her hand. "I appreciate everything you guys have done for me, you know?" she whispered.

"I know," Nikki pulled her into a warm hug. "You still planning on having everyone over tomorrow?" she asked. "No one will mind if you cancel."

"Oh, my God, I entirely forgot!" Amara slapped a hand to her forehead. She had arranged a small gathering a few weeks back. It was something she occasionally did, an easy way to stay in touch with everyone.

"Do you want me to cancel it? I can make the calls; you wouldn't have to do a thing. By now the news is out, and already in the paper," Nikki said decisively.

"No," But Amara didn't sound like she meant it. She was grappling with the decision, which really wasn't like her at all. She was beyond tired, but never went back on her word. And Nikki, of all people, knew how important that was to Amara. "No," she repeated, more firmly this time. "It's okay. It will be a welcome distraction, and I promise to keep it simple."

"Still serving enchiladas?" Nikki asked pointedly.

"Yes, both veggie and queso," Amara stated decisively, "I thought I'd serve rice and beans on the side, and of course chips and salsa. I already have most of the ingredients, and I'm making your guacamole."

"Okay, I'll be here early," Nikki replied. "We can prepare the food ahead of time. That way we won't have to hurry. And I'll bring the guacamole; I noticed you were out of limes."

Amara laughed softly, "How very astute of you," she said, "and thank you."

Nikki laughed in return. They settled on a time, and then said their good nights. Gregory had slipped out unnoticed, and was enjoying a smoke while he waited by the van. He watched as the girls embraced one last time at the door. "Call me if you need anything!" Nikki called out as she disappeared into the night. Amara nodded, and stood watching until her friends drove away. It felt good to have loyal friends. She loved them both, and Nikki was like family to her.

A loud chattering came from somewhere nearby, and Amara glanced up to see Karma in the top branches of a favorite tree. The baby coon had filled out quickly; she was growing up! She didn't really need Amara to feed her anymore, but Amara still left tidbits where they could easily be found. She called out to Karma, and the coon was suddenly in her arms. Funny how the tiny thing could climb her like a tree without leaving a single scratch! She was a loving little girl.

After she had gone back indoors, Amara looked after the other fur babies. Sampson had stretched out in one of his beloved windowsills, his big feet propped up on the casing in pure delight. She rubbed his tummy, chuckling at how his feet resembled snow shoes; they were that prodigious! She invited both Grim and Solomon to go out back with her. She sat with them in the still of night, relaxing in the tranquil evening. The sky was clear overhead, and she found a mossy seat in which to sit and lean against a tree. Grim stretched out beside her even as Solomon curled up in her lap. It had been a long day.

CHAPTER SIX

*A*mara slept late the following day. She sprang awake staring at the clock as if it were an alien object. After her eyes adjusted she saw that it was half past eight. Yet when she first looked, she could have sworn the clock read ten after twelve. She realized then she had been dreaming, and what a strange nocturnal escapade it had been! In it, she was humming the same tune she so often heard in her head. She looked like herself, yet there were discrepancies. And there was a man in this lucid vision that she very much feared. His features blurred in her mind, but her trepidation was definitely real. He was familiar, but she couldn't place him. Already the dream was fading. Grim nudged her hand and licked her face, and Amara sat up with a giggle. "Okay, boy," she said, "I'm awake!"

She went about the morning chores, gathering eggs, feeding the horses and barn cats in turn. She tossed hay down to the cattle and spoke to them just as she would any pet. Animals never forgot you; they remembered your face, voice, scent, and particularly your kind gestures. And they never forgot how you treated them. She then took the time to harvest enough fresh produce for tonight's dinner. Tanner

drove by in his old pickup truck and tipped his hat in her direction. She knew he was replacing the salt licks and otherwise tending the fields he leased. She didn't pause to talk. Grim stuck to her side like glue. She fingered the 1864 Indian Head coin she wore on a long chain around her neck. What an odd gift for Crow to have delivered! Yet somehow it fit.

She had returned to the house, showered, and changed into fresh garments before Nikki arrived at eleven. The girls shared a quick no-nonsense lunch, and then immediately set about making the enchiladas for the evening ahead. They cooked the beans that Amara had soaked the night before. They would season and mash them when it was closer to dinnertime. Likewise, they set out a pot of water, salt, and oil, measuring the appropriate amount of rice, and setting it aside. This would make for expedient cooking. Once finished, they would add a soupcon of cumin, a sprinkle of red pepper, and a couple of spoonfuls of salsa. By then the enchiladas would be ready to serve. The girls wove about the kitchen in quintessential rhythm as the two of them had cooked together a multitude of times.

Upon arrival, Nikki brought a fresh batch of guacamole which was safely stored in the refrigerator next to the cabinet that housed a quantity of tortilla chips. These would be warmed in those last few minutes before dining. She went out to her car, and carried a six-pack of beer and two nice bottles of wine indoors. The dogs followed in hopes of a reward. They weren't disappointed. Nikki tossed them each a treat on her way to deposit the beer in the fridge. She set the wine aside on the counter where Amara was dicing a nice blend of tangy vegetables. "Pico de Gallo?" she asked. Amara smiled an answer, thanking her for the help. The girls washed their hands, leaving everything in place as they fell into a natural conversation about the previous evening.

"You can take a look in the closet," Amara advised,

"though I don't think you'll see anything in there. I'll get the film leader. I'd appreciate it if you would take the negatives home for closer inspection."

"Of course," Nikki's voice was muffled with her head in the closet, "I'd like to take the time to clean them up and see what's on them." She backed out of the closet leaving the door ajar.

"The one Crow dropped off is probably perfectly innocent," Amara whispered without conviction. "The other one was attached to that light cord," she pointed to the bulb inside the closet. "Honestly, they both give me the creeps."

"Yeah, me too," Nikki agreed, "Yet you didn't turn them over to the police. Do you know why?"

"No, I intended to," Amara admitted. "I just found myself walking out with them instead."

"It's natural to be leery of the unknown," Nikki concluded. "I think you were listening to your gut. When did you make the black sage bundles?"

"Before the break-in," Amara responded without pause. "I knew there was someone out there. I followed my instincts and got right on it. They worked their magic too."

"You mean it could have been worse?"

"Exactly," Amara nodded.

"And the clocks," Nikki pressed? "Why do you think they all stopped at the same time?"

"He wanted me to know who was in charge," Amara answered immediately, "and that he could do whatever he desired."

"In other words, he was bragging."

"Yes."

"Well, the gang will be here anytime now. Let's put this behind us. You need to chill. And I promise to let you know what's on those negatives." Nikki didn't say so, but her intuition told her that Amara already had a pretty good idea what they would find. And she was willing to bet it was just too unsettling for her friend to investigate them on her own.

"Agreed," Amara smiled a brilliant smile for the first time that day, and Nikki couldn't help but notice how beautiful she was in her bright red crop top and black jeans. She was wearing her red knee-high moccasins, and the fire opal pendent sparkled at the base of her throat. Tiny red studs adorned her earlobes. She couldn't remember a time when they hadn't been best friends. They loved each other like sisters.

The girls sat outside watching Solomon at play while they each sipped a small glass of wine. Grim was stationed at Amara's side as was his custom. Nikki wore a bright blue halter top with light blue jeans that somehow caused her blonde hair to appear even paler than usual. Small silver hoops dangled from her ears. They made a pretty picture in their casual attire. They were refreshed and at ease when Gregory's tan van pulled up. Nikki smiled as she watched him approach. He returned the smile with one of his own. If they weren't such close friends, Amara would have felt like she was imposing. It was, however, reassuring to witness the affection between them. When they broke eye contact, Gregory turned to Amara with a steady smile. "How are you today, Amara?" he asked sincerely.

"Much better," she replied with an answering smile, "Thanks to you, I actually slept." She moved to the nearest door and scooted little Solomon back inside. He whined and scratched at the portal before settling down to pout. Grim literally smirked.

"I'm glad to hear that," he sounded genuinely relieved. "You had us both worried."

"I don't know what I would have done without you two," she answered honestly.

"I hate to mention it, but would you be open to meeting Daniel at another time? I kind of feel responsible for what happened last night. Under different circumstances, I think you two might actually like each other."

Amara's laughter chimed. "I would be honored," she insisted. "After all, I owe him an apology."

At that point a bright yellow Ford Mustang arrived out front, and within seconds Cynthia walked up the drive. Amara was ecstatic to see her as it had been a while since their last visit, and she loved her dearly. Though she was from the area, and a lifelong friend, Cynthia lived a life of adventure. She was tall and full figured with auburn hair cut to perfectly frame her well-sculpted face. She carried herself with grace, and turned heads wherever she went. Cynthia was both a brilliant equestrian and gifted artist. She made her living at the latter doing art shows across the country. She had a passion for nature scenes which allowed her to travel, and had acquired a reputation for animal portraits that had become her specialty. Cynthia merely went where there was work, and if that took her to new places, all the better. She was also Amara's only pagan friend. She loved reading the tarot and enjoyed astrology. Cards and charts were a specialty of hers; she excelled at them. "Hello!" she called with a cheery wave, dangling a bottle of Amara's favorite Beaujolais. The two embraced, and Amara looped her arm around her as she led her to a seat.

The last two cars arrived simultaneously. Linda, who was the only married female, was accompanied by her husband Ian. The couple climbed out of their Volkswagen Beetle waving as they did so. Linda was pretty in an earthy way. She had long straight brown hair and extraordinarily large brown eyes. Her nose was slim, her cheeks well rounded. She wore a pair of wire rim glasses that made her look even more adorable and had a penchant for wearing hats, specifically caps. Linda loved to sew, crochet, and sketch. She was a master at crafts, and could turn anything into something. Amara liked to shop at second-hand stores, but lacked patience when it came to sizing. Linda would take one glance and say, "Piece of cake!" True to her word, Linda would take the purchased items and return them custom-made. This never failed to amaze Amara who tired of sewing. Ian walked proudly at Linda's side, the sun beating down on his long blonde mane. He had a six-pack of beer tucked under one arm while Linda clutched a bag of limes. "Thought you could use these?" she offered. The pair smiled as they turned to the occupants of the last vehicle. Amara had reached them by this point, with Nikki bringing up the rear.

This last car stood out in the crowd. It was an expensive car, a shiny new corvette, and one none of the friends recognized. Victoria Beech stepped out of the passenger seat just as the driver's door opened. Victoria was an opulent blonde in every sense of the word who had a tendency to choose her men with care. Amara took one look at the driver and gasped. Grim immediately raised his head with only a semblance of a warning growl. He didn't move a muscle as Nikki reached out a restraining hand, but remained at attention. "You didn't tell us you were bringing a guest," Nikki bit out. Victoria looked momentarily wounded, but recovered quickly enough.

"I didn't think anyone would mind?" she glanced at Amara who couldn't quit staring. There, just a few feet away stood Simon Alexander, the college professor she had openly spurned. His eyes burned as he looked her up and down. He wore a smug expression that seemed to say, "*See? I got my way after all.*" Simon was unequivocally arrogant. Amara could attest to that. She was probably the only girl who had ever turned him down. And now he stood before her looking like royalty with Victoria fairly dripping from his arm.

The couple was overdressed to the point of absurdity especially since she had made it clear they would be spending the bulk of the day in the woods. She glanced at Victoria and wondered why she had let her into their circle in the first place. She hadn't particularly wanted to. Even Nikki, who liked almost everyone, had thought it a mistake. Victoria had been in a few of their classes, but they really hadn't interacted. They had nothing in common. Now that Amara thought about it, she recalled having some misgivings about the invitation from the beginning. It was just that Victoria had blown into town at the exact same time Amara was planning the casual event. Victoria had attached herself to Amara, asking questions about the countryside. Honestly, upon reflection, Victoria had invited herself. And apparently, the one person everyone knew Amara never wanted to see again.

Nikki made a hissing sound beneath her breath, and Amara reacted without thinking. Her gaze flew to Simon who was still staring at her even as he reached inside his precious corvette and pulled out a very expensive Pentax 30 mm camera. It was a nice one, and included a quality zoom. It was nearly identical to the one Daniel carried over his shoulder, and exactly like Nikki's own. Grim was suddenly by her side, sitting perfectly erect. He wore a mean look, and his eyes had narrowed into slits. Amara was more than a little suspicious, and felt comforted by Grim's presence. She couldn't help but

notice that everyone else had brought an offering. Yet Victoria's perfectly manicured hands were empty, while Simon's long fingers neatly stroked his camera. He made the gesture appear obscene.

Grim, who had been well behaved up to a point, bared his teeth. He growled long and low, his eyes trained on Simon. Victoria forced a giggle everyone ignored while Simon fought to appear nonchalant. Amara noticed that his hands shook when he tucked them behind his back. He had stashed the camera in the car in order to do so. Amara watched his movements. They were carefully calculated. She had seen the brief flare of panic cross his aristocratic features.

"I think you'd best be leaving now," Gregory stood tall. His shoulders were wide, his expression grim. "It seems you have worn out your welcome."

"I beg your pardon?" Simon began in the same moment Victoria stuck her bottom lip out in a pout. She was used to getting her way.

Gregory did not soften, nor did he allow an argument from the other man. "I believe Miss Owens has already made her preference known. I will not see her put upon."

"Now see here," Simon tried a second time, only to be rebuffed. Ian stepped boldly forward to take his stand next to Gregory.

"Well, I never," Victoria raised her chin a notch as she managed to squeeze a tear from the corner of one wide blue eye. Grim's hackles rose. He was no longer sitting beside Amara. He was standing at attention. Honestly, he looked about to lunge. Gregory's expression revealed the thought that the couple was a pair of complete imbeciles if they didn't get back into the car right this minute. Thankfully, they did just that, and a gust of wind rose on a sigh. Simon had begun to start the car, but his ego got in the way. He rolled the window down for a parting shot when Grim was suddenly in his face! Karma shrieked from a nearby tree in the very second Grim's jaws gave a warning snap. Simon jumped, dropping the car keys, but managed to get the window up. He was shouting something as he backed away, but his words were muffled. Amara ordered Grim to stay, and the huge dog reluctantly obeyed. Victoria's hands flew up in the air as Simon turned and peeled out down the drive.

There was a moment of utter silence. Grim was first to break the unnatural stillness. He gave an angry bark, still spoiling for a fight. Solomon yapped from a nearby door while Karma shrieked a second time, running up and down the tree. Amara was quick to reassure them. The gang broke into conversation. Everyone was grateful to be rid of the unwanted guests. Yet Amara didn't think she had seen the last of Simon. As if on cue, both Nikki and Gregory were instantly at her side. They were obviously concerned about the same thing.

"We're going to get to the bottom of this," Nikki whispered while pulling Amara into a warm embrace. She was looking at Gregory over Amara's shoulder.

"You bet we are," Gregory chimed in his deep voice that always seemed to provide so much comfort. "Do you want me to call and report this?"

"No," Amara was quick to respond, "No, not right now. I'll mention it to Grant later on."

Nikki and Gregory exchanged a look. "Well, I can stay over any time you want," Nikki promised.

"I know," Amara replied. She had no intention of putting her friends out, "And thank you, but we have a big day ahead of us. We won't let them ruin it for us."

CHAPTER SEVEN

"The Yount's Mill was built in 1864. It was the second mill built on this site, and was one of five in the area," Amara instructed as the gang walked around the circumference of the structure. It was missing all of its windows, but still had a portion of the water wheel on the creek side. "You can climb on in if you want," she continued as she dropped inside from a yawning window frame, "It's not like we're hurting anything. I used to do it all the time, but then so did all the other kids. It's a pretty cool building. I hope they fix it up someday."

"It is awesome," Linda exclaimed. She was fascinated by anything historical. "How did it come to be called *The Yount's Mill*? Or is that a stupid question?"

"You mean like which came first, the name of the mill or the name of the town?" Amara asked in way of answer.

"Yeah," Linda nodded, "I always wondered about that."

"Me too," Cynthia joined in. "I think I'd like to paint it sometime."

"I have some great photos of it," Nikki offered, "if that would make it easier."

"Definitely," Cynthia's smile was sincere. "I could do a quick sketch out here, and then use your photos to follow up. I'd love to see them anyway. You do fantastic work. I have always been so impressed with you. I mean, Nikki James, the great Nick James! Who knew you were a woman?" Cynthia was referring to how Nikki got her start as a professional photographer. She didn't come out with her true story for at least a couple of years. By then, everyone positively loved her work!

"Thank you, I strive to please!" Nikki laughed with a glance in Amara's direction, "Do continue please. I doubt if any of us know as much about the place as you do."

"Well," Amara began, "the Yount family was from Germany. The original spelling was Jundt," she paused to spell this out, "But Daniel Yount was born in Ohio in the year 1807. He grew up working in his father's mill, and in 1828 the family moved to Indiana. The two sons had a great deal of experience by then, and in 1835 they built a mill on the Wabash River in the town that is now known as Attica. The only problem with that was that there was a lack of water. So Daniel came here in 1840, and Rock River did the rest, earning the town the name of Yountsville. As I said before, there were once five buildings in the area, this being the second one on this particular site. But this was the main building, and the only one that still stands. This structure is a three and a half story building of the Greek Revival Period, built of sun-baked bricks and sandstone blocks. It's a fascinating piece of history, wouldn't you say?"

"I would," both Linda and Cynthia chimed in unison.

"Anything about the American Civil War is fascinating," Gregory agreed as Nikki nodded along with him.

Amara liked it that her friends were as engrossed in the past as she was. It made for compelling stories around the campfire, conversations that others might find dull in comparison. They fell into a natural pattern of question and answer that Amara found both challenging and exciting. They talked all afternoon, sometimes sprawled about the grounds, other times up and poking about. Each of them wandered freely and relaxed in turn.

"Was this a woolen mill?" Linda asked. Her eyes behind the wire spectacles were alive with curiosity. The girls were all of an age, and had grown up in the same area, but came from entirely different backgrounds.

"Yes," Amara was quick to respond. "They made uniforms for the Union soldiers."

"Wow," Cynthia expelled a breath, "Imagine that! They employed mostly women, didn't they?"

"Yeah, almost exclusively," Amara nodded. "There were as many as three-hundred at a time; children too."

"Did they stay in the old boarding house?" Linda was full of questions. She could never get enough history. She was a regular bookworm, something Amara loved about her. The friends shared archives from their own personal libraries among themselves, careful to keep them within the group.

"They did," Amara replied, "I think that was its main purpose. It's a cool place, the boarding house."

"Wasn't it also referred to as *The Sleeping Place*?" Ian asked. He made an effort to follow along, but was a little confused by the issue.

"Yes, don't be fooled by the numerous names," Amara sighed. "I have read up on the place a lot. I had a friend who lived there for a while when we were kids. I lost track of her, but I think her family lived there a couple of times."

"I remember you talking about that," Nikki agreed, "They were a nice family, you said. Catholic, I believe. I also recall the place being dubbed *The Inn* at some time or another."

"Yes, it was all of the above, I think," Amara stated. "It's like anything else, depending on where you hail from, or what time frame you grew up in. It sure is captivating though."

"I bet it was beautiful," Cynthia breathed, imagining the place at its peak. She had never been inside. "Can we walk up that way?"

"Sure," Amara answered. "I'm pretty sure it's occupied again, but we can walk around the grounds. It was stunning when I was a kid. It was like stepping into another realm. Anyway, I'm sure they're used to people looking it over, same as the mill. These are the focal points of Yountsville."

"That old church across the road must have been something special in its day," Gregory commented. "Nikki has a million shots of it."

"Get 'em while the gettin's good," Nikki gave a gamin grin. "There's not much left to see now. And don't forget the old school."

"That's true," Amara jumped in. "The school is neat, but that church was beautiful. The locals knocked out most of the windows."

"Stained glass," Nikki moaned. "What a waste!"

"Yeah, well, Cynthia and I saved one of them, didn't we?" Amara shot Cynthia a conspiratorial wink.

Cynthia had the good grace to blush to the roots of her auburn hair. She and Amara had known each other the longest, and when they were just grade school kids they had sneaked out one night to steal one of those windows! "Yup!" her pretty face was pink as she confessed to their escapade. "If we hadn't taken it, someone else would have destroyed it."

"That's true," Amara piped up. "We had gone inside a number of times and never touched a thing. And then one night we noticed only one window was in its original glory. All the others were damaged or gone."

"It's true," Cynthia whispered. "We felt bad about it, but we tore it out in one piece. No harm befell that gorgeous glass!"

"How did you manage that?" Ian demanded. "I mean, two lone females, both so young..." he let the sentence trail off.

"We never said we weren't prepared," Amara laughed. "We saw what was happening, and Grandfather had a whole barn full of tools. We simply 'borrowed' what we needed."

"Uh-oh," Ian teased.

"We didn't get caught," Cynthia snickered. "And the window is still perfectly preserved!"

"Where is it?" it was Nikki who spoke up this time.

"That's a treat for when we all visit Cynthia's!" Amara crowed.

"Amara," Cynthia sounded horrified, "You ratted me

out!"

"One of us had to keep it," Amara actually giggled, "and you had the perfect setting. Besides, your gypsy lifestyle deserves a stained glass window! It's a perfect fit."

Everyone laughed in agreement, and Nikki's voice rang out, "I, for one, think it's nice to know where a piece of history is safely stored."

"Me too," Linda seconded. The gang was in good spirits as they found their way back to Amara's side of the creek. Even though they waded across the shallows, everyone but Amara had removed their shoes. Some had even rolled up their jeans in an effort to stay dry. They all enjoyed a good laugh when Amara made a pun of the sole reason she wore sole-less moccasins. They were comfortable wet or dry!

"What a brilliant day! This has been so much fun, Amara," Cynthia cheered.

"Just what the doctor ordered," Amara murmured, and everyone grew quiet. "Awe, come on," she grinned, meaning every word, "This is the best medicine I could have asked for! Thanks, guys."

It was the perfect medicine for Amara, and she felt blessed to have such wonderful friends. She signaled everyone past the swimming hole she frequented, and led them to the best place to climb in order to gain access to the meadow above. They fell silent as they followed her example of which rocks and roots to use as handholds. The trail was an unmarked one, and fairly rugged, yet she climbed it with ease taking the time to demonstrate the safest route. Nikki had been there the most, and realized how sheer the bluff actually was. She took on the responsibility of acting as guide from the rear of the group. The goal was to keep everyone safe after all, and even this, the easiest incline, was steep. The two men were naturals, but the other girls were grateful for the assistance.

It was a long, slow climb, and the gang literally gave a weak cheer when they reached the top. They also took a lengthy break in the meadow before wandering down to the meandering stream. Ian stayed behind for personal reasons. When he rejoined them he singled Amara out, saying, "Amara, I think you've had a deer or something at the edge of your property. Did you notice the flattened grass?"

Amara gave him a quizzical look. She glanced at Nikki, who in turn eyed Gregory, and the three of them set off back up the hill with Ian in the lead. "It doesn't look natural," he murmured. "I don't want to alarm you, but I thought I should mention it."

"You did right," Gregory said firmly.

As they stood around the condensed area that was large enough to house a man, Amara felt a shiver race down her spine. "This is contrived, isn't it? It was manufactured for a purpose," she stared at Gregory, almost daring him to contradict her. She felt the blood drain from her face as she looked over the bluff. There was a perfect view of her swimming hole from here. Nikki noticed the same. She knew Amara better than anyone, and realized that her friend had been spied upon.

"I'm sorry, Amara," Gregory said simply. He knew there was no point in lying to her.

Nikki wrapped her in her arms. "You need to sit," was all she said. Amara didn't even remember walking the few steps to a nearby log, and taking a seat with her best friend at her side. She was made suddenly aware of the two men discussing the situation quietly when they glanced her way. "I'm staying over tonight," Nikki stated clearly. It was not an offer or a question. Her naturally quiet voice was firm. "You need me."

"Yes, please," Amara whispered. Nikki was the only one who could have gotten her to admit to such a need. Normally, Amara would have called her bluff. But Nikki could see through all that. "Tomorrow, I will clean up those negatives, and we'll see what we have. I don't want you alone tonight."

"We will have to contact the law," Gregory stated in an authoritative voice. "You do realize that?"

"Yes," Amara answered, "First thing in the morning. Let's don't worry the others."

"I am not sure I am in agreement with you," Gregory's deep voice rumbled, "but I will respect your decision. I am, however, sleeping over as well." He gave both girls a look that said they were not to dispute the fact.

Nikki's soft brown eyes searched Amara's darker ones until she received an affirmative nod. Amara looked directly at Gregory when she answered, "You guys can take the spare room."

"Thank you," Gregory nodded, and led the way back to the others. Nikki and Amara took their time catching up.

No one said a word, but allowed Amara to take the lead. And she was determined to show her friends a good time. Slowly they began to relax in the woodlands, sitting on, or around, Flat Rock. The land was named after this particular boulder that was believed to sit atop a host of caves. This was Miami ground, and it was sacred. Amara's family had honored it as such, and Amara carried on the tradition. This spectacular stone overlooked the great waterfalls that had been magnificent when Amara was a child. The falls had spanned all three walls of shale with a rush of water so profound as to drown out all else.

Now in 1970, there was a stream deep enough for fishing, and a fairly expansive waterfall. But Amara was shocked by the damage the locals had done with their dams and explosives. She treasured the view she was given on this piece of God's green earth, and could not fathom how anyone could do less. She pointed upward to the crest that jutted out over the water, and the place where they were seated. She explained to anyone who did not know that the ground above was a hallowed burial mound. Anyone who climbed that mound must make an offering, and always, always show a great deal of respect to the people who had worshipped there.

The Miami, she explained, buried their dead high up in the trees, or on scaffolds they had built for this purpose. They believed this would accelerate the soul's passage into the spiritual afterlife. By the same token the infants were eternally nourished in this manner. Their bodies were laid out with reverence on these consecrated grounds. Grandfather had often spoken of the petrified papoose they had found in the treetops in the 1930's. Amara was in awe of this fact.

The hour was growing late. Everyone was tired and hungry. It was dusk when the guys decided to visit the mound, and leave an offering of tobacco. The girls, in turn, split up to wander freely. There was just enough light for them to climb the intricate paths that wove around the rushing current. They gazed in rapture at the towering walls that could not be breached, and gloried in the foamy white waters that rushed past them. It was both breathtaking and omnipotent making them each feel like a tiny speck in an otherwise immense universe.

Cynthia, alone, had wandered upstream to view the

pond. She was gathering ideas for future paintings. The trees were dense along the path, restricting her view of the others. They were in close proximity, yet for all the peace and quiet of the world it did not seem so. Cynthia startled when a twig snapped up ahead. She froze when she glanced in that direction, and there before her stood the most bewitching creature she had ever seen! It was a white fawn, as pure as the driven snow. She could do nothing more than stare. And when she blinked it was gone; just like that. Cynthia stood peering at that empty spot a moment longer, before turning and heading back to tell the others. She was enraptured by what she had witnessed. It had gained her undivided attention, and she gave thanks to the Great Spirit for this magnanimous gift.

CHAPTER EIGHT

Amara deposited both pans of enchiladas in the oven even as she put the rice on to boil. They fit nicely side by side. Nikki was busily flavoring the beans. She would mash them while Amara seasoned the rice. The chips were laid out on the counter to be warmed last. The fridge was well stocked with dark Mexican beer. There was a bright platter of sliced limes next to the bowl of Pico de Gallo that would be served in individual little dishes much like the salsa and guacamole. Amara kept a colorful set of Fiesta Ware specifically for Hispanic food. The kitchen smelled wonderful.

Strains of music wafted through the house. The Band was on the main stereo in the front room. Amara loved listening to Levon's voice. It never failed to amaze her how such a proficient drummer could carry the vocals. Most lead singers focused on voice alone or accompanied themselves on rhythm guitar. It was rare for a drummer to cover the role of vocal artist. In her opinion, it didn't get any better than Levon Helm, and she said as much.

"Those guys are great," Nikki stated emphatically. "I think they are my favorite band ever. I just love Robbie Robertson. And he is so much fun to watch!"

"They all are, really," Amara agreed. "They are so uncommonly gifted. Their interaction is astonishing. I can't understand why they aren't more popular in the states?"

"People lack taste," it was Linda's voice as she blew into the kitchen. "I came for more beer. I think the guys are getting faint," she laughed as she grabbed a couple more bottles.

"Better go ahead and warm some chips," Nikki chuckled as she popped them, covered, onto the other rack. "They will only take a minute," she shook her head as Linda scuttled off to pass the word.

Amara was finishing up the rice when Cynthia came in and took control of the condiments, "Linda said you could use a hand," she offered with a grin. She proceeded to set the table for good measure.

"Thanks," Amara and Nikki chorused.

"Enchiladas will be out in a few," Amara's voice rang out. Nikki was busily wiping down the stovetop.

"Boy, you can sure tell you two have cooked together often enough!" Cynthia smiled.

"All those catering jobs," Nikki murmured. "This one," she nudged Amara, "would truly make a fantastic chef!"

"Yeah, I can't believe you haven't pursued that by now," it was Cynthia again. "Your cooking is heavenly."

"Well, I still might," Amara said without conviction, "but it is so much more fun this way!"

Amara pulled the enchiladas out of the oven and set

the hot baking pans atop pads on the counter. She arranged the Spanish rice and refried beans conveniently next to them. They had agreed to serve themselves. Amara had three really nice bottles of wine. Nikki opened one and set it out with some glasses. While Cynthia told the guys to go wash up, Linda went about feeding Grim and the little ones. This would allow for a peaceful evening. They all knew that with Amara, the animals came first. Amara smiled her thanks, and everyone took a seat just as Beggars Banquet by The Rolling Stones broke free on the stereo.

"It was a truly wonderful day, Amara," Linda said as she hugged her friend good night. "I enjoyed every minute of it."

"Dinner was delicious," Ian complimented sincerely. "Thank you for having us."

"She is a great cook," Gregory acknowledged with a grin, "Nikki too."

"You sure you guys will be all right tonight?" Cynthia asked quietly. "I mean, we can all stay and camp out if it helps?"

"We'll be fine, thanks," Amara gave Cynthia a kiss on the cheek. "You are such a good friend. Thanks for that." Amara held a special place in her heart for Cynthia. They had grown up together. They had shared all their secrets. There was nothing she wouldn't do for Cynthia, and she knew the feeling was mutual.

"Well, dinner was excellent, and it was a perfect day," Cynthia said in earnest.

"Thanks, we'll do it again soon," Amara said. "Now, is everyone safe to drive?"

"I certainly am," Linda offered. She gave her husband a loving look, and said, "I'm sure Ian is too. But I only had tea. Therefore, I claim the wheel."

"I didn't have enough to matter," Cynthia said, "I was more interested in your enchiladas. You make the best Mexican I have ever had!"

The friends said their good-byes, collected their hugs, and insisted that someone contact them the following day. Everyone was clearly concerned for Amara. Grim wagged his tail as he trailed after them. Sampson purred and wove figure eights around Amara's feet, and Solomon walked on hind legs in his excitement. The little guy hopped along after Amara, his tongue caught between his teeth. It had been a successful evening. Amara watched as everyone disappeared from sight before joining Nikki and Gregory for a nightcap. She carried Solomon back into the house, gave Sam a pat on the head, and then poured herself a glass of wine. She had not had any with dinner, preferring to watch after her guests.

Gregory never drank much, but Amara knew that he was being especially careful tonight. Nikki appeared at ease, but Amara knew her well enough to understand that she could go from one mode to another with lightning speed. Amara folded herself into a comfortable seat and sipped at her wine. No one spoke of the necessary phone call that would be placed in the early hours of the morning. But later when Gregory had gone out for a smoke, the girls discussed Victoria and the way she had attempted to smuggle Simon into their tight little group of friends.

"Well, you were right about her," Amara looked Nikki directly in the eyes.

"You would have seen it for yourself if you hadn't been so busy trying to be nice," Nikki reassured.

"Yeah, probably," Amara responded. "But I don't usually slip up like that."

Nikki could see that Amara was somewhat distressed, an emotion she rarely displayed. She had been through a lot, and it seemed an appropriate time to ask, "What exactly happened between you and Simon? You know, when you made the poor decision to go out with him?"

Amara gave a mock scowl. She sighed as she ran slim fingers through her tangled curls. She knew too well that Nikki was using a diversion tactic. At the same time, she recognized that her friend was honestly intrigued. They had never discussed the details of that day. Afterwards, it didn't seem to matter. "I was edgy," she supplied as she told Nikki about the photographs, "and he was arrogant and much too presumptuous. I merely thought I'd get even." Amara paused to draw breath. Nikki gave a nervous laugh, and when Amara next spoke, Nikki just about fell off her seat. "So, I got dressed and came downstairs, and there sat Simon in all his naked glory! He was that sure of himself. I think he realized his mistake when I spied the kettle on the stove. It was still steaming..."

"You didn't," Nikki literally cringed.

"Sure I did. Did you know a man can scream as shrilly as any girl when he gets hot water poured over his privates?" Amara asked the question in a steady voice. "If it's any consolation, I'm sure they were only first degree burns," she offered with a ghost of a smile, "But judging from the look on his face, it is probably a good thing I hightailed it out of there!"

"Wow," Nikki was literally in a state of shock. She stared

at Amara with a mixture of horror, awe, and newfound respect. "Just, wow."

Amara laughed lightly and topped their wine. "I do feel better after our little conversation," she tapped her glass to Nikki's in a private toast.

Nikki gave a timid giggle, and then began to laugh in earnest.

"What'd I miss?" Gregory had come back indoors causing both girls to jump instinctively. Sampson draped himself across Gregory's big feet stopping him in his tracks, while Solomon demanded to be held. He was full of kisses! The girls fell apart; they laughed until their sides ached, leaving Gregory to shake his head at their nonsense. Grim looked up from a nap, yawned at their tomfoolery, and laid his head back on his paws. "What's so funny?" Gregory muttered.

They called it a night a little early and went their separate ways. They would be up before they knew it. Sure enough, Solomon woke them with a tantrum. He was a routine little guy and his schedule was off. Grim nudged him tolerantly as if to say, "Go back to sleep, little buddy." But Solomon was up and that was that. Amara put on the tea kettle, and then fed the little ones. Grim patiently waited his turn. Nikki put on a pot of coffee for Gregory while Amara foraged for food. She set a variety of ingredients on the counter, and between them, the girls created an easy but elegant breakfast.

After a hot shower and clean change of clothes, Amara was ready to make the call. She dialed the station with some trepidation, and was grateful when Grant picked up. "Sheriff Wheeler," his deep voice rumbled.

"Grant?" she said in a husky voice, "This is Amara, Amara Owens." She allowed the familiarity of his voice to wash over her.

"Amara," he said her name in such a way it felt like a caress. "What's up?" he asked, and the moment was gone. "Has something happened?"

"You could say that," she felt awkward. "Do you have time to see me today?"

He asked a couple of questions, and upon learning the situation, said, "I'll be out shortly. Wait for me at the house."

She didn't question his authority, but hung up and settled in to wait. "Do you want me to stay with you?" Nikki's voice showed concern. "I don't have to work today."

"Could you take a look at the film instead?"

"You read my mind. If you're sure you're okay?"

"I'm fine," Amara insisted, "But I have a feeling the sheriff is going to be awfully angry when he discovers that I withheld evidence."

"Maybe we'll get lucky and it won't amount to anything," Nikki suggested. But they both knew it was highly unlikely.

When Grant pulled up the gravel drive, Amara was outside sitting on the front steps. Although Grim was her only companion, she could be heard talking to something in the trees. Amara stood to greet him. She wore a sleeveless plaid top that tied at the waist. She didn't realize that with such long hair and short shorts, she appeared all legs. Grant tipped his hat, quietly accessing her behind dark glasses. He crooked one finger, and she walked sedately to the car. She could feel his gaze like a hot iron, but didn't let on. She slid into the passenger seat, even as Grim climbed in behind her. He filled the entire back seat, and they drove to the meadow where the grass was compressed.

"You should have called me last night," he grated.

"I had a houseful of guests," she gestured with her hands, "and didn't want to alarm everyone. Besides, Nikki stayed over." She wondered why she hadn't mentioned that Gregory had as well.

"This is a crime scene," he pointed at the flattened grass. "I don't want anyone else near it."

"I thought so," she offered, feeling rebuked. "That's why I called." She was getting angry, "Well, that, and to tell you about Simon."

They stood leaning against the vehicle, talking, at least that's what Grant called it. To Amara, it felt more like an interrogation. There were certainly no laughs in this conversation. "I want the facts," he stated. "All of them."

"Look, it's hot. Grim needs water. I understand you need the facts, and I'll be only too happy to supply them. But let's go back to the house, and discuss this over a glass of iced tea."

She watched as he mentally checked himself. She could tell that he was angry by his ruddy complexion. A vein throbbed in his forehead. He straightened his broad shoulders and told her, "Get in." And for one irrational moment, she almost refused. Instead, she obeyed without further comment.

They were back at the house in record time. Amara fussed over the little ones for a few minutes, more to make him wait than anything else. He wasn't the only one with a temper. She poured two glasses of iced tea while offering lemon or sugar. He declined both. She added a large wedge of lemon to her glass, and led the way to a comfortable spot in the shade. The house had several porches. This one was her favorite this time of day. Grim followed her, and Solomon tagged after him. Sampson lounged in the doorway.

Grant waited for her to be seated, then took a chair himself. She wondered if it was good manners or some kind of strategy to gain the upper hand. "Okay," he began, "Let's start at the beginning. How did you meet Simon? How long did you date him? And exactly how did it end?"

"I already told you he was my English professor," her temper hadn't cooled.

"Which makes it wrong to start with," he pointed out.

"Yes, for him," she snapped. "I already told you, we didn't date until *after* I finished all of his classes."

"Your decision, or his?" he asked.

"Mine," her voice was clipped.

"And how long did you date? How often did you see him?"

"Is this necessary?" she was tired of the juvenile questions, and made the mistake of saying so.

"Answer me," his voice was rough, his manner curt. She wondered how she had ever been even a little bit attracted to him. The thought gave her a jolt.

She repeated the answers she had already given, truly dreading the part about the break-up. It seemed such an intimate detail to discuss, and one that would not likely go over well with any male anywhere. Now she understood why she had kept quiet about the bits of film. She felt exposed, and to her mind that wasn't fair.

"You did what?" he exploded when she had finished describing her position in the grand finale. He was up and pacing, throwing looks her way that made her most uncomfortable. Part of her wanted to crawl away and hide, but mostly, she was spoiling for a fight.

"You heard me," she said succinctly. "And I'm not sorry, he had it coming." There was no way in hell she was going to back down now. She stood watching him watch her for what seemed like forever. She had put the dogs inside quite some time ago when she saw how it was going to be. "And if you don't like me for it, so what? You weren't dealing with the creep, I was!"

She was so mad her face flushed red, and her chest heaved. She shoved her hair out of her eyes in the same second he broke into ribald male laughter, "Well, I'll be! Looks like I got myself a little hellcat!" And the look he bestowed upon her was one of pure masculine delight.

God bless her, for the first time she could recall, she was at a loss for words. Instead, she went weak in the knees, and had to grope for a seat. Sheriff Grant Wheeler was actually laughing at her!

CHAPTER NINE

She fell into her Monday routine with the exception of an impromptu call from Sheriff Wheeler on his way home. She was a little confused as to whether he was checking on her personally, or officially? She decided just to roll with it. Tanner came and went with his usual daily chores. At one point she was certain he had been doing nothing more than spying on her. The whole idea put her nerves on edge. She chose to ignore that as well. Gregory rang that evening requesting a reunion with Daniel so that the two of them could become better acquainted. He wasn't pushing it on her, he told her, but Dan was a close friend and he felt responsible for their bad beginning. She agreed to the meeting, and they planned a casual visit the following afternoon. Nikki would join them when she got off work.

So it was, she met Daniel Collins for the second time that Tuesday. It was mid-afternoon when the men arrived, and Amara welcomed the visitation. She had just changed into a fresh blouse when she answered the knock at the door. Why was she so nervous, she wondered? Grant had called earlier, and in general everything seemed normal. She extended her hand to Daniel as Gregory made the unnecessary introductions. "Hello," Daniel began, "I'd like to apologize for the other day."

"No apology necessary," she responded graciously, "It was just a misunderstanding. Would you gentlemen like to sit outside? There's a nice breeze on the side porch, and I just made a fresh pitcher of iced tea unless you would prefer lemon water?"

"Iced tea sounds good," the two men said in unison.

"Have a seat," Amara escorted them to the aforementioned porch. "I'll just be a moment." She was true to her word, returning quickly with a tray bearing a pitcher of iced tea and a set of glasses. There was a small sugar bowl and a saucer of sliced lemons alongside a neatly folded stack of napkins. Grim followed in her wake. Wind chimes tinkled overhead. There was a lovely view overlooking the creek.

"Nikki tells me you are a reporter," she stated in a neutral tone. "I would appreciate it if you would keep the events of the other night quiet."

Daniel sucked in his breath as if he'd been punched, and she realized he hadn't known how threatened she must have felt. "I'm truly sorry for the confusion, Miss Owens," he said in a sincere voice, "I didn't come here as a reporter, ma'am."

"Amara," she replied without pause, "Then I confess, I am confused. Why did you come?"

"I should have explained," Gregory said, and Amara could tell he felt miserable about what had happened. "I'm afraid this was my fault. I did tell Daniel it was okay to photograph whatever he came across, but I was speaking about the hoof prints," he qualified. "Daniel is an author. His topics are rather unusual. I should have asked you first, Amara, but

I honestly didn't think you would mind."

"I study all kinds of phenomenon," Daniel described his work briefly, "and I would never use anything I found without permission."

Amara visibly straightened in her seat. She cocked her head when she next spoke, "I don't understand. You mean you knew about the white fawn, and were trying to gather information on her?" her voice sounded strange to her own ears. With the break-in, and all that it entailed, Amara hadn't imagined this man, this reporter, might be interested in the fawn.

"Yes and no," he expounded on the topic. "I am curious about the white fawn, but especially intrigued with the creature that was encountered."

"How did you know about that?" she asked her face pale.

"The night of the attempted B & E, I admit I was privy to some bizarre happenings. The information came over the scanner that a creature had been sighted on your property. This is my field," he gestured with his hands making her aware of how big those hands were. "I spoke to Gregory the following morning, and he told me that he would be here to make any necessary repairs, and that I should come on out." He paused only long enough to take a drink of his iced tea, and then continued his story while the sun danced off the copper of his hair. He had beautiful hair, she thought. "The impressions altered drastically as I was following them." She could literally feel his excitement. "I could see the changes as they occurred. It was the most peculiar thing to watch what appeared to be a normal set of deer prints become the tracks of a beast known only as a banshee in certain parts of the world! I captured them as they made each transformation.

I only meant to get the photographs while they were fresh. I would have spoken with you myself before I went any further," he disclosed.

"How do they differ?" she asked, recalling the tufted creature with the curled horns and hoofed feet. She would never forget those wild eyes. They were so intense they chilled her to the very marrow.

"The prints looked like those of a deer before the creature changed appearances. That is the only explanation because the hoofs later had three toes instead of two, and the pads were spread out, rather similar to a rhino's. This creature, this beast, would run with a great deal of speed. I'd stake my career on it."

Amara sat staring at him wondering what to say. She was truly at a loss. "What makes you refer to it as a banshee?" she blurted.

"I am of Irish and Scottish descent," he answered, and for the first time she noticed that he had a slight brogue. "And legend has it that banshees are the only creatures with feet like these," he explained.

"But only moments ago you likened them to a rhino's."

"Yes, well, that is the closest comparison I could come up with," he clarified. "There are differences of course."

"Such as?" she wondered why she asked the question. Or was she picking on him, looking for flaws in his story?

"As I said the pads are different," he murmured, shrugging his broad shoulders. "And of course by looking at the hoof prints, the body size and bulk would vary as well."

She was rendered momentarily speechless. She sank

back into the cushion with the realization that she had been tensely seated on the edge of her chair. She didn't know why, but this conversation was disturbing to her. She shook her head to clear it, and the small gold hoops in her ears jingled merrily. It seemed incongruent with the topic at hand. "Why would I have a banshee on my land?" was all she said.

"In Irish mythology, a banshee usually predicts a death. It can, however, be a spirit haunting of a lost soul," Daniel responded immediately. "Please don't take the myths to heart, Amara, there are probably all kinds of explanations for such a thing."

"Of course," she said quietly, but it was clear that she was troubled. "Do you have the photos with you?"

"Of course," he echoed her words, quickly producing a packet from an inside jacket pocket. He had removed the item of clothing upon arrival, and folded it neatly across the back of his chair. "You may keep these if you like; I have marked the order so you can see how the changes occurred."

She was thoughtful for a moment. "Thank you, I shall look them over more thoroughly tonight," she replied even as she flipped through the prints, pausing here and there as she did so. "What will you do with your copies?" she asked with a very real curiosity.

"That all depends on you," he answered. "First off, I will require your signature to use them at all. Then if you allow it, I would only release as much as you are comfortable with," he said kindly. "There isn't any need to make use of your name, or the name of your property. You are not to be put under a microscope."

"Thank you," she repeated with a small smile. "You're very kind."

"It's the least I can do," he responded just as a county cop pulled up out front.

"Are you expecting official business?" Gregory asked at the same time Amara responded to Daniel's comment.

"I appreciate that," she released a breath she hadn't realized she had been holding.

"And no, I'm not expecting anyone except Nikki."

The conversation came to a halt as the vehicle stopped and Sheriff Wheeler stepped out. He approached the house with something of a smug look. His gaze took in the scene on the porch, lingering for a millisecond too long on Daniel. When he looked directly at her, Amara felt like a child who had been caught doing something naughty. "Hello, Miss Owens," he said in a harsh tone. She did not like the implication of his actions, or the way he made her feel.

"Hello Sheriff Wheeler," she replied stiffly. "We were just having some tea. Would you care for a glass?"

"No, thank you," the officer answered, "None for me. I was just driving by and thought to check on you. It would seem my attention is unnecessary."

"Not at all," she remonstrated politely, "I am grateful for your time."

"Are you?" he asked. "It would appear others beat me to it," he sounded arrogant to her. His attitude annoyed her largely because she did not know where she stood with him. Was he just doing his duty, or something more? And why must he make a competition of it either way?

"You remember Gregory," she ignored his rudeness and made the introductions instead, "and I believe you have met

Daniel. He was just explaining his interest in all of this. Did you know Daniel was an author as well as a reporter?"

"Yes," he said, "I make it a point to know what everyone in the vicinity is up to," he offered smoothly, irritating her further. She nodded a response as her temper soared. If he knew about Daniel, why hadn't he informed her? "Walk me to the car?" he asked idly.

"Excuse me for a moment," she glanced first at Gregory, and then at Daniel.

The two men made as if to leave with Gregory saying, "We won't keep you. We had no idea you had other plans."

"I don't," she was emphatic. "Please have some more iced tea. Grim, stay," she ordered the big dog, and Grim who was about to follow whined in protest. He regarded her soberly and laid back down, his head on his front paws. The men sipped at their tea thinking it best not to cause a scene. Grim's eyes followed her every move.

She walked Grant to the car where he spoke just a bit too possessively. He would have detained her further when she thanked him for stopping, but the sound of car wheels on the gravel road announced Nikki's arrival. Nikki gave a wave which Amara returned. "Thanks again," Amara said to Grant, and though he appeared nonchalant, she was very much aware of his irritation. His lips had turned down at the corners, making his expression cold.

"I'll call upon you again soon," he promised as he took the wheel. Amara nodded and returned to her guests. Grant sat staring after her for a full minute before he turned and peeled out onto the highway.

"That went well," Gregory announced when she and Nikki had joined them.

"Ignore it," Amara insisted.

The men exchanged looks, but remained silent. Nikki raised a brow, and Amara looked uncomfortable. "Who's up for pizza?" Nikki changed the subject. "I'm buying!"

"I'm in," they chorused looking to Amara for approval.

"Sure, sounds great," Amara smiled, grateful for the change of subject.

"I'll call it in, and you guys can pick it up. Okay?" Nikki offered. Everyone agreed at once, and the awkwardness of the moment was forgotten.

The pizza was good; really good. Nikki knew all the hot spots. The foursome sat at the kitchen table enjoying the food, the company, and the quiet of the night. The dogs had been fed, and Sampson was busily nibbling at his dinner, while alternately tormenting the canines. Amara sat engrossed in the tales Daniel shared about his work, travels, and homeland. He seemed the most intriguing male she had spoken with in a long while, and his kindness and generosity of spirit appeared real. She relaxed in the presence of his company. Her laughter rang out repeatedly, and Daniel responded in kind. Nikki glanced up at Gregory on several occasions only to find him watching her. They smiled at each other in the soft light of the candles Amara had placed on the table. At this moment everything seemed right in the world.

They took their beverages outside after dinner, enjoying the weather which was so pleasant they made the unanimous decision that a walk was in order. They set out toward the front of the property, an effort that ended with Gregory veering off into the brush with Nikki, while Ama-

ra gave Daniel an informative tour of the Yountsville Bridge. The Bridge was a concrete structure of gargantuan proportions with open apertures from which a driver could view the creek. It was a solid piece of architecture with an enormous arch spanning the waters below. She laughed when she told him that it was a notorious spot for lovers. He raised his brows comically up and down, increasing her amusement. She moved at a relaxed pace as she began the narrative of the original covered bridge. "That one was wooden, and was there during the 1940's," she explained. "I'm not sure what year it was built, but I guess it was quite unusual in that it had two lanes."

Daniel was hanging on her every word. He asked a couple of questions about the construction of the bridge before they wandered back to the house.

"It was a pleasant evening," Amara said when it was time for the others to leave.

"It was a magnificent evening," Daniel smiled as he spoke. "It was a pure delight getting to know you," he grasped both of her hands in one of his.

"You too," Amara blushed as she gazed into his eyes. He had deep-set, sky-blue orbs unlike any she had ever seen before. She literally fell into their depths, and a wide smile spread across her face. The look was contagious causing him to beam from ear to ear. "Thank you for the pizza," she turned her focus upon Nikki.

Nikki grinned and murmured a response while the guys headed for their individual vehicles. "I'll be along in a bit," she called after them. The girls watched as the guys drove away. They looped arms, and with Grim at their heels, headed indoors.

"So, you liked Daniel, huh?" Nikki couldn't stop grinning.

"Yes," Amara wasn't used to feeling like a love-sick pup, "very much. He isn't at all what I expected."

"Yeah, he's a pretty great guy," Nikki agreed, "and there's no girl in the picture. He is totally unattached, and I'd say more than a little interested in you."

They chattered happily for several minutes, and then Nikki said, "I wanted to give you these when we were alone. I cleaned them with isopropyl and pieced them together as much as possible. As you can see, there are only partial images, and not very clear ones at that. These were deliberately sullied, I'm afraid." She pulled an envelope from her shoulder bag and handed it to Amara. "I'm sorry," she whispered as she nudged Amara into a chair.

"Oh, dear God," Amara's voice trembled. She was staring at images of herself on the sandy riverbank. She had obviously been swimming. And she was nude. The pictures were pieced together reminding her of the condition in which she had first discovered them. Crow had delivered one, and the other had been left for her to find in her bedroom closet. In one partial shot she was wearing a tiny pair of hot pink panties. The matching bra was in her hand. Her head was cut off. "Were these on both pieces of film or just the one?" She asked. She didn't know why it mattered.

"Both," Nikki replied. "I don't know how Crow came to have one. I assume he found it."

"I see. Thank you, Nikki," Amara swallowed hard. It was terrifying to her that someone not only took these shots without her consent, but obviously felt the need to brag about it.

"Are you going to turn them in?"

"I don't know."

That night, Amara didn't sleep a wink. She lay awake wondering when her world had turned upside down. Maybe it had always been that way, she thought. Grim seemed to sense something was amiss as he snuggled close against her bed. As she listened to him doze, she realized she was hearing that song in her head again, the one that continued to haunt her.

She fell into a restless slumber at some point in the night because she awoke with a start at the sound of the most eerie howl she had ever heard. It sent chills all the way through her. It wasn't yet dawn when she climbed out of bed, still caught up in the remnants of a dream. In her altered state, she was following a set of deer tracks that suddenly turned into the bare prints of a human female! She padded across the hall to the bath, brushed her teeth and splashed cold water on her face. She dressed quickly in yesterday's clothes, and after looking in on the little ones, she and Grim left the house. She was armed. Breakfast and a hot shower could wait.

THE CALLING OF CROWS

PART TWO

Awinita

CHAPTER TEN

Amara followed a set of deer prints from the woods to the edge of the stream. When she reached the other side, the tracks had become human just like in her dream! She looked to the sun realizing she had lost a couple of hours. For the life of her, she could not remember climbing down the hill to the creek bank below. Instead, she found herself in the middle of Rock River staring at the old mill. The water level had been lower than usual only yesterday. She could have easily waded across. But the water was too high now! Grim whined, and she realized he still clung to the bank. That was out of character for him. She recognized in that moment that her feet could no longer touch the ground. She would have to swim the rest of the way. The landscape wavered around her, and she sputtered as she swallowed a gulp of water. She felt odd, almost surreal. She didn't know what to make of it. She shook her head to clear it as the song in her head gained volume. It was so loud she could make out some of the words.

The mill quivered and shifted just as the water had done, and when she looked again it appeared fully restored! There was a dam and a vast reservoir of water. The mill was

actually functioning, and the place was populated. Women were sitting on the bank, apparently taking a break. Their clothing looked as old fashioned as the mill itself. They wore long dresses that were badly tattered. Most of them wore their hair up or tied back in a braid or pony tail. Some of them were eating, and from what Amara could see, they didn't have much. There were a few children about, but they appeared weak and somewhat subdued. Occasionally a baby cried. A few of the women had begun to sing. Others gradually joined in. She clearly caught the words *wayfaring stranger* and knew this was the song that had been haunting her dreams. The tune lingered, swelling loudly at times, and the lyrics flowed on.

As she stood staring at this implausible scene, the crowd of females began to disperse. She watched until only one remained. She was sitting closer to the water's edge than any of the others, and with Amara's sharp vision she could see that the woman's hair was damp. She wondered if her clothes were too. At the thought, the woman leaned over and wrung out the hem of her skirt, and then looked directly at her. Her eyes were a soft brown, the same shape and color as a fawn's. Amara found herself being pulled forward, closer and closer to the lady in question. She could not tear her gaze away no matter how hard she tried. It was unnerving.

Amara spared a glance over her shoulder to check on Grim who had hunkered down in the sand. Even at this distance she could tell he wore a woeful expression. His whimper carried on the breeze and she wanted to reassure him, but it was literally impossible to ignore the woman. She straightened, and with great dignity, walked up to her. To her surprise, the stranger was made of flesh and bone. She had half expected her to disappear like the apparition she had believed her to be. But she sat calmly waiting as the water wheel continued to churn, and the sounds and voices carried from inside the mill. It was absurd! Yet here she was, and it was real.

"Who are you?" she asked sounding shocked even to her own ears.

"I am Awinita," the illusion replied.

"How did you come to be here?" Amara asked, nonplussed.

"I took a position here, of course."

"I don't understand," Amara stammered. "This mill was not even up and running yesterday! How is this possible?"

"I think you are misinformed," Awinita said softly. "I have been here for over a month now. There are close to three-hundred women and children employed in these mills."

"But this is the only surviving mill, and it has been down for a very long time." A thought was beginning to form in Amara's mind as she fingered the 1864 Indian Head penny. "What year is it?" she asked suddenly.

"Eighteen-sixty-four," Awinita supplied with a twinkle in her eyes. "Well, it was eighteen-sixty-four when I arrived in Indiana. But it's eighteen-sixty-five now. I am sorry to have made this so difficult for you." Her voice was smooth and steady, her personality sweet and somehow familiar.

"Do I know you?" Amara couldn't resist asking.

Just when it appeared there would be no answer, Awinita spoke softly, "Yes, we have known each other for a very long time."

"How is that possible?" Amara breathed, "And why is

this happening now?"

"Time has an uncanny twist about it. Or perhaps it is more like a second chance," Awinita chose her words carefully. "I am here to help you, just as you are here to help me. It is all part of a whole, I think."

"I don't understand," Amara whispered.

"You will. For now, it is enough that we have met. And that you know we are on friendly terms. That way it will be more comfortable when we meet again." That being said, the words hung in the air as Awinita began to fade along with the formerly functioning mill. Amara gaped at the old mill in its present state of neglect even as she continuously looked askance at the spot where the woman had been seated only seconds before. The grass was slightly compressed, and there were imprints in the sand where Awinita's feet had been planted. As Amara watched, these too disappeared leaving no sign of life except her own. She turned and looked at the creek, and the water level was back to normal. Grim whined as he hunched down and bravely crossed to meet her.

Back at the house, Amara discovered that she was cold to the point of freezing. Chill bumps covered her flesh until she couldn't stop shaking. Grim hadn't fared a great deal better. He was trembling almost as much as she, enough that she could plainly see he was in shock. Amara grabbed an armload of towels from the linen closet, threw them briefly into the dryer, and then briskly rubbed him dry. She had rifled through her animal remedies, and had given him an analeptic for this purpose. He calmed rapidly as she spoke to him, administering lots of intermediate hugs. When he was stable she draped an extra towel, already warmed, around him, and led him to his food bowl. She even broke out the special treats.

She had tossed a heavy blanket around her own shoulders for immediate relief while she took care of the babies. Sampson and Solomon were aware of the present trauma, and demanded a certain amount of attention. It was frightening for them when they saw her, or Grim, upset. She cuddled them briefly, and fed each in turn before going to run herself a hot bath. She added some soothing lavender to the water, and dosed herself with her own restorative. She made one specifically for animal energy and another for humans, and they worked extremely well.

Only after Amara was warm and relaxed did she allow herself to lather her hair. She took her time completing her toilet, knowing that after such a shock it was important to move slowly. She dressed in comfortable clothing, put the kettle on, and settled down with her animal family to sip a hot cup of chamomile tea. When she began to feel better, her appetite kicked in, and she decided a healthy breakfast was in order. An omelet sounded extraordinarily good so she set out the eggs and began to gather her vegetables of choice. A delicious aroma filled the kitchen as she sautéed a nice medley of onions, peppers, mushrooms, and tomatoes. She expertly prepared the eggs, topping them with the veggies before sprinkling the overall dish with shredded cheddar. This she slid under the broiler for precisely one minute before folding the egg smoothly. She placed it on a favorite plate and garnished it with fresh basil. It was delectable, she reasoned, and precisely what she needed.

Later that day Amara went down to the barn to tend the animals. She had gathered the eggs after her bath, and fed the cattle as well. But aside from setting food out for the cats, she had pretty much ignored them. They were fine, of course, but she liked to give them the attention they deserved. After all, they had few creature comforts. Smoke, the long-haired grey she most favored, rode her shoulder while she attended a few of the minor tasks at hand. Merlin, the yellow tom, talked to her from the fence post where he liked to perch. While she shoveled the stalls, a job she did daily in an effort to keep them clean, her mind wandered to the history of tomcats. She had discovered that the term had been around since the fourteenth century, but had gained notoriety in the 1760's with an anonymous book called *The Life and Adventures of a Cat.*

She filled the water trough for the horses, making sure they had plenty of hay after adding a couple of scoops of grain to the bin. She caught both mares and put them in the paddock where she groomed them with infinite care. Later, she would give them apples from the orchard. Shawnee was a paint mare, a gorgeous pinto with a proud spirit. She was almost eight-years-old and Amara had broken and trained her all by herself. She stood sixteen hands, and was Amara's pride and joy. Queen was a prickly appaloosa. She stood only slightly taller than Shawnee at seventeen hands. She had belonged to Tanner Lake, and he had allowed a young Amara to help break her, thus teaching her the ropes. Tanner had been more likable in those days before his wife left him. Raven was a handsome black gelding, and not one to be ignored. He was quite good natured, and easily the most mellow of the bunch. He was also the oldest of the three, and Amara had learned a lot from him. He stood fifteen hands, and had the tendency to follow her around. She never had to call him, much less catch him. He would always come of his own volition. All three horses were a source of pure joy to Amara. She loved them deeply, rode them often, and took more than competent care of them.

After checking and cleaning their hooves, Amara decided to take Shawnee out. A ride would do them both good.

She thought briefly of saddling her, but instead merely slipped a bridal over her head. Bareback would be fine. Shawnee was ever sensitive to her needs, and Amara trusted her unconditionally. She talked to her softly while she worked, telling her what fun they would have. She included the others in the conversation before letting them loose in the pasture and closing the gate. They were agreeable by nature. Shawnee let out a loud whinny as they left the paddock. Raven snorted in return running alongside the fence, while Queen regally tossed her head. Amara smiled a wide smile.

Amara walked Shawnee out the gate, and past the garden, before urging her into a trot. She posted easily, letting the trot build into a gentle canter. They rounded the fencing, and entered the woods, splashing through the stream and up the hill. When they reached the crest that opened into a wide meadow, Amara allowed Shawnee to break into a full gallop. Amara then leaned into her and hugged her back, wrapping her long legs around Shawnee's torso. Shawnee ran free as the wind, and Amara's slim fingers tangled in her mane as it mingled with the reins.

The freedom of the ride was exhilarating! To Amara it was a healing of sorts. Shawnee was in her element. She was happiest when she was with her mistress. It was the perfect remedy for an outré day until they came back downstream. As they dashed through the woods, Amara noticed Tanner's red pickup truck parked up ahead on the road. It was a dirt road, and there was no reason for Tanner to block it. Yet here he was leaning indolently against the truck. He was watching her. His eyes feasted on her chest before sliding down her legs and then up again. He had a hungry look on his face, and she was reminded that his wife had left him a long time back. It had been over a year now. Tanner caught Amara's expression, and surely realized he had been caught staring. If so, he didn't apologize. His look said it all, Amara thought. And that thought made her angry. She felt like she had been violated. She had to remind herself that Tanner was here on business, and that is where she intended to keep it.

"Hello, Amara," Tanner said, his eyes never leaving her form.

"Tanner," she nodded. Shawnee snorted and tossed her head. Amara could have nudged her on around the truck, but it would have been an obvious evasion. "What's going on?"

"Saw you out riding," he gave a nod, "You do it good."

If it was intended as a compliment, it fell short. "Thanks," Amara responded.

"I did a good job teaching you, didn't I?" the way he said it gave her the creeps. It was as if he was bragging on a sexual exploit.

"You were a great help," she acknowledged, remembering her youth when she was in training. Tanner, her closest neighbor, would stop by and give her pointers. He had lent a hand quite a few times when she was unsure how to address an issue with one of the horses. Back then she felt no reason to be shy around him. But that was then. Things change.

"I was wondering what you would think of mating Shawnee with my stallion? Buck is a hell of a good horse. We'd see a fine foal from it."

"No," she said emphatically. "No, thank you. I don't want to breed Shawnee."

"It's the natural way of things," he said, but when he spoke his eyes were on her, not her mare, "Keep it in mind."

"Thanks all the same," she said, kneeing Shawnee

lightly. It was a gentle command for the horse to move around him. At that, Tanner reached out to detain her. In so doing, he grasped Shawnee's bridal to which the horse responded with a loud shriek. She reared slightly. Amara held steady with ease, but her own temper flared. "You know better than that, Tanner!"

"All right, all right," he pulled his hands back, keeping them out in front of him as they both noted a county car bearing down on them.

"What's going on here?" it was Grant Wheeler who called out to them. He climbed out of the car keeping his eyes on Tanner. "You bothering the lady?" he asked.

"No, "Tanner said immediately, lowering his hands. "We were talking business."

"Didn't look like the lady wanted to stop and chat," Grant said. "What kind of business do you have here?"

"I keep my herd here," Tanner was referring to the cattle, "And I sow one of the fields each spring."

"I know who you are," Grant said, his right hand hovering near his holster. "Maybe you better be moving on, or would you like to answer some more questions? I know my boys have been to see you. Could be that I have a few of my own."

"Nah, I was heading out anyway," Tanner turned back to his truck. He was brought up short when the sheriff decided to pin him from behind.

"Mind you, stay away from the lady," Grant snarled a warning, "Or I'll be breathing down your back. Understand?"

Tanner nodded and peeled out, causing Shawnee to

rear again. Amara had anticipated the move and was quick to sooth her mount.

"We were just heading back to the barn," she told Grant, "I can meet you at the house in twenty minutes. I just need to separate her until she cools down."

"Okay, if you don't need any help?" he offered. "I'll make a call while I'm waiting," he gestured at the radio in his car. There was constant activity at the station.

CHAPTER ELEVEN

"**Y**ou did what?" Sheriff Wheeler sputtered, setting his coffee aside. "You chose to withhold evidence? Do you have any idea how serious this is?"

Amara looked down at her hands in her lap. The kitchen had grown utterly still, so quiet one could hear the wind in the eves. It was going to storm, and the silence punctuated the fact. Grim raised his big head looking directly at Amara. Solomon mirrored his actions. Sampson appeared ready to bolt while the dogs continued to watch their mistress. Amara stared hard at Grant, causing Grim to move instantly to her side. He wedged himself up next to her, effectively blocking the sheriff's view and limiting his range of motion. He was every inch the guard dog. And he was bordering on attack. Only then did Amara speak, "Grim. Sit."

"Thanks," the sheriff said sarcastically. Grim growled, and Grant had the good sense to back off.

"Try to look at it my way," Amara said in return, "I found the pieces of film just as I told you, but what you are not hearing is that I fully expected something as perverse as this. I was embarrassed." She spread her hands in surrender and raised her chin a notch. She did not look apologetic, not even a little bit.

"What about the fact that you were totally nude?" he stared at her in disapproval.

"I was alone," she hissed emphatically, "or at least I thought I was. And I was on my own property."

"What about that Tanner guy that comes around on a daily basis? What about the fact that your swimming hole is right off the creek?" his voice had risen to a shout. He was yelling at her now.

Grim was suddenly in his face. He growled low in his throat warning Grant to back down. The sheriff sat back in his chair, and Amara let about two additional seconds pass before she gave the command for Grim to sit. "Do not raise your voice," she spat. "You are a guest in my home, but I will not allow you to yell at me under any circumstances."

"You need a good spanking," he threatened, and she had the good grace to blush. "I may be in your house, but this is official business." Grim did not waver. His gaze remained locked on the uniform. Sheriff Wheeler said, "You need to call off your dog. Your impudence could be mistaken for hostility, in which case I would be forced to act."

"That's low, even for a cop," she was furious now, but she called Grim back to her side. "If you so much as threaten my dog again, I will shoot you myself."

"You are walking on dangerous turf," he breathed. He was even more frightening when he was quiet, and Amara wondered once again how she could have ever considered him appealing. Hell, she had even hoped he might ask her out. He must have read her thoughts because his expression was smug when he looked at her. "You didn't answer my questions," he reminded her bluntly.

Amara was fuming. She put him off by pretending she didn't know what he was referring to. Instead, she watched the vein in his forehead throb. His cheeks turned a mottled red before she finally complied, "Okay," she said in a hushed voice, "Tanner never comes down to the creek bank; he has no call to. In fact, he doesn't come anywhere near the hillside leading to the creek."

"But he could," Wheeler responded with a show of temper.

"He would lose his position here if he did. He needs this land, and I have strict rules."

"Yeah, so I saw," he fairly glared at her.

"He got out of line," she bit out, "and I handled it."

"Again, so I saw," he drawled. He sounded like one of the rednecks she so detested. "Please continue."

"I always have Grim with me when I swim," she said as if explaining something very simple to a child, "and I am not always nude. I was wearing lingerie in the other picture, or need I remind you? Sometimes I even wear a suit. What occurs to me is that it is none of your business how, or where, I swim."

"It is my business because I make it my business," he said bluntly, banging his hand down hard on the table. Grim was dangerously vocal, and Amara immediately stood to restrain him. The untouched coffee cups sloshed over, even as the vase in the center wobbled, and Solomon peed on the floor all at once.

"I think you should go," she announced.

"Not without those pictures," he was seething.

"Why, so you can see too?" she accused. She was so angry, her chest was heaving. "I did not want you and the others looking at them. There, I said it! Are you happy now? I told you I was embarrassed."

"Amara," he was giving her an ultimatum.

"I knew I shouldn't have told you about them!" She stormed out of the room keeping Grim with her. She was back in minutes, tossing a small canister at him with all her might. It hit him square in the chest, and she fairly gloated, "There! You can have the original pieces of film. If you want to see them that badly, you will have to have them developed. Now, will you please leave?"

"I'll be back," he said emphatically, "In the meantime, keep your damned clothes on!" He banged the door on his way out and Amara hurried after him to lock it. She was so mad she was beside herself. She needed some trauma drops, and she knew it. She made her way to the cabinet where her medicinal tonics were stored. It was two doses later before she could breathe evenly again.

The rest of the day was uneventful. She kept an easy pace, cutting herself some slack. She had planned to cultivate a new crop of herbs anytime now, so she might as well utilize those that had already been dried to make a new batch of tinctures. As this was a chore she found relaxing, the timing was perfect. She left the kitchen only long enough to gather a mélange of the desiccated bundles. She had sanitized the work surface beforehand. The aroma was wonderfully pungent, and in no time at all her kitchen smelled heavenly. Amara smiled in spite of herself. Her anger was slowly dissipating. Solomon, who had been curled up for a while now, wagged his tail in his sleep. His dreams were obviously cheerful ones. Amara chuckled glad that he had forgotten about his accident. He was a nervous little guy, and it troubled her when he was upset. Sampson opened one eye to peer at him before dozing off again, and Grim thumped his tail in contentment.

Amara collected more than a dozen small glass vials, and laid them aside. She would sterilize and label them later. She had already prepped four large jars complete with lids, adding the stripped leaves of each individual plant. She carefully poured the correct ratio of alcohol to pure water before capping the jars and carrying them to her pantry. There she provided labels bearing the date and contents. She would leave these on the shelf for a good six weeks before straining and pouring them through a funnel. It was a satisfying task just knowing that she was creating natural medications. She had followed a similar recipe with several of her vegetables. Although the outcome was amazing, the procedure was a bit more complicated. Her mother and grandfather had not missed a beat in her medicinal education. Many, if not all of these remedies, had been passed down in the family until they had become second nature to her. Amara fully intended to keep the tradition alive. These recipes were priceless.

She was now able to look back on her argument with Grant Wheeler in a calmer, more intellectual, way. She knew this was far from over, and as much as she dreaded the next meeting with him, she realized she was equipped to handle it. She liked Grant; usually. But she was seeing another side of him that she did not trust. It is often best to hold people at arm's length, she thought. She nodded to herself, acknowledging that she had allowed him to become too familiar, too quickly.

That evening Daniel Collins called. Amara felt a girlish excitement course through her at the timbre of his voice. "Are you busy?" he asked politely, "I don't want to interrupt if you are. I just thought maybe we could talk for a few minutes."

"No, I wasn't busy," she said breathlessly, "I'd love to talk."

They did just that for more than a few minutes, and when Amara hung up the phone, she was fairly glowing. "I have a date tomorrow night," she told Grim who looked at her and wagged his tail. She bent to hug him only to find that his nose was cold as ice. Grim was always aware of her emotions. He kept pace with her while she went about her normal evening ritual, unrolling her yoga mat and doing her half hour stretches. She offered a yoga class in town during the off seasons when life seemed to slow just a bit. It provided an extra income, and gave her pleasure as well. She had signed up to teach a class in October. Amara was accomplished at everything she did, and she had been doing yoga since high school. Grim relaxed next to her, watching her every move. By the time she was finished, he was happily dozing.

The following evening, Daniel arrived promptly at seven o'clock. Amara answered the door in a smashing red dress that flattered her curves. It fell almost to her knees and clung to her like a second skin. It was slit up one side to allow for easy movement, but it also flashed a great deal of skin. She wore black heels that made her look taller than the two inches they afforded her. Her long black curls were caught up on top with a Spanish comb that permitted them to tumble down her back in perfect profusion. She had lined her eyes with charcoal to compliment her complexion. She wore bright red lipstick. Daniel looked positively beguiled.

"Would you like to come in?" she asked politely.

He nodded as if speech was an impossibility he could not quite attain. As he stepped over the threshold, he said, "You are stunning!" and she realized he had found his voice.

"Thank you," she answered sincerely, "You look nice too. I'll get my bag." She returned in a couple of minutes with a small black clutch bag that looked brand new. "The little ones are already settled down in the kitchen," she offered.

He opened the car door for her, and waited until she was seated, before walking around to the driver's side. His car was immaculate, a quality she admired. He was quite the gentleman on the way to their destination. "I made reservations for seven-forty-five," he spoke easily. "We should make it in plenty of time. I found the perfect place, I think."

She asked the name of the restaurant and he told her. "I hear they have a great wine list," he said. "And I know their menu is fabulous. I think you'll like it."

"I'm sure I will," she responded, "You know I love Italian food. But I admit I have never heard of it before."

"It's relatively new," he answered in an even tone. "Gregory told me about it."

"Oh? Odd Nikki never mentioned it," she sounded surprised.

"Got it through the grapevine," he grinned. "He's planning on taking Nikki for their two-year anniversary."

"Oh, my," she laughed, "I'll have to remember to keep

my mouth shut on the topic."

It was soon apparent they both thought the world of the other couple. Gregory was a close friend of Daniel's, and one he obviously felt he could trust. It was equally clear that he was fond of Nikki. She was the perfect mate for Gregory. They complimented each other like two halves of a coin, making it impossible to like one without the other. "Here we are," he pulled into the parking lot, and Amara was struck with the quaint ambience of the place.

"It is really quite spectacular," she said aloud.

"Yes, it is. I don't think we'll be disappointed."

"Oh, I don't either," she laughed as they walked to the door. The aroma coming from inside was a superb preview. Her mouth was actually watering and she told him so.

He laughed with her and spoke aloud, "I believe I'm salivating as well!"

They didn't realize what a striking picture they made as they entered the charming establishment. Everything he had just said about Greg and Nikki rang true for them as well. Had they been more observant, they might have noticed the wistful glances. Though every head in the place turned to look at them, they were too caught up in the other to notice. A waiter seated them graciously, and Daniel naturally bent to pull out a chair for Amara. She dimpled as she thanked him causing the server to smile with pleasure. He handed them both a menu, and then turned to pour them each a glass of water from a frosted pitcher. There was a separate wine list, and after making a couple of recommendations, Daniel ordered a bottle of their finest Beaujolais.

When the wine steward returned, he opened the bottle and allowed the ruby liquid to breathe. A second server produced a plate of hors d'oeuvres while the steward poured them each a sample of the fruity beverage. They nodded their approval, and the man topped their glasses, at which time they made their selections. Amara ordered the eggplant parmesan; Daniel decided on the fettuccine Alfredo. Both dinners included a crispy salad, complete with croutons, and served with the restaurant's famous house dressing. While awaiting their dinners, the couple enjoyed the cocktails and appetizers. The Italians called this an aperitivo. It was divine.

Amara speared a large stuffed olive, while Daniel bit into a mini pastry. It was neither sweet nor sour, but somewhat tart and spicy all at once. Conversation flowed freely between the pair. They were entirely at ease with the other. Amara marveled at her lack of nervousness. It fascinated her all the more because she really liked Daniel. The food, when served, was cooked to perfection. It made her question her own sanity at giving up on the idea of becoming a chef. She mentioned this to Daniel, and he asked a few pertinent questions.

"So, maybe you just enjoy cooking when you're in the mood, but don't want to make a living at it?"

"That's kind of what I think," she confessed, "but is that normal?"

"Well, I think so," he answered without pause. "I mean, I love to write, and will always choose to do so, but I don't want to work at the paper forever. You don't need to quote me on that," he chuckled, "I still need the job."

"Yes, that is precisely it," she qualified. "I do love cooking, but only when it suits me."

"There you go," he responded with a lopsided grin that she found adorable. She shook herself mentally so that he wouldn't catch her staring, "What would you like to do?" he

asked, "Or are you doing it? It sounds as though you have given it a lot of thought."

She told him about her herbs and cordials and how much she enjoyed gardening. "I will always want a year-round garden," she volunteered, "But I guess I'm looking for a different angle."

"Go on," he prodded gently.

"Well, I don't want to have a vegetable stand forever," she replied without batting an eye. "It's fine for now, but it's just a means to an end. I'd like to grow enough to remain self-reliant, but I think there is more to it than that. Something else I want to tie in."

"Such as?" he was used to conducting interviews, she realized; a real pro.

"I believe I am still searching for it," she replied candidly. "I remember reading every Edgar Cayce book I could get my hands on when I was a kid. And do you know what I thought?" she asked unflinchingly.

"What?" he leaned in, and she could tell she had totally captured his attention.

"I wondered how one learned to do such a thing? I mean, the man actually went into a trance and healed hundreds of people! My word, can you imagine? I want to do that." Her eyes were glowing with an anticipation that nearly melted his heart. She had so much intensity, so much drive that she nearly lit the room like a shooting star.

"Wow," he said. "I am utterly mesmerized. I honestly think that if anyone can unlock that kind of secret, it might just be you. You are literally on a quest, and I'd like to see you find it."

The ride home was pleasant. They talked quietly with the radio in the background until the song *Spill the Wine* by Eric Burdon and War sounded. Amara looked at Daniel and grinned as he cranked it, making them both laugh. "That is the greatest song," Daniel gasped as he glanced in Amara's direction. She was more than a little tipsy. "Did you know that this song was inspired when the keyboardist, Lonnie Jordan, actually did spill the wine on a mixing board?"

"No way!" she giggled despite herself, "You're making that up."

"It's true," he said, noting her flushed expression, "Scout's honor."

"Now you're just teasing me," she insisted. "I did know the whole band had a hand in the writing of it," she admitted. "I just didn't know what had prompted it. I guess I thought it was a female thing." For some reason that struck them both as hysterically funny, and she realized that Daniel had kept her glass topped while he had enjoyed a single glass of wine. She sobered when she recognized that he was the type to take his responsibilities seriously, so much so that he had cut himself off because he knew he would be driving. She liked that she could rely on him. It felt good to know that he was looking out for her. When they arrived at her place they were still talking animatedly. He walked her to her front door and unlocked it for her. She wanted to ask him in, but knew it was too soon. He asked instead that she stay put while he stepped inside. After a few minutes, he came back out and announced, "All clear."

He cupped her face in one large hand, capturing the back of her head with the other, and kissed her like it was the only thing in the world that mattered. She kissed him back and felt herself go limp. She was shocked to find that she was actually wet for him and he had not touched her anywhere except her face. Good Lord, it was difficult to say good night!

CHAPTER TWELVE

Nearby and unnoticed, a shutter clicked persistently. The man in the brush stared angrily after shooting a new roll of film. He was enraged that Amara gave of herself so willingly. The slut, he thought. He wanted to teach her a lesson then and there. Instead, he opened his trousers and gratified himself. He ejaculated into a pair of hot pink panties that he carried in the right front pocket of his jeans. He was particular about that. He had been holding them close to his face breathing deeply as he did so. They smelled of her. They carried her scent. His tongue had slipped in and out lapping at them until he tasted her. He was momentarily stunned by the need that washed over him. He wanted her right then and there, on the ground, in the dirt. It made him furious all over again and he felt himself growing hard a second time.

He licked the panties over and over, nipping at them as he wanted to nip at her. He didn't want to stop. Instead he wanted to bury himself in her, and rip her apart with his teeth. He deliberately ground his cigarette out with the heel of his boot in a gesture of dominance, being careful to leave a tendril of smoke even as he rifled through his pockets. He grabbed a handful of the torn pieces of film he carried with him as he continually rubbed his engorged crotch, and scattered the negatives on the ground with the cigarette butt, remembering the swollen globes of her breasts and the silk of her thighs. He visualized her spreading those long legs at his command. He would cram his fingers into her, maybe even his whole hand, then flip her over roughly and grip her soft bare flesh in his large calloused palms.

He would hurt her deliberately, make her beg. He ached to ravage her rounded bottom. It was an exciting ritual to imagine his member filling every orifice of her. He was pumped. He was all-powerful as his sperm poured into her panties a second time, after which he collected himself before urinating on the film, making sure to saturate it. It was as though he was urinating on her. The remaining wisp of smoke from his cigarette hissed which he found somewhat satisfying. He imagined it was similar to the sound she might make when he plunged into her. Only she would be much louder. He might have to stuff the panties into her mouth to subdue her. He mopped himself dry, and then returned the panties to his pocket. One of these days he would carry out his fantasy. One of these days he would make her pay for what she had done to him. For now he would leave her this trail of sullied film, and if she was as smart as he believed her to be, she would be terrified when she realized who was stalking her. He chuckled at his own cleverness.

From the treetops, Crow watched in silence. His beady eyes didn't miss a thing. He understood the actions of humans far better than they might have imagined. He did not like this human, but he liked the lady Amara. The nasty man finished his ritual, zipped up, and stuffed the panties into the pocket near his groin, dislodging a crumpled ball of paper. The man turned and walked away unaware of the token that dropped to the ground. Although Crow didn't know what the paper contained, he swept it up along with a jagged piece of the torn negative. He would come back for more later on. For now, he must deliver what he could.

Amara stepped outside when she heard Karma calling. She dimpled as she answered her in kind, and the now plump raccoon scampered down the tree and straight into Amara's waiting arms. Amara laughed at her antics, promising her some cat food and a juicy bite of fruit. She allowed the coon to ride her shoulder to the porch, told her she would be right back, and returned with the promised goods. Karma trilled a thank you looking decidedly content. Amara smiled and turned to let Grim out. He wasted no time in joining her, and the pair set off down the lane toward the chicken shack.

Amara's long legs carried her onward quickly enough. Grim enjoyed the brisk walk and it showed in his demeanor. His tail wagged as he glanced back and forth across the lane and his tongue lolled lazily from his mouth. Amara kept a running conversation with him until she became aware of a ruckus overhead. She looked up and spotted Crow circling above.

"Hello Crow!" she hollered even as she scattered seeds from her pocket. Crow swept down on the ground before her and literally laid his gifts at her feet. Amara drew back slightly when she noticed the torn piece of film. It looked as damaged as the others, and she had a sick feeling in the pit of her stomach. Crow slowly blinked at her, holding her attention. He was trying to communicate with her and she knew it. "Thank you, Crow," she said in all seriousness. "I am afraid this is bad news, isn't it? But bless you for the warning, my friend." Crow's lower lids slid back into position as he gathered up the food. He cocked his head in parting, and

she waved. She had the unbidden thought that she would see him again soon. What was going on here, she wondered?

As she went about gathering the eggs, Amara admitted to herself that she would have to call Grant. She found herself lagging on the job, making excuses to put this off. She dreaded making that phone call so badly that she considered contacting Nikki instead. That would gain her nothing at this point. She tucked the items away in her pocket feeling unclean as she did so. She was so nervous that she forgot to look at the scrap of paper. She would tend her garden before returning to the house, she decided. It wouldn't make the ugliness of the situation go away, but it would give her time to organize her thoughts. She could use a few moments of sanity. After all, she hadn't spoken to Grant since their argument, and she didn't particularly want to.

When she arrived back at the house, she was in a calmer state of mind. Working in the earth always did that for her. It was such a wonderful way to ground. She felt she had made the right decision and was looking forward to a bite to eat. She would enjoy a light meal first, she thought. That way she would be better able to deal with Grant. He could be very nice at times, but she had seen his other side a little too often. What difference would another half hour make?

Amara cared for the little ones, and made sure Grim had fresh water, before fixing herself a cup of noodle soup with a watercress sandwich on the side. She tried to relax while she ate knowing that she would have her hands full in just a short while. Grim sensed her mood and remained close at hand. She patted him absently as she steeled herself to make the call. It took only minutes to clean up the kitchen, and as she dried her dishes she became aware of a commotion outside. Crow was back, she realized. He rarely came twice in one day, but there he was now. She tried to shake off the sense of doom that had begun to settle over her as she walked outside. He was standing on her porch with a small pile before him. Negatives! Oh dear Lord, he had brought more negatives! And not just a couple, but a rather large collection of cut or torn negatives, each one as sullied as the next. Amara felt a trifle dizzy; she almost staggered. She stammered a thank you to the bird, gifting him with a small portion of the uneaten sandwich. He nodded, gathered the food, and took flight. Amara was pale when she dialed the telephone.

Sheriff Grant Wheeler was actually extraordinarily cordial when he came to see Amara. He looked at the small pile of evidence, and said, "Looks like our boy has a real fetish for you. You do understand you are in danger, don't you?" He nudged her chin with the knuckle of one finger so that she was forced to look him in the eyes. But he was gentle about it, and Amara didn't mind the gesture. She saw what she thought was concern in his steady gaze, and she knew some relief at being able to connect with him.

"Yes, I am afraid of him," she whispered. "But I have Grim with me, and I know how to shoot."

"Good," he said, "you need to be afraid, but you call me any time, even if you only think you are in danger. Don't wait to find out." The sheriff had been studying the assortment of ruined negatives under a bright light as he spoke. He looked troubled, like he was putting the pieces of a puzzle together. He cleared his throat before speaking aloud, "I can't be sure until we get these developed, but I have an uncanny feeling we are going to find a lot of replicas in this pile. You need to be prepared for the worst. Meanwhile, keep your doors locked and your gun at your side."

"Oh, yes," she dug into her pocket and withdrew the scrap of paper that Crow had provided, "I almost forgot. This was with the negatives." She handed him the paper, and he frowned when he spread it out flat.

"Bingo!" he sounded excited, "This is a drug store re- ceipt," he was talking more to himself than to her as he examined the slip she had given him. "Our boy got careless. This not only proves where at least some of the film came from, but what kind of film as well! We needed a break. I will be back in touch, Amara. You call me if anything comes up. And I do mean anything!"

"I will, Grant, and thank you."

She walked him to his car, and for a split second she was positive he was going to kiss her. The moment passed and they said good bye. Amara went back inside and locked the door.

Later that evening Nikki stopped by with Cynthia in tow. She had called ahead to make sure Amara was up to company, and though Amara was down in the dumps she welcomed the change of scenery a visit would afford. Cynthia had a bottle of wine dangling from her fingers, while Nikki conveyed a relish tray containing a variety of cheeses, whole grain crackers, and other healthy goodies. Amara realized they were checking up on her, and greeted them with open arms. They had the sort of sisterhood that encouraged looking out for each other. Since the weather was nice and they still had plenty of daylight, Amara suggested they take the horses out. Cynthia, who was quite the horsewoman, jumped at the opportunity. Nikki giggled wickedly as if she had known perfectly well that's what they would wind up doing.

"I call dibs on Queen!" Cynthia crowed in delight. The other girls laughed good-naturedly. Cynthia always chose

Queen. She had bonded with her years ago.

"I'll take Raven," Nikki smiled, knowing Amara's preference for Shawnee.

They followed the trail to the back meadow where they let the horses enjoy a hearty gallop. It was a beautiful day for a ride, and the girls lost themselves in the moment. They finally slowed and walked their mounts back to the barn, talking all the while. Amara had left Grim to guard the house. She knew he would be anxious for her return and said as much.

"I don't think he likes to be left out," Nikki agreed, "He is so used to being by your side."

"Yeah, but I'm in good company," Amara stated, "and this way, the house is fully protected."

Nikki and Cynthia exchanged a look. They were aware of the fact that this whole mess was getting to Amara. "Have you seen the white fawn lately?" Cynthia asked curiously. She was enraptured by the vision she, herself, had witnessed.

"A couple of times," Amara was deliberately vague, unsure of how much she wanted to disclose. It was an odd feeling since the girls rarely kept secrets. Cynthia looked hurt by her response, making Amara regret her lack of confidentiality. "Honestly," she said to lighten things up, "I'm still trying to figure out her roll in all this, but she is beautiful. She would make a nice painting."

"That's what I thought," Cynthia nodded eagerly.

"Go for it," Amara and Nikki chorused.

"We're not likely to catch her on film," Amara concluded, "But you've seen her. And you have a terrific memory for detail."

"That's true," Nikki encouraged.

"Okay, I'll do it!" Cynthia laughed, and her smile was brilliant.

After tending the horses, the girls returned to the house where Grim met them at the door. He practically knocked Amara over in his eagerness. His nose was cold as ice and his tail swished continuously. He had a habit of giving Amara what she called "eye kisses" by getting directly in her face, and without using his tongue, gently sniffing at her eyes. The girls fussed over him, and took turns making up to the little ones as well. Outside in the trees, Karma trilled. Everything felt right with the world. They popped corn and set out the relish tray, opening the wine as they did so. Amara had left sweet potatoes on low in the oven along with a savory stew from the freezer. They burned incense, and Cynthia did a tarot reading. It was a pleasant evening. When it came time to leave, both Nikki and Cynthia gave Amara a hug, and then waited to leave only after they heard her lock the door. She smiled and padded off to the bath to get ready for bed.

Amara lay awake reflecting on her day. Although she found the photographs unsettling, there was some comfort to be had in Grant's kindness. She never knew what to expect from the man, and that in itself was exasperating. She pondered that moment by his car when she had been certain he was about to kiss her. But what she didn't know was whether she wanted him to or not. At times she really liked Sheriff Grant Wheeler. But then he would go and ruin it all. Amara's mind drifted to Daniel and a smile tugged at the corners of her lips. Now there was a man she could understand. Her thoughts went in circles until she finally dozed off. From a distance she could hear the song *Wayfairing Stranger*.

CHAPTER THIRTEEN

mara's eyes flew open! Where was she? And what had happened? The last thing she recalled was falling asleep in her bed at the farm. She looked around at her surroundings, noting that she was in a mill. But it wasn't the mill back in Indiana. And it didn't appear to be modern times! She glanced down at her plain cotton dress in pure shock. The funny thing was she recognized it as her own. It was grey with a faded pink floral print. She raised the hem just a hair so that she could see her feet, and discovered that she wore a pair of plain black boots. They were sensible boots that laced up the front; nothing fancy. They, too, were familiar. For a second, Amara lay still on the floor where she had found herself. She was in the process of sitting when a voice caught her unawares, "Awinita! What are you about? Did you get sick again?"

Amara turned to face the speaker whom she recognized as her closet friend, "Oh, Caroline! You startled me!" she cried. "I must have fainted." Amara, now Awinita, winced as she lifted one hand to rub her neck. She had moved too suddenly when Caroline called out. As she massaged the crick in her neck, she observed Caroline hurrying over to help her

up.

"You must move quickly!" Caroline tugged at her hand. "You can't afford to lose your job anymore than I can."

"Of course, Caroline, thank you," she whispered. "I'll be back at my station in just one minute." Awinita drew a small compact from the pocket of her skirt and studied her reflection. How odd it seemed to look in the mirror! On the one hand, she knew she was Amara in a different time, yet here she was known as Awinita. She studied her features recognizing the woman she had seen at the Yountsville Mill. Yet comprehension set in that she was at home in Roswell, Georgia. She also realized that this was the year 1864! For a single nauseating moment, she saw one face superimposed over the other. They looked a lot alike, she thought. Funny she hadn't noticed that the day at the Yountsville Mill. Tucking a few stray strands of straight black hair behind one ear, she hurried to her work station still fingering the change in texture.

Caroline smiled wanly when she spied Awinita back at her spindles and looms. The French manager was headed their way, and both women said a silent prayer that he had not noticed the lapse. They breathed a collective sigh of relief when he walked on by.

Awinita completed her work for the day marveling at how it was second nature for her to produce uniforms for the South. Yet as Amara, she had only a mild curiosity about the woolen mill in Indiana. She had never had a desire to learn how to spin. The irony struck her as amusing.

"What are you grinning about?" asked Caroline who missed little of what went on around her. Caroline had been a mill worker far longer than Awinita. She had, in fact, procured the position for her friend when they first met. Awinita's situation had been bleak. And Caroline had the ear of the manager. She wasn't proud of it, but Caroline had lost her husband in the war, leaving her to fend for herself and the child she carried. She was a pragmatic soul, and had done what she had to in order to survive. And survive she did! Caroline owned a small one-room cabin on the edge of town. She had taken Awinita in and nursed her back to health, and in exchange Awinita had taken care of the child and the cooking. They would have left it at that if they could have. But times were hard, and money was scarce, causing Awinita to accept a position at the mill. The women took turns watching baby Chloe while working at the mill six days a week.

Awinita was pregnant when Caroline discovered her in the woods just a few feet from her cabin. She had been beaten within an inch of her life. The man who committed this atrocity had shown no mercy. Awinita was half Cherokee. The assailant had coveted, stalked, and captured the Native American adolescent upon her mother's demise. And he had used her with a lack of honor, leaving her young body with a host of permanent scars. Yet he had, under no circumstances, broken her spirit. She had run time and again, until at last she had made it as far as the forest, where Caroline found her hidden in a copse. Caroline had buried Awinita's stillborn infant, and somehow managed to transport the unconscious female the short distance home.

The two had become fast friends. They were both alone in the world. And they were both accustomed to hard work. Chloe was newly born at the time, and Caroline's milk was dry from malnutrition. Awinita, on the other hand, had an abundance of the life sustaining liquid. She took over the task with a happy heart. Thus it was Awinita became the child's unlikely Godmother. Caroline had once asked how she and her mother had managed to remain in Georgia when President Andrew Jackson had approved the removal of the

Cherokee people in 1838. Awinita had smiled sadly saying only that they had hidden deep in the forest where they lived off the land.

What Awinita had not said was that the city of Roswell had once been known as *The Enchanted Land*. It belonged to the Cherokee people, and the white man was not allowed on, or in, its waters. The Chattahoochee, dubbed *The River of Painted Rock*, was believed to be cursed by an ancient tribe. Awinita's mother, Gola, was a native of this land, while Awinita herself, had grown up hearing the tales of the greed of the white man. It was such a man who had fathered her, and her mother had taken her and gone into hiding. But gold had already been discovered in Northern Georgia, bringing the white men in hordes. Their greed could not be assuaged, and the bulk of the Cherokee had attempted to adapt to their presence.

Many became farmers or shop keepers. Gola had learned much during this time, and ran such a business on the outskirts of town. She grew a proficient garden out back while caring for her daughter. For a time it seemed as though this might work. They had a great leader named Warsaw who ran a ferry across the Chattahoochee. But it was to no avail. Eventually the state of Georgia took possession of the land, declaring the Cherokee Nation illegal, and the people were removed.

Gola was wise enough to take Awinita's father back when he came for her. He was a cruel man, but he was now her only chance. He was a trapper by trade, and he took over her shop, leaving her to raise their daughter. He gave her three sons, each of whom she buried on their small strip of land. Or so he thought. In reality, Gola gave the third, and only, surviving child to a Creole woman named Nonie. Nonie was known to have magical powers, and this was Gola's only way of assuring both of her children's safety. She never told anyone about the boy's survival, but when Trapper was away on a hunting excursion, Gola took young Awinita and fled. Nonie had given Gola a key that led to a hidden cave. And this, Gola had been careful to bury in place of the babe. When she retrieved the key, she took the last name Hide since her husband made a living tanning hides. And the pair went deep into the forest for the second time in their lives.

Gola had often spoken of the powerful men who had taken over their land. She was afraid of Roswell King, who was a former slave taskmaster, from the notorious Butler Plantation on the coast of Georgia. King saw prosperity in the rushing waters of Vickery Creek, and invited his friends to help form a community. His son, Barrington King, founded a mill along Vickery Creek, and by 1839 the Roswell Manufacturing Company was in full swing. The company made cotton supplies allowing the city to grow and thrive.

By the time Georgia seceded from the Union in 1861, the majority of the residents who could afford to do so, had packed up and moved to safer havens. Little did Awinita or Caroline know of the personal turmoil that was about to unfold. Now in 1864, the American civil war had blazed a trail of destruction across the South, and Roswell was in the path of that searing inferno.

Awinita and Caroline were in the thick of things when Union soldiers arrived in mass. It was the fifth day of July, and the women had begun a typical work day when the town erupted! The enemy had come from Marietta, and they were ready to destroy everything within their path. Caroline took Awinita by the hand, and carrying her small daughter, they attempted to make their escape through the smoke and destruction. They had never seen so many soldiers. There were thousands upon thousands of them! Later they would learn that the numbers of troops that overran their city were well over thirty-some thousand. But for the time being they knew only what they could see. They watched as the sheets, tent canvases, and ropes were stripped from the cotton mills. These, they learned, were destined for the field hospitals in Marietta. By then, the soldiers had closed in on those of them trapped at the woolen mill.

The Roswell Covered Bridge was captured after the retreating Confederates torched it. The Union soldiers had easily adapted by fording the river, but the women were effectively cut off. It is said that this was the first time in history that a rifle fired underwater was effective during battle. The commanding officer was Union General Kenner Garrard, and he was acting under the direct orders of General Sherman. The sobbing women knew great remorse when Garrard celebrated the capture of Roswell by supplying his men with whiskey. Caroline's blond hair hung limp in the crowd. She feared for her life, and the life of her child. Awinita stood tall against the soldiers, affording poor Caroline some relief. But the men were unruly. The women had, so far, been lucky to protect Chloe, but it was useless to think they could save themselves. Caroline thought of her small cabin and realized they would have to be clever if they wanted to see it again.

Disorder flared when it was discovered that a tricolor French flag flew high over the Ivy Woolen Mill. Unbeknown to many, the mill manager had hoisted the flag in an attempt to regain control, hoping to prevent the mill from being burned. It was a trick that had nearly worked as General Sherman was many miles away. When the general received word of the commotion, he stated that he had not realized the mill was in full operation. He commanded the flag examined. When lowered, the Union soldiers noted that the initials CSA had been sewn into the wool, and the ruse was up.

In fact every single material item, whether cotton or wool, that came from any of the three mills were stamped with the initials CSA. The mill itself was promptly torched, and the mill workers were accused of treason. They watched in mute silence as the mill burned to the ground, after which they were made to walk to Marietta to stand trial. These orders included all women and children. Awinita's head snapped up at the news. As she mouthed the word "Treason", Caroline paled and swayed on her feet.

Tempers were frayed. The soldiers were restless. Awinita gave Caroline a steady look so as to judge how her friend was holding up. Caroline, who was usually so tough, looked defeated. Her wide blue eyes were pinned on Chloe who was slumped between them. Chloe had just turned three years old, and up until now she had been a brave little girl. But Chloe had had enough. She was sobbing hysterically, wiping her eyes on the back of her sleeve. Caroline could see that the child was weak with hunger. So much time had passed! Her little face was pinched and dirty, her garments obviously soiled. The child needed food and water. It was as simple as that. Caroline watched with pleading eyes as a man approached. He stared hard at Caroline before producing a half loaf of bread. Caroline gave him a weak smile knowing she had made her choice. He handed Chloe the stale loaf, and the deal was done. Awinita cringed as the man's nostrils flared and his chest puffed.

The women were allowed to gather what few possessions they could carry. Some of the ladies who had fallen on hard times were assigned a guard to escort them to their fine homes where they could salvage a keepsake or two. Awinita was happy for them. These ladies had worked as hard as any. Awinita didn't have a jealous bone in her body. She only wanted to survive. She cast a look around and froze. *He* was here! *He* was close enough to touch! And far more frighten-

ing than any other ever could be. He had not seen her as yet, and Awinita meant to keep it that way. The officer in charge was trying to maintain control over his men. Awinita glanced first at Caroline, and then turned her face away. Caroline gave a slight nod. She had witnessed the look of pure un-adulterated terror that had stolen across Awinita's features, and understood what had transpired. She spoke softly to the man at her side. He agreed to accompany them to their cabin, and she was grateful for his protection.

The women were now officially prisoners of war. A few days later, they were marched to nearby Marietta where they were placed in the Georgia Military Institute. There, they were denied trials, leaving them no opportunity to de-fend themselves. Awinita blanched; Caroline broke down and wept. The only thing they knew for certain was that they were to be sent far from home and all that was familiar. They were shipped out in railroad cars on the tenth and eleventh of July, knowing their families would never be able to find them. It was highly unlikely they would ever be able to make their way home, if indeed there were any homes left stand-ing. They made stops in Chattanooga and Nashville along the way, but the women remained unaware of their final destina-tions.

Many were sent on to Indiana, while others were held in Louisville, where they were imprisoned in a local hospital. Typhoid and measles had spread among them, and only the strongest survived. All of them were hungry and exhausted, with few possessions and no money to begin anew. There was little air in the barren cars. Creature comforts were a thing of the past. Caroline and Chloe clung to each other, just as they attempted to hold tight to Awinita. But Chloe was singled out and separated from her mother, and Caroline fell ill with fever.

Awinita mopped Caroline's brow and tended her

needs, all the while promising they would find her daughter. It was a promise she did not know how to keep. She watched it all through saddened eyes, putting forth a show of bravado she did not truly feel. She kept a brittle disposition around the soldiers, but was known as a savior among the women. Awinita had conditioned herself long ago to withstand more than most. She gave freely of herself in an effort to help the others. She shared her food which was in short supply, and watched many a child so that another woman, another mother, could rest. She became something of a legend among the women, and they came to both love and respect her. Caroline gradually got well, but she remained silent so long Awinita feared for her sanity.

Meanwhile, Awinita asked after the child, Chloe, at every stop, every opportunity. She was determined to reunite mother and daughter even though she had no idea where Chloe had been taken. Still she could do nothing less, and so she continued to buoy Caroline's spirits with dreams of a reunion. In short, she provided hope. Caroline clung to her tightly, and Awinita realized she had become a tenuous lifeline of sorts.

Finally during a pit stop, where they were allowed to get out and stretch, Awinita saw a familiar face. Margaret whom they had known from the mill was also exercising her cramped muscles. Awinita approached, "Margaret?" she called, "I cannot believe it is you! We thought we had seen the last of you!"

"Awinita," Margaret smiled brightly, "I'm so happy to see you! Are you well? What of Caroline and her child?"

"Caroline is well enough," Awinita murmured, "but we have lost track of Chloe. We were separated some time ago. I am afraid for Caroline's state of mind."

Margaret who had no children of her own was highly unlikely to recognize one child from another. The women had worked a solid eleven hour shift each day with time only for lunch and necessities. But Margaret was a kind soul and understood the grief poor Caroline must be suffering. "There are two cars headed for Indiana," Margaret confided. "I am on the second one. It is possible Chloe got mixed in with us. We have a group of children we take turns tending. They appear to be lost. Let me look among them."

"Oh, Margaret, we would be so grateful!" Awinita cried. "Chloe is fair-haired like her mama, with big blue eyes. She is a shy little girl, but she is bright. If you speak of her mother, she will respond."

Margaret assured her she would do as requested. She had always liked Caroline and wanted to help. She told Awinita that there were several such children that fit the description. The only thing Margaret did not say was that most of them were in dire condition. They had lost their mothers, and with that, their will to live. Some were so ill they no longer spoke. Awinita noticed the look of hesitation that crossed Margaret's pale features.

"If Chloe is among them, no matter her condition, it will give her something to aspire to if she knows her mama is looking for her. Tell her, please, that we will not stop searching. We will never give up!" She had read Margaret correctly.

Margaret cried when Awinita hugged her, and the guards herded them back into their separate railroad cars. Only Awinita dared to look back.

CHAPTER FOURTEEN

mara sat up in bed. Whoa, she thought, what the heck just happened? One minute she was Awinita, and living in 1864. And the next thing she knew she was back in Indiana, and in current time! She jumped to her feet causing Grim to move quickly away from her. His eyes clouded over, and he sat back on his haunches, and emitted an unusual keening sound. When she reached for him, he took another step backward. "What's wrong, Grim?" she crooned. "It's me." He whined as he nudged her hand before coming closer, and she realized that whatever happened was real. She spoke softly as she smoothed his thick coat. Grim was rarely shaken by anything. But he was very definitely disturbed now. She hugged him to her, glad to share his warmth. Grim was her best friend and constant companion.

The dog sensed his owner was herself again and visibly relaxed. She could feel the steady beat of his heart against her palm. Amara had glanced at the clock upon waking and nearly shrieked at the time! It was exactly 12:10 in the afternoon! To all intents and purposes, she had slept the morning away. Yet she felt there was a nefarious reason for this particular hour. She took a glance around and was relieved to see that her surroundings looked normal. Still, she was almost afraid to look in the mirror. When she did, it was her own image gazing back at her. She examined the face so similar to Awinita's, and wondered how she had ever missed the resemblance. Yet, here were her golden-brown tiger's eyes instead of Awinita's chocolate-brown ones, and her naturally curly hair in lieu of the straight black curtain she had come to associate with the other woman. Aside from these small changes, however, the women were mirror images. In truth, Amara admitted to herself, Awinita could easily pass for her mother, Alina. Alina had died when she was a child. Amara shook her head as she set off for the shower, wondering at the meaning of it all. It was then she decided to spend some time with the family photo album later that evening. Maybe she would find some answers there.

Amara stepped from the shower and pulled on a short summer robe. It was a pleasant shade of lavender that complimented her pigmentation and clung to her curves. She fed Grim and the little ones, and then set about cooking a late breakfast for herself. She was just about to sit down to eat when she heard a knock at the door. She pushed her plate back and went to see who it was, surprised that the dogs hadn't alerted her. Solomon barked loudly, sounding much larger than he really was, while Grim led the way to the door. Her protectors, she thought fondly. She was taken aback to see Sheriff Grant Wheeler standing on the porch. He held a manila envelope in one hand that he tapped absently against one muscled thigh. His mood was serious. She frowned in response. Grant usually gave her the courtesy of a call before stopping by. She unlocked the door, and he stepped inside without further ceremony.

"You're not dressed? Are you ill?" he frowned.

"No, just running late. It has been an odd day," she mumbled. "I was just about to eat. Would you care to join me?"

"No," he brushed the invitation aside, "I brought you these. I think we should sit down and discuss them." As he spoke he held up the envelope, and Amara's stomach lurched.

"I haven't eaten yet today," she admitted, staring at the casing he carried. "And I'm afraid I don't feel well. Why don't I put some coffee on? I just poured myself a cup of tea and I know your preference."

For once he didn't argue or take control, but followed her into the cozy kitchen. He watched as she measured out his coffee, and then proceeded to fix a second plate. "I don't like to eat alone, and I made enough for two. I don't know why I did that."

She was nervous, and it showed. And she was fidgety. It was unlike her. "Are you sure you're okay?" he asked, causing her to turn and look him full in the face. He wasn't the soft type, she thought, and now that she was paying attention, she realized he was checking her out.

"I'm fine," she reassured. "I overslept, that's all."

"How late, until noon?" he asked without preamble, "Your hair is still damp from the shower."

"No, of course not," she denied what sounded like an accusation to her, "I just got a late start. You know how it is. You get up late and before you know it, your whole day is askew."

"You're being defensive," he accused.

"You're reading too much into it," she shot back. "What is it with you? Do you think I had an overnight guest?"

"It had crossed my mind," he was getting angry now.

"Well, I didn't. And if I had, it wouldn't be any of your business," she snapped. "Look, let's cool off and have a bite to eat. I am running on empty, and you are surely in need of a meal?" She was trying to call a truce. He accepted.

She handed him a plate of scrambled eggs with sour cream and chives. There was a batch of warm biscuits and a side of fresh fruit. He grunted his approval as he took a large bite of the fluffy eggs. She was a good cook, he acknowledged. They ate in silence for several minutes. When she glanced up she caught him staring at her chest. She cleared her throat, fingering the fire opal pendant that was nestled there. He raised his gaze slowly to her face. The motion was deliberate, she thought, as if to say, "So, you caught me." He picked his empty plate up and carried it to the sink. She followed suit, offering a refill on the coffee. "No, thanks," he said pointedly, "It's time to get down to business."

Amara poured herself another cup of tea and set it aside to steep. She took her time wiping down the table. When she finished, she looked up and said, "I'm going to get dressed, it will only take a moment." She did not give him a chance to argue, but left the room immediately. She felt, rather than saw, his gaze scorch her back.

When she returned, she was wearing cut-off jeans and a tight black tee. Her curls were pulled back in a loose pony tail. For the first time he noticed how tired she looked. "Are you sure you're okay?" he asked, sniffing as she placed her cup in front of her. "What is that stuff?"

"Mugwort," she answered shortly. "It's the root."

"Then you are ill?" he queried.

"No," she sighed, "I'm tired, that's all."

"Look, I'm sorry to put this on you right now," he

sounded sincere, "but it's important." He handed her the manila envelope. When she didn't take it as quickly as he would have liked, he set it near her elbow. He had already broken the seal and the contents scattered across the table. Amara's eyes were huge as she stared at them. It was exactly what she had expected. There were dozens of torn and damaged photos of her, all nude except for the hot pink panties.

"There are so many," she gasped. "Are they identical?"

"For the most part," he nodded, understanding her distress. "We think he took the same shot several times. But he definitely made a multitude of copies with subtle variations. For some reason our boy is fixated on this particular pair of panties." She drew in a ragged sigh, allowing him to continue, "The question is, do you still wear them?" Her eyes met his in a state of momentary shock. "Or, more to the point, do you still have them?"

"Well, I don't know," she shook her head, "and stop calling him 'our boy'. I haven't worn them since all this began. I guess I hadn't really thought about it," her voice shook when she spoke.

"Well, think about it," he said crisply. He knew he was pushing her, she was sure of it. Maybe that got him faster results.

"No, I haven't seen them in a long time," she admitted. "I didn't think to look," she splayed her hands in an innocent gesture.

"Okay, look Amara," his voice was softer, kinder, "the perp gets off on these particular panties. We need to know why. It might help us solve the case."

She caught that he now referred to the creep as the *perp*, and for some reason that put her mind at ease. She swallowed hard as she allowed herself to think back to the day of the break-in, "I haven't seen them since he broke into my house," she said in a flat voice.

"Are you sure?" He nudged her chin up with one blunt finger to get a better look at her.

"Yeah, I'm sure," she whispered, "It just hadn't registered with me. I'm sorry."

"Would you mind checking for me?"

"No. Not at all," she stood and walked out of the room. She had an empty feeling inside like she had been more fully violated. Well, she had, hadn't she? She checked her lingerie drawer thoroughly, repeating the process twice. She went through every stray item of clothing in her closet as well. The results were the same. She swallowed a sob, wiped her eyes, and returned to the kitchen where Grim sat staring at Grant. The dog relaxed when she sat back down. "They're gone," she said simply, "They're not there."

"Thank you," Grant said to her. "I'll be checking in regularly," he reminded, "but you call if you need anything."

He let himself out, and she watched him get into his car and drive away.

Amara went through the motions of the day, feeding the animals, tending the crops. She looked up once to find Tanner pulling out of her drive in his red pickup truck. She had not even known he was there until he made a show of it. That fact sent a chill down her spine. She had thought she was alone. Now her mind kept returning to the perpetrator, and to the events of night before. It was mind-boggling.

Somewhere along the way she had either slept more hours than ever before, or she had literally lost time. And to top it off, she was dealing with yet another nasty piece of the puzzle with the local police. It was becoming difficult for her to focus on just one problem at a time. She could no longer divide the past from the present. Was it possible that it was all tangled up together? Amara didn't know. She sincerely wanted to confide in her friends, but was unsure of what their reactions might be.

Nikki was used to turning up the unusual in her line of work, while Cynthia literally thrived on things that others might shy away from. It might be smart to go to them. Her mind wandered to her date with Daniel and the easy conversations they shared. Would he understand all this? Or would he think she was off her rocker? She wasn't sure. One thing she did know, she had read every Edgar Cayce book ever written. And he, the sleeping prophet, had gone into a state of semi-consciousness to achieve his goal. She had also read many other books on out-of-body experiences and past life regressions from Hans Holzer to Frank Edwards. Maybe what she was experiencing wasn't as obscure as she thought? Maybe it was something she should delve more deeply into before sharing it with anyone else?

That evening Amara settled down with the family albums just as she promised herself she would. There were millions of pictures of her with her grandfather at all ages. There he was alongside her at every important commencement of her life from her first day of school to her college graduation, and everything in between, including powwows, cars and horses, and father-daughter dances. There were, however, very few of her mother, and most of them were taken on specific holidays. Tears filled her eyes and she reached for the phone. "Nikki? It's me," she said into the receiver.

Nikki arrived like the speed of light. The friends had

a pact that if any one of them was ever in need, they had only to call. And Nikki didn't need a pact to know that Amara was nearly at her wit's end. She had heard the desperation in the other's voice, and felt it like a physical blow. Amara, who was usually so collected, literally threw her arms around her friend the moment she set foot inside. Grim whined in such a primal way that Nikki actually paled. It was such an unearthly sound that Solomon whimpered and Sampson hid. Somehow Nikki managed to maintain her calm demeanor long enough to brew a fresh pot of tea and carry it to the enclosed porch where she set it on the work table, automatically setting two places. She gently led Amara to a seat and told her to drink. Then she waited for Amara to speak while smoothing Grim's fur. The big dog's eyes were liquid with human emotion and Nikki had to hold back tears. Good Lord, what had happened here?

When Amara concluded the narrative about her time spent as Awinita, Nikki sucked in her breath. Amara was not the type to fabricate anything. If she told Nikki she had been to the moon, Nikki would have believed her. Besides, Amara was different from other people. Her lifestyle alone reflected that. One didn't have to question her integrity. Honesty was the fabric of her very existence. "There's more, isn't there?" Nikki asked fearfully.

"Yes," Amara murmured, and told of the newest development on the case. "It's just all so confusing, Nikki. I don't know what's what."

"Well, we know the police case is solid. And I suspected there was more to it than just a white fawn, rare as they are. Are you suspicious there is a parallel of some sort between the two happenings?"

"I'm certain of it," Amara admitted, "I just can't get a grip on it."

"That's because you are too close to it. You can't observe what you are living."

"Do you think I am crazy?" she asked pointedly.

"No. Definitely not," Nikki assured her. "You are the most level-headed person I know. We do, however, need to document the facts. And it wouldn't hurt to bring Cynthia into this either. That girl's seen more than her share of paranormal happenings. Hell, she seeks them out!"

"Agreed," Amara sighed in relief, "And thank you for believing in me." Before Nikki could respond, the most preternatural sound she had ever heard pierced the night air. "That's the banshee," Amara whispered, "Awinita must be chasing someone off the property."

Suddenly there was a scratching at the back door. "Karma," Amara crooned, holding her arms out for the furry creature. It was the most natural thing in the world to watch Amara scoop the young raccoon into her arms.

CHAPTER FIFTEEN

Amara was up early the following morning. She had fallen behind and needed to get caught up. She showered and let her hair air-dry where she sat on the sun porch enjoying a strong cup of black tea. She ate buttered toast cut into triangles, all the while talking to Grim and the little ones. She wasted no time getting ready to run into town. She needed a few things from the grocery, had to stop by the post office, and tucked a short list of supplies from the feed store into her purse. This Saturday would be a busy market day for her. She had baking to do, sage bundles to make, and as always, tinctures to complete.

The groceries were loaded into the back seat, and the feed was in the trunk by the time she pulled away from the post office. She hadn't seen the man in the car behind her. He had been following her, and on the seat next to him was a manila envelope. She had almost made good her escape when she decided to make a quick dash into the drug store. On her way back to the car, she bumped into Grant. They spoke for a moment, but before she could reach her destination, he asked her to lunch. It was a simple thing really, certainly not a date. He said he was headed to the diner across the street and thought she might tag along. That sounded harmless enough and certainly difficult to sidestep since she had pushed breakfast on him the day before. She accepted reluctantly, but didn't let on.

He ordered a full plate of meat and potatoes along with a tall glass of milk. She opted for a fresh green salad and glass of iced tea. She laughed when he gave her a lop-sided grin which said what he thought of her light meal. They joked a little about their differences, and he ended by saying that opposites attract. She didn't have a ready response so she gave him a saucy smile. And that was where they were when Daniel walked in.

Dan spotted them immediately, and if he felt like a fool, he stopped by their table all the same. Grant seemed to visibly heighten in his seat. Amara forced herself to sit up straight. She looked Daniel straight in the eye when she asked how he had been. He said he was fine and that he had meant to call. She smiled wider and suggested that he should. Grant watched the two of them like a professional analyzing a couple of suspects. Amara thanked him for the meal and stood to leave. Grant stood, and both men watched her walk away. No one noticed the man in the corner of the room who had been observing her the entire time. He was drinking coffee while pretending to read the newspaper.

When she got home, the phone was ringing. She half expected it to be Daniel, and was more than a little disappointed. Disappointment rapidly turned to anger at the smug voice on the other end of the line. The words bordered on obscene. And Amara was fairly positive of the caller's identity. She hung up with a show of temper, slamming the receiver harder than necessary. She had only begun to walk away when it rang a second time.

"What do you want?" she demanded.

Heavy breathing filled the silence. Before she could end the call a second time, the voice whispered, "I've been watching you." His voice was distorted.

Amara didn't say a word. She disconnected, backing away from the phone as if in slow motion. She had the creepiest feeling that all the pieces were falling into place. And she felt sullied. When the phone rang a third time, she almost didn't pick up. Then she steeled herself, straightened her spine, and answered in an angry tone, "Leave me alone or I'll call the police. This is harassment."

"Amara, are you all right?" Daniel's warm voice came over the wire. "What's going on?"

"He called me, Daniel," Amara's voice was clipped, almost staccato. She was speaking rapidly as if in shock. "He admitted that he'd been watching me."

"Whoa, slow down," he spoke with authority, "Who called you? And what precisely did he say?"

"It was Simon," she breathed slowly now, "I'm almost sure of it. And he said he was watching me. He was bragging about it."

"You have to report it," Daniel responded without pause. "He's not only harassing you, he is threatening you as well."

"I know. I just hate having to talk to Grant about it. He's so hot-headed," she sighed.

"Do you want me there with you? Just say the word."

There was a momentary pause before Amara spoke again, "No, I'm a big girl," she answered, "I can handle it."

"You're sure?" Daniel didn't sound happy. "If you

change your mind, you've got my number."

"I'm sure."

"Have dinner with me tomorrow night? I'll take you somewhere nice," he was trying to put her at ease now while scoring a second date. She could almost see his grin.

"Tomorrow," she teased lightly, "I can do tomorrow. What time?" He told her and she smiled in spite of herself. He was good at healing her emotional state, she thought. "I'll be ready."

"If you have any more problems of any kind, you promise to call me?"

"I promise." They hung up with expectations for a second date.

Grant showed up immediately after receiving Amara's phone call. He said he wanted to make sure the bastard hadn't been on the grounds. He took a look around and sent a couple of his men out to check the woods. "All clear," they chorused when they returned to the house. Grant nodded in approval before dismissing them. Amara liked the officers. They were just doing their duty. But she caught a snippet of their conversation and knew without a doubt that she was the topic of their attention. She ignored their shared laughter when they got into the patrol car.

When Grant told her to forgive their lack of manners, she gave him a small smile, "I'm the talk of the town," she spread her arms, "Why not them too?"

"I'm sorry," he said, and he sounded sincere, "You

want to tell me exactly what he had to say?"

"He said that he had been watching me," she replied.

"And," Grant prompted?

"And he said he had seen me naked," she swore beneath her breath.

"That's grounds for questioning," he said seriously. "You sure it was him? Did he admit it?"

"Not in so many words, but it was Simon."

"I'll see if I can loosen him up," Grant's eyes gleamed. "I'll be in touch. I'm going to go have a nice long chat with your former professor. Keep your door locked."

It was late in the day when Amara finally took some time for herself. She went to the backwoods with Grim at her side and climbed downhill to the creek below. The water was warm in the late afternoon sun. She removed her cut-offs and moccasins and allowed herself to bask in the feel of the current against her skin. The sand was soft beneath her feet. The sun beat down upon her. Grim lay on the bank and watched as she waded further from shore. He whined when the water closed over her head. Amara resurfaced, sputtering as she caught her breath. It was happening again! The water was suddenly deeper than only seconds before! It rushed by her, pulling her along. She regained her wits and set out for the opposite waterfront. The mill was again fully functional, the grounds crawling with women and children. No one seemed to notice as she regained her footing; no one except Awinita. And she met her eyes serenely, "I've been expecting you," she said.

There was a whirring sound in Amara's head that was difficult to ignore. She trained her gaze on Awinita, watching as her mouth moved. She could see that she was speaking to her. Yet the words were somewhat delayed. Like everything else, it was as if time had to culminate before Amara could continue on her journey. And in that moment of suspended breath it did just that. Amara gasped slightly and swept her wet tresses from her face, "You knew I was coming?"

"Of course," Awinita smiled at her shocked expression. "I summoned you after all."

Amara was nonplussed. She stood in a daze, half in, half out of the water. With her hair dripping down her back, she glanced down at her partially clad body. "What must they think of me?" she cried.

Awinita acknowledged her embarrassment by way of explanation, "They cannot see you," she said calmly. "Do not fret. It is only I who can lay eyes on you."

Amara took the time to process this new information. "And what do you see?" she asked curiously.

"It is like looking in a mirror," the other responded.

"So, we are alike?" Amara asked.

"I am an aspect of you. And you are an aspect of me. It is simple, yet complicated. Common, but nearly unheard of," Amara thought Awinita spoke in a riddle. Yet when she said as much, Awinita merely shook her head, "I am trying my best to explain something that is inexplicable. It baffled me in the beginning as well, you see."

Amara took her time digesting this bit of news. As she did so, she stared at the scene around her. It was like being a participant in a play. Only this was real. "When was that?"

she asked at long last, "How long did it take for you to fully comprehend this?"

"Oh, mercy," Awinita paused in thought, "I'm not sure. I believe it took half a century for me to grasp every angle of it. Most of it filtered in fairly quick, I suppose."

"Half a century," Amara muttered to herself. "How is that possible?"

"Well, one must start somewhere," Awinita reasoned. "I thought it best to begin at the beginning. At least that is what I believed you'd have me do," Awinita appeared slightly offended. "But if you would like, I will try to forge ahead?"

"No, no. Of course not," Amara shook her head. "I meant no offense. I am simply trying to keep up."

"Well, for now, you really only need to understand that we are the same, and yet we are different. No need to overcomplicate things," Awinita smiled as if she had laid the matter to rest and Amara should feel greatly relieved. When Amara's brow furrowed in confusion, Awinita frowned slightly.

"Why am I here?" Amara asked, trying to sound far more patient that she truly felt.

"Why, you are here to help, of course! By aiding me, you too, will receive the assistance you need! It is rather like we are joined at the hip. Does that make sense?"

"Not entirely, but it is a beginning," Amara stated matter-of-factly. "But what can I do?" Amara was desperately trying to stay focused. She could hear Grim whining in the background. And that whirring sound was filling her head again. She was starting to feel caught between worlds.

"We have to support each other in order to reset time. Gola tried to talk to your mother, but it ended badly for them both. We cannot have that happen again!"

"Gola," Amara prodded?

"My mother," Awinita conceded. "She was your mother's aspect. They were like us in that regard. Gola did not shift, nor did your mother. It would have helped immensely if they had. They worked well together, but they never put time back in place. *He* shifted, as do I, and we shall make the best of the gifts we have."

"*He?* Who is *he*?" Amara called. She felt despair washing over her as she realized she was fading away.

She heard Awinita's last words as they carried on the wind, "The dark one who stole your mother! And mine before her! He will steal you too, even as he steals me!"

When Amara found herself washed up on the bank on her own side of the river, Grim was licking her face. She choked briefly on the brackish water, and then gathered Grim close to her in a tight embrace. The big dog was panting heavily as if he had labored long to save her. And Amara had mental images of him tugging her back to shore. She looked down at the summer top she had worn and witnessed the teeth marks in the torn fabric. Likely Grim had saved her life, she thought. She had been so determined to capture all the details of the excursion that she had run out of energy altogether! Amara shuddered, and the pair returned to the house where Amara took a hot soak and treated Grim to a special dinner.

That evening when Amara cleared the table and wiped down the cabinets, she put the last of the clean dishes away before setting out for the enclosed porch. There, she loaded a box of sterile bottles and carried them to the kitchen where she placed them on the counter next to the sink. Returning to the solarium, she gathered up several large jars and carried these to the table as well. The jars each contained a natural base which she would transfer to the half dram bottles. She always had a nice stash of the finished products on her shelves, and kept a constant rotation of those in transit at all times. These particular jars would be finished quickly enough. She completed the herbal concoctions first, and then proceeded with the vegetable bases.

Simon and Garfunkel were on the radio. Amara listened in silence to the song *Richard Cory*. It was a good piece, she thought, and a popular one. But it always made her sad. As if sensing her mood, Solomon stood erect and walked on hind legs to the work area. He hopped up and down much like an ecstatic rabbit performing a bunny binky, and then stood stock-still, back straight, until she noticed him. When she looked at him, he held her stare. Amara laughed as she gave him a gentle squeeze. He nipped playfully at her nose, proud that he had accomplished his goal.

Amara sighed and patted his back as Solomon curled up next to her chair. She wiped her hands and reached for her jar of choice. Broccoli was up first; she opened it and mused that she stocked this mainly for herself. *"Broccoli stabilizes the body and soul,"* she could almost hear her mother's voice beside her, *"It is so powerful that it is a tremendous aid when one encounters a power struggle of any kind."* Amara added the correct ratio of liquid to the already preserved base, mixing thoroughly before filling the jar to the brim. She then poured the vegetable mixture into each one of the small bottles using a funnel so as not to spill. After sealing each one of these, she wiped the bottles dry before adding a label.

Next, she started on celery which restored balance to the immune. There were a lot of people with damaged immune systems which made this medicine invaluable. This done, she went to work on both comfrey and cucumber. Comfrey was a must as it treated both people and animals for arthritis and other diseases of the joints. Her grandfather had always claimed that comfrey, when given to humans in this form, worked wonders on repairing soul damage, especially when related to past life. She missed her small family and thought of them daily. They were her teachers, her friends, her closest companions. They were her world. She spoke to them in Cherokee as if they sat beside her. The connection brought comfort.

Lastly, she manipulated the cucumber base and proceeded to finalize her mission. Cucumber was a wonderful cure for depression, and she sold a lot of it. When the last jar was empty, she wiped down every individual bottle checking the labels once again. She then placed the empty containers in the sink while she cleaned up the table and put away the vials. The activity gained the attention of the sleeping Maine Coon who stretched to his full length of thirty-six inches. She scratched his ears and called him, "Yardstick." It was a term of affection. Sampson's ears twitched in response as Eric Burden and War filled the room making her think of Daniel and their dinner date tomorrow night. She smiled at the thought of seeing him again.

As she loaded the now vacant box with the half dram vials and headed for the sun porch and her pantry full of medicinal, all three of the animals followed in her wake. They were comedic in their camaraderie. Grim was at her heels with Solomon close on his tail, and Sampson brought up the rear with his perpetual smile. They were all quite complacent as if they had done the job themselves and were proud of their accomplishments. Glancing back at them, Amara couldn't help but notice that her three companions thrived on evenings such as this. They liked the quiet time together. They were easy to please, and very routine. Amara made a mental note to give them all a special treat.

Grant called right at bedtime. Amara had just curled up with a book when the phone rang. She stood and stepped around Grim, padding barefoot to the phone in the narrow hallway. She picked up the receiver with some trepidation. It came as a relief to hear Grant's no-nonsense voice on the other end of the line. His slight Scottish burr resonated with her. "Hello," she said in a sleepy voice.

"Did I wake you?" he asked politely, his tone familiar.

"No, no," she countered, "I had just settled in. What's up?"

"I just wanted you to know that we have interrogated Simon Alexander. He won't be bothering you anymore." Amara pictured Grant Wheeler's face. She imagined the sheriff was pretty proud of himself.

"Really, that's great," she replied, "So it was him all along?"

"Looks that way," Grant answered with authority. "We don't have enough solid evidence to do any more than give him a warning. Still, I get the feeling he will be leaving you alone from now on." She heard the smile in his voice. She did not know about the bruises on his knuckles.

"Thank you, Grant," she whispered.

"You're welcome," he said in response. "I hope you sleep better now."

"I will," she assured him. "Good night."

CHAPTER SIXTEEN

Amara bathed after a hot day in the late summer sun. The weather was beautiful. The trees were a lush green with a dash of cochineal. Amara dressed with care. She was looking forward to her date with Daniel. She selected a short little black number from the rear of her closet. It was backless, and sexy, and perfect. She slipped it over her head, smoothing it down over her hips as she twirled before the mirror. She wore a pair of black, high-heeled boots with a concealed zipper that made for a snug fit. They were decorated with the same black sequins as the little black bag she had paired them with. Her hair was loose in all its glory, and she sported matching jet earrings. The fire opal pendant was snuggled in the valley between her breasts. Amara had just touched up her lip color when she heard his knock at the door.

"Wow. You look fabulous," he complimented, and she could tell that he meant it.

"Thank you," she dimpled, snatching up a light wrap. "The boys are down for the evening so I am ready any time."

"Good," he nodded approvingly. She called good bye to her animal babies before locking the front door. He grinned and steered her toward his car. As he helped her in, he said again, "Wow, I really like that dress!"

She felt his fingers graze her bare back, and thought how much she really liked this man. "Thanks," she said in a husky whisper, "I hoped you would."

They enjoyed a quiet conversation on the way to the restaurant. He had chosen a colorful Chinese palace in Lafayette called The Ginger Cow. They were promptly seated upon arrival amid bright lanterns and handcrafted murals. There was a Zen-like simplicity in the clean lines that created the serene atmosphere. They ordered tea and took their time viewing the menu.

When their tea arrived, the waiter produced a complimentary platter of eggrolls. Amara almost squealed in delight! Vegetarian eggrolls were practically unheard of. They looked amazing, smelled delicious, and were served in abundance. "I took a chance on these," Daniel grinned at her excitement when the waiter confirmed that Mr. Collins had indeed placed a special order just for her. Amara was impressed. Daniel was very definitely a thoughtful man!

They finally decided on two contrasting vegetable dishes, ordering both for the table so that they could share. After much discussion, they ordered fried rice instead of steamed, and once again Amara discovered that he had made special arrangements to accommodate her needs. "I never get to order fried rice or eggrolls," she admitted, "since they always contain either pork or chicken." She beamed when the food was placed before her devoid of meat. It was a banquet set for a queen and she said so. The waiter looked pleased by the compliment, and Daniel encouraged her to sample everything. The dinners were served with an entrée of soup and the steaming bowl of hot and sour was a delightful concoction of tofu and vegetables. Its aroma was pleasing, and Amara's expression was curious as she took a tentative taste. Truth be told, she was trying to identify all the ingredients so that she could duplicate the recipe. When Daniel guessed as much, she was surprised that he had come to know her so well in such a short period of time.

"I'm pretty good at that," she admitted, "but it is such a pleasure to sit back and relax." They talked while they ate, allowing the conversation to flow naturally between them. And laughter was a thing contagious. Daniel had a keen sense of humor making it obvious to all that they were enjoying themselves immensely.

After dinner he surprised her further by inquiring if she would like to stop and listen to some live music before heading home. "There is a jazz band down at the corner pub," he told her, "I hear they're quite good." She accepted gladly, thinking it would be a shame to end the evening prematurely.

The music was astounding in its professionalism. The band was well versed. The crowd was small and appreciative. It was an intimate setting with dim lights and small round tables covered in clean white linens. They had a corner all to themselves. He ordered them both a drink and they sipped quietly. As the music turned sultry he moved his chair closer to hers and placed an arm around her shoulders so that his warm fingers brushed her flesh. He whispered something in her ear, stood and extended one large hand, and without further ado she found herself in his arms swaying to the music. When his lips grazed her temple, she felt chill bumps. She looked into his deep-set blue eyes and saw a world of longing. He didn't say a word. He just looked at her as if he could devour her. Her gaze landed on his mouth, and she desperately wanted to kiss those lips that were entirely too full for a man. She settled for touching one slim finger to them instead and instantly realized her mistake as he gently suckled it. She gasped. When the song ended she allowed him to lead her to her seat where she polished off her drink.

They took a long walk when they left the pub. Daniel had given the waiter a generous tip, and paused at the door to do the same for the band. The players had really outdone themselves. There was a misty rain that was both warm and pleasant as they admired the architecture of downtown Lafayette. It was full of exquisite old homes that were meticulously kept, every one of them worth a small fortune. They made quiet comments between themselves, scarcely noticing when the rain stopped. They had walked full circle back to the parking lot. He unlocked his car door, circled around, and politely assisted her. She nearly swooned at his manners. He was absolutely perfect.

On the ride home, they discussed the band. "The music was great, wasn't it? Did you enjoy yourself?"

"Oh, yes," her eyes shone with satisfaction. It was clear that she was extremely content. "The vocalist was amazing. I loved her voice," she said sincerely, "and I thought it was terrific that she could blow sax so darn well too."

"She was good," he agreed. "They all were. It took a lot of talent to do what they did. Did you like the keys in that last song?"

"Why, yes! The player was brilliant. I always wanted to be a musician," she admitted. "I love music, but it does not appear to be among my gifts." She made a face and he laughed.

"That's because they make it look so easy," he chuckled. "Nothing that good is ever easy. Those people worked hard to get where they are. It can be intimidating."

"You play anything?" she asked coyly.

"I took piano as a kid," he admitted. "I'm not very good, but I enjoy it."

"Oh, that's wonderful!" she clapped her hands in excitement. "I have a set of bongos," she laughed.

She chattered on about how she couldn't wait to hear him perform. He grinned and suggested they listen to the radio instead. She pretended to pout, but was the first to comment on the station he had chosen saying that they played some really good blues on that channel. Next thing they knew they were back at her place. He pulled in her drive, helped her with the door, and escorted her up to the house. They could hear Grim sound the alarm with Solomon joining in. He escorted her inside, checked out the place, and put a sack of leftover Chinese in her refrigerator. She hadn't even realized he had carried the bag of food out of the restaurant!

Daniel had already gained Grim's trust, and Solomon obviously adored him. Sampson purred and stayed nearby which was a compliment in itself. He had been accepted, it seemed. He gave each one a pat in turn, and then headed for the door. "It's late," he said, "I need to let you get some sleep."

"Would you care for a nightcap?" Amara asked quietly. Her voice was barely a whisper. She looked all wide-eyed and innocent when he faced at her. "You don't have to go in early on Friday, do you?"

"Ah, no," he said matter-of-factly, "I don't. But I think I should be going."

She let her white teeth sink into her full lower lip, and stood watching him. "Or you could sleep over," she said breathlessly.

He closed the distance between them in two long strides, taking her into his arms. He kissed her long and hard, and then peered into her eyes. "Are you sure? I don't want to pressure you."

"I'm sure," she smiled shyly, "Grim won't mind." The joke was intended to lighten the mood. But his eyes were serious when they found hers. He studied her features thoroughly before extending his hand. She put her small hand in his much larger one and allowed him to lead her to the bedroom.

Amara awoke with a sleepy smile. She stretched and cast a look about the room to see what had awakened her. Daniel was pulling on the black jeans he had worn the night before. Her smile widened. She tossed her curls and patted the side of the bed he had occupied, "Don't go," she pleaded. "It's early yet. Come back to bed."

He smiled back at her, his deep-set blue eyes piercing the depths of her golden brown ones, "I have to," he said quietly, reaching down to stroke her hair. "I don't have a fresh change of clothes here."

"Maybe you won't need them," she whispered confidentially.

"I knew you'd say that," he leaned down and kissed her. She clung to him making it incredibly difficult for him to break away. "Yeah, I will," his eyes creased at the corners when he smiled. She reached up and gently touched his face, her fingers caressing those sultry lips. She was so comfortable with him! She couldn't believe how natural it felt.

"Oh," she groaned in distress, "I suppose you feel honor bound to go to work?"

"Yeah," he nodded, still grinning, "And it's kind of a giveaway if I show up unshaved and in rumpled clothing."

"Oh, all right," she said the words sadly as if it took great effort. "Well, I can at least feed you before you go." She was already pulling a short little gown over her head to cover her nakedness. "I'll get the coffee going."

She was in the narrow hallway where Grim had slept when he spoke again, "Tea would be great. And we have egg-rolls," he reminded her, "If that sounds good to you?"

"Oh, yes," she grinned back at him, "It does sound good. You sure you don't want coffee?"

"No, tea is good. I like your tea."

Amara smiled and headed to the kitchen with Grim in her wake. She put the kettle on, preheated the oven, and laid a pair of plates on the range. While the water was heating she fed Grim, talking to all three of the boys at once. She stooped to pick Solomon up knowing how much he liked to be held and carried him with her. Sampson followed all the while telling her about the bottom of his bowl. She grabbed the bag of cat chow and poured some into his dish, topped off the communal water bowl, and set Solomon down on the porch where his food bowl was waiting. She filled it and patted his bottom while he wagged his tail. "Such good boys," she told them in unison, "I have such good boys, don't I?"

She returned to the kitchen where she washed her hands before slicing a loaf of French bread. She had already popped the eggrolls, now in aluminum foil, into the oven. She slid the bread in next to them. While the bread toasted she set out a tub of ricotta cheese, then opened a container of basil pesto she had made the day before. She retrieved the toast, spreading each slice with ricotta before topping the cheese with pesto. She slid a slice on two individual plates and switched off the oven. She was rifling through her tea bags when Daniel entered. He had had second thoughts about that shower and was dressed only in his jeans. There was a clean towel around his neck and his feet were bare. Amara thought he looked absolutely gorgeous, like an avenging angel with that copper head of hair, broad shoulders, and lean physique. His build was so gloriously muscular that she found herself staring until he spoke directly to her. "Would it be too presumptuous of me to assume I might leave a razor here?"

Her generous mouth curved into a broad smile as she said, "I was hoping you would see it that way! If you tell me what you use, I'll pick you up some supplies? I need to run into town anyway, and you might as well be comfortable."

"Can I help?" he nodded at the stove.

"No, it's all ready. Have a seat," she bustled about the kitchen while she spoke, setting a plate before him. When she returned with a plate for herself, she carried the eggrolls in a warming basket which she set in the middle of the table. Before she seated herself, she filled two mugs with strong hot tea.

"Looks good," he said.

"Go ahead and eat," she grinned. "You've got to be hungry?"

"Oh, yeah," he looked her over as he said it, and they both chuckled.

Grim barked, interrupting the conversation momentarily. Daniel stood and peered out the window. He thought he'd heard a crunch on gravel as if someone had pulled into the drive. But as his eyes swept the winding road that led up the hill to Amara's house, he saw the lane was empty.

They said their goodbyes at the door. She returned his kiss with enough fire to make him want to beg for more. "Later?" he asked, and she gave him a very slow, decisive nod.

CHAPTER SEVENTEEN

mara watched as Daniel drove away in his light green '64 Rambler. It was a reliable four-door that allowed for easy storage, and he kept it immaculate. She was on cloud nine as she headed for the shower and a clean set of clothes.

Daniel pulled off the gravel drive and turned onto the highway. There was practically no traffic this time of day so he was taken off guard when a vehicle sped up behind him. It must have come from one of the obscure side roads because it appeared as if from nowhere. He didn't think anything about it when he noticed it was a police car, but naturally began to pull his car over so the officer could get around him. There was no oncoming traffic. Still, he followed protocol. And that was when the car slammed very deliberately into the rear of his own vehicle!

Startled, he glanced in the rear view mirror while he gained control of his ride. The county car was on his tail! He scowled when recognition set in. It was that cop! The one that was on Amara's case, and he was pissed! Daniel laid on the horn, and the cop slammed him again. What was his name? Grant something, he thought. Yeah, Grant Wheeler. Daniel would have pulled over and put an end to it right then, but Wheeler was enjoying the game. He slammed into Daniel a third, and then fourth time!

Both cars were squealing now. They were burning rubber, yet the cop didn't show any sign of slowing. Daniel floored it and swerved onto a dirt road where he was able to spin his car about so that the nose faced the highway. Dust flew; tires spun. He hopped from the vehicle, his own temper exploding. Grant almost missed the turn altogether, he was that close on Daniel's tail. When he did pull in, he stopped alongside Daniel so that the men stood nose to nose. Daniel got the first word, "What the hell?" he roared.

"You were speeding," Wheeler accused.

"Bull shit!"

"If I say it's so, it's so," the sheriff sneered.

"What's really going down here?" Daniel exclaimed, as if he didn't already know the answer.

"Like I said, you were speeding," Grant repeated, "Caused me to lose control in a high speed chase."

"That's a trumped-up charge, and you know it," Daniel pressed. "You try to make that stick, and I'll get the best damned attorney money can buy!"

"Nah, I'm going to give you a warning this time." The sheriff made as if to turn and walk away, veering back at the last moment, "You stay away from her, you hear?" He pointed a commanding finger in Daniel's direction.

"That was you in the drive," Daniel accused. "I knew I heard a car."

"Yeah, and you had no business with her, you got that?"

"The lady is capable of making her own decisions. I didn't force her."

Grant's face turned beet red. He stepped close enough to jab the other man in the chest, "She's spoken for. Back off," he muttered.

"And if I don't?"

"Now, you don't want to do that. You don't want to come up against me," Grant's features were harsh in the early morning sun. His complexion was mottled, he was that angry.

"Like I said, I didn't force her."

For a long moment it seemed that Wheeler was going to contest the comment. Instead, he turned on his heel, and with one foot on the bumper, said, "Maybe I'll go see what the little Indian girl has to say for herself."

Daniel was thoroughly shocked by the parting remark. It was a cheap shot. Surely Wheeler didn't actually mean that? "Leave Amara out of this!" he grated, "This is between you and me."

"We'll see," Grant snarled as he slammed his door shut behind him. He sped off down the highway in the opposite direction leaving Daniel to worry over Amara. Daniel checked out his vehicle, which except for a slight fender bender was remarkably undamaged. He climbed into the driver's seat and drove off. He would have to think on how best to handle this new situation. Who knew the sheriff was such a bigot? What a cad.

Amara saw Daniel again on Friday evening, but he didn't stay over since she was busy preparing for Saturday's sale. Instead, he helped her gather the late root vegetables from the garden and the salad greens from the herbary. She even had plump red tomatoes and crisp cucumbers! Amara baked bread while Daniel took care of the boys and fed the horses. They shared a simple meal she had pulled from the deep freeze along with a warm loaf she had set aside for the two of them. Daniel was a grateful man. Home cooking was scarce in his world!

At length, Amara finished a new bunch of sage wands and set them aside with her elixirs which were neatly stacked in boxes by the door. Daniel carried them out for her and locked them in the trunk of her car. "Would you like for me to take them on down to your stall?" he offered, "Might save you a little time in the morning."

"No, I'll get them when I set up, but thank you," she smiled. She was happier than she had ever been as she went about humming some vaguely familiar tune. When he mentioned it, she blushed and said, "Oh, that! I've had *Way Faring Stranger* in my head of late."

They showered together at the end of the evening, and the intimacy of it was more mind-blowing then Amara could have imagined. She gasped out orgasm after orgasm. When they finished, she took his hand and pulled him across the hallway where they fell together on the bed one last time. She didn't want him to leave, but he insisted she would rest better, "You have to get up early," he reminded, "and I would probably be in the way." She only gave in because she knew she would be swamped, and Daniel usually worked until noon on Saturdays. "I'll call you tomorrow night," he promised, "or maybe I'll stop in."

"Do that," she pleaded. "Come for dinner."

"I sense a trap," he teased, and she was fascinated by the creases at the corners of his eyes. He was a man who laughed easily, she thought. She liked that. "I'll tell you what, I'll bring pizza," he promised, "Your favorite; mushroom."

Amara hid her disappointment when he went to leave, but she knew it would be easier for them both. And he'd be back the next night. She tucked the boys in, poured herself a glass of wine, and carried it with her to bed. Grim settled down at her side. She fell asleep much more easily than she would have imagined.

Amara sold every single bit of produce and product that she set out! She looked satisfied when she gathered her cash box together, locked it, and slid it under the front seat of her car. She was just about to drive the short distance to the house when Tanner pulled alongside her. She gave a brisk nod to his friendly wave hoping to avoid any conversation with him. Even knowing Simon was the culprit, Tanner still made her jumpy.

"Given any more thought to my proposal?" he asked bluntly.

"What? You mean mating our horses? No," she shook her head.

"We could make beautiful babies," he grinned slyly. Amara didn't like that grin. She slid behind the wheel of her car just to put some distance between them. Tanner was on her like a flea on a dog. He leaned into her car, placing one hand on the wheel, effectively trapping her. "Sure you don't want to reconsider? We still got time to think on it."

"No. I told you I won't breed Shawnee," her face was

set, her voice firm.

Neither of them noticed the sheriff pull up until he was practically on top of them. Are you bothering Miss Owens again?" he spoke with deliberation.

"No, sir," Tanner drawled in his best redneck voice, and then spat in the dirt between them. He had taken a mighty dislike to the sheriff.

Wheeler smiled an evil smile. He said, "I didn't think so. Why don't you go on about your business?"

"Yeah," Tanner never broke eye contact with Wheeler, but he climbed back into his red pickup truck and said, "I was just about to do that." His tone of voice dismissed any respect he might otherwise have shown. Tanner roared on up the hill and past the house.

"I don't trust him," Grant said. "I don't trust him at all."

Late afternoon had Amara finishing up with the hors-es. She had spent extra time with their care as well as the with the necessary barn work. It had been a while since she had cleaned their tack so she chose to do that today. She had just released the animals into the pasture, put away the curry combs, cloths, and neatsfoot oil, and laid fresh straw down in their stalls. Earlier, she had draped their saddles out over the fence along with their pads and bridals. She stepped out to carry these back indoors when she was startled by the sound of the double wide doors nearest her. She turned to find Tanner lounging in the open cavity of the structure as if he owned the place. He must have been observing her while she worked because he had effectively cut her off. His stance was rigid, his expression hard. He looked like he was about to pounce. "I already told you, no," she stated firmly, but a frisson of fear trickled down her spine. Her shotgun was only a short distance away. She had left it just inside the barn door, but Tanner was blocking her path. She pretended not to notice as she tossed her head. She didn't so much as bat an eye.

As if he read her mind, he turned and glanced right at it. "Been keeping that thing awfully close of late," he snorted, kicking up the clean straw in an insolent gesture. "What you need is a man. Then you wouldn't be so jumpy."

"I am not jumpy," she snapped, wishing she hadn't left Grim to guard the house.

"No? Then you won't mind thinking on what I have to say," he shrugged. "We could make it work, maybe combine our farms. We'd both stand to gain." She sucked in her breath at his arrogance. "Hey, I'm not laying down any claims, just making some suggestions." He spread his hands out to his sides. He had shifty eyes. "I've been working this land for some time now," he stroked his chin. "We get along well enough. Maybe it's time we took it to the next level?"

Amara was shocked, completely and utterly shocked. They had a business arrangement, nothing more. They had never even seen each other in any other capacity, not to mention that she had absolutely no interest in him. "I think not," she said succinctly. And in that moment he looked like nothing other than an outraged bull. Before she knew what he was about, he charged. She staggered under the weight of him, twisted in his grasp, but went down all the same. He kept a firm hold on her, and they rolled a few feet in the dirt, his hands invading her clothing. Amara shrieked in anger. And that's when she noted a passel of blackbirds overhead.

Crow separated from the group and dove in upon them,

providing that fraction of a second she so desperately needed. Amara frequently kept a sheathed blade in her booted moccasin. She drew it now and expertly buried it in his shoulder. He roared like the beast he was, freeing her just long enough for Amara to leap to her feet. She snatched up the shotgun as she bolted through the barn door. In the pasture the horses shrieked. They were kicking up enough of a ruckus as to give Tanner pause. He backed away from the double barrels of the shotgun, raised his hands in the air, and spat. Amara recognized his distain, but stood her ground. She kept the shotgun trained directly on him, "I want you out of here. Now!" her tone was one of authority. "Make arrangements for your cattle elsewhere." She didn't give him a chance to respond, but forced him off the property.

Daniel was surprised to find the house unlocked when he arrived with the pizza. Amara never left her door unlocked. He set the box down on the outside table and cautiously entered the front room. He could hear Grim snapping and growling in the kitchen. In response to Daniel's voice, Grim barked sharply. Someone had locked the dog in the kitchen, or more precisely, out of the rest of the house. A wooden straight-back chair had been propped against the door for further security. There had been one missing from the front porch. Daniel ignored the dog for the moment, choosing to search for Amara instead. As he opened his mouth to call her name, Amara emerged from the shadows.

She was wild-eyed where she stood in the doorway. Her clothing was torn, her hair unkempt. And she had him in the sights of her shotgun, reminding him of the first time they met. He blinked as he stopped short, speaking softly to her, "It's me, Daniel," he crooned, "You're safe, honey. I found your door unlocked," he continued to speak until he saw a spark of recognition in her eyes. He stood stock still allowing his words to register. When Amara slowly lowered the gun, Daniel expelled his breath, and she flew into his arms.

Amara took a dose of her shock and trauma drops while Daniel phoned the police. The thing that scared them both was the fact that there was no sign of forced entry. Amara had turned that over in her mind, finally concluding that someone must have found her spare key. She cautiously opened the cellar door, and there in the dark recesses of the stairwell, discovered that her key was indeed missing. She reported this to the police as soon as they arrived.

Sheriff Wheeler was among the officers at the site, and had, of course, run the show. His insistence of a formal statement was nerve-racking. Amara had undergone a routine examination by the paramedics who were actually quite thorough. When Sheriff Wheeler demanded she accompany him to the hospital, she referred him to the EMTs. The sheriff had wanted to argue, but Amara turned her back on him. It was as though he was bent on getting her alone, she thought. Now why would that be?

"She already declined any further exams," Daniel spoke for her, "the paramedics have a list of every single bruise on her. They were thorough enough to photograph her torn clothing as well as any contusions, and you've taken her statement."

"You're interfering with the law," Grant replied. A muscle ticked in his cheek.

"I am carrying out her wishes," Daniel expounded. "She returned home after the assault to discover someone had been in her house. I think it only natural that she went

into shock."

"She is not in any position to make such a decision," the sheriff ground out, at which point Amara turned and gave him a chilly look.

"I'm perfectly capable," she said distinctly. "I will answer any further questions you may have, Grant. But I'm staying home." It was not the response he was looking for. "If you want to help," she called after him, "make sure that Tanner Lake never steps foot on my soil again. He had no right to attack me. And someone has a key to my house!"

Wheeler turned and faced her. He was angry and it showed. "How can you be sure when the key was stolen?" he persisted. "You told me there was nothing stolen at the time of the break-in. Then, you discovered that your lingerie was missing. Now, suddenly, you find that your key is missing as well."

"I didn't realize the key was missing," she repeated as if speaking to a belligerent child. "I didn't figure that out until today."

"We assumed it was another break-in," Daniel intervened, "until it became clear there was no indication of one."

"Truly, Grant," Amara attempted to smooth things over, "It wasn't until Daniel noticed that the lock was not broken that I even thought to look for the key. I have always kept it in the cellar. No one else uses that door. They couldn't. I keep it bolted from inside. It is simply an escape route should I ever need one."

Wheeler gave a terse nod. "Yet someone knew to look there," he said flatly. "How would they know that, Amara?"

"I don't know," she answered honestly, "unless they

knew the outline of the house. Tanner has been a neighbor for a long time. He knew my grandfather. Perhaps he had been in the cellar years ago? Then again, we know Simon broke in recently. Perhaps he searched the place more thoroughly than we thought?"

"I'll look into it," Wheeler said, but he appeared agitated.

"It could have been either one of them," She insisted. "You, yourself, said that you didn't trust Tanner. And you sure as hell don't like Simon! But Tanner's actions today were premeditated."

"Oh, I'll have a talk with Tanner Lake," he ground out. "He's facing a charge of attempted rape. Anyone else you been stringing along?"

"That's dirty, and you know it," Amara sneered.

Wheeler threw her an insinuating glance as he turned on his heel, muttering something beneath his breath.

After everyone had gone, Daniel insisted on heating their dinner while Amara showered and changed into fresh clothing. Now he handed her a glass of Beaujolais to go with the warm pizza. He had picked up the wine on his way home, and Amara was grateful for his thoughtfulness. She had taken a second dose of the trauma drops, and was much calmer as a result. The couple shared a quiet meal, and settled in with Grim and the little ones for the remainder of the evening.

CHAPTER EIGHTEEN

*D*aniel was just leaving when the girls arrived as planned. He had spent the morning helping Amara with her chores. She realized that he was worried about her, and suspected that he was reluctant to leave. If he acted a bit too possessive, she didn't mind. He wasn't the type to boss her around. He was simply looking out for her.

Nikki was the first to pull in. She had discussed the menu with Amara beforehand and therefore knew how best to help. She had picked up some wine that would complement the meal. She met Daniel in transit, and he briefed her on the events of the night before. Nikki grew up concerned about her friend who seemed to draw too much negative attention from men. You couldn't find a nicer person than Amara, so Nikki had long ago concluded that Amara's ill luck must have some kind of karmic roots. The two of them had discussed it openly, going so far as to include college courses that might aid their cause.

Amara believed she was born into a particular archetype that provoked the issue, thereby making it her goal in life to correct the imbalance. Nikki thought it went deep into past life. It was possible they were both right.

Nikki let herself in and carried the wine into the kitchen where Amara was busily stirring a pot of red lentil soup. While the collective aroma of onion, garlic, carrot, and tomato permeated the air, the selection of cumin, oregano, and rosemary was pungent enough to tease the senses. As the soup simmered over a low burner, Amara boiled three cups of sunflower seeds and set them aside. These would be used to make sunflower cakes. By this time the soup was ready to puree, and Nikki automatically leant a hand. Amara thanked her and returned to the sunflower mixture. She added a couple of scoops of blue cornmeal, plus a tablespoon of sugar, and began forming the cooled dough into rounds. She placed these in a skillet with just enough oil to allow the cakes to fry, flipping the patties expertly so that they browned evenly. By this time Nikki had transformed the soup into a thick stew. She looked at Amara and said, "Lemons?"

"Yes, two," Amara replied, nodding toward a fruit bowl. Nikki juiced the lemons and poured the extract into the stew. Amara had by this time produced a pair of hot pads and was pulling a pan of roasted mushrooms from the oven. She slid a pan of seasoned chickpeas in where the truffle had been, covering the spores to keep them warm. She then retrieved a side dish of stuffed eggplant, and placed it on the warming pad on the counter alongside the mushrooms. "All we have left is the salad," she smiled, "and we're good!"

"Something smells phenomenal!" Cynthia called as she entered the kitchen. She set a bottle of wine on the counter along with a homemade batch of Naan bread. "Yum!" she exclaimed in enthusiasm, "Linda is right behind me."

Linda walked in at precisely that moment. "I locked up," she said by way of greeting. "I brought a rice stir-fry. Nikki said it would go well with whatever else you are making, and oh, my gosh, that smells amazing!"

Amara glanced up from the spinach and arugula salad she was tossing. Nikki grinned and slid a bowl of diced tomatoes and cucumbers her way, while Amara leaned in and pulled the roasted chickpeas from the oven. She tossed in the veggies, topping the salad with the legumes. "Dinner is ready whenever you all are," she said, "The stir-fry will be a huge help," she told Linda, "And Cynthia, your bread smells fabulous!"

The girls set the table while Amara fed the boys. Solomon's eyes were bright with excitement. He liked company. Grim looked on in pure adoration, and Sampson settled down with his arms wrapped around his water bowl. Amara had added the desired ice, and the Maine Coon fairly preened in delight. The girls all laughed at how he let his long, wet chest hair go unnoticed while he lapped at the cold drink. Amara joined in the laughter as she opened the wine commenting on how much she adored his tufted toes.

After dinner the girls settled down for some serious conversation. Linda and Cynthia listened in rapt attention while Amara told them of her out-of-body-experiences. They were fascinated by her past life or time travel excursions, whichever they were, and never once questioned their reality. In truth, Amara's friends had always been more than a little in awe of her. She had always been different, they said. And she stood out without even realizing it. If Amara said she had gone back in time, then she had gone back in time. End of story. So now they must discover what they could do to help, because somehow the things that were happening to Amara were all tied up with those very experiences.

"I don't understand, "Linda said pensively. "Are you implying that the break-in and the photographs are somehow related to the out-of-body experiences?"

"It's a definite possibility," Nikki said solemnly. "Remember, Simon was her lover, and is involved in one, or both, issues."

"He wasn't my lover," Amara protested weakly.

"Almost," Nikki amended. "He wanted to be, and had gone to a great deal of trouble to make it happen."

"True," Amara agreed, "and he had an obsession with photographs."

"Then what about Tanner," Cynthia asked, "and how does he fit in? He's up to something."

"That's what we're trying to figure out," Nikki answered.

"I am not sure who did what? Or why any of it is happening for that matter," Amara sighed. "I don't even know how Simon popped back up, yet alone why Tanner has gone berserk."

"Think of the Jungian archetypes," Nikki instructed.

"Which ones," Amara countered, "the four main ones?"

"I don't know," Nikki supplied, "We have a blank canvas."

"Well, the four main ones being the Self, the Persona, the Shadow, and the Anima should include, or help explain, any of the others," Amara stated.

"I keep getting hung up on the victim archetype," Cynthia interrupted. "How do we determine when, and what, came first?"

"Or if we are talking Jungian, or pagan, or something altogether different?" Linda inserted. "I am not as well versed on this stuff as the rest of you, but I do know there are similarities in every category."

"Yeah, maybe we're being too fundamental," Nikki agreed, "And you, Linda, are remarkably well read. Please do not undermine your knowledge."

"Victim could fall in with the shadow," Amara spoke in a whisper, "And I agree with Nikki, Linda."

"Sure, Sexual and life instincts. That fits," Nikki murmured.

"Or even the anima," Cynthia volunteered.

"Yep, the feminine image in the male psyche represents the true self," Amara stated.

"Everything is sexual in the Freudian world," it was Linda who had spoken. Her self-esteem had been restored. "How does Jung vary?"

"Carl Jung would look at the libido as a generalized source of psychic energy motivating a wide range of behavior. Freud, on the other hand, would say that the libido is a source of psychic energy specific to sex," Amara translated. "There's a big difference."

"What we're looking for is a kind of pattern," Cynthia asserted, "and we can find that in any reading."

"So, do a reading," Amara invited. "I am open to just about anything right now. All I have is what Awinita has provided, and that is precious little."

Cynthia pulled a deck from her purse and shuffled the cards. She didn't even look to see which pack she placed before them. Cynthia carried a variety of pagan and mythological decks wherever she went. The topic was open to discussion. To her they all spoke the same language. It was the translation that mattered. "That's interesting," Cynthia whistled. "One could read that in several ways, I suppose, but it's fairly clear to me. Who else gets it?"

"You laid down hearts," Nikki responded, "love and happiness. But the cups are upside down."

"Meaning the opposite," Cynthia said authoritatively. "Now it depends on the draw," she shuffled the major arcana, giving Amara a gentle nudge.

Amara reached out and plucked the first card that spoke to her. She placed it face down on the surface of the table. Cynthia turned it over slowly and sucked in a breath, "You drew the queen," she whispered. "It's the soul, thus you are on a soul journey, and none other."

"What else?" It was Amara who asked the question on everyone's mind. "Can you read the whole?"

Cynthia nodded thoughtfully, and said, "The cards represent a psychological study of man, and his relationship with Spirit. These are drawn from the collective unconsciousness. I see a duplicity only you can alter, and a vast timelessness. I also see waves that bridge the gap," she paused, regarding Amara for a long moment, "Do you understand this?" Amara nodded to the positive causing Cynthia's brow to furrow, "There is a bird. No, two birds," she pronounced slowly. "These birds are somehow instrumental. They are of the same color, yet they are polar opposites. They hold completely different energies. What did you withhold from us? There is something you have not shared."

Amara stared at Cynthia, and then turned her gaze upon Nikki. "Nikki, we did not explain Crow. Or mention the magpies."

Nikki returned her stare, horrified. "I forgot," she said helplessly. "I didn't connect the dots, did you?"

Amara shook her head, "Crow is a trusted friend. And the other, an enemy, I think."

"And the waves," Cynthia asked, "Do you comprehend the waves?"

"My passage to the other side," Amara replied.

"Then that is your answer. The key lies with the corvid," Cynthia said as she laid down the last card. "Not the good one, but the other. That is your new focus."

"Okay," Amara said slowly, turning a riot of thoughts over in her mind. The conversation shifted to the birds, and the girls discussed Amara's friend, Crow, finding both strength and integrity in the creature. They then considered everything that had now surfaced about the magpie, especially what it represented, and how it affected Amara.

They ended up with a diagram showing the positive and negatives of each winged creature. Linda had drawn the graphs and charts, taking note of the conversation as a whole. After learning of Amara's grandfather's experience with the magpie shortly before his death, as well as the fatal feathers in the grill of Alina's car, Linda paused midsentence, "I think we have forgotten one very important component to the riddle." Her wide brown eyes looked at each person in turn until she saw it dawn on them.

Nikki was the first to comment, "Amara is Native American!" she exclaimed. "How on earth did we discount that?"

"That's true," Cynthia swallowed, "but not full blooded. Does that still count?"

"Definitely," Amara said decisively. "My mother always said I was *of the people*. The Cherokee are a proud people. Why didn't I see that from the beginning?"

"I don't think you, or any of us, truly overlooked it," Nikki spoke up. "I think it's just so normal to us that we didn't perceive it as part of the problem."

"Now if we look at all the facts," Linda suggested, "and put them together with a person of Native American blood, what do we have?"

"A totally different picture; a contrast," Cynthia said. "Your background, Amara, your life, and past lives, would be altered greatly by such a *simple* thing as blood."

"It's huge," Nikki breathed out a sigh. "It changes everything!"

"Yes, it's true you are regarded differently in this life, but can you imagine the distinction your very blood made in any given past life?" Cynthia stared at her friend. "It is so freaking obvious!"

Amara sat stone still. She was remembering all the interactions with Awinita. She was listening to her mother's words from long ago. She had a thousand memories that spoke to her, and she was humbled. "I cannot believe I didn't comprehend this sooner," she said. "Now that we have a new pattern, I will give this much thought."

"How long has it been since you went to a powwow?" Cynthia asked. "I remember going with you when we were girls. Some of the most profound experiences of my life followed those assemblages."

Amara didn't utter a sound. She was nonplussed.

That night the girls stayed over. Aside from having plenty of room, Amara kept extra blankets and bedrolls. After everything they had shared, and all that Amara was going through, the friends agreed it would be best to stick together. No one really felt like leaving her alone, and Amara herself was grateful for the company. They were a tight group, each relying on the other. They talked late into the night, settling in during the early hours of the morn.

Amara awoke to the smell of strong coffee coupled with a familiar voice urging her to get up. "What?" she murmured sleepily as she curled more tightly into a ball. The morning air was damp and chilly and she had no cover other than a scratchy bit of Confederate wool that she shared with another female. "You'd best be rising," it was a roughened tone that sounded in her ear. "You planned on heading into town today," the woman wheezed, "and I brought you some coffee. It's the last of our stash."

That did the trick. Amara opened one eye and realized what had happened. She was back in time again. And she was Awinita. She straightened her spine and did as suggested. Coffee was a lifeline under these circumstances. Of course it was not real coffee. But it was hot, and it was strong, and it was extremely bitter. Awinita nudged the woman beside her only to be met with solid resistance. There was the real source of the cold, she thought.

They were set upon the northern shore of the river the night before, forced to sleep wherever they landed upon the hardened earth. For the most part they had seen little in the darkness; except for Awinita. And Awinita, with her keen eyesight, had seen enough to know that the river was alive with activity. There were other boats besides their own that were overloaded with human cargo, and if Awinita had to guess she would say they were amid the company of soldiers. How this would affect them, she didn't know. But Awinita was wise enough to shy away from crowds, particularly those in uniforms.

Awinita was in with a group of women who by now had no money, food, or prospects. She had shared what scrap of warmth she could find with a woman named Alice. Alice was a young widow with little spirit and no expectations. They had been abandoned back in Louisville where the Manchester and Roswell mill workers ceased to exist as individuals. They were no longer referred to as humans, but were now considered only numbers, and treated as refugees or exiles. They had traveled all the way from Roswell, Georgia, in this God awful heat under some of the worst conditions known to man. They had ridden in box cars so cramped they could not stand erect, and in temperatures so intense they could not breathe. They had walked when there were no available cars. They had gone without food for days at a time when rations were cut, and they had leaned on each other for support.

Alice had lost hope long ago, and finally succumbed to the elements. They had once been members of the Roswell mill, and had numbered as many as four-hundred women and children. Now after weeks of disease and starvation, they were less than half that. Awinita could still see Alice's pinched features and clenched fists in the early morning mist. The women formed a burial detail. And after placing Alice in a shallow grave, they said a prayer over her. When they left Alice behind, it was painfully difficult to go forward. Awinita could not help but think of her friend, Caroline. Would she ever see her again? She had no idea of her whereabouts. Awinita raised her head and placed one foot in front of the

other. What would they find in New Albany?

THE CALLING OF CROWS

PART THREE

The Plight of the Roswell Women

CHAPTER NINETEEN

A meeting was called near the edge of town. Awinita was the elected spokesperson. She had shown both courage and compassion on the journey north, and she was good at bargaining. She knew how to read, write, and figure, and due to her mobile life style, she had a wider scope of discernment than most. She accepted the responsibility with aplomb, comprehending the weight that went with it. She would be entrusted with the meager amount of coin they shared. And she would act as leader. They had voted among themselves, concluding it wiser to send a small detail of women into an unsuspecting environment. They did not wish to overwhelm the entirety of the town. Awinita quietly walked among them, carefully making her selections. She chose three reliable companions.

Apparently, their imminent arrival was well known. They were greeted by a group of townspeople who had, in fact, caught wind of their whereabouts when they were set upon shore the night before. It was no secret they were heading this way. And everyone knew the particulars. Though they were not criminals, they had been charged with treason. Because of this, the citizens of New Albany were a wary lot.

Whispers rippled through the crowd, most of whom were women. At a loss for words, the majority simply stood and stared. Awinita's gaze darted among them, noting random soldiers here and there. It was a threatening atmosphere. Everywhere she looked, copies of The New Albany Daily Ledger met them head on. Articles from the local paper were plastered on storefronts. They even adorned the occasional tree or post. Awinita's sharp gaze caught the bold words in black and white print.

"I have ordered the arrests of the operators at the Confederate manufactories at Roswell and Sweetwater to be sent north. When they reach Nashville have them sent across the Ohio River and turned loose to earn a living where they won't do us any harm."

Signed, General William T. Sherman

Many in the crowd appeared uncomfortable with the situation. They couldn't help but wonder what they would do in a like position. A few were jealous of a new populace of females. A lady in a pale blue cotton dress tore an article down as she stood facing Awinita. "I'm sorry," she said as she crumpled the offensive story. "I feel so sorry for all of you. Come inside, won't you?"

Awinita appreciated the woman's show of kindness, and followed her indoors. She flashed a cordial smile even as her chest tightened in apprehension. Up until now they had a single goal. Reaching the nearest town north of the river had been more than a landmark; it was their salvation. Now that actuality felt shaky. The mill workers were about to discover that the town of New Albany had little to offer. There were no jobs to be had. And in their desperation, there was nowhere to turn. Awinita picked up a paper near at hand, and sighed as she read the following words:

"The women of the South kept the war alive and it is only by making them suffer that we can subdue the men."

Signed, Jeremiah Jenkins, Union Lt. Col

She was standing at the counter of the grocery store where the lady in blue had poured her a refreshing glass of water. She tentatively asked about lodgings and where she might find a job. The Union lady across from her was not unsympathetic. She simply had no sage advice. The town had suffered the war like everyone else. Their loyalty was to the Union. The local hospitals were the recipients of anything they had to spare. She named a couple of farm families that might provide a meal or two in exchange for some hard labor.

"That's all you would get," she said knowingly. "Those folks have no cash to spare, but they always have work. Maybe that would help until you can figure something out? Are there as many of you as they say?" she gestured to the newspaper.

"My group numbers over fifty women and children," Awinita replied, "but there are more heading this way." Awinita held eye contact, "Thank you for the water."

The lady in blue looked saddened by the thought. "I came to purchase food," Awinita reached into the deep recesses of her skirt, and from a hidden pocket, counted out several pennies. "I need enough for a large cook pot," she stated matter-of-factly, "Can you help me choose the best selection for the price?"

The storekeeper counted the coin as she walked to the shelf on the far wall. "That'll buy you enough beans to make a mighty fine soup," she said competently, "and a decent amount of cornmeal."

Awinita brightened and said, "That will feed us for a spell. And it will taste awfully good too."

The woman put the purchases into a small bag knowing that even the bag would come in handy. She caught the gleam of appreciation in Awinita's gaze and smiled slightly. "If you stay close to the edge of town, you will be safer, I think. And you should be able to find kindling easily enough. I know for a fact that old Mister Johnson leaves a trash heap out yonder. Sometimes one man's trash is another man's treasure?"

"Thank you," Awinita smiled in return even as her stomach growled painfully. Her new friend looked uncomfortable, and Awinita realized how much weight she had lost. No doubt the poor lady was fretting over a stranger she couldn't save. Awinita put on a brave face as she started toward the door. "What was the commotion on the river?" she asked in veiled curiosity.

"Oh, you mean The Nashville," the other responded. "She is one of four *floating hospitals*. They are the result of The Western Sanitary Commission. We are well staffed to tend the injured." The autonomy of the river town carried a hubris known only to those accustomed to hard work and dedication.

"That's commendable," Awinita nodded. She was from a proud heritage, and admired the trait in others.

"Thousands of soldiers come here for help," the storekeeper gave a small smile, "We have eleven hospitals total. We even have one for injured Confederate soldiers. I will ask if they are willing to come to your aid, should any of you need it."

Awinita was impressed and said as much. "That's very kind of you," she added.

"I believe you dropped something," the Lady said hurriedly as an older man stepped into the room. He leaned heavily on a cane and glared at Awinita who had begun to shake her head. But at the look in her new friend's eyes, she checked herself. She remained silent as the lady reached out to her. Awinita took the small pouch that was dropped into her hand as she realized the man had almost certainly been spying on them the whole time!

"Thank you," Awinita murmured, "That was clumsy of me." She hadn't missed the glint of cruelty in the old man's faded visage.

The lady looked relieved as Awinita swept out the door. When she was far enough away to ensure privacy, Awinita peeked into the pouch. Chicory! The real stuff, she thought excitedly! Why, it had been ages since any of them had tasted anything close to chicory! Coffee was a distant memory, and the brew they had this morning was bitterroot. This would taste like a dream! She must remember to thank the lady for the bonus, because she knew without a doubt, she did not have enough coin to have purchased the beverage along with the food.

Awinita met her comrades at the designated spot. They had each one taken a different route, checking into jobs that were the antithesis of the others. In this way they hoped to find at least some gainful employment among themselves. But their hands were as empty as their eyes. Awinita saw their defeat and spoke briskly, "Look, I have food enough for a couple of days!" she exclaimed, "And something more will turn up."

"I found this on the ground," the smallest in the group stated hesitantly. Her name was Ellen, and she was speaking of an old newspaper she had tucked beneath one arm. "I thought there might be something useful in it."

"I like the way you think," Awinita smiled at Ellen's effort. It was a source that might provide information on nearby towns. "It's worth a look. And we need to know our whereabouts."

"It's dated the twenty-first of July," one of the ladies murmured. "And it contains an unflattering article about us."

"I dare say we may benefit from that as well," Awinita said shrewdly. "The more we know, the better equipped we are to handle what comes our way."

The woman who had spoken opened the Daily Ledger and began to read, *"Two-hundred and nineteen women and children are headed to New Albany where they are an unwanted burden to the state. If they are not fit to live in the South on account of their disloyalty, are they fit to live in the North?"*

Awinita lifted her chin a notch at the other woman's grimace. "Don't let it disturb you," she ordered.

"She's right," Ellen said. "We can't afford to take it personally. We have a right to make a living just like anyone else." Awinita smiled at Ellen's show of bravado. She was such a little thing, reminding Awinita of a wren. In truth, Awinita had chosen her for her spirit. Wrens were considered harbingers of spring and rebirth. Because of their constant song, they symbolized the arts, musicians, and authors of the written word. Among their many talents was their flair for protection. The wren might be small, but they were well gifted, intelligent creatures who flew close to the ground and moved quickly. Others might see Ellen as shy and unobtrusive, but Awinita applauded the subtle qualities hidden just beneath the surface.

They were silent the rest of the way. When they reached the campsite, they were pleasantly surprised to find that those who remained behind had kept busy. The bivouac had been swept clean. The fire sported a cook pot along with the tin they had used for morning coffee. They had piled their own meager belongings together, and after tallying everything up, had discovered that they had enough plates and utensils to make do. They even had a large tin that would serve as a griddle, as well as a couple of smooth flat stones. The main cook was elected based on her skill and knowledge alone. She appointed a secondary cook to act as her helper. Between them they would keep the site clean, and the dishes washed. They immediately put beans to soak, and turned cornmeal into grits. Some of the scouts brought them plants which were examined to determine if they were edible. Anything that required culinary skills fell into their laps. Everyone was in a good state of mind as the fire blazed high, and the scent of corncakes and chicory filled the air.

Over the course of the next few days, Awinita put everyone to work. She instructed several of the women on how to clean and sharpen sticks to be made into spears, showing them how to fashion a tip that could accurately be used as a weapon or tool. The women were eager to learn, and went out of their way to seek Awinita's approval. Awinita was pleased by the number of knives, scissors, and other sharp objects they had among them. She would see that each woman was armed and able in one way or another.

A second group was taught to weave saplings together. The saplings were coated with mud and used to create shelters that would keep them dry at night. Awinita was a proficient teacher, and by nightfall they had made remarkable progress. But the women were limited. They were not well muscled men, and they lacked axes and other tools. This meant they had to rely on what they could pull from the earth, or discover on the forest floor.

A third group was put in charge of collecting sticks

and branches, including fallen tree trunks. Awinita told them of Mr. Johnson's trash heap, and assigned some of the younger girls to check on it regularly. A board could be fashioned to create a lean-to. A piece of metal might complete their cookware. And fabric scraps were to be cherished for winter wraps and clothing. Anything that could be used for walls and roofs were willingly handed over to those building huts.

Awinita handpicked two members of her crew to accompany her to the water's edge, where she put a finger to her lips and silently communicated how to procure a good fishing hole. She demonstrated the use of a spear, leaving the others to watch in awe as one fish after another was tossed onto the beach. Soon the selected partners followed her example. It was slow progress, but they were learning. At least they would eat.

They slept at night in partial shelters with hope in their hearts and food in their bellies. It was enough for now, though Awinita knew it wouldn't last. While the women were willing, they were not skilled. There was a false sense of security about living like this, and Awinita knew it only too well. There would be good days at the river, and days when there was no catch at all. There would be days when they would have coin, and days when there would be none. They would have to beg, and they would have to take whatever jobs came their way. And the coin would be used to feed the whole group. Predators were everywhere. Men were greedy, and women were easy targets. Wild animals were on the prowl, and they were in unfamiliar territory. And the months would grow cold, and they were threadbare with no winter clothing or coats. Disease would begin to sweep through their numbers. In all fairness, Awinita realized they were simply buying time. They needed to find permanent jobs and real homes, and she didn't know how to accomplish this.

Those who could read poured over the newspapers

they had managed to collect in hopes of gleaning information. What they discovered was disparaging. It seemed that all of the river towns were busy tending their own, and Jobs were nonexistent. It was now early August, and The Louisville Daily Journal gave a bleak account of the refugees on the northern side of the river. Awinita, along with everyone else, had been held in either refuge houses or female facilities while in Louisville. They were literally prisoners without benefit of food, water, or heat. But they were the first to cross the river. Now that The Female Military Prison had opened its doors under the care of Dr. Mary Walker, many would remain indefinitely on Kentucky ground. Awinita worried over her friend, Caroline, and the child, Chloe. Where were they?

Despite all the improvements, the nights were downright chilly here on the river. And they would become increasingly more so. Fights broke out among the women. Rules were defined with the intention to put an end to the violence. Women, it seemed, could be just as headstrong as men. Soon, small angry groups set out on their own. It wasn't long before their numbers were reduced by half, and Awinita watched with concern.

So it was Awinita offered to send scouts ahead to explore the surrounding towns. She would have liked to go herself, but knew that she was needed here. She had spent a great deal of time studying every individual municipality in the vicinity, and honestly, none of them sounded any better than where they were. She was still tempted to go in person, but whenever she broached the topic some of the women became hysterical. They were used to relying on her, they said. In the end, Awinita appointed four of her most loyal hands, and sent them in her stead. They were to go to Jeffersonville which appeared to be their best option. It was only about a five mile walk. Awinita gave strict orders for their safety. She prayed she had made the right decision.

It was during this time that The New Albany Daily began announcing unidentified bodies discovered on the banks between settlements. The newspapers stated only that the deaths had been a result of the elements. The scouts had been given food enough to last two days if they were careful with their rations. It was up to them to provide the rest. Their reality was becoming darker by the day. Awinita had no way of knowing if her friends had perished, or if the bodies were those of deserters. Either way it cast a pall over the camp.

Awinita went to sleep each night with dim memories of another time, another life. She wondered if she would ever see those in that lifetime again, or understand why she was here in this one now. She kept her confusion to herself, understanding whatever the reason, she must live each day at a time. But in the wee hours of the morning, she missed being held in the arms of her lover. His beautifully chiseled features continued to haunt her.

CHAPTER TWENTY

Something wet touched her face. Grim whimpered, and someone hushed him in a gentle voice. Amara moaned softly as a cool cloth was placed upon her brow. She ran her tongue across chapped lips. A gentle hand cupped her head, pressing a cup of cold water to her mouth. She drank greedily, coughing as a result. "Slow down," a familiar voice cautioned, "not so fast."

Nikki, she thought. It was Nikki! She cracked her eyes open. The light from the nearby window hurt, and she moaned. Nikki got up and closed the curtains. "Oh, my God, is it really you?" Amara cried. Tears streaked her face. Grim was quick to kiss them away. She broke into sobs and drew him to her, reaching for Nikki at the same time. Nikki sat back down and took her hand. Grim settled next to her with his big head in her lap. Amara squeezed Nikki's fingers. "What happened? Have I been ill?" she asked.

"You've been out for over twelve hours," she whispered, her own voice breaking, "Oh, God, Amara! I didn't know what to do! We were so worried!"

"Twelve hours?" Amara was in shock. "How can that be? I've been gone for weeks!"

"You fainted last night," Nikki whispered, thinking how inappropriate the word truly was. "Your breathing was so shallow it was barely perceptible. We took turns at your bedside," she resumed in a quivery voice, "Amara, I was terrified!"

"I'm sorry," Amara's voice was quiet. "I don't remember."

"You said you were gone for weeks. What did you mean? You were back in time again, weren't you?"

"Yes, it was awful, Nikki," Amara's voice broke on a sob, "We were starving. There were so many deaths!"

"Where were you? Were you in Indiana?"

"We got detained in Louisville after all those miserably long days and nights in the confines on the rails. We were held captive in refuge houses, but there was no food or water. They took us across the river and dumped us like garbage on the shores of Indiana. I made it into New Albany, but there was no work to be had! Babies screamed until they choked on their own breath! Women and children died in our arms! There was so little food I could feel my spine against my stomach. When I laid my hand across my middle," Amara placed a hand to her waist as if to demonstrate, "I could literally feel my spine." Nikki bent close and wrapped an arm about her as Amara wept, "Oh, God, Nikki, why is this happening?"

"I don't know," Nikki said quietly, "Just hush now. You need your strength. I'm going to go fix breakfast."

In the kitchen, Nikki put a light meal together, and

loaded a tray for Amara. "She's way too pale," she told Cynthia who looked over her shoulder like a lost pup.

"Amara is typically the strong one," Cynthia protested. "Are we doing the right thing, do you think?"

"What else can we do?" Nikki replied crisply.

"I didn't mean anything," Cynthia shrugged. "But what if we're missing something? I'm worried about her."

"Yeah, me too," Nikki said more calmly, "I didn't mean to snap."

"It's okay. We're all under a lot of pressure. I think we need to tell Daniel," Cynthia replied defensively. "There, I said it."

"We probably do," Nikki agreed, "But Cynthia, it has only been twelve hours, and she is nearly emaciated," Nikki's voice was horrified. "She has lost an incredible amount of weight for those few hours!"

The girls looked at each other in shock. They knew what had taken place, and as far-fetched as it may sound, they believed every word. But seeing Amara this ill was not only out of character, it was unreal. How could her body be so thin after such a short amount of time? How could they explain it to Daniel? Amara needed rest. She needed nourishment. And she needed understanding. Would Daniel be able to provide those things?

"We'll take turns sitting with her," Cynthia spoke up. "I don't have to work tomorrow so I can stay until Daniel comes. Hell, I can stay as long as she needs me. My schedule is flexible."

"Thank you, I was worried about that. I can come any

time after work, or sleep over when Daniel can't," Nikki ventured. "We've got to get her back on her feet. I'm really worried. What if it happens again?"

"We'll be here for her," it was Linda's hushed voice. She was standing in the doorway looking as terrified as they felt. "I just looked in on her. You guys are right. She needs us. Ian won't mind if I stay whenever needed."

"Then it's settled. We'll talk to her and get permission to speak to Daniel. She's too exhausted to have to explain everything, and she's going to need him."

"I think he'll be okay about it," Nikki ventured. "He's crazy about her, and Gregory has told me enough about him to know that he has seen some pretty wild stuff himself."

Cynthia had spoken to Amara, and it was agreed that she would explain the situation to Daniel. That way the ground work was laid, and Amara could catch up on her rest. While Amara napped, Cynthia cooked a simple, but filling meal, after which she helped Amara bathe and wash her hair. She had known Amara forever, and had never seen her so frail. It was truly terrifying. She was determined that Daniel would understand, because if he didn't, she, Cynthia would set him straight.

Amara was so exhausted after her catharsis that Cynthia brought her tea and toast. Grim stayed at her side the entire time. Even the little ones were subdued. The three of them guarded their mama with loving care. Sampson stretched out on the bed beside her, while Solomon mimicked Grim's actions. He circled two or three times before curling up in a ball. None of them made a peep.

When Daniel arrived, it was Cynthia who met him. Amara was resting, she told him. She led the way into the kitchen and handed him a cup of tea. By the time Amara awoke again, Daniel had heard the entire story. "Well?" she gave him a pointed look. "What are we going to do?"

"I am going to check on Amara," Daniel said firmly. He didn't hesitate a second. "I'll see if she's up to coming to the table while you take care of dinner."

Cynthia broke into a radiant smile, "I knew you were good for her," she said triumphantly.

Daniel put an arm around her shoulder before he left the room, "I won't let you down," he stated firmly, "I'm in love with her."

Amara dined at the table that evening and managed a good portion of her meal in spite of everything she had endured. It was obvious that she had suffered acute starvation. She complimented Cynthia repeatedly even as she begged for seconds. "This is incredibly good," she praised, and Cynthia knew that she was sincere, "You couldn't have chosen a better menu."

"Mac and cheese is always good when you're sick," Cynthia responded.

"Yes, but this is the best I have ever had," Amara insisted.

"I made an extra pan for the freezer," Cynthia smiled, "just in case."

Amara dimpled and lingered over the meal.

Cynthia cleaned up the kitchen, and fed the animals. She had taken care of the horses earlier in the day, and was leaving Daniel strict orders to call if they needed anything. The girls all left contact numbers by the phone. Amara's eyes shone with gratitude. She had the best friends in the world, she exclaimed between yawns when Cynthia prepared to leave. Cynthia kissed her lightly on the cheek, took one last look at Daniel, and swept out of the house.

That night while Daniel held her, he ran his large hand down her ribcage, and in his deep voice said, "Angel, have I told you how much I love you?"

Amara's dark eyes filled with tears when she looked at him, "I was hoping that was the case," she whispered in a husky voice. "I think I've loved you from the first, even if I didn't trust you."

Daniel's chest rumbled with suppressed laughter, "That was love? You, staring down the twin barrels of your shotgun at me?"

Amara chuckled in response, "Well, I always have expressed myself poorly," she said as she looped her arms around his neck, and kissed him soundly on the mouth.

"You do just fine," he said as he gently spread her hair across the pillows. He looked her deeply in the eyes, registering the bluish smudges beneath them. "You need to get some rest."

"Stay with me?" she asked shyly.

He responded by fitting her small body against his larger frame. As the nights were beginning to get chilly, Cynthia had placed a soft blanket at the foot of the bed. Daniel reached down and pulled the cover over her, tucking it beneath her chin. They talked in quiet companionship. Amara liked the way he doted on her. It amazed her how easy it was to confide in him. He didn't treat her like she was daft, or question her sanity in any way. He merely nodded in understanding, and proceeded to share some of his own weird experiences. This brought them full circle to the day they had met, and the creature he had tracked in order to obtain photographs of its prints. They had discussed his books and photography since, and Amara knew how badly he ached to get an actual shot of the banshee. Daniel's work took him into all sorts of strange phenomenon that others might balk at. So, when they returned to the topic at hand, it was a comfortable conversation.

"It seems to me we have to figure out how to keep you safe in case this happens again," he said succinctly.

"Not if," Amara corrected, "When."

"You're sure?"

"Yes, I'm sure. There is a purpose behind all of this. Awinita once said that we must complete each other. That I must help her so that she can help me. I don't really understand it, but I am trying."

"Okay, so how do we talk to her? How do we find out what we need to do to protect you?"

"I can start with intent," Amara answered without pause. "I will call in my grandfather, and ask for his assistance. Maybe call in other ancestors as well, so long as they are healthy aspects. If I do that, maybe they will help me find what we seek."

"We'll start there then," Daniel agreed. "Is there anything I can do?"

"You're doing it," Amara whispered. Daniel held her

close until she fell asleep. And during the interim, he asked her to focus on the intention she had set. He watched as she breathed softly, and just before she dozed off he witnessed a kind, but authoritative male presence. His was a proud visage, and a fairly solid one. And he called her, "Granddaughter".

Amara dreamed of her family that night. Grandfather sat on the side of her bed, holding her hand. Alina, her mother, leaned over her and blew something cool into her ear. There was a familiar scent of herb, and spice, and something mystical. A cloud in the shape of a man rose above them, and a great blackbird streaked across the sky. Amara was trying to make sense of it all when she realized the scent was one that she had partaken of at certain powwows. She felt her body quiver like a stringed instrument, watching as her mother split into two beings until Alina and Gola stood side by side. They could have been sisters, they looked so much alike. They spoke inaudibly, and then faded into the night. Amara cried out, wanting her mother to come back, but she only glanced over her shoulder, and disappeared with Gola.

Daniel was hovering over her urging her to wake up. His face swam before her when she opened her eyes. "You cried out," he stated quietly, but he sounded concerned. Grim whimpered on the other side of the door, and Amara was certain she heard Solomon imitate the urgency of that whimper from the kitchen.

"I'm okay," she said in a hushed tone, "It's time to get up in any case."

"I'm up," he replied. "I can hang around a while if you want to go back to sleep?"

"No, I'd rather be with you. I can fix breakfast while you clean up for work."

"Keep it simple," he ordered, but his words were sweetly spoken.

Amara found that the girls left things in good order. There was a bowl of spiced fruit salad she recognized as Cynthia's own recipe, and a freshly baked loaf of bread. She set these out as she heated the tea kettle. When she turned to look into the cupboard, she was pleasantly surprised to find a full jar of sprouts. A serving dish sat just below on the counter with freshly ground nuts, and a note tucked beneath. The note advised to toss with watercress, which she found when she reopened the fridge. She wondered how she had missed it the first time. She followed the instructions and yielded a delicious sandwich spread. Daniel entered just as she set the table, and they shared a pleasant meal.

Cynthia arrived before Daniel left, and a routine was established. Someone was always there to watch over her. She gradually regained her strength as she worked alongside her friends. And then one day, she knew she was capable on her own. The first morning she walked to the barn with Grim at her side, Crow circled overhead. "Hello Crow!" she called with a smile, "It's good to see you!" Crow swept down from the sky to drop a gift at her feet, and Amara was surprised to discover a key. It was an ancient key, a skeleton key, like the ones used in old houses. She stared at where the serrated edge had been removed, and knew that it was a master key. Amara tucked it away in her pocket where she could ponder it later.

That evening Daniel took Amara to his house for a private recital. She was in such a state of rhapsody as she watched his lean fingers skim the keys. He had a beautiful piano, and an appealing dexterity. He didn't give himself enough credit. He was literally one with the instrument as he leaned into it, and the strains of music that filled the environment were exquisitely haunting. Amara could have listened for hours. Daniel played like it came from his soul. No one could have been taught to sound like that. It wasn't the type of performance one could learn, but a gift that poured from him naturally. Amara was in awe.

CHAPTER TWENTY-ONE

Amara sat with Nikki near the falls in the back of her property. There was such peace and reverence in nature. She held the skeleton key out for her friend's inspection, "I wonder what it opens?" Nikki's eyes sparkled the way the sun played on water. Amara couldn't help but admire the other's love for life. Nikki was such a vibrant being.

"That's the question of the day," Amara laughed, "I have been turning this over and over in my mind! And still no answer."

"Ask and you shall receive," Nikki said knowingly.

"Yes," Amara breathed. "Maybe I am making too much of this, concentrating too hard," she said as she took the proffered key away from Nikki, and placed it safely in her pocket.

"I don't think so," Nikki replied, "Perhaps you just have to wait until the time is right?"

"I am ever impatient, am I not?" Amara laughed.

"No one could fault you for that!"

The girls stood and brushed themselves off just as Grim gained his footing and vigorously shook out his coat. They walked back to the barn to check on the horses. It was a nice fall day, and what was referred to as Indian summer here in Indiana. Amara had grown a couple of rows of Indian corn. The colors were brilliant. "I bet you sell it all at the next market," Nikki giggled.

"Oh, no, I will keep some for myself," Amara laughed at Nikki's delight. It felt good to enjoy life again. She hadn't been bothered by anyone of late, or taken any more worrisome trips into the past.

Nikki was relieved that her friend had been given a break from all the stresses of her reality. It showed in the healthy hue of her cheeks. "I should get going," she said. "Daniel will be here soon, and I know Gregory is wondering where I am."

"No, he's not," Amara corrected, "but he is wondering what time you will be home. I guess it is selfish of me to keep you any longer."

"You know I love our time together. I treasure it."

"As do I," Amara responded. "And I love this time of year."

They walked companionably back to the house. "Call me if you need me," Nikki said as she eased one long leg into the driver's side of the car.

"I will," Amara smiled. The wind blew, and the fragrance that was unique to the Midwest filled the air. She stood and watched as Nikki drove away before going inside to cook dinner. Squirrels chased up and down the trees, busily stashing their winter supplies. Karma trilled from somewhere nearby. Birds chattered in their very own dialogue.

Amara was at peace with her surroundings.

Amara was stirring a pot of hearty potato-leek soup when Daniel arrived. She grinned as she pulled a fresh loaf of cheesy-chive bread from the oven, knowing how much he loved her homemade breads. She was just about to go out to meet him when the front door opened. She had left it unlocked specifically for him.

"Amara!" a voice boomed, "Why is your door unlocked?" Amara frowned in consternation. It was Grant who stood inside her doorway.

"Hi stranger," she said in an effort to disguise her aggravation. Why hadn't he knocked?

As if reading her thoughts, Grant said, "I know, I know, I should have called," he began, "I just wanted to lay eyes on you! It's been a long time."

Amara swallowed her annoyance and accepted his explanation with grace. "What brings you here?" she questioned, "Is there anything wrong?"

"Nah, not technically," Grant responded. "I just got news of another break-in," he explained, "and wanted to make sure you were all right. You will be reading about it in the morning paper."

"Oh," Amara's lips turned down in a slight frown, "I hope no one was hurt? Was it anyone I know?" Amara knew pretty much everyone in this neck of the woods. Most folks came to her open markets, and many of the families had been permanent residents for generations. There were few strangers in these parts.

"It was close, Amara," Grant told her. "It was one of the homes across the bridge from you. I will be looking into it more fully. I can tell you there were photographs involved."

Amara had a sickening feeling in her gut. She paled and gestured for him to sit down. "Did it involve a young woman?"

"Yeah, I'm afraid so. That's why I'm here," he answered. "You can't let your guard down. You understand?"

"Of course, thanks for letting me know," she said, humbled. It had been nice to stop worrying for a spell.

Daniel pulled up just as Grant was leaving. Amara waved to him from the window. He came inside with a worried frown, "What did he want?" he asked. Daniel and Grant had not spoken since the incident on the highway. Amara told him about the break-in across the creek. "Do you know the family?" he wondered.

"Yes, it was Mira Thompson. Her father passed away recently. Mira is my age."

"And you're wondering if there is any connection?" Daniel tilted her chin up with one long, lean finger.

"Yes," she admitted, looking him in the eyes. "Mira and I attended school together, including the same college. Wouldn't you be suspicious?"

"I am," he said automatically. "When will Wheeler be talking to that professor of yours?"

"He was headed that way when he left here."

"Good. I don't like the sounds of the guy," he gave her a little squeeze. "We will not drop our guard," he said possessively. Amara gave him a brave smile. She was glad he was on her side.

Grant was back the following morning. As Daniel had left only seconds before, the timing was uncanny. "I'm on my way to see Mira," he told Amara, "Thought you might want to know that Professor Alexander had photos of her in his possession. That guy is all kinds of creepy."

"Oh," was all that Amara managed. "She was in some of his classes," she added lamely.

"Do you happen to know if she went out with him?"

Amara knew that Grant would ask Mira, and probably others, the same question. He was just doing his job. "Hmm, I'm not sure," she answered honestly. "Mira didn't date much in college. Neither one of us did."

"But?" he waited expectedly.

"But from what I saw, she was definitely his type."

"Dark hair, great build, bookish," he responded, "He likes them smart. Probably finds it more of a challenge," he looked Amara up and down as he spoke. It made her uncomfortable. As if it suddenly dawned on him, he made an effort to meet her eyes.

"Tell Mira I'll stop in later today," she said.

"Will do," Wheeler turned to leave, and then paused, "Oh, by the way, he claimed he got the photos in the mail." This last was said with a laugh as though it was an obvious lie. Amara looked at him sharply. "He knew the house. These shots were taken without her consent as she was stepping from the shower." Amara was still thinking over their conversation on her way to visit Mira.

Mira cracked the door open. She met Amara with a trepid smile. "Amara, I haven't seen you since the funeral," she said as the two embraced. "How are you?"

"I'm fine," Amara replied, though in truth her own nerves were shot. "I was sorry to hear about the break-in."

"Same here," Mira responded, "I've been meaning to come by."

"It's okay," Amara assured her, "I knew you had your hands full since your dad passed. It's hard, isn't it?"

"Yes, I mean, Daddy was ill. But he wasn't that old. It came as a shock."

"Have you been getting on okay?"

"Yeah, I'm still getting used to running the place," she admitted. "I don't know how you do it! I feel so lost at times. But now, now I'm scared." Mira's face flamed as she said this last. "And I'm so embarrassed!"

"Don't be, we're old friends. You've been through a lot," Amara said in total understanding, "You have every right to be afraid. It's only natural."

Mira looked completely at a loss. She just stood there, her eyes welling with unshed tears. "You've always been so strong," she told Amara, "I wish I were more like you."

"No, you don't," Amara assured her. "You are perfect the way you are. But you do need a friend right now, and I am just across the creek. If you need anything, call me," Amara pressed a card with her home phone into the other's hand. "Keep this by the phone. And if anything comes up, you call me. I don't care what time it is, do you understand?"

"Yes, thank you, Amara," the other girl whispered, "You

always were nice."

"Mira, did you ever go out with Simon? I mean, Professor Alexander?"

"No," Mira answered, and just as Amara started to relax, the other girl added, "But he asked me often enough. I just wasn't into dating, especially not the teachers," she said.

Amara's lips rounded in an O, but she quickly hid her concern. "I understand," she gave Mira a parting hug, "One more thing, was anything missing?"

"I don't think so. The police asked me the same thing," Mira chewed her bottom lip and Amara knew she was worried, "But my lingerie drawer has been violated. And I can't find my spare key."

Later that afternoon, Amara brought Daniel up to speed. She could tell he disliked Grant, and was concerned about Simon. She could also see that he was aware that this break-in mirrored the one that had happened here on her property. "Do you think Gregory would mind checking her place out?" she asked. "It's smaller than my farm, but it's fairly isolated, and she is alone."

"I'll speak to him. I'm pretty sure he'll do what he can," Daniel assured her. "I don't think any of us want to see someone get hurt."

"Thank you," she paused with her hand on his arm, "Let's walk upstream." Daniel took her hand in his, and they set off in the opposite direction. There was still plenty of daylight even though it was getting late in the year so Daniel had his camera with him. He was always ready for a nature shot,

and hadn't given up on finding more hoof prints. The earth was soft here near the water, making it easy to spot prints of any kind.

Amara was vaguely becoming aware of the song *Way Fairing Stranger,* when all of a sudden an inhuman howl rent the evening air. She swung to face Daniel, but it seemed as if she was moving in slow motion. She heard him call her name as if from a distance, saw his features freeze as he motioned to something up ahead. Vaguely, Amara heard the shutter speed of his camera. And in a flash, there *it* was, standing right in the path directly in front of them! The banshee! The thing screamed again, and even knowing as much about it as she did, Amara felt her skin grow cold as she broke out in goose flesh. She was so unusually numb that she lost sight of Daniel completely. All she could see was the banshee. Its cry filled her, possessed her, and for a single moment Daniel ceased to exist. Instead, the banshee wavered before her even as her head swam and her stomach lurched. She felt ill like she was going to be sick on the ground. And then she was lying on the earth with Awinita leaning over her. "What happened?" she croaked, her throat dry. "Where am I?"

"You're right here," Awinita assured her, "On your very own land. Do not fear."

"But, Daniel," she began.

"Will be waiting for you," the voice finished calmly.

"What am I doing here with you? And am I in the past again?"

"You are between worlds. But only for a short time," Awinita placed a heated hand on her brow, and Amara's body temperature increased dramatically. "There, are you warming up?"

"Yes, how did you do that? And why am I here?"

"You will learn the answer later in the caves of New Albany. They are, in a sense, one and the same," Awinita often spoke in riddles and sometimes it rankled. "I came to tell you to hold onto the key. Keep it with you always. It will bring the story of Gola into play, and you will understand the purpose. It will also unlock the door to Nonie."

"But..."

"Do not be alarmed, you can trust my mother as well as your own. And Nonie is to be revered. You must rest now, dear."

Amara felt her eyes close, knew complete and total darkness for an endless moment. She awoke to Daniel's worried voice as he hovered over her. "Angeni," he called, using the Native American name for Angel, "Are you all right?" he patted her cheeks a little too roughly.

He had such big hands! She sensed he was trying to be gentle so she kept her thoughts to herself, and instead put her focus on opening her eyes. Daniel looked terrified, but not of the banshee. No, he was concerned about her. She struggled to sit and reassure him, but found she was astonishingly weak. He lifted her from the forest floor and carried her back to the house, where her all-knowing, entirely too psychic fur babies were waiting.

Grim met them at the door as if to say, *"Don't ever leave me behind again!"* Daniel found himself muttering to the dog as he laid Amara on the sofa. She blinked a few times before speaking. "I'm all right," she whispered, "I'm fine." But Daniel was hovering over her, and three additional pairs of eyes were trained on her as well. Grim, Solomon, and Sampson sat in a row directly across from her. Amara managed a convincing smile.

CHAPTER TWENTY-TWO

Amara was fine, just as she had promised. And Daniel had gotten some extraordinary shots of the banshee. He was exuberant about the images, and talked about them at length. Amara giggled at his excitement. She knew he wanted to do an exclusive, and she was agreeable because she realized he would be both sensitive and professional. She had read everything that Daniel had written, and though all of it was true, none of it sensationalized the subjects. Daniel was good at what he did. His photographs were absolutely stunning, and in a sense, told a story of their own. Yet not once had Daniel ever exploited anyone. In spite of everything Amara was dealing with, she held no worries about living with Daniel, or allowing him to get too close.

What was truly unforeseen to both of them, was the fact that Daniel had managed to get a shot of Awinita leaning over Amara. She was merely a wisp of energy, but she was clearly visible. Her form and features were explicit. Amara was partially transparent as well. It was a ghostly type of photograph, and somewhat chilling. Both females were clear to the eye. That is to say that both women could be fully viewed, even though each of them appeared as apparitions.

Awinita was by far the paler of the two, but Amara was definitely translucent.

"What do you think she meant when she spoke of Gola and Nonie?" he asked. "Do you think you will meet them?"

"I'm not sure, but I rather think I will meet Nonie. I don't know why."

"But you think it's important, don't you?"

"Oh, yes, very much so," Amara answered. She had considered every possible angle she could think of, and so far meeting Nonie seemed invaluable.

"What do you suppose the key means?" he asked.

"I don't know that either, but I think it's symbolic. Awinita said I would find the answers in the caves."

There was a sober moment when Daniel looked at her with consternation. "Maybe we are not taking this thing seriously enough?" he said. "I mean, how do we know you will be safe? How can I be sure you will come back to me?"

"Oh, I'll come back," she grinned at him, but a look of apprehension crossed her features. It was a daunting reality. And one that seemed a bit far-fetched. They were admittedly grateful that she had protectors like Awinita. And they were both hopeful that Nonie would be a staunch ally. But the fact was, neither of them really knew anything when it came to her safe return. "All I know is that the next trip is crucial if I am to meet Nonie. There is something about the key that will get me there, and somehow, the combination of the two will assure my safety."

"So we had best make certain that the key never leaves your possession."

"It won't. It's securely tucked away," she demonstrated the point by pulling it free of her brassiere.

"That's a good plan," he agreed, and she realized he hadn't noticed the sturdy cord her hair and clothing had concealed.

They talked quietly for some time before the conversation evolved into the other topic on both their minds. "I'm worried about Mira," Amara whispered, "She isn't very strong. She was born with asthma, and has always depended on her father. It was a terrible blow for her when he passed so suddenly."

"Gregory is going to stop over this evening," he said. "I am sure he will do everything he can."

"I am grateful for him," Amara agreed. "He really is thorough. And I know Mira is terrified. She needs friends right now."

"I wouldn't be at all surprised if we didn't see something of him tonight; Nikki too. She remembers the two of you being close."

"Mira was shy," Amara said. "She didn't make friends easily, and if Simon was hounding her, it probably frightened her more than anything."

The phone rang and Amara hurried to answer it. It was Gregory's voice on the other end. "Amara," he said, "Everything is fine. I just left Mira, and she locked up behind me. I am going to do some work for her first thing in the morning."

"Thank you, Greg," she said solemnly, "I am so thankful for you."

"You're welcome," he said gently. "Get some rest. I'll

be in touch."

Amara took Gregory's advice and went on to bed. Daniel stayed nearby until she fell asleep. He planned to go back to his place in the morning to develop the remainder of his film. He wouldn't stay up much longer. His mind drifted to an odd event earlier in the day when he was cleaning his equipment. He had looked up and caught Amara's eyes on him. When he asked what she was thinking, she shook her head vaguely, "Nothing important," she had answered absently. But he remembered her expression. It was as if she were analyzing his equipment, scanning it for some nefarious purpose. He shook his head. He had just settled back with a book when he heard a shrill scream. Daniel dashed into the bedroom to find Amara sitting up, eyes wide. "Amara, what is it?" he asked.

"I'm not Amara," she said in a strange voice, "I'm Awinita. He did it to get even. He said he'd get back at me. And he did." Before Daniel could respond Amara curled up on her side, facing away from him. She was sound asleep, and it was past midnight. He had best turn in. The next morning Amara did not remember a thing.

It was early when the dogs sounded the alarm. Grim's bark was ferocious. Solomon did his best to echo him. Sampson hid under the table. Daniel was up and nearly at the front door when the knocking commenced. Amara looked stricken where she stood by the stove. She still held the kettle in one hand when she followed Daniel to the door. It wasn't normal for Gregory or Nikki to pound so loudly. And Grim's bark

was not just an alarm, it was a warning.

They heard a car pull into the drive so fast its tires screeched. Amara peeked out in time to see Nikki and Gregory scrambling up the walk. Then who was on the porch, Amara wondered? And then she saw the cop car that followed on their tail, and realized that another one had slipped up from behind. She expected Grant's big frame to fill the doorway, but when Daniel opened the door, his deputy stepped boldly inside. Amara snapped an order for Grim to sit, and he obeyed but sat gnashing his teeth. The growl he emitted was downright scary. Solomon wasn't quite as well behaved and she scooped him up, admonishing his manners as she did so. He yielded with a sheepish look. "What's happened?" Daniel demanded in his deep voice, and Amara found herself holding her breath. Nikki slipped around the cop and wrapped an arm around her waist.

"The sheriff sent us to check on you," the deputy said in his straight forward way. "I regret to tell you that Miss Thompson is dead."

"But I just saw her yesterday," Amara stammered as Nikki led her to a chair. Amara's legs had turned to jelly, and her skin had paled drastically.

"We found her this morning, Amara," Gregory interrupted, "There was nothing anyone could do."

Amara's eyes were wide, "How?" was all she said.

"She was murdered," the deputy said without preamble, "Strangled."

"Mira was terrified of suffocating," Amara said in a tiny voice, "She always kept an inhaler with her."

"He used a nylon stocking," the officer informed her.

"That's off the records," he amended in case he had made an error in saying as much as he had. Or at least that's how it sounded to Amara.

"We arrived to find the door standing open," Gregory told her. "I had Nikki wait outside while I went in to check on her. It was too late, Amara."

"There was no sign of a break-in," the deputy said, "Whoever did it had a key."

Amara heard Mira's voice telling her, "*But my lingerie drawer has been violated. And I can't find my spare key.*" She repeated Mira's words to the officer and watched as he wrote it down. The two cops glanced between them. It was apparent they didn't know whether the sheriff knew this or not.

"Amara, there's more," it was Nikki's steady voice speaking directly to her. Nikki never took her eyes off her friend when she said, "Honey, the thing is all the clocks were set at 12:10, every single one of them. We are waiting for the official time of death, but based on everything we know..." she let her voice trail off.

"I'm sure Sheriff Wheeler will be in touch as soon as possible," the first cop spoke up. "We were to make sure you were safe, and see that you weren't alone." He glanced at Daniel for confirmation.

"She won't be alone," Daniel responded, leaving the officers free to go while Nikki fussed over Amara, and he and Gregory stepped outside.

Mira's death cast a pall over the small town of Yountsville. Her death had been called at 12:10 a.m. Murders didn't happen in towns this size where everyone knew everyone else, and people felt safe leaving their doors unlocked. The thing was, in a town such as this, only a select few locked their doors. Amara and Mira were both known to do so. It was as if it was part of the killer's game.

Amara and her friends attended Mira's funeral. Amara was deeply shaken by something she felt could have been avoided. The others went mainly to show their respects, and to lend Amara the support she deserved. Nikki remembered Mira from their college days as a bookish girl who kept to herself. Mira, the introvert, that's what they called her. No one meant anything by it. It was just an obvious depiction. Cynthia and Linda had known her only as Amara's shy neighbor.

Amara stood alone in the cemetery while her friends waited respectfully by their cars. She stooped to place a bouquet of freshly cut flowers on the gravesite. Daniel and Gregory stood nearby. Everyone knew it could just as easily have been Amara in that grave. Tension coiled thickly around every individual present.

Anger tightened the skin around Daniel's eyes and mouth. Nikki wondered specifically who he was angry with. His jaw clenched when Sheriff Wheeler walked over to where Amara stood and took her in his arms. The hug he gave her was more than a little possessive. Nikki couldn't help but glance back at Daniel. His eyes narrowed when he strode in their direction. Wheeler saw Daniel approach just as Amara whispered something in his ear. Nikki knew she blamed him for Mira's death. Had he taken Simon into custody, Mira might still be alive today. Daniel was within earshot when Wheeler said succinctly, "Forgive me. I thought he just had a thing for squaws."

Amara's gasp filled the quiet of the cemetery. Nikki's mouth fell open. She was relieved to see that Gregory had followed Daniel and was attempting to ward off a fight. Daniel sucked in his breath as he took hold of Amara's arm, addressing Wheeler as he did so, "You will apologize for that remark."

"What? Still sore about that day on the highway?" he sneered. Amara's eyes cut directly to Daniel where he stood trying to shelter her. What was Grant talking about? But the sheriff wasn't finished. He was pent-up angry, "Or are you jealous because I got to her first?"

Cop or no cop, Daniel's fist would have slammed into Grant's jaw if Gregory had not been there. And now that Daniel's movements were restrained, Grant was ready to throw a punch. "That's enough," Nikki voiced furiously. "Everyone knows nothing happened between you and Amara." Amara's chin went up a notch. She was surprised to find that every single one of her friends had her back. Where had Cynthia and Linda come from? She hadn't even seen them move.

Sheriff Wheeler looked up as if he had just noticed the same thing. His eyes went around the circle of unfriendly faces. He straightened his jacket, smirked at Amara, and then quickly strode away. Everyone was speechless for a long moment, and for the first time Amara wondered if Grant Wheeler could have been behind this entire mess? She would never have imagined such a racist comment coming from him. And he did have the exact same camera as Simon, Daniel, and Nikki. Could he have been her stalker all along? Did things get out of control with Mira? A badge could go a long way as a cover.

It wasn't until after things had calmed that Daniel confided the happenings on the highway that day. "Why didn't you tell me sooner?" Amara's eyes shone.

"To what purpose?" he answered to which she had no response. The fact was Mira was dead, and there was still a murderer at large.

CHAPTER TWENTY-THREE

*A*winita dreamed of bovines that night like the kind she had seen on Amara's small farm. She was gaining strength over Amara, and needed to merge with her more fully. Hence, she snatched Amara from her sleep, forcing her to awaken to the tragedy of infant fatalities in a bleaker time and place. In spite of their best efforts, the elements were harsh and food was scarce, making it nearly impossible to persevere. This prompted Awinita to visit the New Albany grocery store later that morning.

Her prize possession was a bag of sucrose. It was a small bag, but perhaps it was a life-altering substance for the remainder of the mothers? It was her hope that their babies might better survive with the aid of the occasional sugar tit. She hung her head for just a moment; it was such a tiny contribution! Then she squared her shoulders, adding a few other selections to her basket while the benevolent lady in blue stood waiting. Ellen was on guard outside the door.

It was obvious to her they made the townspeople nervous, and the soldiers in turn, did the same for them. But Awinita knew Ellen had her back, and she had learned that

her new friend's name was Mary Ann. The crabby old man she had glimpsed on her first visit was Mary's husband. Today Mary Ann had confided that her spouse had attended a local meeting. "I'm worried, Awinita," Mary Ann kept her voice low. "I don't know what they're planning, but I fear the meeting is about you and the others. There are those who see you as a threat."

"That's ridiculous," Awinita was incredulous, "We don't bother anyone."

"Just be warned," Mary Ann replied, "And alert."

"We will, thank you," Awinita noticed that Mary Ann was visibly shaken. "I promise to take care," she told her, knowing that Mary's situation was nearly as dire as her own. She had not missed the angry contusions that matched the color of her faded dress. Given that Mary was the owner's wife, one would have expected her to sport a bright ribbon or some other pretty bauble even on these dark days. But so far Mary always looked the same. Only the bruises changed. Mary Ann did her level best to cover them, and this brought out Awinita's protective nature. While it was abundantly clear that Mary Ann was badly abused, her sorry circumstances brought them closer together. Both women had known brutality, and thereby each had gained a wealth of empathy.

Mary Ann summoned an impish grin. She had packed Awinita's purchases carefully, commenting on the packet of salt Awinita had added only after making sure she had enough coin to include it. "Food is mighty boring without proper seasoning," Mary said. "For some, a sweet treat is just as important." Awinita gave her a quick hug when she spied the penny candies that had gone unnoticed in the bottom of the bag. There would be happy children in the camp tonight! Awinita collected herself, pleased with the rice and flour she had managed to add to the sack of sugar. The salt would add flavor while the candy would bring joy.

"I'm going to find a way to head further north," she whispered, "I hear there are jobs to be had up there."

"Did you catch the latest about the rails?" Mary Ann returned. "I lined your bag with newspaper," she added under her breath, "They're current. It would seem General Sherman is willing to help move you along. He has passed an ordinance giving all of you a ride on the rails to accomplish his goals."

"To what do we owe this turn of good fortune?" Awinita replied. "I doubt it is given out of pity."

"No, but rather a way to put a lid on a badly handled situation," Mary Ann agreed. "There has been a lot of speculation as to what to do with you."

"What to do? He seems to have a great lack of compassion."

"I couldn't agree more, but there have been a lot of folks asking for donations, and to no avail," Mary Ann sighed. "Apparently women and children matter little when it comes to war. However, it is reputedly believed that many of the children were taken in by the Sisterhood of Nuns of Nazareth in Bardstown, Kentucky. They were said to have been given to families in the general area. Unfortunately, these children were taken from their own natural mothers! I have nothing but sympathy for those poor women."

"I worry something like that may have happened to Chloe, my friend Caroline's child."

"I will pray for her," Mary said sadly. "I also read that Dr. Mary Walker opened the women's prison in Louisville. She is well known for her contributions at the First Bull Run.

You may have friends there as well, but I do not think they will have an easy time of it. Dr. Walker was recently a prisoner of war herself." At that Mary Ann's green eyes darkened.

"What is it?" Awinita had heard the warning in her friend's voice.

"There are rumors of abductions, women and children being trafficked to Mexico. I wouldn't put anything past a group of people with mob mentality. They are desperate to be rid of you!" she said knowingly, "And if there is a profit to be made, you can bet they will do their best to make it happen."

"Thank you for the warning, dear friend," Awinita said as she squeezed Mary Ann's hand, "I will spread the word."

There was a slight disturbance behind the curtain that separated the shop from their home, causing Mary Ann to still. Awinita saw the whisper of motion, and knew Mary's husband was eavesdropping. "Well, I must be off," she said formally, "Thank you for the goods."

"You're welcome," Mary Ann whispered politely. Yet she clung to Awinita with her eyes. Awinita recognized loneliness when she saw it. Mary Ann had few friends. She lived instead under her husband's thumb.

Awinita made up her mind right then and there to help this poor soul. She looked directly at Mary Ann and said for her ears alone, "There are opportunities everywhere, my friend. Sometimes one just needs a change. You can come with us if you dare?"

Mary Ann watched Awinita all the way out the door and down the street. Her own shoulders straightened as she admired the way Awinita carried herself. But her smile fled when her husband roared. She turned in time to avoid a blow to the head. He looked shocked by the look of superiority she wore as she walked away unscathed. It was as though she had taken a dose of confidence. He couldn't allow that, not if he intended to maintain control. But Mary never so much as glanced at him as she made her way out of the room, leaving him to watch the store.

Conversation buzzed around the campfire that night. Awinita read aloud from the newspaper before passing it among them. *"It would seem as though we are a public nuisance,"* she commented before she turned to the next page of the article she was reading, *"Louisville provost marshal Captain Steven E. Jones has turned to General Sherman about the growing problem of refugees on the shores of Indiana. Sherman responded to Jones's request by issuing General Orders No. 22 on the 12th of August. Refugees of either gender shall be forwarded at the expense of the United States if unable to pay their own way to any point not over 100 miles by railroad."*

"Refugees of either gender?" one of the older women said in wonder, "So they seek to rid themselves of us, do they?"

"So much so that we are to be given a ride, so long as we head further north," Awinita agreed with a sparkle in her eye.

"On the 16th ,The New Albany Daily Ledger goes on to say," Ellen squinted at the small print as she read, *"They will be better able to procure employment, and earn a livelihood, relieving the border counties of the abundance of this lowly class of persons."* With a look of distaste, she tossed her long brown hair.

"Well, we won't be missing them either," another voice chimed. Excitement fed the crowd of homeless women who saw this as a chance to begin a new life. Sadly, they had by this time acknowledged, there was no going home.

"We will make ourselves ready," Awinita announced, "so that we all have rations in case we get separated. We must be prepared to leave at a moment's notice."

The conversation carried late into the night with Awinita warning the others about the meeting Caroline had mentioned. "It would seem this opportunity has come just in the nick of time," Ellen countered.

"In the meantime, we will post twenty-four hour surveillance around the camp," Awinita stated. "We cannot afford to drop our guard."

"Agreed," everyone chimed as children fell asleep, and mothers prepared to do the same.

"I will take the first watch," someone offered.

"I second that."

"What about you, Awinita? Will you be back in time?" Ellen had become dependent upon her, as had the others. Awinita was their leader, and she had told them before she shared the contents of the newspaper, that she must leave on a brief mission first thing in the morning. No one had thought to question her destination.

"I'll be back," Awinita promised. "I'll only be gone a short while. But should anything happen before that, you must go. I'll find you."

Awinita closed her eyes allowing the worry and anticipation to dissipate. The others followed her example.

In the dark before dawn, Awinita slipped quietly away. Only Ellen was awake to bid her goodbye. Ellen was a worrier. She had attached herself to Awinita from the beginning, and it bothered her that she was taking off on her own.

Awinita traveled the short distance following the directions that had been provided that day by the water. *As the crow flies*, she thought to herself as she followed the single bird that led the way. Had the journey been less arduous, she might have called out to him. Part of her mind snagged on that other life where Crow was her friend. As if attuned to her thoughts, the corvid circled once, cawing as he did so. "It IS you!" she gasped aloud. Though her voice was quiet, Crow swooped down and dropped a *gift* at her feet. "An amulet?" she wondered. The gift was a braid of golden hair wrapped around an oblong gemstone. The hair was streaked with just about every color under the sun, and the stone had been carefully crafted into a barrette so that the owner could easily wear it. "Thank you, Crow!"

Crow responded by swooping low to the rocks. Awinita studied his actions, allowing her eyes to explore the many boulders. Crow continued to hover over the same general area until Awinita found the opening to the cave. "Hello!" she called, crawling inside. The sight that met her was astounding. The cave itself was charismatic with all its stalactites and stalagmites. The minerals that had formed were truly beautiful. The colors were well lit by a host of torches on the walls. But the real shock, the thing that amazed her most was the woman who came forward to greet her.

"I am Nonie," the vision spoke in a cultured voice. Her maple-syrup skin gleamed in the firelight. She was the most exotic creature Awinita had ever seen! Her eyes were large

and deeply set. They were cerulean blue, and somewhat at odds with her skin tone. Awinita knew there were Creoles of all colors, but she wasn't prepared for the exquisite beauty before her. Nonie's long, thick mane was a hue as golden as the sun, streaked with vibrant shades of red and brown. She carried herself like a queen, and her voice was nothing if not elegant. Awinita immediately realized that the hair talisman belonged to her. When she thanked her for the gift, Nonie's response was gracious.

"You are most welcome," the woman said in measured tones. "You had need of it."

Awinita nodded as she pulled the cord from her clothing only to find that it came up empty! What happened to the key? She started to panic when she glanced up at Nonie who was already wearing the object around her neck! "What magic is this?" she asked.

"Only the true owner ever really holds the key," she explained. "I merely allowed you to borrow it for safety's sake."

"Thank you," Awinita breathed, "So it is also a talisman?"

Nonie smiled for the first time. Her lips were full. Her teeth were white as pearls. And her smile could melt mountains. She had a tiny beauty mark at the corner of her mouth. Awinita was stunned. Nonie towered over her, and her apparel was encrusted with gem stones; everything about her sparkled. "Come, we have much to do," she said. "But first, you must dine."

Awinita's stomach growled in response. Nonie waved a hand causing Awinita's vision to blur, and a table of polished rock shimmered before her. A collection of dishes cluttered the iridescent surface with each new dish more tantalizing than its predecessor. All were fragrant enough to make her salivate, and Awinita felt she might swoon. Nonie bade her sit, and suddenly Awinita was seated on a small throne that matched the table to perfection! A plate was set before her. Awinita did not hesitate. She had been back in time only a short while, and was already starving! Her clothes fairly hung on her frail body. She filled the plate with a variety of succulent flavors, and savored each and every bite. These were decidedly the best foods she had ever imagined. She cleaned the entire plate before Nonie stood and walked away, "Come," she called over her shoulder.

And so it began. Whatever request Nonie put forth, Awinita was quick to comply. She found herself excelling at each, and every, topic. They discussed magic, and Awinita immediately found herself scrying. She was especially good at water scrying, but did fairly well with stones too, so long as they were smooth. She learned how to create a conscious link between her third eye and an object, by visualizing a ray of light coming from her pineal gland, also known as the *Seat of the Soul*. She could program a specific crystal in this manner. She was fascinated by the wealth of Nonie's knowledge, and had finally gotten comfortable enough to ask how the food had simply appeared out of nowhere. "It was there all along," Nonie dimpled. "You just didn't see it!"

"Or smell it! How is that possible?"

"Our conscious mind limits us to the five senses. It cannot comprehend more than that. Once you learn to open and utilize your other senses, it becomes quite natural."

"Like the way the key found its way back to you?"

"Something like that," Nonie blinked those gorgeous eyes displaying long lashes as golden as her hair. "The key was actually with me all along. I simply loaned you its energy."

"I see," Awinita had one thought after another, "How does one scry if there is no water, no stone?" she asked, looking completely lost.

"In that case, you open a window," Nonie said sagely, "and produce what you need."

Awinita admitted that she was confused. She asked Nonie to demonstrate. After some time, Awinita was finding windows of her own accord. "Remember," Nonie advised, "You can find whatever you need. Energy is everywhere. It is everything. We only need to open ourselves to it. It merely takes practice."

"Like shape-shifting?" she asked.

"Exactly like shape-shifting," Nonie agreed, "Only It is not in the stars for you right now."

Awinita cocked her head, "Why not?"

When Awinita would have continued asking questions, Nonie hushed her, "It is time now for you to meet your brother. He has been a guide for you, and I would have you know him. Before you go I will do a healing on you, and you will possess the skill. Your brother will lead you safely back to your campsite. You have learned much this day."

"How long have I been here?" Awinita asked, "How is it possible to learn so much in so little time?"

"Time is not linear," Nonie answered, "it is an illusion. We will meet your needs."

With that, Nonie waved a magical hand and Crow flew into the room. Awinita had not been aware of his presence, but the cave had many rooms. Her eyes grew wide as saucers when Crow landed and stood before her. Her vision blurred as it had with the table of food. The air rippled. There was a sizzling sound, and Crow slowly materialized into a nice looking young man. He was tall and well-built with black hair and eyes. His features were beautiful and Awinita could only stare. She couldn't help but wonder if she had been drugged! After all, many cultures used plant-based drugs to alter experiences. There was so much to internalize, and still more to process!

Soon the two of them were talking like old friends, which they really already were. And before she knew it, she had received the healing Nonie had mentioned. It was a "laying-on of hands", and it was awesome. Awinita had a million questions that would have to wait. It was time to return to camp. "Go," Nonie insisted, "Crow has been following the train schedules. We will meet again in another time and place. For now, remember to stay near the camp, and near the tracks."

CHAPTER TWENTY-FOUR

It was the month of September when Tanner removed his cattle from Amara's land. She had not had any contact with him since their last quarrel. She was glad to see the last of him, glad to sever the tie between them. He had left in a foul mood, making it obvious to everyone that he didn't consider the matter closed. Amara honestly didn't know what to make of that. She had already signed a new agreement with another farmer in the area. Farmland was always in demand. The new man's name was Luke, and he was to plant in the spring. An additional crop of corn or soybeans was just good business, and Amara was ready to move forward. Luke and his family lived on the opposite side of the creek. They were honest folks who would provide an extra income without all the headaches. Other options were still open for the time being, but Amara was fine with the current arrangement.

It wasn't until late in the day that Amara returned to the house. She had groomed the horses and cleaned out the barn, laying fresh straw in the stalls. Now it was time to wash up and get started on dinner. Daniel had gotten into a routine of coming over in the early evenings. They shared dinner on a regular basis with either Amara cooking, or Daniel providing the meal. Their nights out were special, but on occasion he would surprise her with takeout. He had offered to do so tonight, but Amara had a new recipe she wanted to try. She enjoyed cooking for Daniel. They liked the same foods, and she knew for a fact that he appreciated her culinary skills. It wasn't that Daniel couldn't fend for himself, but rather that he didn't enjoy the task.

On her way to the house she carried on a conversation with Grim, who seemed to hang on her every word. She felt good today, even after snapping back to the present not so long ago. She knew that her good health was due to the healing Nonie had done, and she couldn't wait to start practicing on her friends. Only Nikki knew about this last trip, and the overall consequences. She would bring the others up to date on their next gathering.

When they arrived at the house Amara was immediately concerned to find the front door unlocked. She had definitely secured it earlier that day. She opened it cautiously and stepped inside. Before Grim could follow, the door slammed shut! Grim let out an indignant howl. Amara never saw a thing. She felt a hard shove and stumbled, catching a whiff of something strong. Simultaneously, a sheer fabric tightened sickeningly around her throat. She was suffocating, struggling to breathe as her fingers fumbled with nylon. She heard coarse male laughter, but failed to recognize the voice. She identified the scent, but it was too late. She was already lost. Her last thought was of Mira.

She awoke to find Daniel calling her name. Grim was whining in the most hysterical tone she had ever heard him emit. Solomon had been shut in the kitchen with Sampson. They were her babies, and they were crying. She was worried about them. Daniel opened the door and carried her outside, allowing the fresh air to fill her lungs. He told her he would

be right back, and then ran to her pantry and brought back some smelling salts and a bottle of trauma drops. She declined the salts, but managed to prop herself up in order to take in the sweet Indiana air. She coughed when he attempted to give her the drops. He waited a minute before trying again. When finally she was breathing evenly, he went and picked up the phone.

Grant appeared with his deputies in tow. He asked several questions while they checked out the property. Amara answered everything as accurately as possible, but when he asked her why she wasn't armed, she glanced away briefly before responding, "I was," she hesitated, "I didn't follow protocol."

"Meaning?" he glared at her.

"I should have had my gun in my hand, ready to fire," she said sheepishly. She was embarrassed by her lack of common sense. The thing was, she knew better. "I was worried about Solomon. Besides, Grim was with me."

"Yeah, that worked out real well, didn't it?" Grant's voice was smug.

"Look, I know I made a mistake," her cheeks were warm. "Didn't I just say so?"

"Lay off," Daniel growled, "Anyone could have done the same."

"Amara isn't anyone. She's the target," Grant snarled. "Were you aware that Simon Alexander was in town early this morning?" Grant glared at Amara.

"No, how would I know that?"

"You were in town yourself, weren't you?"

"Yes," Amara said, "What does one thing have to do with another? And why are you spying on me?"

"Probably nothing," Grant returned, "And I merely wondered if you had seen Alexander?"

"No, of course not," Amara's temper was rising, "I would have said so if I had."

Grant let the matter rest while he poked around the front room. He bagged the stocking, noting the odor, "Chloroform," he muttered. "This guy is serious, Amara. You cannot drop your guard until after I've got him behind bars." They glared at each other for a full minute, before one of the deputies stepped inside and announced that all was clear. "I'm going to go have a chat with Alexander," Grant said tersely, "Don't lose your focus again."

"Just one question?" she stopped him where he paused at the door. "Why didn't this happen at 12:10?" she asked. Her lower lip trembled, and he knew she was frightened.

"My guess," he said, "is that this was a game. He didn't intend to kill you, this time."

"Why were you in town this morning?" Daniel asked casually.

"I had to drop some things off," Amara looked surprised by the question, "and bring some forms home to fill out for my upcoming yoga classes." Her voice was brittle. She was aware that her tone was defensive. "Why do you ask?"

"No reason," Daniel looked directly at her, but she couldn't fathom what he was thinking. "You didn't mention it, that's all."

"Well, I didn't exactly get a chance, did I?" Amara looked surprised by her own outburst. She turned to Daniel who was sitting at the kitchen table where Amara was busily cleaning up the last of the takeout containers. They had settled for salads from the pizza place where they made really good vegetarian sandwiches as well. "I'm sorry," she said quickly, "I didn't mean to snap at you. It's just that Grant was right. I can't afford any mistakes. *He* was playing with me. Next time I won't be so lucky."

Daniel let out a sigh, and reached for her hand. "I was thinking the same. And even if you didn't see him, I bet he saw you."

Amara dropped into the chair next to him. "You think that's why he was here? In town, I mean?" her voice was husky with emotion.

"Possibly," he admitted. "Then again, he lives and works nearby. Would he risk showing his face in town if he had plans to assault you?"

By this time Amara was deeply confused, and incredibly terrified. "I don't honestly know," she admitted. She had been wondering the same thing. "Do you think Nonie knew this was coming? Is that why she gave me the amulet?"

Daniel had no answer for that. "I think we have to keep our eyes open," was all he said.

Nonie was sitting across from her, and Awinita couldn't help but admire her natural beauty. She was an avatar, and for an instant Awinita wondered if she was primeval. Nonie was one of those women who actually glowed. Her skin was flawless, her hair stunning in its profusion of color. And her physique was perfect. It didn't occur to Awinita to wonder how she had come to be here. She had simply found herself back in the caves that Nonie called home.

"Tell me about Crow," Awinita said, staring into Nonie's deep-set Mediterranean pools. "I do not understand how I came to have a brother. I thought my mother had buried them all."

"Gola planned to tell you when she deemed it safe," Nonie said. "Unfortunately, the evil one got to her first."

"I was quite young, but I remember her losing the babies. She buried them in the forest," Awinita's eyes were moist. "My mother would have given them a Cherokee burial, but *he* wouldn't allow it."

"He wasn't Cherokee. He would have insisted she bury them as she was told. But your mother had a mind of her own. She marked the earth as sacred ground and buried each with an amulet."

"Except for one," Awinita spoke quietly. "Which one survived? And how did she come to give him up?"

"Crow was the third born," Nonie said in response to the plea for information. "Gola did not take him away from you," she assured, "I was her Godmother. I had watched over her all of her life. She knew that if he got hold of his son, the boy would have no future. She also knew that I would protect you. The decision to give me the child was an easy one, I think."

"How did she come to marry such a monster?" Awinita asked.

"He wanted her," Nonie said calmly. Her features remained smooth, masking her emotions. "White men take what they want. There is no honor in them."

"But she would have fought," Awinita replied with fire in her eyes.

"She did. But she had you to protect," Nonie said gently. "Gola loved you far too much to put you at risk. Instead, she took you and ran. And for a time it worked, and the two of you were happy."

"Yes, we were happy," Awinita agreed. But Nonie knew she was thinking of her baby brother.

"There is much you do not understand. When you have children, you will grasp the sacrifices that were made."

"Did she ever visit him?" Awinita couldn't help but pity the boy who grew up without a mother. She realized Nonie loved him, but he must have felt abandoned all the same.

Nonie smiled and the caves lit with the grandeur of the heavens. Awinita was in awe of this woman whose name literally meant *Gift from God*. "Of course, she visited," Nonie allowed, "Often. She planned to bring you when you were old enough to understand."

Awinita looked perplexed by this. She believed she had been a very wise child, one who had grown up too quickly for her years. She gave this away in her next comment, "I would have understood."

Nonie reached out and stroked her smooth dark hair, "You had enough on you. Your mother thought to spare you."

Awinita's expression was mulish. Nonie chuckled and leaned in to kiss her forehead. "You must go back now," she said, but her words sounded far away. They echoed in Amara's ears even as she blinked up at Daniel. He had come to check on her.

"I brought you some tea," Daniel said lightly, noting the contrast from a short while ago. Nowadays when Amara went back, she took on Awinita's personality so completely that Amara was nothing more than a dim memory. It was as if the two women were consolidating on a permanent basis, and Amara couldn't help but wonder if Daniel had noticed the change in her.

"What is it?" Amara asked.

"You dropped your book," he spoke quietly. She had been outlining her October yoga class. He handed her the appointment book, and the braided amulet that had belonged to Nonie fell to the floor. "It's happening more often, isn't it?" he asked holding eye contact, while alternately fingering the hair barrette. "You just came back, didn't you?"

"Yes," she said defiantly, "I no longer know who I am, or where I belong."

CHAPTER TWENTY-FIVE

mara awoke to find Daniel manning the stove. Whatever he was cooking smelled amazing. She slipped up behind him, and wrapped her arms around his lean waist, causing him to turn and fully embrace her. "I'm sorry," she whispered in his ear, stirring up an entirely different kind of appetite. He gave a boyish grin, and let his free hand wander.

Solomon, apparently feeling left out, did the puppy crawl. He crouched low to the floor, and wiggled his way over to where they stood by the stove. He gained their full attention when he flipped onto his back, and with his feet in the air, caused them both to laugh. Amara bent to rub his rounded tummy, and the pup's tail wiggled with a life of its own. He was proud of his new trick. Amara's smile was watery when she looked up at Daniel.

"You have no reason to be," he kissed her, and then turned back to the stove.

"Yes, I do," she insisted. "It bothers me that I am so moody. I don't feel like myself."

"Cut yourself some slack," he told her while she watched him expertly flip a couple of pancakes, "Anyone would have trouble keeping up with all that is happening."

"You think?" she asked sincerely, "I worry that it is turning me into someone else. I am afraid I will lose you."

"You're not going to lose me," he whispered back at her. "You are still the same sweet girl I fell in love with."

She pressed her cheek to his back and sniffled, demonstrating how distraught she had become. That was when Sampson grew tired of Solomon hogging all the attention. He arched his back and leaped from the chair on which he had been perched. "Uh-oh," Amara giggled as Grim loped over to join them.

"It's a bit crowded at the stove just now," Daniel chuckled. He slipped them all three a morsel of pancake, and laughed as both dogs wolfed theirs down, while Sampson chose to bat his around like a toy.

"Now you've done it," Amara giggled a second time, "You'll come to regret that."

"I'll take my chances," he quipped. "I hope you like blueberry?"

"I do," she smiled, once more at ease, "I'll set the table."

Daniel watched as she bustled about, and then seated her as if she were royalty. "I am serving this morning," he said firmly. "We are having the special." He brought her a stack of blueberry pancakes along with an earthenware pitcher of warm maple syrup. He set the syrup in the center of the table along with a stick of softened butter. Amara clapped her hands in glee at the expression on his face. He looked so pleased with himself.

"Thank you," she said with emotion. No man had ever cooked for her before and she told him so. He dropped a kiss on the top of her head before seating himself.

When they were finished eating, they cleared the table together, and then Daniel carried two large mugs of tea into the enclosed sunroom. "Wow," she said, "You really do want to impress me," she said.

"No, I want you to relax," he corrected. "I am a firm believer that when things are spinning out of control, it is time to simply rest and rejuvenate."

"That's a good way to look at it," she agreed. "I do feel out of control."

"Do you want to talk about it?"

"Maybe," she hedged, wishing her situation was a little more normal. He laughed when she voiced that opinion, and she joined in without a thought. "You do know how to put a girl at ease," she said quietly. When he failed to respond, she put her chin in her hand, and with a pensive look, said, "I was thinking maybe it would help to visit the southern part of the state."

It was not a question. It was a statement. Daniel nodded, and in all seriousness agreed, "That's probably not a bad idea. I will go with you if you want? Or I can stay here and take care of the place?"

She loved him for that. Most guys would have insisted on taking control of the situation. Amara didn't have a clue what she was looking for, yet Daniel was willing to do whatever she needed. "I'm not really sure," she said. "I would be happy to have you along, but I will need someone to fill in for me here."

"Take your time and think about it," he advised. "We could go over the weekend, do some sightseeing; chase a few ghosts. Maybe we'll learn something. Or if you prefer to go alone or with the girls, that's okay too. Any way you go, you'll have someone here to take care of things." Grim gave him a regal look that said he understood every spoken word, and they both laughed.

Amara shook her head, "I don't want to go alone," she offered, and was rewarded by the relieved expression he was incapable of hiding. "You are such a dear, sweet man," she cupped his cheek with her palm, "I have no desire to worry you further."

They agreed upon the weekend, and planned to make an outing of it. Amara wasn't concerned about leaving her animal family, but only because she knew that they would be well cared for. "If Nikki and Gregory are free, I would prefer that. I don't want any of the girls to stay here alone," she ventured.

And so it was settled. It was just for one night, after all. They invited Nikki and Gregory to dinner, and set the wheels into motion. The other couple agreed easily enough saying it would be fun. Amara smiled at Daniel when she realized that this would be another first for them as a couple.

As it was, they discovered they were both light packers. Amara made one single stipulation, and that was to include one sexy little garment. They agreed to take the Rambler because of its space and accessibility.

The town of New Albany was a vibrant river town.

When they explored the shops that lined the streets, Amara was pleasantly surprised to find a grocery in the exact same spot as the one she had frequented as Awinita. She looked around half expecting Mary Ann to pop out of the woodwork. She could see the pretty redhead almost as clearly as if it was the year 1864.

When another young woman in faded blue jeans stepped forward, Amara actually got the chills. The girl's red hair had Amara staring blindly. Once she got her wits about her, Daniel politely retreated, allowing her to take the lead. She noted the changes and similarities, both in and around, the grocery. The town was well kept, and somewhat touristy, which only added to its charm.

The couple checked into a hotel dating back to the Civil War days, and had lunch at The Old Pike Inn. The Inn was built in 1840, and was owned by the Kreutzer family. It was a two-story brick building with a hipped roof that was a familiar sight to Amara. She remembered it well, but had no idea what its original function had been. Now it was a tavern, and a quaint place to stop for a suds and sandwich combo. They lingered only briefly to get their bearings before setting out on a tour of the town.

There were several landmarks among the mansions that lined the riverfront. New Albany was a rather wealthy town, and it showed in its architecture. She had the strangest feeling as they stood on the banks of the Ohio River. It was a surreal moment, and one that disturbed her peace of mind. Of course, she and her mother had done the very same thing many times in her youth. Those were wonderful memories with Alina laughing down at her tiny daughter. It was incredibly nostalgic, making her miss her mother all the more. She wished Daniel could have known her. The thought had Amara shaking off the sadness that threatened to overwhelm her as she studied the mansions in much the same way her mother must have.

When they came to the section where she and the other women had set up camp, Amara's skin prickled. The winds seemed to pick up, and there was a bite in the air that had not been there a second ago. She walked across what would have been their campsite with echoes of the others ringing in her ears. *"Here now! Don't be a bully!"* someone said, and just as clearly Ellen's high-pitched voice rang out in stern authority, *"Straighten up, all of you! Awinita assigned our chores. And that is precisely what we are going to do!"* Bless her, Amara thought. Ellen was such an honorable little woman; she handled herself with aplomb. And she had worked her way into Awinita's heart so quickly, and so deeply, that Amara would never forget her. She was as precious to her as Caroline and Mary Ann. She didn't quite know when it had happened, but these women had claimed a piece of her heart, and she loved them dearly.

She sniffled and turned her face toward the river so that Daniel wouldn't see her tear up. A steamboat blew its whistle in that same moment as it chugged upriver. She and Daniel planned to go out on a riverboat ride tomorrow afternoon. It was something they were looking forward to. As they walked on past the campsite in the direction of Jeffersonville, Amara noticed an enormous shift in the energy. Even though the town had expanded, Amara saw only the vast density of the forest. She felt threatened as if she needed to be armed and ready. Something terrible was about to happen, and Amara felt the tremors shake her very core.

"Are you all right?" Daniel asked. His concerned voice penetrated the shadows that threatened to consume her. She felt small and frightened, and so very alone. She no longer saw the people, or the buildings that surrounded them. And she had totally forgotten Daniel. He no longer existed.

The muffled cries of the women had seized her attention. They had been forced to walk into the deep recesses of the forest away from the safety of civilization. She reached for her spear, shocked to find that it was no longer at her side. Yet she found security in the weight of the blade strapped to her thigh. Awinita was good with knives. She was well experienced, and could throw with deadly precision. Amara had long since been forgotten as Awinita took over.

This cloud that was about to break overhead would bring death to many, and capture to most. Awinita needed her wits about her. It was a matter of survival. Men screamed. Horses reared. The black mass overhead roared. And Awinita saw through the smoke that hell yawned before her. She screamed in fury as she let go the blade. It buried itself deep in the belly of her enemy. Above her something large and black swooped down and carried her to seclusion. She fought with the strength of ten men. She was as sleek as a tigress, all teeth and arms and legs. Her muscles rippled. The man that held her would pay dearly for his transgression for Awinita was a thing to behold. No mortal man could ever tame her. And as it turned out, no mortal man had.

The creature that restrained her had the persona to terrify even a warrior such as Awinita. He had shifted into a beast right before her eyes, and without raising a hand he had her bound and gagged. He held her prisoner in the back of a wagon, and Awinita knew defeat when she was dumped to the ground in the presence of others. Above, the magpies circled. She heard their vicious cries even as they swooped down to pluck at her skin and clothing. And her despair was great.

"Amara, are you all right?" It was Daniel's dear face

peering down at her. The concern showed in the creases around his eyes, the tightness in his voice. He stroked her hair as he cradled her head in his lap.

"What happened?" she asked her mind foggy.

"You blacked out," he answered, his voice strained. "I don't think you were entirely yourself."

Amara was relieved to know that he understood. "No, I was Awinita," she confirmed in a whisper. "I do not understand why I become her. But I do know at least vaguely what will happen here."

"What can I do to help?" he asked. "There has to be something, or I wouldn't be a part of this thing."

Amara swallowed as she considered his words. Her throat was parched, and she longed for a beverage. "I'm not sure," she said. "I know that I am meant to stop this massacre, because that is exactly what it is going to be if we are not very, very careful. Maybe if we put all the facts together as in a puzzle?" she suggested.

"You mean by tying the past with the present?"

"Yes, precisely," she gave a brisk nod. "I believe our lives today will be badly altered if we do not correct the past."

"Then we must work through this together," he said strongly, and she felt that strength in the very fiber of her being. If a man, or partner of any kind, could stand by her side in this, Amara knew without a doubt it was Daniel. She smiled up at him as he helped her to her feet. His big hands skimmed her lithe body in one fluid motion, making sure she was unharmed. They walked hand in hand back through the city.

They dined that night in an Italianate villa built in 1851 by a man named Pepin. The current owner of the house had turned the ballroom into a first-class restaurant. Mary was a gentle, but wise business woman, who served fine meals on the formal china she sold in the basement gift shop. The place was dubbed *The Yesterday House*. Amara raved about the food as she delighted over the various patterns of porcelain. In the end, she proclaimed the set of dogwood her favorite.

The Culbertson mansion that her mother had been obsessed with was located right across the street. Amara dimly recalled seeing it when it was nothing more than a bare lot with a structure of frame work. It seemed so odd being with Daniel in the here and now. This pretty little town was loaded with history. They had a wonderful dinner, after which they retreated to their hotel room. Amara didn't notice when Daniel signaled the owner to wrap a set of the chosen china.

They set out for the caves first thing in the morning. Amara half expected to see Nonie. But the caves she knew were nonexistent to the public eye, and even if they did locate the entrance it would be dangerous to explore them on their own. At times like these Amara questioned her sanity. Daniel, however, was quick to assure her that her mind was intact. She did, however, have the overpowering feeling of being observed. They wound up taking a tour of the more popular caves in the area and enjoyed themselves immensely. If Amara found herself looking over her shoulder a great deal of the time, neither one commented on it.

They finished in time to grab a quick lunch since they had passed on breakfast. They had chosen the comfort of their hotel room instead. It was one of the rare occasions when Amara enjoyed a steaming hot cup of coffee as much as Daniel. It gave them the boost they needed.

After a light meal they walked down to the river, reveling in the architecture that brought the masses for tours. They took great pleasure in the riverboat, lounging on deck with rum runners while taking photographs of the ship, the shore, and the surrounding waters. It was a scenic view. Afterwards Daniel chose a seafood dinner complete with French fries and coleslaw while Amara ordered the batter-dipped veggie platter. It was unusual fare as she generally avoided fried foods, but it came with a lavish salad featuring every color of the rainbow.

They talked the entire ride home trying to gain a new perspective on the strange turn their lives had taken. It had been an interesting trip that was both fun and educational. And somewhere in the peripheral scope of her mind, Amara sensed she had learned more than she realized. It was as if a door had opened, and she had yet to access it. She told Daniel this and was relieved to know that he understood what she meant.

CHAPTER TWENTY-SIX

*I*t was great to be home again! Grim remained in position by the door the entire time they were away, Nikki said. And Solomon acted like he wanted to play, but couldn't quite pull it off. Instead, he curled up in a tight little ball keeping his eyes trained on Nikki all the while. Even Sampson was lackadaisical. In lieu of stretching out in a sunny window somewhere, he huddled on Amara's pillow as if that would bring her home more quickly. He would get up periodically to check on Solomon, creeping silently through the house, going nose to nose with his little buddy before wandering back to the familiar spot. After a while the two of them began to check on each other in some kind of soundless communication, before settling back down in their individual places. At night when they slept in the kitchen, Nikki took to looking in on them, only to find them cuddled together in one solid ball of fur. Gregory backed her up on this, claiming that even bribery had failed to work. No matter how hard they tried to entertain Amara's animal family, it was as if the troops were on strike.

Daniel laughed at the description they painted. Amara crooned soothing words to the little ones while Grim snuggled against her. "I rarely leave them overnight," she acknowledged, "It's so difficult to do. Look at those little faces!"

Now they were all making jokes, laughing as the two little ones showed off for their mama. Only Grim remained seriously by her side as if afraid she might slip away again. "Awe, come on, babies," she called, "Let's get you guys some fresh chow."

She caught up with the others in the front room where Nikki had set up a terracotta tea tray. There was a fresh pot of an herbal concoction with an intoxicating fragrance, and a side dish of mint leaves and orange slices. Tidy rows of selected cheeses and accompanying crackers lined a sturdy platter of the same design. "Did you make these?" Amara asked as she examined a detailed cup and saucer.

"No, Linda did," she said with a smile, "and Cynthia supplied the contents as a sort of homecoming. Everyone's worried about you," she added.

"They should have hung around!" Amara said with emotion.

"That's what I said," Nikki agreed. "But I have a feeling they will be back soon enough. Maybe we girls could get together one night this week?"

"Sure," Amara readily agreed.

"Well, I have some work to catch up," Daniel said. "Why don't you girls pick a night, and we'll coordinate our schedules?"

"Yeah, "Gregory chimed, "I've fallen behind too. And I'd rather be busy when you guys are." He ogled Nikki letting her know he wanted to be free when she was available. She cracked up causing Amara to do the same.

"Okay," Nikki giggled, deciding to settle the issue, "If you guys are ready to get back to work, I happen to know the others have a movie they want to catch. We girls could meet at the theatre for the early show tomorrow evening, and then come back here for a late dinner. I left a pan of lasagna in your fridge," she winked in Amara's direction, "It's all ready to pop in the oven. And, it's eggplant."

"Oh, that sounds delightful!" Amara exclaimed, "Thank you!"

"You're welcome. Just looking ahead," Nikki laughed.

"I'll toss a salad," Amara offered, "But let's go casual. I have a lot of catching up to do as well."

The girls met as planned with everyone in high spirits. It was good to hang out with friends. They saw the movie Love Story with Ali MacGraw and Ryan O'Neal. Linda was a sucker for romance, and the one who chose the flick. No one really cared; they just wanted to have fun. They had taken Cynthia's Firebird to better enjoy the ride. They were walking down the street to the parking lot next door when they overheard a nearby couple.

"How dare you?" a female voice hissed. "You were practically drooling over her!"

"Don't be so damned melodramatic," her partner responded in anger. "You asked me out, remember?"

"Oh! I cannot believe you are rubbing that in," she huffed. "You are insufferable!"

"Well, then you shouldn't care who I look at, should

you?"

"I should have known there was more to it than you said," the girl sneered. "Why else insist on crashing that stupid dinner party last summer?"

"So what if I've got it bad for another chick? I still have fun with you. You're good in bed, or anywhere else for that matter."

Amara let out an involuntary gasp. The others heard her and turned to see that she had stopped walking and was standing stock-still. The color had drained from her face as she stared at the couple a few feet ahead of them.

"Oh, no," Nikki whispered.

"I can't believe this," Cynthia muttered. "Of all the theatres in the world, why did they have to come to Crawfordsville?"

By this time Simon and his date, Victoria, were in the middle of a heated argument. "I'm not going anywhere with you," she said as she began walking in their direction.

"Don't be ridiculous," he snarled. "Get in the car." He grabbed her arm, and was attempting to physically force her into the vehicle. But Simon not only had good taste, he always had to have the best. It only took one swipe of her nails at the paint job on his corvette for him to slap her; hard. Victoria staggered backwards with an incredulous look, her hands shielding her face. Her eyes welled with tears as she backed away from him. When she removed her hands, Amara and the others, could see that she was bleeding.

"Don't come near me," she hissed again, but the venom was gone from her voice. She was frightened, and most likely in shock. Amara felt sorry for her. She called out softly as Victoria stormed past. "You," Victoria screeched, "This is your fault!"

No one noticed the black Chevy that stopped to give Victoria a lift.

Nikki put an arm around Amara. Linda did the same. Cynthia rushed ahead to unlock the car doors. Simon pulled up right in front of them as he was leaving the lot. He stared at Amara as if drinking in every detail. He didn't speak; he didn't have to. It was all right there in the way he looked at her. Amara couldn't help it, she stared back at him. She heard him laugh as he drove away. It was an astonishingly cruel laugh.

They talked about the movie on the way home. It was reputedly one of the best movies of the year, and Linda was weepy through the bulk of it. "It *was* sad," Cynthia chimed, and the conversation shifted to dinner by the time they pulled into the drive at Yountsville.

"Greg and Daniel are already here," Nikki said, "Is Ian coming?"

"Are you kidding?" Linda grinned, "He wouldn't miss your lasagna for anything!"

"I invited Todd too," Cynthia said, "That's all right, isn't it?"

"Of course," everyone sang out in unison. Cynthia liked to date around, but she had fallen for Todd and they all knew it. He was a nice guy; good looking, and interesting as well. Cynthia smiled to herself, and the others laughed.

Dinner was superb. The lasagna was a favorite among the friends. And Amara had made an enormous salad complete with fresh basil from the herbary as well as a side of her homemade blue cheese dressing. Cynthia and Todd supplied the wine. And Ian brought a dessert that Linda had put together that morning.

They listened to music and enjoyed the meal while Grim lay at Amara's side and the little ones romped in the front room. "They'll wear themselves out soon enough," Amara predicted. And she was right. They soon plopped down near the kitchen table and fell fast asleep. Sampson stretched out to his full length earning him the use of his nickname. Amara had affectionately dubbed him 'Yardstick' referring to the fact that he was a full three feet long. Solomon slept with his mouth agape and his pink tongue caught between his teeth. When he began to snore, everyone laughed. He must have been having good dreams because every so often his tail wagged furiously, reminding them of the ducks on the pond. At least for the time being, Amara had forgotten all about Simon. She looked up and chuckled.

After dinner Gregory said he had an announcement to make. Nikki's eyes sparkled when she raised her glass. Her lips widened into her most stunning smile, gaining the attention of the populace of the room. The candle light brought the stone on her finger to life, and suddenly everyone was speaking at once. Nikki looked at Gregory, and the couple shared a kiss. The friends broke out in applause. "We are making it official at Christmas," Gregory said in his deep voice.

"We were wondering when you were going to make it legal," Ian spoke for all of them, and the girls gathered around Nikki to admire her ring.

"That's why Linda chose *Love Story*," Nikki admitted, "She overheard us making plans."

"What a spectacular Christmas we will have!" someone said, and they all cheered.

It was late when everyone left. Daniel elected to stay over, and Amara wasn't about to argue. Even though she felt competent on her own, she liked having him around. She thought about Nikki and Gregory and wondered when her time would come.

It was a busy week, and summer was behind them. The changing seasons were a normal part of Indiana, and Amara welcomed the fall weather. She loved this time of year. The colors were glorious to behold, and she made it a point to watch as the leaves turned from green to red, and then to gold. She knew she was extremely fortunate to have this piece of property. It was one of the prettiest little farms around with its waterfalls and easy access to the creek. She walked the path to the woods a hundred times a day. She hadn't mentioned it to anyone, but she was worried about Karma. The little coon hadn't made an appearance in a while. Of course this would be her first winter on her own and Amara knew she would be busy preparing her den. She watched for her nonetheless.

Life seemed to settle a bit with Daniel working on an upcoming book, and Amara engrossed in her markets. She would be teaching yoga in a couple of weeks. She taught a beginners' class as well as an advanced one. It supplemented her financially, and satisfied her physically, and she was good at it. She practiced running energy every chance she got. She would put her fingers together, and then pull them slowly apart just to watch the life force, or vital principle, stretch like rubber bands before her eyes. She delighted in the chi that sparked from the tips of those fingers, and the way she was comprehensively beginning to see halos. She was thorough in following Nonie's instructions, and still found herself speaking to the phantom-like Creole late at night.

These nocturnal visitations just happened nowadays. Sometimes she simply heard Nonie's voice and responded. Other times she would find herself back at the caves. It didn't frighten, or upset her, any more. She knew she was going through training. And then one night in the cave, she had a very clear awakening as she received yet another attunement. This one was different from the others in that everything she looked upon gained great clarity. The halos became far more pronounced, the lights more distinct, and her observations more intuitive. She was gaining insight as a healer, and as a psychic. She knew she had come a long way, and was grateful to Nonie.

This form of healing was called Reiki, Nonie told her. The exotic Creole explained the Reiki principals, and the meaning of the word itself. She taught her the sacred symbols that must always receive grave respect. And she instructed her on the many hand positions and the steps she would need to take to qualify as a teacher herself someday. She taught her to hold this training in high esteem, for it must never be compromised. The symbols were the work of the Ascension Masters. They were iconic, and there had been hundreds of them at one time. Nonie had traveled, and received her training in other countries, she said. She was pleased that Amara was a natural, thus making it possible to teach her both the Usui and Tibetan systems at the same time. She told her that she had great potential, and never to underestimate the power she held in her hands. This energy, this sacred light, would save her life time and time again. It was to be revered. Amara bloomed under Nonie's tutelage, and was in turn loved like a daughter. Her genealogy was akin to royalty.

On occasion, her brother would join her at the caves

or in the woods. They would sit and talk about everything from magic to family. She was thirsty for knowledge, but she craved family even more. Crow was an unusual young man. He always appeared in human form except when he came to her aid. They looked a lot alike, and she was glad they had both taken after their mother. In truth Awinita didn't know her father any more than Amara knew hers. It was something they had both come to accept. Now as Awinita, she wondered more than ever about that shadowy figure who was her father. On that topic Crow kept silent.

CHAPTER TWENTY-SEVEN

It was early evening, and Amara was at the grocery store. Daniel was away on a story, and wouldn't be back for a couple of days. Amara was accustomed to living alone and knew she could handle herself, but under the current circumstances, preferred to be home before dark. She glanced at her list as she went along, and as she reached for an item off the top shelf, she had the disconcerting feeling she was being tailed. She looked up, and caught a glimpse of a figure disappearing around the corner of the next aisle. She was as curious as she was cautious. And as she pursued her subject, she watched as the same thing happened again. Just as she navigated one corner, he rounded the next. Amara was not one to back down to anything, and she was now fairly certain she was being stalked. By the time she was at the checkout counter, she looked up to see the supermarket door swing shut directly behind a tall, shadowy figure. Amara frowned in consternation. She knew darn good and well that man had been spying on her. But he was little more than a blur. Was it Simon, or someone else? She was still uneasy about the scene in the parking lot the other night.

She paid the checkout clerk just as the boy who was

sacking her groceries put the last item in a bag. "Thank you," she called as she scooped up her purchases and hurried on out the door. The boy would have carried them for her, she knew, but she didn't wait for him to offer. She reached her car safely, put her bags in the trunk, closed the lid and looked straight into Simon's cunning eyes!

"So it *was* you," she accused, "What do you want? And why are you following me?"

"I think that should be obvious," he said succinctly. But she was relieved he kept his hands to himself.

Amara stared at him, at a loss for words. And she couldn't help but observe how one of his eyes strayed off into the distance as though viewing two separate destinations at once. What was he looking at? Or did he have difficulty focusing? She never noticed that before. He was actually a good looking man, except that Amara saw in him what others did not. And she was seeing it right now. There was something about Simon that was just plain unnatural.

She held a pepper spray concealed in one hand; she kept it close to her side. She had a license to carry, and was comforted by the fact that she had a small handgun in the glove compartment of her car. It would take only seconds to snag it. Simon must have read her train of thought because he laughed lightly, and said, "You look like you're about to bolt. Don't tell me you're afraid of me?"

"Don't be ridiculous. I'm not afraid," she lied, "I just don't like you. There's a difference."

"Well, now, that was uncalled for," he said in a sing-song voice. "You always were too blunt." He sounded slightly demented when he talked like that, and Amara felt sensations prickle down her spine.

"Too bad," she whispered raggedly. She never took her eyes off him as she moved toward the driver's side of the car.

"I don't mean you any harm," he said slyly. "I just want to call a truce. We left things in bad standing between us."

"I left things exactly as I meant to," Amara's voice was steady despite the tension of the moment.

"Look, just let me buy you dinner," he wheedled, "It would make my day, give me a chance to make amends, and all that other good stuff one is supposed to do." He spread his hands out to his sides in a gesture of surrender and looked at her with puppy dog eyes. Except that Simon's eyes never looked innocent. He had a slight tic that was probably nerve related, yet somehow made him look charming. And Amara was all the more uncomfortable by his subterfuge.

"That isn't necessary," she said in a brisk voice. "Now if you don't mind, I'd like to be on my way." She had somehow managed to unlock the car door, while still holding the spray in her other hand. Her motions were sure and smooth giving the illusion of calm. At the same time, Amara was listening for anyone nearby who might come to her aid should there be any altercation. She saw movement out of the corner of her eye, and knew someone was getting into the car next to hers. An engine roared to life in a black Chevy across the way. Voices buzzed as two women walked past.

Amara took the opportunity to slide into the driver's seat and promptly close the door. Simon took a step back, and Amara pulled away without a second thought. She caught a glimpse of him in her rearview mirror. Anger made his features appear harsh. It wasn't until later that she realized she never did see his parked car. Why not? Had he parked elsewhere in order to fool her? Amara shook her head, and continued to drive home.

She arrived home without incident and carried her bags inside, locking the door behind her. She had left Grim loose in the house, and took comfort in his greeting. The telephone was ringing, and she hurried into the kitchen to set her bags on the counter. Solomon hopped excitedly up and down. Sampson stretched. And Amara went to answer the phone. She was expecting Daniel's smooth burr when someone hung up on her. Amara replaced the receiver on the phone, thinking she had probably just missed him. She hadn't so much as taken a step away from the alcove where she kept the telephone when it started ringing again. She snatched it up with a happy little laugh.

"You should have taken me up on that dinner," Simon's voice sneered, "That was a mistake, Amara. And trust me, you will pay for it."

Amara quickly hung up the phone, wrapping her arms around her middle. She felt like she had been punched in the solar plexus. She was glad she had Grim, but she would keep her gun handy just the same. She had the handgun tucked into the back of her jeans, and the shotgun loaded and at the ready. She left the flood lights on that Gregory had installed outside, and took comfort in all of these factors. She considered calling Grant and reporting Simon, but in the end decided against it. Grant made her just a little too jumpy these days. Maybe she wouldn't bother him after all. After that day in the cemetery she wasn't really sure whose side he was on.

She paused to feed her animal family before fixing a late meal for herself. She gathered up some potatoes from the vegetable bin in the cellar, and selected a nice butternut squash while she was at it. She had some leeks upstairs in the kitchen she wanted to use. The combination would make a savory soup. She quickly cleaned the leeks, careful to rinse all the sand out of them, before adding them to the pot where she sautéed them in her own mustard vinaigrette. Next, she heated several cups of vegetable broth, and brought the potatoes to a boil. By this time, the squash was ready to come out of the oven. She cut it into cubes and tossed it into the pot. Soon she was happily blending the mixture into a smooth soup. She let it simmer while she toasted some whole grain bread and made a watercress sandwich. It was a delightful little repast, and there would be leftovers for another time. She enjoyed the flavorful combination while listening to some soft Blues.

Daniel called right after she washed the last of the dishes. She poured a cup of peppermint tea and curled up on the sofa to chat. She wanted to hear about his day, and the job he was doing. She was interested in where he was staying, and hoped he found a nice motel. They had talked for over an hour when she thought to tell him about Simon. His voice roughened, and she realized she had disturbed him. "Don't worry," she told him, "The doors are locked, and I have Grim with me." Grim raised his big head at the mention of his name. She rubbed his ears, and he settled back down.

"Did you call anyone? Nikki? Or that cop that's always coming around?" he asked. "You ought to leave the flood lights on tonight."

"I plan to," she answered. "It's been quiet so far." She was willing to bet that Daniel would call Gregory as soon as he hung up. He had a way of making her feel safe, and she smiled at the thought. That was a good quality in a boyfriend. "I was going to see if Cynthia would want to come over, but then I remembered she would be spending the night with Todd. I don't want to mess that up."

Amara snagged a book and went to bed soon after she

disconnected from Daniel. She missed him. They had fallen into a routine of sleeping together in the extra bedroom, and it felt empty in the larger bed without him. The house was drafty this time of year. She hadn't turned on the heat yet, opting for an extra blanket instead. She tucked the extra pillow into the curve of her body, and dozed off more easily than she would have imagined, allowing her book to fall unnoticed to the floor.

It was the dark of night that woke her. It was pitch black, and far too quiet. Even the steady tick-tock of the clock had stilled. Amara opened her eyes, and wondered what was wrong. She sat bolt upright, fumbling with the flashlight she kept in a drawer by the bed. It was clear outside with no inclement weather reports, and she had left the grounds well lit.

She swept the flashlight around the room, freezing when its beam fell on the electric wall clock. The clock read 12:10. She raced to the telephone only to find it dead. Most likely someone had cut the electrical wire precisely at ten minutes after midnight. Amara reached for the shotgun, racked it, and propped it beside her while she slipped into her jeans. She tucked the handgun back into the waistband of her pants, leaving her pajama top intact. She didn't want to be caught off guard.

Grim followed her every move with his eyes. She could feel his coiled strength, and knew he sensed something was wrong. Carefully, they made their way around the house, checking every window and door. All was airtight, but when she approached the front door a second time, she nearly slipped on something slick. She crouched down slowly, keeping her gun at the ready, and reached for what she now recognized as a sheet of paper. Someone must have slipped it under the door. It had not been there a minute ago. She shone the flashlight directly on it. There, in bold block letters, the note read, "ITS ALL YOUR FAULT."

Amara gasped, crumbling the letter in one fist as she got to her feet. What did it mean? What was all her fault? Her mouth felt as parched as a desert. She filled a glass of water at the sink, tucking the little ones out of her way as she did so. They didn't make a peep, not a single protest. Since she couldn't call for help, she settled for perching on the edge of a seat, fully armed, until daylight streaked the sky. Grim sat with her, his ears pricked at an angle.

Grim went off a fraction of a second before someone pounded on the front door. She jumped in spite of herself, but kept her hands steady as she approached the door. "Who is it?" she shouted in the most aggressive voice she could muster, at the exact same instant Grant called out. She did not lower her gun, but stood to one side of the door.

"Police! Open up!" Grant's voice was harsh.

Amara cautiously removed the chain, and peered out at Grant and his deputies. She kept a firm hold on her weapon even when she let him in. "What in the hell is going on?" she yelled at him. She hadn't realized how tense she had been.

Grant rewarded her with a respectful look, but his jaw was tight. "I've been worried about you. Your house is dark, sealed up all tight. Phone is dead. I got an emergency alert out this way."

"What happened?" she paused for air, "Was someone hurt?"

"Someone's dead, "Grant said bluntly. "I was afraid it was you. You stay here. Lock up behind me."

"But I know the land," she protested. "I can help."

"I said, stay here," he ordered when she would have argued. "Look, Amara, there's a killer out there. A body has been dumped in the creek. It's female; same size, build and age as you. Now, stay put."

She nodded in a way that signaled she was frightened. *Good, it's about time,* his expression said. He stepped outside with his deputies, and before she could move, snapped, "Lock up!"

Amara complied. She shot the bolt without hesitation. She left the little ones closed up in the sunroom, while she took Grim to the back of the house where there was a clear view of the creek. She had deliberately avoided the windows until now.

There was suddenly a lot of activity in the stark morning light. Several car doors slammed nearby, and she realized they were parked in her driveway. County cops were canvassing the banks below. She could see them through the trees that covered the sharp incline to the water. She couldn't have done so a couple of weeks ago, but now with the leaves down, she had a pretty clear panorama. She snatched up the binoculars she used to watch the birds and other wildlife, and focused on the creek where several cops had gathered. She stiffened when she saw them haul a body to the sandy banks. She wasn't positive, but she thought she saw a stream of yellow blonde hair before they covered the victim with a tarp. Amara's stomach churned.

The electrician arrived just before the coroner's vehicle pulled up. Her lights came on, and she was told that the telephone was in working order once again. She watched as the deceased was carried from the woods, and then set the binoculars aside, and went to put on a clean blouse. Inside she was shaking, but she kept a calm demeanor. She was asked to identify the cadaver. She did so with deep remorse.

Had she acted sooner, had she called the police after the theatre, or the grocery, or especially after the phone call from Simon the night before, Victoria might still be alive. That was a possibility she would have to live with. What a terrible burden to shoulder!

She listened as most of the county cops dispersed, knowing that Grant would stop back by. She busied herself making a pot of hot coffee. She warmed some biscuits, and placed them in the center of the table. She didn't want anything herself, but the men would need something. The waters were cold this time of year, and some of the deputies were pretty young. It had to be an awful shock finding a corpse. It sure as hell was identifying one.

Grant stopped in as predicted with two of his deputies. They welcomed the coffee, and thanked her for the trouble. "No trouble," she said quietly. She was humbled by the faces of the younger men. She gave them their space, waiting patiently for Grant to address her. He lingered until after the deputies went outside. He needed them to check the grounds, including the doors and windows of the house, for anything that might have been overlooked. It was a known fact that the killer had been on the front porch. The note claiming that it was Amara's fault was proof of that. And then of course, there was the matter of the electrical wires. The murderer was too close for comfort. Grant rechecked the inside of the house himself, testing the telephone as he went. He glanced at each of the clocks. He was nothing if not thorough.

Grant studied the note again while he sipped his coffee. He had read it a hundred times by now. He had her repeat the exact words that Simon had said to her at the grocery store, and then again in their brief phone conversation. He was angry that she had not called him immediately after those incidents, and the strain showed in the timbre of his voice. But he didn't rebuke her, and she wondered if It was obvious how deeply affected she was. The tragedy wasn't really her fault, he told her. But the fact of the matter still remained that Victoria Beech was dead.

THE CALLING OF CROWS

PART FOUR

The Calling of Crows

CHAPTER TWENTY-EIGHT

mara took the curry comb to all three horses before taking the time to pick each set of hooves clean. Queen's ears pricked up as she stepped like royalty through the gate. Shawnee nickered and nudged her chin, while Raven stood placidly by watching Merlin perform like a tightrope walker down the length of the fence. Amara shoveled out the barn while Smoke rode her shoulder. And Erebus, the caliginous feral tom that had taken refuge in her barn, skulked behind the hay bales that were stored in the loft.

Erebus had shown up one dark and turbulent night. He was a nefarious soul who had seen countless fights, leaving him with the remnants of a once proud face. Amara could never have turned him away, for he was a pathetic creature in need of a home. She could feel his greedy gaze upon her. He was relentless in his quest for food, an ugly beast with calloused layers of scar tissue, and an empty eye socket. The other cats were smart enough to be afraid of him. They gave him a wide berth, and he in turn left them alone. Amara addressed him in a melodic voice as she tossed him some scraps, and was rewarded when he snatched the food away without grousing. Erebus loomed out of nowhere and merged with the night, clarifying the name she had chosen as he was the personification of darkness. But he took only what he was given, leaving the rest untouched. And Amara wondered at the mystery of him.

In the herbary Amara's plants were thriving. The seedlings were fragrant, the lettuces and other salad vegetables, abundant. She didn't want to dwell on the events of the night before, but Victoria's death lay heavily on her conscience. She felt responsible. Everyone assured her it wasn't her fault. The police, the press, even Grant, was kind about it. Daniel, her dearest love, sought to console her. He proposed to come home early, but Amara knew he needed to finish his story. She didn't want to cause him any work-related problems. Her friends offered to take the day off to come and stay with her. She declined them politely. In the end, Amara chose her own company. She needed time alone to reflect on the murder. Hard work was in order.

Truth be told, she already knew she was stepping into another world. She had been aware of it all day. She was lightheaded, yet her feet felt like she was sinking in quicksand. She wore Nonie's amulet in her hair and her 1864 Indian Head penny on a cord around her throat. She realized she was simply putting things in order before she left again. In a weird way, it made perfect sense. If they were going to ride the rails, it had to happen now. She had a sense of urgency about her that wouldn't let up. She knew her history, and understood that they were running out of time.

Set ashore on the banks of the Ohio without food or money, the Roswell women received little help from the residents of Indiana. River towns, like New Albany and Evansville, were too impoverished to support such a large number of refugees during the years of the American Civil War. They had their hands full taking care of their own, and there were no agencies to fund these desperate people. General Sherman merely passed order number 22 in an effort to move the homeless to a place where they might possibly learn to take care of themselves. It was not an act of kindness, but rather a way to clear the slate. Amara knew that Sherman wouldn't honor the mandate for long. When it came right down to it, he simply didn't care. She also knew that the disappearance of the Roswell women would remain a mystery. If she wasn't there to lead those in her care, many would die, and many more would be sold. There was no going back. Amara realized that Barrington King believed the operatives were responsible for the loss of the Roswell Mill. He would not welcome them back. And the Cannelton mills here in Indiana were not an option either.

She allowed her instincts to take over and guide her while she soaked in a rose scented bath, and in the rippling waters her perception cleared. She had the strangest premonition that the women in her care were reliant on her to rescue them from a devilry that was about to descend. She did not fully comprehend what this abyss was, but she sensed a massacre was about to take place and a yawning chasm of some kind was about to swallow them whole.

She toweled off and donned a suitable garment, then hugged and kissed both of the little ones before tucking them in for the night. When she padded barefoot to the bed, Grim was at her side, and she bent down and buried her face in his stygian fur. He whimpered, and she felt the dampness of her tears on his coat. And then, after lying upon the bed, she allowed herself to let go. A single droplet slipped down her cheek as she heard Grim's faint mewl, and her fingers ruffled his thick fur one last time as she drifted off and literally detached.

Amara was conscious of the transformation more than ever before. She and Awinita had so neatly coalesced that they knew each other inside out. Amara watched as she stepped into Awinita's self, leaving Amara on the bed in her old room. She didn't look back, but moved forward with new purpose. She had left the caves behind, and was heading toward camp when Crow swept down from the heavens. He flew ahead and circled three times, and when he returned, he presented a gift from the campsite. It was a broken dish, and it accelerated her step. No one ever broke, or wasted, anything. These women were destitute. Everything they owned was a treasure.

"Here now!" someone said clearly enough for Awinita to hear, "Don't be a bully."

"Straighten up, all of you!" It was Ellen's high pitched voice, God Bless her! It was odd how sound carried.

Within a quarter mile of camp, Awinita heard the screams of the women mingled with the battle cries of their attackers. Awinita knew she was walking into something vicious, and much bigger than herself. She carried a spear, wearing her knife in a sheath at her thigh. She was essentially preparing for war. The scent of blood filled the air. She was terrified she would be too late as the sound of shrieking horses met her ears. As she slipped quiet as a cat into camp, she heard Mary Ann's voice sounding an alarm. Her sweet friend had tried to warn them! Mary Ann held a pistol at the ready. She had a bundle of her worldly goods tied around her waist. She was one of them now. And their camp was under invasion. Awinita wasted nothing; no breath, no kindness, no thought. She took Mary by the arm, pushing her on ahead just in the nick of time, "Go, and lead the others," she cried over the cacophony of sound, "You're in charge!" she screamed as her blade deftly sliced a man's throat.

Mary Ann wanted to argue, but she had no stomach for it. She had no wish to leave Awinita. But Awinita had already turned away, and was fighting hand-to-hand combat. For a split second Mary Ann froze in disbelief, for Awinita was a fearsome warrior. Her movements were fluid and graceful; her knife and spear took the lives of many. Mary Ann stumbled in the direction she had been shoved. The black mass overhead roared, and Awinita peered through the smoke as Hell yawned before her. She screamed in fury as she let go the blade. It buried itself deep in the belly of the enemy. Above her something large and black swooped down upon her, and Awinita knew she was lost.

Later, she opened her eyes to the cry of magpies. She had been dumped to the ground, her clothing torn, her weapons missing. She turned her face away from the evil one, and the flapping of wings came to a halt just as the man emerged before her. Awinita had foggy memories of this human. Much had been swept into in the deep, dark recesses of her subconscious mind, but the thought of escaping him was of phenomenal significance. She felt her body shudder in revulsion. She knew her intellect had sheltered her from a past that was too painful to recall.

"You are a grand prize," the man roared triumphantly, "Much more so than your mother!"

She raised her head and looked him straight in the eyes. Those opaque windows stripped her of her worth. They were entirely devoid of emotion. This man had no honor, but knew only avarice. He survived on animal instinct alone. The sight snapped off a memory in Awinita, much the same way a shutter clicked off a photograph. She remembered a harsh man shoving her skirts up when she was a little girl. His large member had penetrated her child's body; she had bled for days. Her mother, Gola, had tried to protect her by hiding her in the forest, and for a time they were safe. Then one day he discovered their whereabouts. Awinita was in the water, fishing. Gola was on shore. *He* watched as Awinita hitched her chin to show her mother her catch. He relished the look of pure horror on her young countenance as he butchered Gola right before her eyes. He dumped his wife's body into the river without ceremony, and watched as Awinita's mind went blank.

The memories came flooding back. With tears in her eyes, she said in a bitter voice, "Hello, father." In that single basic greeting there was a wealth of hatred. And Awinita had sustained it for a lifetime. Her cheeks burned when he laughed at her.

"Hello daughter," he guffawed rudely, "Did you really think you could escape? You will never run from me again," he warned in a threatening tone.

Awinita closed her eyes against the sight of him, offering a prayer to the Great Spirit. The man who was her biological father reached down to fondle her where she lay on the ground. She moaned in protest, gaining an audience. The men were deeply aroused by this warrior woman, and equally impressed with the man who had defeated her. They leaned in, hoping for some sport, but were immediately dismissed. Even as they sought their own conquests, their shifty eyes darted back to Awinita.

Awinita was sickened by the outcome of the battle, and the pain and humiliation that was cast upon her women. She pretended indifference even as she vowed to get even. She would kill this monster, and all of those who followed under his leadership. She went to sleep, at long last feeling his limp tool slip from her bruised body. His loud snores overrode the sobbing of her female friends. Unlike most, Awinita shed no tears. The time for such weakness was past. She had not been deaf to the conversation that buzzed around the wagons. She heard every single comment these men made. It was their intention to sell her friends into a lifetime of slavery down in Mexico. Once there, they would never be seen, or heard from, again.

Awinita covertly watched as the men put their plans into motion. There was to be another party arriving later in the day. She put all of her lessons to use as she focused first on her connection with Nonie, and then repeated the process with Crow. Of course, they knew where she was, and Crow was watching. Hence, Awinita sent meticulously precise telepathic messages. She had learned much as her counterpart, Amara, and Awinita felt certain it would take the effort of both personalities to beat the man who called himself *father.*

Meanwhile, his men would continue to take advantage of her friends. Therefore, it was imperative to get her comrades to safety. Awinita knew that the men believed their leader had been successful in breaking her. She played on this, pretending docility. They were given a few precious minutes throughout the day to take care of their needs. Awinita used the opportunities to manifest their freedom, watching as Crow circled the wagons. She glanced at Mary Ann in such a way as she had been taught. Naturally, Mary didn't have the skills both Amara, and Awinita, possessed. She did, however, pick up the on urgency directed at her. Next, Awinita did the same with Ellen. After some time, Ellen's head swiveled slowly about, until she met Awinita's gaze. Awinita smiled with her eyes.

When she next answered the call of nature, Awinita kicked sand in the eyes of the man nearest her, and dove for his weapon. Though her hands were bound, Awinita knew Crow would come to her aid. He acted on cue, expertly freeing her of her bonds with the tip of his beak. She drew back the hammer and fired, belatedly realizing her extremities had gone numb. She frowned when her shot went astray. The man snarled as he pulled a knife. Crow swept down from the heavens, and plucked out one of his menacing eyes. The man screamed in agony as blood poured down his face. Awinita swept up the blade, and buried it to the hilt in the soft belly of an oncoming opponent. When she boldly pulled it free, the weapon produced enough suction that a river of blood gushed from the fatal wound. The sound was atrocious. Yet Awinita had little time for reflection. Instead, she wiped the mess on her skirt. And that's when she looked up to see a third man advancing out of nowhere. He turned, and fired directly at Crow. And for one suspended moment everything went black.

Feathers flew in all directions, and Crow tumbled to the earth. Awinita wanted to cover her eyes and weep for the loss of her friend and brother. But in the heat of the moment she took revenge instead. The man died at her hands while a look of astonishment crossed his features. He had underestimated her rage. Awinita didn't bat an eye, but ran to where Crow's body lay. She called to Nonie, and to the Great Spirit. Nonie's voice filled the wind that exploded violently as if from nowhere. And Awinita cursed these men who had brought destruction upon so many innocent souls. As the clouds roiled the skies above, thunder broke loose of the elements.

A great rain flooded the forest, cleansing it of all bloodshed. The remaining men escaped the wrath of something far more powerful than they could have imagined, leaving Awinita free to look after Crow. But Crow was gone. All that was left in his place was a mass of black feathers. Awinita picked one up from the ground noting the blue-black sheen of it, and placed it in her hair. She stared in horror at the scene before her. Many of the women and children were dead, their limbs tangled together on the sodden ground. Others had been taken when the men fled. Only a handful remained with her. When she caught Ellen's eye, and saw that both she and Mary Ann were unharmed, Awinita covered her face and wept. She didn't notice the fire opal that belonged to Amara winking from the battlefield.

While Awinita was busy caring for the survivors, her father managed to flee the forest. He met with the party who came for the captives, and they shared food and drink. Awinita caught a glimpse of him when he took flight. She cursed when her arrow merely grazed him, for he was an evil man with supernatural powers. He was, when he chose, a magpie. And now, there was a war between the two strains of birds. Awinita wore Crow's feathers proudly. She had gathered all that she could find, and made a headdress of them.

She had taken roll call, and out of her entire camp there were thirteen women, including herself. There were no surviving children. They had learned a great deal in that awful day, just as they had known a terrible loss. They buried their dead, later gathering in prayer. And they found a small stream where they located some edible plant life. Ellen was silent when she handed Awinita a small string of fish. Her catch was nothing short of a miracle. Mary Ann's eyes gleamed as she emptied the bundle she had tied to her waist. From it, she produced dried fruits and nuts, along with other edibles she had taken from her husband's store. She even had a bag of loose tea. They would honor the dead by nurturing the living.

CHAPTER TWENTY-NINE

The women managed to egress the forest under Awinita's mastery. They had rested only long enough to tend their wounded. They saw Awinita as a hero, and followed her without question. She had drawn a crude map to help them find the main road. The sun was rising when they caught sight of the railroad tracks, and Awinita warned them to keep moving. They had no way of knowing if they were being followed. It was wise to assume they were.

Awinita cast her gaze to the sky in the hopes of seeing Crow circling high above. The depth of her despair was so great that the only thing that enabled her persistence was her commitment to the others. She needed to see them to safety before she could seek out Nonie. She kept her mind on the matter at hand. There was a small train station some miles ahead. She would lead them there. They might have a bit of a wait, but the station would offer a modicum of protection. They had already been warned to stick together. No one was to wander off.

They walked for miles on only the occasional bit of food and water. Early in their journey they kept quiet conversation in order to stay awake and aware. Now their chatter ceased altogether. Their overall pain had escalated without proper care. These women had been abused. Some were badly injured. All were sore, tired, and hungry. What if the engineer refused them? They were beginning to worry about the possibility. Awinita continued to encourage them. She told them what they needed to hear, that there would be food at the station, and that they could rest comfortably on the train. It would not be like the trip from Marietta to Louisville. Here, they would be treated like human beings.

Awinita kept her worries to herself. She could only pray that she was correct. She was used to being the responsible party, but she had gradually become aware of her other self leading her. She had flashes of insight that let her know she was on target. She heard snatches of conversations with the one called Amara. Awinita had faith in the Great Spirit. She had to believe that this was the way things were supposed to unfold. She kept to her path, as always in tune with nature. She was constantly on the alert for any sign that they were being followed. She had become familiar with the noise of blaring horns, the rattle of cars on rails. They made a peculiar vibration that reverberated in her mind. She could hear them from miles away. She trusted her own logic, valued the gifts she had been given. When she first heard the rumble of a distant train, she felt like shouting. Instead, she waited until it was close enough for the others to hear. It was safer that way. She needed the crew to remain low-key. They could not afford to draw attention to themselves.

At length they reached the station. It was small and crowded, with a mass of potential passengers. The women went from excited to fearful in seconds flat. Awinita talked to them in a soothing tone. She glanced over her shoulder, wanting to circle back to the caves. She wanted to find Nonie. She needed to know Crow's fate. Was there any chance he was alive? Nonie was a gifted healer. But she had seen the man pull the trigger, watched the bullet hit dead on. She had witnessed the explosion of feathers. But when she searched the ground, there was no sign of her brother. She had begun to see this as a chance he may have somehow survived. She had discovered hope. After she saw the others safely aboard, she decided to circle back. She promised to join them as soon as she could. Somehow, she would keep that promise.

Awinita cast one final look behind her, and froze. There, in the distance, was a familiar figure! She was thinner than she had ever seen her. She was limping, threadbare, and emaciated. And she wasn't alone. She determinedly dragged someone along with her. The smaller figure bounced ahead of her, and Awinita knew a thrill of excitement. As she gazed at the scarecrow, her tears flowed unchecked. "Caroline! Oh, dear God, Caroline! Is it you?"

Amara awoke with a start. She was in her room at the farm. She and Daniel had been frequenting the master bedroom, but here she was all curled up in her own colorful space with tears streaking her cheeks, and her stomach growling like she hadn't eaten in a week. She was absolutely starving! Her memory blurred like a transfer print of one image on top another, and she realized she had been out of body again. But this time she could recall every detail of her experience as if it had happened to her personally!

Before she could do anything, she must eat, shower, and take care of the animals. Daniel would be home tonight, and they had made plans to meet at the new bistro in town. Amara was looking forward to seeing him. She had so much to tell him, and wanted to hear all about the story he was working on. She hoped it was going well. Tonight was her first yoga class of the season, and Daniel had said they should celebrate. She liked that he took an interest in her work. She told herself she must put all her troublesome emotions on hold.

While she busied herself preparing brunch, she allowed her mind to wander. She would make her way to the caves. She would speak to Nonie, and check on her brother. Funny, she had always thought of Crow as Awinita's brother. Now she saw that he was her brother, as well. She loved having a sibling! She had missed family more than she ever could have imagined. And she would do anything in her power to protect him. Amara could not allow herself to believe that Crow was gone forever. It just wasn't possible. She held on to that thought with everything she had.

She made spinach quesadillas because they sounded good, and she was craving spinach. She poured herself a cup of tea, and sat down at the table. She took first one bite, then another, and was glad she had made two. Astral travel depleted one's system, she thought. Of course, it probably didn't help that she was starving in her past life. That thought made her think of Caroline. Oh, dear God, she had never been so relieved to see anyone in her entire life! Caroline was her best friend and spiritual sister. She could no longer separate her from her current reality. Something had shifted. When had that occurred?

Amara pondered these things all morning long as she went about her chores. Grim was even more protective than usual, and Amara knew it was because this OBE was somehow different from the others. Solomon eyed her suspiciously, and went so far as to yap when she approached. Sampson, too, behaved strangely. Yet he wove his way over to her kitchen chair, stretching out to his full three-feet, as he stood and wrapped his arms around her neck and shoulders. He purred in his warm kitty voice, while he began massaging her with his strong paws. Those tufted toes amazed her with their intensity, but he seemed satisfied and Amara certainly knew that she was loved!

All three of the horses shied from her. Shawnee stamped and snorted for a full minute before Amara put a halter on her, and led her into the adjoining pasture. Raven nickered, and shook his head stubbornly. And Queen rolled her eyes, bucking for several minutes before Amara could calm her. Amara realized what a big impact this had had on all of them, and hoped that it would get easier. She hopped on Shawnee's back in the same fluid manner Awinita might have. She couldn't help but gasp at the vaginal discomfort she experienced. She had tucked the source of it away in the dusty corners of her mind. It hurt to think about it, she acknowledged. It was physically painful, but the mental-emotional conflict was worse. She gave Shawnee a nudge, and they broke into a smooth gallop. The ride was cleansing, and that's how she came to realize she needed to speak to Nonie about clearing work. Subconsciously, she sensed there was another lesson coming.

She went about the rest of her day with a bit more confidence. When it came time to get ready for class she took a steamy shower, soaping her hair and rinsing, before wrapping herself in a clean towel. She slipped into a matching set of purple lingerie, and went about towel drying her hair before applying a little makeup. She dressed in her yoga clothes, stepping into a bright print skirt that she wore over her leotard, and allowed her curls to finish air-drying. On her way out the door, she snatched up a bag that contained her purse as well as a change of clothing, and a pair of high heels.

She parked in her designated space behind the building where she taught. As she stepped from her car, she spied a black Chevy moving slowly down the alley. It revved to life when she glanced at it, and disappeared around the corner. She knew a moment of discomfiture. Was someone following her? Or was she being paranoid?

Her class was a success. She had more than enough students to make it worthwhile, and they were a pleasant bunch at that. She enjoyed this particular job, and was considering adding a meditation class next season. After everyone had gone, and she had locked up behind them, she took the money from the cashbox, adding it to her wallet, and dropping it into the bottom of her purse. She changed into a casual dress that was an all-time favorite, and released her hair from the ponytail she had worn while she was teaching. Now she shook it free, allowing it to cascade down around her shoulders. She had a light wrap should she need it, but it was a clear night, and unseasonably warm. She was just about ready to head out, when a man's shadow filled the doorway. She stopped and stared, rooted to the spot. He did not knock, but tried the lock instead. He jiggled it a second time, and Amara knew a moment's panic. She was about to ring the police when he called her name. Amara was furious when she opened the door.

"Why didn't you knock, Grant?" she didn't care if she sounded angry, "You scared me to death."

"I was just checking on you," he said soothingly, "Settle down."

"I always lock up," she swore at him, "You know that."

"Someone's following you," he said without preamble, "I thought you should know."

"If you're talking about the black Chevy, yes, I know,"

she fumed.

"I spotted it a couple of times. Whoever the driver is, he's elusive," Grant replied. "I arrested Simon Alexander," he added before she could say anything further, "We don't have enough evidence to hold him."

Amara merely closed her eyes. Would this nightmare ever end?

As if he could read her thoughts, Grant added, "We'll get him, Amara. We just need something more concrete." He looked like he was about to touch her, and Amara didn't know why, but she took a step backward. She wrapped her arms around her waist as she looked at him, and waited for him to leave before she went out to climb into her car.

Amara met Daniel at Joe's as planned. He stepped out of his vehicle when she pulled into the lot, and went to greet her. When he folded her in his arms, she had the strange validation that this was the first time she had felt safe since he'd been gone. She had missed his strength, his male presence at night. But inwardly she scolded herself. Amara was a capable woman. She was not in the habit of allowing anything, or anyone, to frighten her. Still, she liked it when he pulled her close and led her inside.

They ordered risotto and stuffed mushrooms to go with the light German beer they were drinking. Joe had an entire menu based on beer from around the globe. He had such a wide variety of foods it was difficult to choose, but the risotto was one of the best she had ever tasted, and the mushrooms rivaled her own. They sat in a quiet booth, and looked into each other's eyes, while they savored their dinner. Joe's was relatively new, but it had been an immediate success. He had good taste in background music, and his patrons could request the ambience they wanted by simply indicating which room they preferred.

Daniel said something amusing and Amara laughed, making the man sitting alone in the shadows cringe. He hated that laugh. He used to think it was musical, but now he found it mocking. Did they know he was sitting there? Was she laughing at him? He would wring her neck if she was laughing at him. He would take her in every single way he had fantasized about. And then, he would slip a silk stocking around her throat from behind, and mount her in that very same moment. He licked his lips at the thought. It was far more fun when he imagined punishing her. He would make commands, and she would do exactly as she was told. It would be fun to string it out. He had a lot of patience when it came to someone special. And Amara was special. He had been waiting for her for a long time. It couldn't end too quickly. No, he might even release the stocking just in time, tie her to the bed, and start all over again. Yes, that could go on indefinitely.

His arm bumped the beer bottle on the table, and it almost toppled over. He had gotten so carried away that he had opened his pants, and was fondling himself. He was glad he had chosen a darkened corner of the room. Grateful, too, that he had caught the beer before it spilled all over his clothing. That would have been humiliating. He would never let a woman humiliate him again! *She* had done enough of that already. Soon it would be his turn. He stuffed the pair of hot pink panties back into his pocket where they belonged. He hadn't been able to resist the scent of them. He looked around just in case someone had seen him. Everything was as it should be. The room was still. He put his middle finger into his mouth and suckled it, working it in and out, until he felt himself explode again. Amara would be doing that

for him soon; very soon. He withdrew the panties he carried with him, and mopped himself dry. Now their scents were mingled. He had made them one.

They kissed when they reached Amara's vehicle, "Do you want to come home with me?" she asked in a husky voice.

"Oh, yeah," Daniel smiled into her eyes, "Why don't you go on, and I'll follow you?" he said.

"That works," she whispered, sounding pleased.

They drove off in the direction of Yountsville, with Amara a car length ahead. She glanced back in her rearview mirror, too happy not to grin. A siren sounded a few seconds later. Amara glanced back a second time to see Daniel being pulled over. She frowned, and pulled her car over to the side of the road as well. "What is this about?" she asked in indignation.

Sheriff Wheeler slanted a look in her direction, "Couldn't help but notice Mr. Collins here was going a little too fast," he drawled. His burr was thicker than usual.

"That's nonsense, and you know it, Grant," she said hotly.

"Amara, don't," Daniel said steadily, "Let me handle this."

"Just doing my job," Grant muttered. "He was over the limit, and I know he's been drinking," Sheriff Wheeler looked smug.

Amara was so irritated, she blurted without thinking, "Not as much as me. Or you, for that matter."

"Is that so?" Grant squinted at her, and she felt herself blush. He was angry, and he had been drinking. "Well, well, well, aren't you the smarty-pants?"

"I'm sorry, Sheriff," Daniel answered for her. "She just got carried away, that's all. You didn't mean anything, did you, Amara?" he looked straight at her, and Amara realized she needed to back down.

"No, I didn't mean anything at all," she responded quickly.

Grant appeared to reconsider the situation. He stared hard at Amara, laughed at something beneath his breath, and straightened to his full height. "Well, all right then," he said, "I guess I can overlook it this one time. But don't let me catch you two at it again," he warned. "You head on home, Amara," he said as he climbed back into the county car.

Amara reached out to Nonie on several consecutive nights. She was worried sick about Crow. But each time she called, her voice came back empty and alone. She had not been able to make the connection with Awinita either, not from the house, nor even from the water. With each passing day, Amara became a bit more distracted, and far more withdrawn. She picked at her food, too upset to eat. What was wrong? What had happened to Crow? She had been so sure Nonie's magic would save him. What if he had died because of her? What if it was a permanent death that could not span time and what about the fate of Caroline and the others? Amara was at a loss as to what to do. It was Daniel who made the connection.

CHAPTER THIRTY

"You need to talk to the Elders," he told her. "You've been talking about that since we met."

"I have been thinking on it," she nodded solemnly. "I have fallen out of touch since Grandfather's death."

"Maybe it's time you remedied that?"

"You're right," she concurred. "The Blood Moon tells the tale of the Cherokee Nation, and how it became divided in the 1830's, when the people were forced from their ancestral homes in Georgia, and the Southeastern parts of the United States. They were required to resettle in the territory west of the Mississippi, in what became known as The Trail of Tears. Awinita's mother, Gola, lived through that time. Most of Awinita's family was run out of the state of Georgia," she paused, "There is a Blood Moon in two weeks."

"Is there some way you can connect with Awinita through the moon ritual?"

"I don't know. Grandfather had many friends from the old days," Amara said thoughtfully. "I could reach out to them. They are not so very far away," she said excitedly. It was the first display of positive emotion she had shown in a long while.

"The main thing is to reconnect, isn't it?" he queried, "So that you can communicate with Crow?"

"Yes, Crow is Gola's son, and Awinita's brother," she said thoughtfully, "and I am one with Awinita. So Crow is my brother too."

Daniel looked relieved, and Amara perceived that although she had only voiced part of what had happened in her last journey, Daniel had probably guessed the rest, or at least some of it. He looked Amara in the eyes when he offered his support.

"You already are a huge help," she grinned at him. "I have been so worried, I could not think straight. I will get in touch with my grandfather's friends immediately."

Grandfather's people were due to arrive. The Blood Moon was upon them, and Amara had welcomed them to her property. They had asked her to fast, and she had eagerly complied. She had also set aside an hour each night to speak specifically to her grandfather, asking him for guidance. She gradually began to feel his energy building, gaining strength. Soon she felt his immense presence more strongly than if he was in the physical realm. And while she relished his scent and welcomed him home, she didn't miss the multifaceted display of faces flickering over his features like a movie projector. Amara now knew she was on the right track. She had regained confidence in herself, and Grandfather was here to guide her if she stumbled because he had his wise and well ancestors to lead him.

She spent her time creating festive dishes, knowing her guests would honor the fact that she was a vegetarian. She would serve all the traditional fall cuisine in a colorful array of corn, potatoes, squash, and eggplant. She made flatbreads, cornbreads, and sunflower seed cakes, until the house held the aroma of the season. She baked pumpkin pie, and pureed sweet potato soup. She swept out the house, cleared the clutter, and filled the place with colorful mats and Indian corn. She made homemade cider and herbal tea blends that would enhance the occasion. At last, she was ready to greet them.

"Maybe I should stay at my place for a while?" Daniel offered, and Amara grasped for the first time that he might feel awkward.

"You are with me, are you not?" she asked almost shyly. "You are more than welcome to stay. The people will know we are a couple as soon as they see us together. It would be wrong for us to pretend otherwise."

Daniel nodded once, and said, "Wrong as in an insult?"

Amara smiled with her eyes, and the matter was settled. "I would be honored to stay," he laughed down at her, and she hugged him close.

She was still smiling when her guests arrived. She met them out front with Daniel beside her. "Tom Long Feather, this is Daniel," she introduced the Elder first. Tom was Grandfather's peer. The two had attended school together. Tom sized Daniel up in one quick assessment.

"I am proud to know you," he told Daniel sincerely.

"And this is Sam," she continued, her eyes alive as she gave Sam a swift hug. "Sam is Tom's son, and my childhood friend. I'm afraid I had quite a crush on him back in the day."

Sam shook hands with Daniel, and Daniel took note of the glimmer in the depths of the black eyes regarding him. Though he appeared friendly enough, Daniel was fully aware of his scrutiny. "Amara followed me everywhere when we were children," Sam acknowledged, "I called her *My Shadow*." The timbre of his voice told Daniel more clearly than words ever could that Sam would be watching. His interest in Amara was certainly not reserved for the old days.

Amara feigned ignorance of any conflict among the men, and made the last of the introductions, "And this is Leon and Anna," she said. Leon was tall and muscular much like Sam, and Anna was part Hispanic. She was as little as her spouse was large. She had beautiful liquid brown eyes in a kind, round face. Anna and Amara broke into easy conversation. Soon Amara had everyone seated and comfortable with a beverage in hand. It was funny how after all the fuss and worry, it seemed like only yesterday when she had last seen her friends. They were good and caring people, and Amara set a place for Grandfather among them.

They became reacquainted over the next couple of days. Anna helped Amara in the kitchen while the men talked and shared a pipe. Amara asked Anna what she would be wearing, and Anna showed her the dress she had made of softened buckskin. It sported colorful beads and silver conches. The beadwork was elaborate, and Amara praised her for the fine work she had done. It was perfect for the pretty little Hispanic woman with the beautiful eyes. Amara openly admired her handiwork, commenting on her own lack of talent.

"My mother, Alina, made her ceremonial dress," Amara offered shyly. "I had my own miniature version," she laughed. "I stored them away in the event that I may one day have a

daughter. Here, I will show you," Amara lifted the tiny duplicate of her mother's dress from the cedar chest, and showed it to a beaming Anna.

"Oh, it is precious!" Anna clapped her hands in joy. The dress was small enough to have belonged to a doll.

"I plan to wear my mother's dress," Amara announced.

"Let's take a look at it," Anna suggested. "Have you tried it on? I can help you with the measurements if you'd like?"

"Oh, would you?" Amara's eyes lit up, "It is a beautiful garment, but I am taller than my mother, and not quite the same proportions." She carefully lifted her mother's costume from its place in the chest, and gently shook it out. It smelled of lilacs.

Anna was delighted with the work Alina had put into the frock. "It is a piece of art," she told Amara, "and one that deserves to be perfectly displayed. It will be a simple matter to adjust the fit," she said seriously. "We can have this ready in no time."

Amara hugged Anna with emotion. "I am so excited," she confessed, "I have worried over this to no avail. I am no seamstress. Thank you so much for this kindness, Anna."

"It is my pleasure," Anna assured as she completed the task that same evening, "I think you will find this acceptable," she spoke shyly as she returned the garment and watched as Amara slipped it over her head.

Anna's eyes were shining as she looked upon Amara where she stood before the beveled mirror. "You are beautiful!" she breathed.

"And you are incredibly gifted! I cannot fathom how

you worked such wonders!" Amara twirled before the dressing glass, and they both laughed, "Thank you, my friend."

Anna's face was flushed with pride, and Amara knew that the other girl was honored to have repaid her hostess for her hospitality. Her voice was heartfelt when she whispered, "I only made the adjustments. It is your beauty that makes it shine."

When the full moon peaked both girls took special care with their appearance. Amara smoothed the silver bells on Anna's costume, while Anna combed Amara's multiple layers of fringe. The men were busily setting up in the back meadow where they could safely have a campfire near the woods and water. There would be a drum circle, and each man would have his own instrument. Tom would lead the circle with his kettle drum. He had looked ahead and brought ancillary hand drums, both double and single headed, as well as rattles and shakers in the event that Amara might have friends who would want to attend. They would keep the circle going for two consecutive nights.

The Blood Moon ceremony was something to behold. Nikki and Gregory were thrilled to be a part of the group. Cynthia arrived with Todd, and Linda with Ian. They were all finely attired, and intrigued with the cultural exchange. Sam and Leon were seated on either side of Tom. The rest of the men chose a drum, and entered the circle. Since this was not an official powwow, the women were allowed to join in as desired. Cynthia chose a rattle, and Linda a tabla. The rattles were made of rawhide or leather, and filled with corn or beans. The tabla was a twin hand drum. Linda was a proficient drummer, having played for years, and took great joy in joining the circle. Nikki held a mallet in one hand, and an idiophone in the other. She joined Anna and Amara in dance.

Tom's voice was strong and sure as he led the vocals. His words were clearly enunciated. Sam and Leon joined in with modulated syllables that rose and fell in harmony with Tom. Their voices filled the night as the other men quietly chanted along with them. As the women danced, the conical bells that embellished Anna's costume jingled. Amara gave herself up to the beat of the drum, rejoicing in the stability it provided between heaven and earth. Nothing mattered now except the spirituality of the moment, the connection with Unetlanvhi, the Great Spirit. The beat carried them. It addressed Lune, otherwise known as Nvda. And in this connection the two hemispheres of the brain exhibited balance and harmony.

Tom kept the heartbeat going, and when Amara felt compelled to ease from the dance, she moved gracefully to stand behind him at the kettle drum. She played a lovely solo on a hand-carved flute, then holding it before her she began to hum along with the men. Her position never altered as she remained respectfully behind Tom. But her voice, which had begun as a quiet melody, built in volume and swelled with emotion. Daniel looked up in surprise. He had never heard her sing before. Her voice was pure and sweet, yet it carried strength and beauty as it rose above the voices of the men. Everyone had become one with the night, magically allied with Spirit.

Negative energies were released and gently transmuted in the light, giving birth to a healthy effervescence. The group's spirits were uplifted. There was an abundance of food and drink. An aromatic smoke rose from the campfire to merge with that of the pipe. Every single mood was euphoric as each person relaxed into a world of unity and spirituality. They took breaks as needed, sometimes switching instruments, or joining in on the dance.

At some point, Daniel respectfully receded from the group in an effort to photograph the circle. The fire was bright, and Daniel was competent at his craft. He noticed that Amara appeared to be experiencing something the others were not, and that in the density of the tree line behind her stood a man in black. He was Native American, and he was partially transparent. Daniel prayed that he had managed to capture the image, and by the time he had finished, he had decided to develop the pictures immediately.

Amara was caught between worlds. When she saw Awinita they embraced, merged, and then separated with aplomb. Next, she spotted Nonie in the fog beyond, and at midpoint between the two, she spied her brother. Crow was solid, yet fluid. Awinita called out to Nonie, but her words were muffled. Yet when Nonie whispered from the shadows, her voice was strong and vibrant. Amara was mesmerized. She gave a sharp affirmative nod. Crow was alive, but he was ill. And this was a *Calling*. Amara was forever a part of Awinita, just as she was strongly linked to Crow. But he was more than a brother to her, he was a blood brother. He held a part of her soul, and she did the same for him. And in that instant Amara realized what she must do.

By the end of the evening, everyone was ready to call it a night. Amara walked trancelike to the house, automatically seeking her bed. When the sun rose they gathered to break the fast, and though Amara served her guests, it was obvious that she was preoccupied. She spent the afternoon conversing with Tom who gave the occasional nod, but otherwise remained quiescent. Amara surmised that Tom must have seen everything in his long life because nothing appeared to shock him. He was respectful in the way he kept her counsel, and at one point he looked up to his right and nodded, and Amara realized he was listening to a beloved manifestation. When she inquired about the matter, he told her that his dear friend

James Asher had been guided to join them. Amara straightened her spine, and stared at the space beyond Tom's right shoulder. Tears filled her eyes when she whispered, "Hello Grandfather!"

When evening fell Amara was more than ready to return to the circle. Her senses were heightened; her perception honed. The events played out much like the night before with everything coming in and out of focus. Amara had no doubt that she was preparing for a journey, and that aside from the fact her brother needed her, she was also determined to see the Roswell women to safety.

Earlier that day, Anna had used Amara's stall on the highway to sell her wares. She had beautiful handmade jewelry and woven blankets. Amara selected a graphic blanket and soft shawl for the winter. She paid Anna with a mixture of cash and medicinal, knowing that natural cures were coveted and sometimes difficult to obtain, especially those that worked at soul level. Anna took the medicinal appreciatively, but handed back the cash. She said, "I was given that you would need the money. But you must go to Tom as the Elder of the group. There is something he is to handle for you."

Amara thanked her as her fingers curled around the cash. A sensation sizzled down her spine, and without thought she reached up to grasp her fire opal only to find it missing! When did she lose her pendant? Her vision blurred with unshed tears. That necklace was a significant tie to her mother. It was the last gift Alina had given her before she departed this world.

Amara went to Tom as directed, and without a glance at the amount of cash she handed over, Tom gave her the exact sum total in coin. Amara studied each piece in surprise. They were dated 1864. Each and every one of them!

As the hour grew late, and Amara rejoined the dance, she paused to look at Daniel. Their eyes locked, and Amara thought he looked worried. And then he nodded as if to say goodbye, and Amara understood that he already knew she was leaving again. She attempted a reassuring smile, and he grinned back in the sweetest way. Amara took courage from that look. And Tom Long Feather observed them in silence.

That night Amara tucked the coins from 1864 into a drawstring bag which she slipped around her wrist. Wrapped in the warm blanket she had purchased from Anna, she raised her arms to the heavens, and disappeared from the grounds. She literally faded right before Daniel's eyes! Tom stood behind him, and Nikki approached, camera in hand, and caught the shot Daniel had been too grief-stricken to shoot. Her eyes glittered with unshed tears. There was no guarantee that Amara would be back. When Amara's physical body vanished from sight, the only thing that remained was the patterned blanket. Nikki stooped to pick it up. She smoothed it with care, folding it as she did so, and handed it to Daniel. Tom laid a reassuring hand on his shoulder, murmuring something in the Iroquoian language. Daniel sat out in the woods alone for the remainder of the night. His grip was tight on the blanket.

CHAPTER THIRTY-ONE

Awinita hustled everyone onto the train, holding tight to Caroline who was too frail to manage on her own. Chloe didn't need to be told to stand fast. She had no intention of losing track of her mother ever again. Even as Awinita told Ellen to look after the newcomers, she thrust the bag of coin into Mary Ann's loyal hand. "This is for food. I know you will get the best bargains to be had," she said succinctly. Her gaze lingered momentarily on both women, "I trust you two to look after the others. Please take special care of Caroline. I will follow the tracks, and catch up with you as soon as possible."

"But, where are you going?" Mary Ann's voice quavered just as Ellen looked over her shoulder at Awinita, her fine brows arched. "You can't go back. They will kill you!"

"Do as I say," Awinita hissed as the engineer blew the whistle, "and stay at the station in Indianapolis. I will find you there. And remember to take care of each other!" With that, Awinita jumped off the steps, and hit the ground running. She glanced back only once to see her friends securely onboard. Mary Ann's mouth was open in a perfect O, while

Ellen's nose was pressed against the glass. These were common expressions for both of them as Mary was accustomed to taking orders, and poor Ellen frequently found herself squinting in an effort to improve her vision. It was a whole lot harder leaving them behind than she ever would have imagined. They had become an integral part of her life, and she vowed to find them once Crow was safe. Nonie could not reach him, and Awinita would find out why.

"I would know why you cannot come with me?" Awinita faced Nonie with a tenuous scowl. She was at the cave, and knew that her stint here would not cost her.

Nonie gave her a wounded look, her large deep-set blue eyes shone like twin pools. "Do you question my honor?" she asked softly, but her body was rigid with tension.

"No, I simply do not understand. Surely, you can aid me?"

"Of course," Nonie sighed, and her earrings tinkled like wind chimes, "But I must do so from a distance." When Awinita refused to respond, Nonie continued in a guarded voice, "I cannot approach Crow directly. The dark one cursed me long ago. My strength is at its peak in the caves."

"But you are my teacher, and a magnificent healer," Awinita protested.

"I am an aspect of Gola," Nonie explained. She disliked being interrogated, and saw it as a form of disrespect.

"And I am an aspect of Amara, as Amara is an aspect of me."

"Exactly," Nonie started to turn away, but Awinita would have none of it. Her frown deepened until Nonie silenced her with a look. She laid a slim hand on the other's shoulder, and Awinita felt the energy course all the way through her entire body. It was enough to still her tongue, but Nonie graced her with an answer all the same. "I will be backing you all the while, just as Amara will be transferring much of the energy. She is a natural, thus you have all the help you need."

Awinita allowed the energy to fill her, but argued the wisdom of Nonie staying behind. It made no sense. Nonie saw her doubt, and sighed, "The dark one raped me long ago, just as he raped you," she said heavily. "It is often wise not to speak of such matters as they can bog one down. He claimed a part of you, which in turn, weakened your protective walls, and therefore lowered your defenses."

Awinita was truly shocked. After a moment she said, "Amara remembers the rape. Therefore, she too, is his victim."

"No," Nonie was shaking her head of golden curls, "She experienced the rape from your perspective. She was in shock and felt the repercussions, but she was not personally assaulted. That is a part of what we must stop."

Awinita sucked in her breath. She hadn't realized the possibility, and it came as a blow to her solar plexus. Nonie shivered delicately, "Amara will soon know this in her lifetime if we do not act soon. Likewise, Crow will be defeated at the hands of his father. *He* carries nothing but hatred for the both of them. Amara has eluded him, and Crow did not grow up in his image."

"I'll leave at once," Awinita was embarrassed she had questioned Nonie's integrity.

"You are excused," Nonie had read her mind. "My energy, and Amara's, will go with you. Remember, many of us are multiple souls," her voice had gentled even as she verified Awinita's earlier thought, "The caves know no time so you have lost nothing."

Awinita silently circled the campsite. She noticed a man with an eye patch, and recognized him from the battle. He was the one Crow had maimed. Now the man sat near her father where the evil one conversed with a group of Mexicans. Honor among thieves, she thought. They were a rowdy bunch, drunk on whiskey, and bragging about the fine purchases they had acquired. Awinita had picked up enough Spanish to understand the gist of the conversation.

Her eyes darted to the covered wagons that were located on the far side of the fire, and suddenly everything clicked into place. These conveyances housed the missing women! She was certain of it. She had rescued only twelve, and had wondered how they could have lost so many! Now, as she examined the prairie schooners, she was beginning to understand. Her gaze wandered to the tree line beyond. And that's where she found Crow.

He was in human form, and tied to one of the trees! His straight black hair hung limp like his body. She could see, even from this distance, how badly he'd been abused. Awinita moved soundlessly, stealthy as a shadow. She held one slim finger to her lips as she peered first into one wagon, and then another. Several heads moved in tandem as they swiveled in her direction. Tears pricked the backs of her lids. The wagons were so tightly packed, the occupants could scarcely move. So many women bound and gagged! They were a cluster of tangled skirts and frightened faces.

Awinita assessed the situation. The men were careless in their drunkenness. There was no guard on duty. Instead, they had chosen to leave the females bound in much the same way the horses were tethered. In this case, male ego would be their downfall. Awinita's mouth stretched into a grim smile. They were sitting ducks, she decided as she took a quick inventory. There were as many as thirty horses, all of which were no doubt stolen, yet there were no more than a dozen men. And every last one of them was inebriated.

Nearby was a pile of munitions, which she discreetly transferred to a different location. While she worked, she spied a number of rifles propped along the length of one of the wagons. Awinita recognized them as contraband, and took pleasure in removing them from their convenient locale. What rich irony!

She returned to the front of the wagons, and slashed the bonds of the first two women, signaling them to remain silent. She then motioned them to free those trapped behind them, before clearing the space themselves. As each dropped quietly to the ground, they grabbed a gun from the stack that was awaiting them. Each individual took her training seriously. They understood it was imperative to move as one large body. The first wagon was empty, and the women were in position by the time Awinita cleared the second.

She moved on to Crow, pleased to discover that he was not as weak as she had feared. She applied energy with one hand even as she slit the ropes with the other. This gave him the strength he needed to stand on his own two feet. She escalated the energy in a burst that surged like a bolt of lightning, and he jumped to arms more quickly than she could have anticipated! All guns were now trained on the circle of men who were shocked by what was taking place right under their very noses.

Crow's war cry sliced the night. It resonated off the density of the forest, sending chills down the spine of the most seasoned soldier. Crow squeezed off a round as Awinita released her blade, at the same time positioning her rifle. The knife landed square in the heart of the one-eyed man. Her bullet took out the marauder seated next to her father. She grimaced as *he* moved to save himself whilst her troops bombarded the enemy with rifle fire. The Mexicans made a bold attempt to return fire, but their reflexes were dulled. They died in a pool of blood and vomit. The women continued to blast away until every man was down, later kicking their guns aside to make sure they were dead. There were no survivors. The rear rank of female soldiers dropped back to take charge of the horses during an evaluation of their own troops. There were two wounded, and two casualties. But to Awinita's horror, there was no trace of her father. The bastard had managed to escape.

Time was of an essence as they must reach Indianapolis as quickly as possible. Yet in Awinita's mind, Crow's health must be restored in order for him to travel the distance to the caves. He went along with his sister's mothering only to a degree, and only because he knew they were safe enough for a spell. They moved camp a few miles north, leaving their enemies lie. These men deserved no graves.

They each selected a mount, and carried what was needed. Awinita had taken stock of the camp, and was glad to find there were plenty of provisions. Only the captives had gone hungry, it seemed. A good night's sleep would prove beneficial. Therefore Awinita divided the troops into categories, allowing everyone some rest. There was a detail for burials, and another to aid the injured. Guards had been assigned to take rotating shifts. Cook was among the survivors, so Awinita allowed her to summon her assistants, and take charge of the food. No one would leave here without supplies of their own, and everyone was congratulated for their courage. Crow smiled down at his sister. He didn't say a word, he didn't have to. His eyes shone with pride.

When they set out the next day, there were twenty-seven women including Awinita. They had lost three. Aside from the two casualties, one of the injured succumbed to her wounds. The others were in good enough condition to travel. They were a bedraggled lot, but they were grateful to be alive, and willing to carry their share of the burden. Awinita had marked her trail well, and the part of her that was Amara had a natural sense of direction as true as her own. Plus, the Amara facet had the benefit of knowing Indianapolis, albeit in a different era. It was beginning to occur to both of them that they were more than aspects of the other. Awinita now knew, and Amara wondered, if it was possible for one to house multiple souls.

When they came to a fork in the road, Crow headed home to the caves. Awinita watched him go with a sense of gratification. She had come to love this brother of hers, and would miss him immensely. But she was now able to peer ahead, and see that he would be fine. "Tell Nonie I will be in touch," she called after him, "And take care of yourself!"

She could have sworn she heard a chuckle as he leaned into his mare, and disappeared in a funnel of dust. Awinita straightened her back, and led her troops onward to Indianapolis. It was a lengthy ride, but they had an abundance of food and water, and were well protected from the elements, thanks to the canvas they had dissevered from the prairie schooners.

They kept a steady tempo, pushing the horses only when necessary. Awinita found the train station without difficulty, and was rewarded by numerous cries of joy. It was a relief to see that her original group was intact. Even from a distance she spotted Caroline's yellow hair. Chloe stayed close to her mother, and it was obvious that Mary Ann had befriended the newcomers. Ellen came running to meet them, she was that excited. A smile curled the corners of Awinita's lips as she pulled Ellen into a strong embrace before greeting the others.

They camped near the tracks that night, marking their whereabouts with care. "We have horses enough to get us the rest of the way, "Awinita said proudly. "Mary Ann, you have done well with the coin. Everyone looks well fed."

Mary Ann beamed at the praise. She knew they were a scrawny bunch. But they were well rested and gaining strength every day. She nodded in answer.

Caroline looked at Awinita with gratitude, "You saved my life," she breathed, "Mine and Chloe's."

"I am grateful for your life," Awinita assured her, "It is precious to me."

"Mary Ann tells me you no longer hold your most prized possession," tears welled in Caroline's sky-blue eyes. Awinita had secretly shown her the fire opal when they lived together in Roswell. It was just a ghost of a memory, and yet Awinita knew after all that had occurred, it was seared in the other's mind.

"What good are possessions without family, my sister," Awinita smiled again, and her teeth flashed in the dark of night, "It will return to me someday," she added in confidence.

It was a happy reunion for all. They were granted a clear night, and were comfortable against the chill. Cook hosted a fine meal. They had become a tight unit, intent on looking after one another. These women had become ripened soldiers.

"We must get some sleep. We head out at dawn," Awinita spoke clearly once everyone had eaten. "There are mills up here where we can work until those of you who wish to marry find men." Everyone laughed at her announcement.

"How will we know where to look for these mills?" someone called out.

"How will we know where to look for the men?" another joked, and everyone chuckled.

"I have been doing some research," Awinita replied, and the women stilled. "There are mills at Connelton," she said evenly, "But..." Awinita drew out her announcement, "they will not take us." She had anticipated their excitement. "It would be a waste of our time."

"How do you know this?" someone asked. By now everyone knew Connelton was the nearest worksite. It was certainly the most talked about.

"Others have been turned away. And now those mills have closed. When they reopen they will want Indiana women," she said with certainty, and the crowd moaned.

"Where will we go?" they chorused.

"Yountsville," Awinita announced, and again everyone gasped. "There is a town called Attica that is situated north of Yountsville. A pair of brothers built mills there, but these mills failed for lack of water. The family's name was Yount. They came from far away, and when the first mills were unsuccessful, they built more. These new mills thrived, and the town was dubbed Yountsville. We will go there." Everyone spoke at once. Awinita allowed this for a time as she sat back grinning. It was good to see her friends happy.

Eventually someone asked, "Will they take us?" It was Ellen's shy voice that rose above the crowd.

"I feel positive," Awinita stated calmly. There was a suspended moment in time when no one made a peep. All eyes were on Awinita. She knew they were wondering how she could be so sure of herself. She held her ground, and the instant of doubt was gone as quickly as it had occurred. The women broke into excited conversation. She had long ago earned their trust.

CHAPTER THIRTY-TWO

Amara shivered and reached for a blanket, causing her to collide with a solid male body. The man groaned bringing her instantly awake. It was Daniel lying next to her with a death grip on the Indian blanket she had purchased from Anna. They were in the back meadow of her land at Yountsville. Amara's head spun for a sickening moment before she whispered, "Daniel, I'm home."

Daniel was so relieved to see her that he wrapped her in a bear hug. She clung to him, breathing deeply of his clean earthen scent, vowing she would never let him go. He didn't release her for several minutes. "I was afraid I had lost you for good," he said in a ragged voice.

"I'm sorry, my love," she smoothed his hair away from his face, "I would have warned you if I could."

He kissed her deeply while they held each other, sharing a quiet conversation before returning to the house. The sun was overhead when they arrived to find that everyone had gathered in the front room. Grim met them at the door, his long tail thumping animatedly. Tom Long Feather stood stock-still when she entered. He looked her over, nodded once, and the eyes that had been so serious only a second before crinkled at the corners. He laughed and clapped her on the back, and Amara broke into a wide smile.

Anna launched herself into Amara's arms while everyone gathered close. Sam and Leon had been talking with Gregory in the background where an anxious Nikki stood quietly conversing with Linda and Cynthia. She held a squirming Solomon in her fine-boned hands. Cynthia cradled Sampson like a sack of potatoes, and Linda jumped from one to the other in an effort to lend support. Ian looked uncomfortable where he stood talking to Todd. Todd nodded toward Amara as she walked in, and Ian glanced up with a curious expression. Amara wondered if she had become overly paranoid, or if the two of them were up to something. No one really knew Todd all that well, and Ian had always been the quiet type. He shot her a grin, but his features appeared strained.

Both Sampson and Solomon sprang free in unison and scurried to greet her. Nikki heaved an audible sigh of relief as all three girls clustered round. Linda automatically burst into tears. She was the sensitive type. She wiped her eyes, pushing up her wire rim glasses, before hurling herself at Amara. The gang had obviously been discussing her disappearance.

Amara stooped to plant a kiss on top of Grim's big head, even as Solomon thoroughly washed her face with kisses. He clung to her with both front paws wrapped around her arms, his bright eyes alive with excitement. Sampson kissed her toes, and wound figure eights between her legs, and Amara giggled with pure joy. "Hi *Yardstick!*" she cried as she scratched his ears before scooping Solomon into her arms, "How are you, *Little Toes?*" she giggled as she hugged the miniature pup. She had gifted him with the Indian name after the arrival of her indigenous friends. *Yardstick* purred loudly as his tufted toes spanned her waist. *Little Toes* hic-

cupped, and hid his face. It was good to be home.

A quick glance at the room told her that Tom and the others were already packed. They obviously weren't leaving without a farewell, but had been patiently awaiting her return. The air was stagnant with unreleased tension. Tom spoke for the group of Native Americans when he said they should to be on their way now that she was home safe. Sam's eyes lit with pleasure as he stared at her unique beauty. He had a way of gazing deep into her soul as if he saw something that others did not, and Amara blushed at his close scrutiny. Leon smiled, and Anna simply couldn't stop beaming.

"Do you have time to join us in breaking the fast?" Nikki asked politely. "I have corncakes and sweet potatoes warmed and ready, and a black bean frittata in the oven. There's plenty of hot coffee and spiced apple cider. I can have it ready in minutes."

"Sounds good," Tom exclaimed with a grin, and the tension dissipated as though it never existed, "I guess we can linger a while longer."

Sam, Leon, and Anna nodded in unison. Their appetites were back now that Amara was home. "I'll admit that I'm starving!" Sam announced, and they all followed Nikki into the kitchen. She had a stack of plates and utensils at the ready. She pulled the quiche from the oven, uncovered the remainder of the food, and began pouring coffee. There was a bowl of mixed berries on the table. She placed a pitcher of fresh cream next to them. "Grab a plate, everyone," she sang out, "and dig in!"

It was a pleasant gathering after such an intense weekend. Everyone broke into easy banter, while Amara hurried to Nikki's assistance. She was grateful to her friends for taking care of things. Nikki flashed a reassuring smile, while Cynthia smoothly mopped up the countertops. Linda fed the fur babies, knowing that Amara would pause to do so if someone else didn't beat her to the punch. Amara grinned at her, and mouthed the words, *Thank You.*

Just as she was about to seat herself, Amara felt a frisson of fear tingle the base of her spine. *That is your root chakra.* It was Nonie's voice guiding her. *It not only grounds you, but holds much of your childhood within its depths. Feel that twinge in your heart? Listen to your gut.*

Amara straightened and glanced at the clock in the same instant that she noticed the punch to her solar plexus. *Tap head, heart, gut,* Nonie instructed for her ears alone, *Head, heart, gut...* The clock read 12:10, and Amara wondered if life would ever be *normal* again, whatever that was. Tom Long Feather's head swiveled in her direction when she deftly corrected the hands of the clock. Though her actions were subtle, Tom's obsidian gaze caught hers, and she felt him willing her to be calm. Amara took enormous comfort in the gesture. She nodded with renewed strength and sat down to eat.

"I will miss you, My Shadow," Sam whispered, as Amara gave him a quick kiss on the cheek. Leon and Anna closed in for a hug, with Anna squeezing her hand before walking away. Tom was the last to approach, and stood apart from the others. His position was revered. "I am never far away," he said emphatically. "You call if you are in need. Do not hesitate."

Amara's head dropped as her eyes filled with tears. Tom lifted her chin with one finger, and waited. Amara gathered her armor about her, and said in a steady voice, "You have my word."

"We are family, little one," he said in a warm tone, "Your grandfather and I were blood brothers. I will see you at the Spring Festival." It was a promise of better things to come. "Until then, I will be watching." With that, Tom too, disappeared into the vehicle. Everyone waved as they drove away.

The couple enjoyed a peaceful evening. It was an opportunity to renew their love for each other. They lingered in the woods listening to the sounds of nature. Water babbled downstream, gurgling as it pooled over and around ancient rock formations. The falls roared to life. Birds chirped even as an owl hooted somewhere nearby. The horses whinnied in the distance. There was an occasional plop in the water and the rustling of bare branches overhead. When they stood, there was a crunch of fallen leaves under foot. Neither of them spoke. Instead they held hands and cherished the solitude.

Life returned to normal with the rising of the sun. Daily rituals somehow resumed the regular pace and pattern, regardless of what else might be unfolding. Amara was ready for the playful moments with the fur babies, and treasured last night's romantic episodes with Daniel. She welcomed the earthy work of the greenhouse, and was joyful about toiling in the barn with the horses. She took pleasure in their grooming, and in the antics of the barn cats. She breathed deeply of the aroma of fresh hay, and didn't mind cleaning the grounds. She was prideful of her land.

She had yoga classes to teach, and studies of her own to pursue, while Daniel returned to the book he was writing. He came and went, but stayed at her place more often than not.

He had her over for another piano recital, thrilling Amara all the more with his talent. She wondered if he would ever permanently live with her, and what that would be like. She imagined how amazing his piano would look in her house, and speculated on the changes they could make so that he would feel at home.

Daniel surprised her that evening with flowers from Milligan's. They were a variety of exotic blooms she had been eyeing. He knew that she would take starts for the greenhouse. She was as touched by his thoughtfulness as with the gift itself. They shared a quiet dinner, and retired early. The next day she had a class to teach, and Daniel planned to spend his time in the darkroom at his place. Afterwards, they would grab some dinner in town. Amara looked forward to the treat. Joe's had become their favorite local food establishment.

Daniel left early the following morning, allowing them both time to catch up with their various jobs. Amara had another major sale before the holiday season. People bought all kinds of goodies this time of year. She worked on more medicinal and other popular items before preparing her class. As usual, she dressed appropriately, and carried an easy change of clothing in an oversized bag.

When she arrived at the downtown building she rented, Amara had a queasy feeling in her gut. She parked carefully, looked around with caution before leaving her car, and unlocked the back door. Everything appeared as it should, nothing out of place, nothing out of the ordinary. She had just begun to relax when she glanced at the clock, and saw that it had stopped. It read exactly 12:10. Amara felt her world tilt sidewise, and automatically took a seat.

By the time her students arrived, she had resumed her regular balance, and taught her class with aplomb. No one would have suspected her fear of a short time ago. She smiled and spoke as everyone filed out the door, and then locked up behind them. Amara was totally and completely in charge. She took a few minutes to tidy the room, musing about whether to call Grant or not. She decided against it, and went about changing her clothes. She applied fresh lipstick, shouldered her bag, and walked out the door.

As she pulled out of the lot and onto the street, she was almost struck by the black Chevy that loomed out of nowhere! That darned car had lain in wait. Its lights had apparently been turned off, and its engine had roared to life, and come right at her! She swerved, nearly hitting a parked car on the opposite side of the narrow lane, but managed to right herself just in the nick of time. She was so angry, she saw red. She laid on the horn in an unusual show of temper, and stepped on the gas. Before the Chevy realized that she was on top of it, she had it corralled.

Amara reached into the glove box, and slid her handgun down the back of her pants. Her long, loose blouse obscured the weapon from view. She walked cautiously to the driver's side of the car, ready for anything. It was an act of bravado. But the tinted window didn't budge. There was absolutely no way she would display even a trace of fear. She had too much of the warrior in her. Amara was smart enough to be cautious, but wise enough to be bold. She knocked loudly, stepping slightly to the side, keeping her gun at the ready. Her feet were braced, her body coiled for action. She was fully aware of Awinita's presence. It was as if the two women were allied in every single account of danger. She was, nevertheless, slightly shocked when the driver's door slowly opened and a woman alighted!

The woman looked her in the eye with more than a touch of bitterness. Her mouth curved downward in an ugly frown. Amara was certain she had never seen her before in her life, yet there was something vaguely familiar about her. And this was one angry female who was very much looking for trouble. She raised her chin in a look of pure defiance, and with an attitude that was meant to be insulting, spat in the dirt at Amara's feet.

"You almost hit me," Amara accused in a strong voice. "It was no accident. You did it on purpose." Amara hadn't missed the tight muscle tee shirt and compact frame. The lady in question had a skull tattooed on her muscular bicep that matched the one on her shirt. She had the look of someone from the wrong side of the tracks.

"Huh," the woman snorted as she tossed her lank brown hair. She wore it short, cropped close to her head. It was so greasy Amara couldn't help but wonder if she knew the meaning of the word shampoo. The thought made Amara's lips curl in distain. She caught the look of cold calculation that crossed the hardened features as the woman shifted her weight, at the same time packing a powerful punch to Amara's stomach. But Amara's instincts were on target; she tightened her abs even as she sidestepped the steel-toed boot that would have incapacitated an unsuspecting victim. Amara allowed herself a smirk as her opponent's foot smashed uselessly into the side of the car. When the woman stumbled, Amara wrenched her arm sharply behind her back. *Muscles,* as she now thought of her, breathed fire when the nose of Amara's handgun dug into her side.

"One more smart aleck trick like that," Amara hissed, "and I'll shoot you. You got that? Come on, I dare you."

Muscles continued to stare, refusing to speak, but it was obvious that she wasn't going to back down. Amara gave a sharp twist, wrenching the limb up hard until she heard it crack. Muscles gasped in pain, and sagged against Amara's unyielding form. The warrior in her did not budge. She let

the woman slump to the ground, planting one booted foot atop her, and grinding until she heard the bones crunch. A distinct moan accompanied the sound. "You wanna tell me why?" she asked, but the woman remained mute, staring up at her with pure hatred. There was something odd about that stare, something *off* with the eyes, apart from the small scar that stretched the skin on one side of her face.

"Okay," Amara spoke coldly, her face a brittle mask. She felt Awinita's blood pumping through her as she held the gun trained on the enemy while opening the back door of her Buick where she snatched up a coil of hemp. Muscle's eyes bulged, and Amara realized that she had a prosthetic eye. That's what had been gnawing at her. Still, Amara didn't blink, but proceeded to bind the woman's wrists. She, then, tied her wrists to the wheel of the Chevy, removing the keys from the ignition in one fluid motion, and tossing them into the back seat of the car. "Let's see if you'll talk to the police," she said in a controlled voice, "They're more civilized than I am."

CHAPTER THIRTY-THREE

"Are you sure you're all right?" Daniel asked for the tenth time. Amara had called and informed Daniel that she would be late for dinner. Her voice sounded hollow even to her own ears. It was over an hour later when she walked in and calmly explained what had transpired. He looked at her as if seeing her for the first time when she shrugged away his concern.

"I'm fine," she answered smoothly, as she dipped her spoon into the soup Daniel had ordered for her. She followed with a sip of wine, watching him closely. He seemed unsettled, she thought. Well, she had every right to defend herself. What did he expect?

"Do they know who she is?" he asked.

"No, not yet," she replied, "Grant will be in touch. He will get to the bottom of it, I suspect." It must have seemed strange to Daniel when she told him that she had felt Awinita's presence during the entire altercation. She felt like herself again now though.

"Rhonda Sue Cummings." Amara looked up in surprise.

She hadn't noticed Grant approaching their table, nor had she spotted him when he entered the restaurant. Daniel had; she would bet on it. "Don't know much about her, except that she has a rap sheet a mile long: assault, petty theft, and a couple of B & E's." He pulled out a chair and seated himself next to Amara, "You roughed her up pretty good," he added with a grunt. She couldn't decide if it was an accusation or a compliment, but it sounded like he had gained a measure of respect for her.

"She asked for it," Amara stated.

"Yeah, got a broken arm out of it too," Grant announced.

Daniel whistled, wide-eyed.

"Like I said," Amara said sedately, "she asked for it."

"I wasn't arguing the fact," she thought she heard Grant chuckle, "Just stating the obvious. She attacked you. You had a right to defend yourself. She had a blade at the ready. And I don't think she would have hesitated to use it. The question is why?"

"That's what I'd like to know," she muttered.

"Well, we are holding her for questioning. And you not only have a license to carry, but you were the injured party," Grant had a gleam in his eye. "You turned that around right enough didn't you?"

Amara very deliberately selected a dinner roll from the basket in the center of the table. She slathered it with softened butter, and bit into it with purpose, washing it down with another sip of wine. For all intents and purposes, she looked entirely demure.

It wasn't lost on Amara that this business with Rhonda, who she now thought of as Muscles, had not truly bothered her all that much. It had angered her. That's for sure. But it hadn't really upset her. She realized that Awinita had a lot to do with that, and decided to confront the issue.

She found Awinita at the mill. It no longer seemed strange when she crossed into the other's time frame. It was just as natural as waking up. Someone was singing in the background. The voice was hauntingly familiar. Awinita looked at her with a small smile. Her lips tilted up at one corner, proving her amusement. "Don't you dare laugh at me," Amara exclaimed. "You have no right to *step in*. You can guide, assist, and help me. But you cannot take over."

"Oh, my," Awinita fanned her flushed face. It was a hot day in the mill, and she had only stepped outside upon Amara's arrival. "I see the amusement was lost on you," she emitted a wicked laugh, and Amara scowled.

"You were expecting me, weren't you?" it was a demand, and an irritable one at that.

"Of course," Awinita answered simply, "and I apologize. I suppose I had forgotten that I was playing with your world. And besides..."

"Besides what...?" Amara demanded.

"Besides, you do not understand who Rhonda truly is," she said mysteriously. "If you did, it would make all the difference in the world."

Before Amara could inquire further, Awinita had achromatized, and the mill had returned to its current status.

"Wait!" Amara called after the diminishing figure as she faded into nothingness. "I am not finished! I have some questions for you!"

"So that was Awinita the other night?" Daniel ran his hands through his hair as he contemplated the circumstances. Amara admired his loyalty. She followed his movements with grateful eyes.

"Yes, thank you for understanding," she whispered. "I have occupied her body during battles, Daniel. And now she has occupied mine. I know her pain, and rage, and range of emotions. I have experienced them. But this is new to me."

"You don't know her memories. You don't know who Rhonda is," he nodded to himself as he stated the facts.

"No, I'm not that fully in her head," she admitted. "Only part of me understood the other night. It was like I was watching myself act out, but I was not in charge. I called her on that."

"I get it," he said thoughtfully, "let me show you something." He got up and went to the desk he now claimed for his own use. He pulled out a thick folder that she knew contained his manuscript and with it an overstuffed envelope. She wasn't surprised when he handed her a stack of photos. "Take a look at these," he said, "The first few were the last of the ones taken at the stream the day Awinita first appeared to me. The rest are from the drum circle."

Amara studied the first batch of photographs closely. She was as between worlds as Awinita. The funny thing was that the pendant her mother had given her as a child was barely perceptible around her own throat. But the fire opal now glittered strongly on Awinita. It was as if it had gained new purpose, and with it, a new owner. Amara wiped a tear from her cheek. She hadn't realized she was crying. "Have I changed so very much?" she asked.

"No, Angel," he stroked her hair, "You haven't changed. You are simply in the middle of something you can't completely understand." His touch was so gentle, so reassuring that Amara felt the tears fall in earnest. It was Daniel who wiped them away as he took her into his arms.

Amara had culled enough petals for the sachets she was planning to make. Her herbary had yielded enough to fill an entire shelf at the upcoming market, and the tantalizing array of colors and choices brought her joy. The perfume was so powerful that in spite of all the disturbances in her world, Amara couldn't help but smile. She was happiest amongst the flowers and animals in her life. These were the things that nourished her soul.

Grim sat at her side, her silent companion. He was her constant friend and protector. Her heart swelled with love for him. He looked up and smiled at her as though reading her mind. Amara laughed, a rich sound, "I love you too," she dimpled. "The market is only a few days away, you know," she told him. "We must have everything ready, although I admit I relish the peace it brings most of all. I like the scents, the preparation of the blooms," she qualified as she gingerly fingered several plants before selecting those to pinch off, serenely adding these to the basket on the counter. She would take her choice cuts back to the house to dry, and savor a tranquil evening while Daniel was busy writing.

There was something elusive niggling at the back of her mind that wouldn't leave her alone. That day at the mill, she had wanted to ask Awinita about the significance of 12:10. What was it she was blocking? *Don't you know?* It was Nonie's steady voice. It reverberated all the way through her so strongly that Amara actually jumped. *Look to the past. Awinita could tell you, but she wants YOU to make the connection. REMEMBER!*

Amara caught the staggering recollection so quickly it rushed over her like a flood of ice water! Oh, dear God, how could she have forgotten? She left her wicker carrying case on the counter, and rushed back to the house. She would retrieve it later. She wanted to complete her mission while everything was still fresh. Grim easily kept her pace, and the two hurried into her old bedroom to dig into the treasures of her youth. There, amid the mementos of her childhood, were the newspaper clippings about her mother's demise. The time of death was given as 12:10 in the afternoon.

She carefully smoothed the articles that were a link to her past, and therefore her mother, and was setting them carefully aside when another voice interrupted her private reflections. *See, you didn't need me for this particular riddle. Your mother died at the same precise moment as mine.* It was Awinita's voice, ragged with emotion. *They both drowned. They were murdered.*

Amara looked up in wonder to spy Awinita standing in the doorway. She was solid flesh and blood. And she was soaking wet. Water dripped from her hair and clothing, running in rivulets onto the floor. Her skin was ashen, her eyes sunken as she stood in a puddle of her own making. She was wearing the fire opal, and made no apology for it. She fingered it as she spoke, and the stone came alive. The sparks that flew from it were so starkly visible that they wielded a power of their own. Amara was mesmerized. "Why didn't you tell me?"

"Because you knew all along," came the outrageous remark, "Of course, you had forgotten, but that is how we gain insight. And you need your wits about you now more than ever."

"Why are you so always so darned dramatic?" Amara sounded annoyed, "You are dripping all over everything!"

"I'm not dramatic," Awinita said in a hollow voice, "I'm dead."

"Well, of course you're dead," Amara sounded exasperated when suddenly she stopped ranting, and looked closely at Awinita. She gasped at just how pale her skin really was. For the first time she noticed the emptiness in those hollow eyes, and she began to break into uncontrollable tremors of her own, "How old were you when you died? What year was it?"

Awinita sighed softly, and the air in the room was so frigid Amara could see her own breath. Grim whined, and tucked his tail. He stuck to Amara like glue. Solomon, who had been circling out in the hall, backed away with a whimper. He quickly pursued Sampson who had taken flight immediately upon Awinita's arrival. Everything was just a little off kilter as if the room was tipping sideways. Amara snatched a blanket from the bed, and wrapped it snuggly around her shoulders. She was so cold she was shaking. Awinita's next words made her heart skip a beat. "I was your age precisely. We share the same birthday."

"And the year you died?" Amara swallowed audibly.

"1865," she whispered in a hoarse voice, "At Yountsville. Caroline sang at my service."

Amara slapped a hand over her mouth. Tears were streaming down her face. Her own slim body was wracked with real physical pain. She felt suffocated as if there were invisible hands closing around her throat. "I failed you," she choked, "It's my fault!"

Amara stood there sobbing until the room spun away, and just like that she found herself riding hell bent for leather in the direction of the little town of Yountsville, Indiana. Only she was Awinita, and she was accompanied by her band of female warriors.

"We are nearly out of food," Ellen confided when they stopped for the night. She was sitting on the ground next to Awinita. Her trim, well-toned body was thinner than Awinita remembered, and her stomach growled so loudly it was torturous to hear. "I overheard Cook complaining that there is scarcely enough to go around."

"We'll break into groups and hunt in the early morning hours before we leave again," Awinita replied without pause. She peered into Ellen's myopic gaze, and thought that someday they must find her some glasses. Ellen was never one to complain. But Awinita could see how much she struggled. Everything was made more difficult for her. "We have enough to manage for one more night."

"We have a lot of mouths to feed," Mary Ann approached, "I saw evidence of a small town a few miles away. And we still have some coin. I can go a few more miles this evening," she offered.

Awinita considered her words. "I, too, saw what appeared to be a town," she agreed, "It didn't look like much, but they surely have a general store." The girls waited patiently while Awinita weighed their options. She didn't know exactly why, but she felt a *pull* to this town. "Okay, a handful of us will go," she said at length, "We do need to replenish our provisions. The others can take turns on guard duty while alternately resting. Who's with me?"

"I am," Mary Ann didn't falter.

"Me too," Ellen said evenly.

"Count me in," Caroline was not to be left behind. She had been silently studying them, while keeping an eye on Chloe.

"Chloe can help Cook," Awinita announced, "She has a love for children. We will be back by the time supper is ready. Perhaps we can enhance it? Let's ride."

CHAPTER THIRTY-FOUR

The town was tiny. It was nothing more than a cluster of barns and houses. But it did include a decent general store, post office, and of course a blacksmith, as well as a local sheriff. Mary Ann was as impressed with the selection of groceries as she was adept at negotiation. Her years spent running her husband's business had paid off, and she wouldn't take no for an answer. But Awinita was the obvious leader. Her protectiveness went a long way. No one would have questioned her authority, or missed the way she handled herself.

Awinita experienced hyperesthesia as soon as they entered the General Store, and her head swiveled in the direction of the rear window where she stared at the sign across the street. It was a doctor's office, and she didn't wait long before asking if he was in residence. The store keep said that he was. "He's probably closed for the night," he warned, "But if you knock loudly, he'll hear you. He's not likely to turn you down since you've come a ways."

"Be all right if we pay the bill after we see the doc?" she asked. She didn't miss the worried glances of the other women, but focused solely on the clerk. "We can split up so that we don't waste your time. I know it's late."

The store keep nodded, "I reckon that's all right," he said looking directly into her eyes. "Don't see the harm in it."

"Thank you," Awinita shook his hand before heading for the door. She was sizing him up, and everyone knew it. "Mary Ann, you and Caroline stay here and finish up. Ellen, come with me. We won't be long," she told the others.

Caroline followed her to the door all the while wringing her hands. "Are you all right?" she asked, and Awinita realized she had frightened her.

"Yes, but you're on guard duty. You should be safe enough, but I'll be watching from the window," she nodded across the street. "Stay within sight. Mary Ann can finish gathering the provisions. I'll pay up when I'm done."

Caroline nodded uneasily. She never took her eyes off Awinita as she crossed to the opposite side of the street. She noticed, as Awinita raised one hand to knock, that the other hand hovered ever so subtly above her holster. Ellen looked fidgety even from a distance. She had a nervous disposition, and didn't know what to make of the unexpected stop. They all knew that even when injured, Awinita would do her duty by them. They had great faith in her, but they were worried.

When the doctor opened the door, Awinita tossed a glance over her shoulder. She saw Caroline's perceptive nod, and returned it. "How can I help you ladies?" the doctor asked. He had been fixing himself a bite to eat.

"I noticed your sign," Awinita explained, "while at the General Store. Go ahead and eat, we can wait."

"It'll keep," he responded kindly. "It looks like you've

come a ways."

"We're on the road," Awinita offered. "I noticed you are an optometrist? My friend here," she nodded at Ellen, "has trouble seeing. We won't be staying over, so I know it's a long shot, but I thought it might be worth asking if there's anything you can do?" She didn't add that a voice in her head kept encouraging her.

Ellen jumped at the reference to her own particular problem. She had no idea what Awinita was up to, but she was both touched and embarrassed. No one had ever paid her any attention, leastways not good attention. She looked at Awinita like a long lost puppy that had suddenly been noticed, adopted, and adored.

The man had not missed the exchange. He stroked his chin for a moment while he thought about her question, the whole while glancing from one to the other. "Well, I'd have to examine her," he said at length, "and see what I have in stock."

"Okay," Awinita promptly replied, "We can spare the time if you can?"

The doctor directed the shy young woman into an examination room where he busied himself with lenses, and lights, and a host of questions. Awinita divided her time between the room and the front window. The doctor whose name was Perry was aware of Awinita's vigil. It was obvious to him that she was the responsible party. At long length he finished his calculations, walked with determination to a corner cupboard, and returned with a pair of spectacles. "Let's see what these do for you," he fitted them to Ellen's small face, and bade her read the letters on the viewing screen before her. To her surprise, Ellen could see every single one of them! Her face lit up, her eyes danced, and a gorgeous smile curved her lips! Ellen was a beauty! Dr. Ian Perry grinned broadly.

"How did you happen to have these on hand?" Awinita asked, although she had known he would. "I mean, the prescription is perfect!"

"Some time ago, a young woman ordered these glasses," he replied. "It was all very odd because she didn't even ask for an exam. She merely handed me a prescription, ordered them, and asked me to hold them." He looked directly at Awinita, and continued in a queer voice, "She looked a great deal like you, and she said they were for a friend. She said that I would know when the right person came through the door."

"That is odd," Awinita agreed, wondering how Amara had accomplished such a feat. She heard a tittering sound, and realized that the Amara aspect had joined her.

"Yes, I've never forgotten her," he mused. "She was dressed rather strangely, but otherwise could have been your twin!"

"How much do we owe?" Awinita asked. Mentally, she was calculating the math.

"That's the other thing," the doctor said, "they're already paid for. The lady only said that I should remember to ask you to send me a forwarding address when you get where you are going!" He looked at Ellen with a fond smile, and added almost timidly, "I think I would appreciate that very much."

Ellen blushed for the first time in her life. She liked this man, and had hoped to see him again. Awinita caught the exchange, and promptly gave her word.

The preholiday market went especially well for Amara. People came from far and wide for her tonics and tinctures. Her sachets, dream catchers, and other specialty items were a hit. And her baked goods sold out immediately. She was finished by noon, and the best part was that she had an enormous order for her homemade noodles, carob candies, and jams. She closed the booth with a warm feeling in her solar plexus.

Yoga classes were finished for the season. They would pick up again next spring, and while Amara enjoyed teaching, she was ready for a break. It was the all-inclusive balance that kept her productive. She liked variety, and didn't want to stagnate on any one thing.

Daniel had completed his most current book and was wading through photographs while adding the final touches before sending it off to print. She was proud of his efforts. What he was able to accomplish astounded her. The fact that he could take any topic, no matter how intense, and present it while keeping his subject anonymous, pleased her immensely. He truly was an artist.

With Christmas around the corner, the most special event of all was Nikki and Gregory's upcoming wedding. Amara had accompanied Nikki on dozens of shopping trips aimed at discovering the perfect gown. They had finally stumbled upon it in a small bridal shop in Greencastle. The gown was glorious in its lines with a tiny pinched waist and low-cut bodice. The only thing missing was perhaps some form of adornment. They kicked it around, and then called in the troops. Cynthia took one look, and pronounced, "Seed pearls, it needs seed pearls scattered across the bust. That would make it perfect."

"Do you think they have a seamstress who could add them?" Nikki asked reverently.

"I'll do it!" Linda chimed. "It'll be fun. It can be your wedding gift!"

"Oh, that's marvelous!" Amara clapped her hands. "Let her do it, Nikki. You won't regret it."

"All right," Nikki laughed. "I love the idea of all my closest friends having a hand in the final touches."

And so it was that Linda labored over the delicate details. She was a genius with needle and thread, and sewing was perhaps, her top talent. With her at the helm, the gown would be stunning!

Nikki and Gregory were married at one o'clock on Christmas day. The couple had chosen an outdoor wedding despite the cold. They were blessed with both sunshine and a newly fallen snow, and Nikki stayed warm by wearing a mantle of soft white fur. The extravagant cape was her *something borrowed*, as it belonged to Cynthia. Nikki was the most gorgeous bride Amara had ever seen, and Cynthia had been correct about the seed pearls. Linda's intricate detailing was majestic as the pair stood in the woods among snow laden branches with the waterfalls as a backdrop. Nikki had selected an arrangement of lavender and long-stemmed yellow roses for her bouquet. She wore her newly washed blond hair long and straight with a crown of orange blossoms. An attached veil made her appear mythical, and Gregory couldn't take his eyes off her. Her smoky "Peggy Lipton eyes" were carefully rimmed with charcoal, and her lips were lined with only a hint of color. She was a natural beauty. She carefully allowed the cape to fall from her shoulders when they paused to exchange vows. Amara stepped forward to collect it. The small group of friends gasped in unison at the vision the bride presented, and Daniel caught it all on film.

After the ceremony, Amara and Cynthia served a light lunch of cucumber and watercress finger sandwiches, alongside pecan logs and assorted fruits in lovely lace doilies that set atop the delicate antique dogwood dishes Daniel bought Amara at The Yesterday House in New Albany. Soft jazz filled the front room. Fine Champaign flowed freely. When they raised their fluted glasses to the bride and groom, Daniel remained busily occupied with his camera. Nikki flashed a smile when she revealed the *something blue* as the lace garter from Linda's wedding.

The cake was Amara's creation. It was a masterpiece with triple layers of almond frosting embellished with lifelike leaves and ornate flowers. Everyone applauded as the happy couple drove away with all the trappings of a pair of newlyweds. It had been a glorious day.

Amara and Daniel had settled into the solitude of winter when the New Year arrived with a bang. The small town of Yountsville was in such a remote setting that many of the locals who were firework enthusiasts got a trifle carried away. The couple didn't mind ushering out the old, but opted to stay in for a romantic evening. Amara had planned a special dinner for the two of them that they would share before the rustic little hearth her grandfather had built. It was a practical move on his part, allowing for an alternative method of heat. It had proven beneficial so many times in the past that Amara never failed to keep a cord of wood. She lit some candles and checked on dinner, while Solomon licked his lips and danced across the kitchen on hind legs. Sampson swished his thick plume, swatting with his huge paws as he passed. Grim lay curled in a quiet corner of the room, watching the activities of the others. Only his eyes moved, and Amara laughed at the three of them.

Daniel had run into town to retrieve a few necessities from his place, giving Amara plenty of space to cook. She was listening to Chuck Berry, and enjoying a glass of wine. She had records strewn about the room that reflected her moods of the day. So far Billie Holiday held her captive with an early collection of tunes, while Nina Simone entertained her with her version of I put a spell on you. Amara was enjoying her time alone.

She was shutting off the oven when Daniel called to tell her that he would be a few minutes late. Her lips curved into a smile when she assured him everything would keep. Daniel was never truly late. He was overly conscientious. Amara covered the dishes, knowing he would be home before the food could get cold. She opened another bottle of wine, set the table, and grabbing a jacket, carried the garbage out to the trash bin. Grim followed at her heels.

There was a thrashing in the bushes, and Amara looked up in time to see a fat raccoon disappear from sight. "Karma!" she called, "Is that you?" Amara cupped her hands around her mouth, and called a second time. Feeling dejected, she hung her head, allowing her hands to cover her eyes. She missed the baby she had raised from birth. In that moment, a barrage of fireworks exploded from across the creek. On the tail of the detonation, a heavy silence hung in the air. It was so pronounced that Amara was aware of every nuance of her distorted reality. She smelled the fumes as they drifted across the waters, felt an unnatural spray from the river that could not possibly have reached her, and wrapped her arms around her middle as she struggled to maintain control. She was numb with shock when she recognized that her clothing was damp.

Suddenly, the air was rent by a primal scream that caught Amara off guard. It startled her that the sound could still give her the creeps after all that had transpired. But there was something so horrifying about the cry of the banshee that Amara physically trembled. In her mind's eye she saw Awinita as wet and cold as when she had appeared in her bedroom doorway. She was pale as death, and her eyes were as hollow as the scream of the beast. When Amara had remarked on it, Awinita said in all seriousness that she was dead. Now without full comprehension, Amara realized that something was terribly wrong. Even as she came to this conclusion, Grim bared his teeth, and bolted for the bushes. He had become a wild thing, and Amara lost her grip on him. She ran after him into the woods.

She was shaking when she re-entered the house alone. Grim hadn't come back. Daniel hadn't come home. Sampson was nowhere to be seen, and Solomon whimpered from his hiding place beneath the sofa. Amara felt like she was walking sideways when she heard the song, and no one had to tell her that it was Caroline's voice doing it justice. Amara choked on her tears when she noted the silence in the house. The clocks had stopped ticking. They all read 12:10. Someone came in the door unannounced, and Amara shrieked as she reached for her gun. It was Ian and he looked deranged.

"What's wrong, Ian?" she asked, as she backed carefully away from him. Linda's husband had been acting strange of late. She had been aware of it that day she came back, and everyone was gathered at the farmhouse. She shouldered the shotgun as she regained her poise. With her feet braced, she drew back the hammer. Ian's breath hissed between his teeth. And Amara warned him not to move.

CHAPTER THIRTY-FIVE

*D*aniel was halfway to Yountsville when his engine started smoking. He managed to pull off the highway, and get safely to the side of the road, despite the fact that the pavement was as slick as the engine was shot. He was worried about Amara. He had attempted another call before setting out, but her line was dead. The weather was rocky. It was already icy, and they were predicting snow storms later today. Now, as he studied the engine, he suspected foul play. He could hoof it, but Amara's farm was a good three miles down the road.

He had set out on foot when he heard a police siren directly behind him. He turned and saw a county cop car pull up behind his vehicle. "Oh, for the love of God," he mumbled to himself.

"What's up?" Grant called in an antagonistic tone, "Need a lift?"

"Yeah, my car's down," he answered, but resented the time wasted, "Look for yourself," he walked the few feet back to the abandoned Rambler.

"Looks like you got an enemy," Grant scoffed. "That engine's been tampered with."

"I know," Daniel didn't waste another second, "Look, Amara's home alone. I tried to call, and her line's dead. I'm worried."

"Hop in," Grant's tomfoolery ceased. He instantly dropped the attitude when he realized how concerned the other man truly was. A car pulled out in front of them as they approached the Yountsville Bridge. Grant's vehicle swerved narrowly escaping a head-on collision, causing his temper to escalate. He jumped out of the car, and confronted the other driver. It was Ian. And he looked like a wild man! He was babbling something about being on the wrong end of a shotgun. He climbed from behind the wheel, hands in the air. His clothing was disheveled, and he looked somewhat demented. Daniel shook his head; he had never seen him like this before. Ian was generally a pretty level-headed kind of guy.

Amara found the phone lying on its side. The door to her old room was ajar. It was cold inside. She hadn't even removed her jacket, and she felt the drop in temperature. The wind howled, and the broken glass in the window rattled. Had Ian done this? She didn't think so; he had entered through the front door. Then who, she wondered? She stepped cautiously over the threshold, still holding the shotgun. The room was empty, but there was a surrealistic quality about it. The little ones hadn't come out of hiding, and Grim still wasn't home. The house was dark. The electricity had obviously been cut.

She kept a flashlight by the bed. She had several located at strategic points throughout the house. As her eyes adjusted, she realized she would abandon the light immediately in favor of the gun. Amara had a pragmatic mind. She cast a look about the room, knowing without a doubt, that she wasn't alone. It was then she saw the skid marks, like something had been dragged across the floor. When she looked more closely, she could see streaks of blood on the soaked carpet. Whoever was in here was hiding, and probably injured. Her gaze flew back to the window. If someone climbed in that way, they would have been cut on all that jagged glass. She thought she saw a scrap of fabric on one of the broken shards. She didn't allow her gaze to linger. Her lingerie drawer was standing open, and her personal garments were scattered across the floor. The obscenity of the sight made her skin crawl.

She heard a shuffling sound like someone moving in a repetitious fashion. It came from inside the closet! *You've got the gun,* she told herself. She angled the flashlight at the closet door, wishing she had her handgun. Instead, she laid the flashlight on its side, and positioned the shotgun. Slowly, she turned the doorknob, and the door creaked open. There was a figure huddled on the floor of the closet. Amara braced herself as she blinked in surprise. As she drew the hammer for the second time that night, she heard a ragged sob, and the man looked straight at her, his expression vacant. "Simon!" she gasped his name aloud, and her eyes widened at the scene before her. There were nude photographs of her all over the surrounding floor. His pants were unfastened, his member exposed. He held a pair of her panties to his nose, causing his breathing to escape in a labored manner. He made unnatural grunting noises, and she understood she had interrupted him during ejaculation. Amara was both repelled, and alarmed. Anyone who would do this would do anything. She held the gun trained on his chest in a moment of indecision.

"Amara, Amara! Where are you?" It was Daniel. He

had come home! His strong voice reverberated throughout the house. It was a voice she loved, and Amara had never been as grateful in her life as she was in that moment. Daniel would know what to do. She stayed put, but responded in kind.

"I'm here! In my room," she called, never taking her eyes off her captive. "I need help!"

So it was, on New Year's of 1971, Amara's house was once again a crime scene. Grant had his men on the job in no time. Simon was arrested, and hauled off to jail. The electrical company was brought in to repair the wires. And Ian said he would like to stay and help, but that he had to get back to Linda. "Why did you come here?" Amara pinned him to the spot with her direct line of questioning.

"I was worried about Linda," he said without pause, "I was hoping you could help."

"Help how?"

Before he could answer, the lights came back on, and the telephone rang. "Ian? It's the hospital," Daniel said urgently. "Linda's been admitted. Cynthia is with her."

"I'm on my way," Ian called over his shoulder.

"Daniel, I've got to go to her," Amara's face had paled. She caught up with Ian, leaving Daniel to deal with the situation at the house. As she climbed into the passenger side of his car, it never occurred to her that she had pointed a shotgun at him only a short while ago.

Daniel was on edge. After the officer read Simon his rights, and took him away in cuffs, Daniel remained troubled. Oh, he knew Simon was a sick son of a bitch. That much was clear. But somehow, this was not enough to relieve his mind. Something was *wrong*. Whatever was going on here, there was more to it than a psychotic college professor who had the hots for his girl. So *what* was he missing? As soon as the police were finished, Daniel took Amara's car and drove into town. He didn't know Ian had taken a different route.

Meanwhile, Ian had started out for the highway. He noted the number of police, and other emergency vehicles, and immediately turned off on the old Country Club Road. Amara scarcely noticed the change in direction. She wasn't feeling well. She recognized that her worlds were shifting when things began to get fuzzy. She heard the song in the background, and knew a moment's panic. Ian wouldn't know what was happening! He had never experienced any of her shifts.

Amara attempted to speak, but Ian was distracted. She moaned, and he pulled over to the side of the road, and got out of the car. There was a loud popping sound, and Amara disappeared into the past.

"Yountsville," Caroline cried, "We made it!"

Awinita grinned, "We sure did," she said in agreement as the women dismounted to stand and stare at their new beginning. It had never occurred to any of them that things wouldn't work out. They had no room for pessimism, and had kept one foot forward the entire way. Now, they exchanged

nervous glances. It was such a small town! Somehow, the women had expected more. Awinita saw their uncertainty, and was quick to reassure them, "We'll like it here," she said with ease, "You'll see. There will be plenty of jobs, and rooms at the Inn, and most importantly, we are among friends."

"Yes, that's right," Caroline chimed, "We have ourselves a new beginning!"

Mary Ann smiled a broad smile, and lifted her canteen, "To new beginnings!" She took a sip, and passed it to the next person.

Ellen followed suit, "To new beginnings!"

No one noticed when Awinita tossed an anxious glance over her shoulder.

Awinita stood by the river bank enjoying a brief respite. She was deeply troubled, but that was her secret for the time being. She could hear Caroline and the others laughing and chatting as they shared the noonday meal. They had not only managed to secure positions for all of the women among the multiple mills of Yountsville, but the four of them had managed to stick together. They were fortunate to have been able to land jobs in the main mill as well as to rent rooms in the nearby Inn. The mill was clean as far as mills went, and the boss was fair. They received regular breaks, and were treated reasonably well. It was a huge boon to be among friends, and such close friends at that. It made all the difference in the world when it came to living in a foreign place.

The rooms at the Inn were exceptionally nice. They were sparsely furnished, but had all the basic comforts of home, especially to women who had lived on the road for an extended period of time. A few of the women had suitors from the first. They giggled among themselves, happy to be so lucky. Life at Yountsville was just as Awinita had promised. It was a new start filled with hopes and dreams. It was almost more than they could have asked for.

Mary Ann darted briefly outdoors and handed Awinita a kerchief full of bread and cheese. Ellen's contagious laughter spilled out the apertures of the mill. She stayed out of the elements, watching as Awinita flashed a conciliatory smile, and Caroline watched through veiled lids. Awinita knew that Caroline was on to her. She had a suspicious nature, and knew her more intimately than the others. The two of them had lived together before they had been charged with treason after all. And though the charge had been dropped, Awinita never relaxed her guard.

Awinita caught the silent inquiry, but chose to ignore it for the time being. She was hoping she was mistaken. But ever since that haze between worlds where she and Amara merged, she had gained new insight. Amara was a part of her now, and she was fully aware of it. She needed her help just as she knew that he was coming. She finished her meal, shook out her skirts, and walked back indoors. Awinita cherished the woods. She loved this riverbank like no other because it brought a new freedom. She would face the dark one when the time came. For now, she would live in the moment. But before this was over, she and her aspect would confront evil in order to alter time. Everything was riding on their success.

He had discovered her whereabouts. He knew exactly where she was, and where her friends were hiding. She had been running from him her entire life. His men, those few who were away from camp that fateful day, wanted those women. They had been thwarted, and intended to get even. And he, Trapper, wanted her. The fact that he was her biological father didn't alter a thing. She would pay for her betrayal. Awinita's torment included the actuality that she was privy to every detail of the bastard's thoughts.

He had watched her grow from a perfectly formed child to a stunning young woman. Even in the days when he was bedding her mother, he had craved the daughter. He would stare at her mouth, and see carnal desire where there was none. He imagined her small body spreading easily as she opened herself to him. She had developed telepathically, and was repelled by his line of thought. She was a child; she was supple with flawless skin and silken hair. It didn't matter how young she was, he never doubted that she wanted him too. He caught her scent, and grew hard. He caught glimpses of her flesh, and fondled himself. He became so fixated on her that each night as he pounded savagely away at Gola's body, he imagined it was Awinita he raped.

She shivered as she became more fully aware of his perversity. And she knew he meant to have her. The obsession grew until he began stalking her. She noticed him watching from the bushes when she was bathing, looking on with rapture when she stood nude beneath the waterfalls. He watched as her lithe young body began to mature, and the hint of breasts began to form. He noticed the initial bloom of pubic hair, and grew ever more aroused. It would be silky like the hair on her head. She saw his gaze rest there. He liked them young. And Gola had grown too old for his taste.

He found Awinita enticing. He liked to think she flicked her little pink tongue across those deliciously ripe lips in deliberate invitation. And he liked to imagine what that mouth would feel like enveloping him. He was positive she was flirting with him, and all the while, the child, Awinita was disgusted. She cringed at what his thoughts revealed.

And knew that he wondered what she would feel like when he buried himself inside her. And he honestly believed she never suspected a thing. He was a stupid beast. He was a brute, and therefore something to be feared. She was grateful when he left.

He had been away on a hunting trip, and came home to the smell of fresh fish cooking over the open flames. Gola was bending over the fire, tending their dinner while Awinita waded deeper into the waters. She was wet enough to cause her skirt to cling to the V at the apex of her thighs. The wind blew, and caused the fabric of her top to expose those tiny little points.

He groaned audibly when she sent her spear straight through the fish she had been stalking. She raised it high in the air, and called gleefully to Gola, proud of her catch. Blood ran down her arms, and streaked the already damp dress. He imagined it was the blood of her virginity. He grew bold just thinking about it. He spared a fleeting glance at Gola, but couldn't take his gaze off young Awinita. And Awinita caught his thoughts. She looked down at her wet blouse when she realized he was there in the shadows. She bent low to avoid being ogled, and heard him smack his lips at the sight of her rounded little bottom. She felt violated when she felt his eyes on her, and shivered.

A mass of magpies screeched overhead. There were dozens of them! Awinita peeked at the sky ever so briefly as he smashed Gola's head against the rocks, releasing her body to the river. She screamed when she witnessed her mother's death, and he came after her. She broke into a run when she reached the shore. But he was faster. Her mind was numb when he took her. She could not stop screaming. He was a monster, and he had staked his claim on her. The shrieks of the magpies intensified. There was no turning back. Now she was his. It was up to her to create a new destiny. She lay on the ground and covered her face.

CHAPTER THRITY-SIX

Amara stumbled from the riverbank, and into the shelter of the woods. The snow was thick, making it difficult to see. The river rocks were slick with ice. She climbed upward to the meadow with care. She was grateful that she knew these woods like the back of her hand. She couldn't shake the images she had witnessed. Her senses were off-kilter, and her hands and feet were numb. The temperature was dropping quickly, making the predicted blizzard far worse than the news had forewarned. Her head ached, and her mouth was dry. Her stomach churned with uncertainty.

Somehow she knew *he* was out there, and that she was walking into a trap. But she only knew his identity from Awinita's world, and that gave her little to go on. She wanted to circle back around to the house, get her gun, and set up a protective barrier. She had begun to do just that when she heard a soft whimper. Her head snapped up. It was Grim! He whined a second time and her heart exploded. Grim was her best friend and constant companion. He claimed an enormous piece of her soul. She would risk anything for Grim. She caught sight of him as she crested the hill. He was tied to a tree, bound by rope so thick he would never break lose. He

was fairly hobbled with little room to move. His joints would be stiff from the cold, his movements impaired. And he had been missing all day! It was dark out now. It had been hours since he disappeared.

Though she tried to be quiet, her breath caught on a sob. She cast about for some way to free him. She was usually armed. She felt naked without a weapon. She talked to him in a whisper, and stroked his back as she cradled his head and kissed him. He returned her affection in kind. Grim had always taken her protection so seriously that wet puppy smooches were uncommon for him. But he kissed her now until tears filled her eyes. "I'll be right back," she promised as her search became frantic. She stepped on something sharp, and knew a moment of pure unadulterated joy. She had new hope as she bent and retrieved the well-honed arrowhead, and then huddling close to Grim, sawed at the heavy rope.

She was halfway through its density when she heard a nearby footfall. Her hands stilled as she swept the panorama of the meadow. Her heart skipped a beat. How could she have missed it? Was it there a minute ago? True, the snow was plentiful enough to obscure her vision, but she blinked a second and third time to convince herself that the black Chevy was real. She swiped at her eyes, unwilling to accept the inevitable. It was still there when she looked again. The driver's seat was empty making the vehicle appear abandoned, but the roof was crowned with magpies. They sat there in a cluster looking at her with beady eyes, mocking her in a vicious tone. She spared a glance at the sky, and noticed still more. She remembered Grandfather saying that magpies were their enemies. Their feathers had been found in the grill of her mother's car. And Grandfather, himself, had been attacked by them just prior to his death. She sucked in her breath when she heard another crunch on snow. It was *Muscles* standing there before the timberline. How long had she been watching her?

Muscles heard her intake of breath, and knew she had been spotted. She laughed a cruel sound, and spat a glob of yellow mucous into the pristine snow. There was something keenly familiar about *Muscles*. She was an odious creature, more male than female. She wore a dirty camouflage jacket, and a pair of snug pants of indefinable color. The sinew bulged in her legs, and her feet were encased in the same steel-toed boots as before. Her grimy, close-cropped hair was nearly covered by a flat brimmed cap that only served to make her appear more nefarious. She walked with a swagger as she approached, and she was well armed. Despite the guns and ammo, her obvious preference was a wicked looking hunting knife. Amara would have bolted, but she didn't dare leave Grim to such a fate. Instead, she stood frozen to the spot. *Muscles* paused a foot away, "Guess it's my turn now," she grinned slyly.

Amara stared mutely, her hand flexing around the arrowhead. Grim fought against the bonds that held him, barking deep in his throat. There was nothing about him that smacked of intimidation. He was in attack mode. But *Muscles* looked past them, snickered, and said, "What do you think? Is it party time?"

Amara's heart sank when she realized there was another presence directly behind her.

Awinita had been dragged from her bed, hogtied and delivered, to the banks of Rock River where the evil one awaited. His lips twisted into a cruel semblance of a smile when he perused her trussed-up form, and Awinita cringed when his nostrils flared in triumph. He licked his blubbery lips when he reached for her, allowing his spittle to drip down upon her. Trapper had spent all of eternity searching for her, and now preened before his conquest. She and her mother had escaped him a number of times, yet he had always found them. Until, of course, he had rid himself of Gola once and for all. It pleased him to credit his daughter for her elusiveness as it had become a blood sport. But those days were done. It was time to finish this thing. As Awinita sought divine intervention, she heard the obnoxious chatter from above. The black mass appeared like a thunder cloud, breaking into individual components of beaks and feathers. The magpies had come, of course. They were his source. He was one of them. And they were here to tear her apart.

Daniel had headed home to Yountsville later than planned. Amara's car had also been targeted, a possibility he had not considered. When he finally did get the Buick up and running, the hour was late. During the short time he was at the hospital, he had learned that Linda had been spotting. She hadn't told anyone except Ian that she was pregnant. And Ian had insisted on calling Amara. When her line was down, he had hopped in his Volkswagen Beetle, and rushed out to Yountsville. The couple had suffered the loss of a child a couple of years ago when Linda had an ectopic pregnancy. It not only cost them the baby, but nearly took her life as well, and Ian had sworn they would never take such a chance again. Linda was his world, and he had no intention of risking her. But Linda had never gotten over the loss. She wanted a baby.

When she started bleeding, Linda had called Cynthia who was on her doorstep in minutes. The couple was on the verge of hysteria when she arrived. While Linda was terrified of a potential miscarriage, Ian was equally traumatized by the possibility of losing his wife. He knew Amara excelled as a healer, and flew out the door when he couldn't reach her by phone. But Cynthia insisted on the emergency room. So where the hell was Ian now? And where had he taken Amara? Daniel was in a dark mood. His concern for Amara took precedence over all.

Just as he reached the juncture to the curving lane that was Amara's drive, he spied someone darting through the trees beyond. There was something familiar about the figure. Daniel hopped out of the car, and was in pursuit quickly enough when he realized it was Ian he was chasing. The man was hobbling at a fairly slow pace as though he had been injured. There was a blood-soaked rag around his head that spurred Daniel on. The slopes were icy making any form of travel difficult, but Daniel was in mint condition, and fueled by his fear for Amara. He caught up to Ian, taking him by surprise, and clipped him lightly on the jaw when the other man would have put up a struggle.

"What the holy hell...?" Ian snarled as he rubbed his jaw.

"Easy," Daniel warned, "It's me, Daniel. What have you done with Amara?"

"I don't know, man! She disappeared!" Ian shouted, and it was plain he was overwrought. "My car stalled. It was probably damaged in the accident. When I went to check it out, someone hit me from behind!"

"Have you been to the house?" Daniel shouted, giving the man a slight shake.

"Yeah, she's not there," Ian freely admitted, "No one's there."

By this time Daniel had put most of the missing pieces

together, "I'm heading to the house," he said. "I'm going after her. You need to chill."

"I'm coming with you," Ian argued, "Whoever hit me was after her. I called the hospital while I was in there, and Linda has been released. I was told Cynthia was planning to stay with her. They would kill me if I didn't help you find Amara!"

"You got that right," Daniel muttered, and the two moved in tandem to the house. The place looked deserted, and it tugged at Daniel's heart strings. He broke out every weapon he could find. "Sure you're up to it?" he asked, "I don't need anyone to slow me down."

"I won't get in the way."

Meanwhile the snow was coming down in clumps. The winds roared as Amara was forced downhill to the riverbank. She hadn't gotten a good look at the man in charge of the operation, and *Muscles* wasn't cutting her any slack. She kept poking her in the back with something sharp. Never mind that Amara's hands were bound. "Keep movin'," she ordered meanly, "It's almost time."

"Time for what?" Amara questioned more to give herself a chance to think, than for any other reason.

Muscles chortled as though she found this amusing, "Haven't you figured it out yet?" she laughed. At Amara's mute response, she jabbed her hard and continued talking, "It's very important that we remain on time," she tapped an imaginary watch, "but we're still going to have a party."

"You talk too much," the big man snarled. "Shut your

trap!"

"And what do you suppose she's gonna do about it?" *Muscles* jeered. "You promised I'd get my turn." She leaned forward, and lifting Amara's hair, slid her tongue up her neck in an obscenely intimate fashion.

"Oh, God," Amara moaned without thought. It was enough to get a ribald response from both of her captors.

"Well, aren't we picky?" *Muscles* sneered. "Don't worry. I'll make it good for you."

When they reached the bottom of the hill, Amara stumbled. The sand was frozen with clumps of snow and ice. The footing was uneven, making it hard to balance with her hands bound. She had only a light jacket as she hadn't been prepared for any extensive time outdoors. *Muscles* faced her with blade in hand. She ran her tongue across her lips, and rubbed her crotch as she eyed Amara. The big man chortled as he spurred her on, "Go for it," he said, "I love to watch."

Muscles responded with one quick slice through the thin material of Amara's jacket. She chuckled at the expression on the other's face. "Don't worry, pretty girl. I won't cut off anything that matters, not yet anyway," she promised.

Amara didn't utter a sound. She stood her ground in an attempt to gain her bearings. There were crows in the surrounding trees, and more overhead. She took comfort in their call. But she wasn't prepared when the knife sliced through her blouse and clipped her bra, leaving her exposed. "Hmm, nice breasts," *Muscles* hissed. She severed the bonds, freeing Amara for the moment. "Take it off. Take everything off," *Muscles* was getting excited, "Don't play with me, girl. Do it!"

Amara's hands shook when she removed the top lay-

ers of her clothing. "The bra too," the man asserted, and his voice sounded identical to Trapper's.

Amara chanced a look in his direction, and gasped, "Tanner? Is that you?" Trapper's face was superimposed over Tanner's, and both voices projected simultaneously. The effect was spooky.

"Surely you recognize your father, Awinita," he crooned. "I've spanned centuries for you."

Amara listened as if from a distance. Her head was spinning as she said in a hushed voice, "I'm Amara, Tanner."

"I know that," the thing laughed, and the sound was grotesque, "and I'm your daddy. Don't you recognize your own father?"

Amara was stuck in a nightmare as the pieces fell into place. Alina never spoke of her former partner because she, Amara, was the product of rape. "You?" her voice quivered, "Did my grandfather know?"

The beast with two faces laughed, and the winds picked up as the magpies advanced. The crows were growing in volume; they squawked overhead as they charged. The collision was bloody. Now was her only opportunity to run.

Amara bolted. They were on her in seconds, peeling her clothes away, tugging at her boots. Their hands were everywhere at once, pinching and groping. Tanner's tongue thrust deep into her throat, and she gagged. In the same instant *Muscles* slid a finger between her legs, quickly following with her mouth. "Not so fast," Tanner's voice was ragged. He withdrew an object from his pocket, and thrust the hot pink panties at her, "Put them on. Now!" he barked. "I've waited a good long while for this, Awinita."

Amara scooted as far from them as possible, but obediently donned the panties. "Have your fun, sis," Tanner said, and *Muscles* dropped to the ground between Amara's thighs.

Sis? Amara's thoughts whirled. This was Tanner's sister?

"You knew me as a man in another time," *Muscles* toyed with the lingerie before shoving it aside. "I was one of the gang. Your brother shouldn't have stolen my eye. It still plagues me. Now it's my turn to torture you for your part in my demise," she ground out, punctuating her words with savage fingers. In the treetops, the crows grew more vocal. Occasionally, one swooped down upon them, and Amara was certain they were calling in reinforcements.

"It's time," Tanner said, and Amara screamed. He shoved her hard into the icy depths of the creek. But Amara was uncontrollable. She didn't stop screaming until Tanner's giant hands wrapped around her slender throat, and he shoved her head beneath the water. When she came up for air, he repeated the process again and again, until he managed to position himself between her legs. His member was throbbing despite the cold, and Amara choked on a sob even as he promised he would hold her captive for all eternity. But when he would have plunged into her, the most unearthly howl split the night, and without pause a great black beast appeared out of nowhere, and hurled itself onto him. Its fangs were as deadly as its claws.

Awinita broke free of the pair that held her down in the depths of Rock River. She had heard the calling of crows and the ghostly howl that belonged to another world, and had responded in kind. She added her voice to that hideous ululation, and the girl whose animal totem was the fawn, gave birth to the energy of the banshee! Her female form rose from the water, making the shift as she did so, and she was awesome to behold as she destroyed her attackers within seconds, leaving their mutilated bodies to be found. Grim's cry had reached her across the boundaries of time.

Daniel's head snapped up at the muted cries. He was already at the riverbank, with Ian a step behind when he witnessed the attack of the beast. In that same instant, a whirring sound sped across the waters. The beast tore Tanner's throat out even as an arrow buried itself in the villain's broad back. The arrow quivered, adding mystique to the trauma at hand. *Muscles* drew her handgun and took aim, intent on the kill. The mandible of the beast gushed blood. And Daniel didn't hesitate. He shot *Muscles* dead, causing the gun to misfire, but the great beast faltered all the same. Its massive head swung in his direction, and there was recognition in its eyes. With his heart in his throat, Daniel watched the transformation from beast to dog, and was humbled when Grim staggered and lay down in the crimson snow. Daniel's eyes filled with tears as the big dog whimpered, and lowered his lids. Grim had found another way to protect Amara, he loved her that much.

Ian removed his woolen coat as he hurried to where Daniel stood in the scarlet waters. He watched while Daniel gently lifted Amara's limp body, wrapping her in the warmth of the dry garment. There was little left of the man they had known as Tanner, but when they fished him from the creek, his wristwatch had been shattered on the rocks. The time read 12:10. And though the shaft of the arrow had disintegrated before them, there was an arrowhead embedded in the dead man's body. Daniel glanced up in time to see the ghost of Awinita on the opposite shore. She lowered her bow, gave a satisfied nod, and disappeared into the mist.

EPILOGUE

The gang convened at Amara's house before she and Daniel took off for the spring powwow. Linda was lovely in the bloom of pregnancy. She was having a boy. She had decided to name him after her husband since she was extraordinarily proud of the fact that he had decided to go back to college and finish his degree. He had always dreamed of becoming an optometrist, and Linda had confided in Cynthia that she somehow knew he would excel.

"I will need a larger paycheck to support a family," Ian said amiably.

"Better get crackin'!" Cynthia suggested with a curious smile. She had just finished a tarot reading, and couldn't shake the image of Ian with a trio of toddlers! "Just a hunch," she laughed in way of explanation, as she placed the cards face up. These were an ancient deck, a set so unique she rarely handled them. The depiction of triplets on the three of pentacles was a jolt to everyone.

"I still can't shake the events that unfolded on New Year's Day," Linda commented. "You didn't see any more threats from Simon, did you?" she asked Cynthia. Linda had been confined to bed rest until recently, and was still concerned for Amara who had been uncommonly silent.

But Amara shone like the sun in her radiance of being free of her troubled past. She felt an inner peace she had not known since before her mother's death. Cynthia and Todd were planning to join them for the powwow, while Nikki and Gregory were going on a belated honeymoon, leaving Linda and Ian to take charge of the farm for a couple of days. They were looking forward to the excursion.

"No," Cynthia stated with certainty, relieved to see Amara looking so calm. "The door is closed on that one. Simon's just a creepy professor with the hots for his students," she said, "especially those who spurn him."

"Do you think he had anything to do with Mira's death?"

"No, sweetheart," Amara chimed. "He's a budding sociopath, that's for sure. He spied on Mira, and on me, but he used his telephoto lens, and his imagination to do it."

"Yeah," Nikki said in an informative voice. "In a strange way, he was a target too. It made it all the easier for Tanner who saw an opportunity to step in."

"True," Amara responded. "Simon will pay for his part in all of this, but we got the real culprit."

"What about Grant?" Linda persisted. She had disliked the sheriff ever since the racial slur he had made that day at the cemetery. Linda firmly believed comments like that were the root of all evil.

Nikki grinned, and took over for Amara, "He's okay, for a cop," she said. "He's got a thing for Amara, and couldn't stand the competition. But he's a straight arrow."

"I have something to share with all of you," Daniel prompted. He sat at Amara's side, and watched as her fingers trailed protectively down Grim's thick fur. The big dog swung his head around to face his mistress, and there was pure adoration in his gaze. He was healing nicely, and took obvious pleasure in Amara's tender care. He had been dubbed a hero, and he looked okay with that too. When Amara moved to hug him close, his mouth spread in an open smile that Amara returned wholeheartedly. Her eyes lit up when she glanced at

Daniel who said, "I'll go get it."

Everyone broke into excited conversation in the same second Sampson leaped into the wide bay window. He lay contentedly grooming his thick plume between his sprawled hind legs, like only a male cat could, while watching the adventures of Karma Coon, who had returned from the bitter winter a new mother. She had brought her entire brood home to the farm, and watched while they sampled the food Amara had put out for them. Karma was a protective mama!

Daniel returned carrying an antique picture frame, and everyone gathered around the kitchen table. Before them was a photograph of Awinita surrounded by three equally charming young women, all posing in front of the old mill. Nikki's pink lips rounded in a perfect O as she eyed the portrait. Amara was obviously one and the same as Awinita. But what amazed everyone was that Nikki's striking features matched Caroline's exactly! And it was equally apparent that Cynthia was Mary Ann, and Linda was Ellen! They were all right there! Awinita was wearing Amara's pendant, while staring directly at the camera, with one eye closed in a cocky wink. They were as tight a group then as they are now! The friends exclaimed in unison, and Solomon chose that moment to roll over and show them his tummy. It was his most recent trick, and he was proud of it. He had a nice tummy!

After their guests had gone, Daniel got down on one knee, and surprised Amara with an engagement ring. It was a fire opal that would have matched her beloved pendant to perfection. He had witnessed the sheen of tears in her liquid brown eyes when she stared at Awinita in the portrait. Yet he had refrained from commenting. Now Amara did the same. It was sweet of Daniel to propose, sweeter still to make the effort to replace her treasured stone. She sank down across from him, and met him on her knees. His strong arms closed around her, and before their lips met in a passionate kiss, she whispered the word, "Yes."

Amara had noticed that Daniel had been behaving strangely this past week, ever since he had taken a solo walk in the woods. When she had inquired, he merely said that he had been preoccupied with something a friend had done, and the matter had been dropped. Now it was time to tell her what had truly transpired. Amara was speechless when he admitted that he had met up with Crow, who was patrolling the sky above! According to Daniel, Crow swept down and dropped something at his feet. When she asked what her brother had given him, Daniel reached into his shirt pocket, and withdrew an object Amara had never expected to see again. At least not in this lifetime! It was the pendant. Daniel dangled it before her, and while Amara cried softly, he stood, and pulling her to her feet, fastened it gently around the slender column of her throat. What a magical world the Great Spirit had created!

FACTUAL ACCOUNTS

Roswell, Georgia, July of 1864, is accurately depicted. This is where some 400 mill workers were charged with treason, and forced to walk to Marietta, where they would be sent by rail, or on foot, to their destination in Indiana. These women and children were herded to Chattanooga, Nashville, and then on to Louisville, until they reached the Ohio River where they were taken across and literally dumped on the shores of New Albany, Indiana. Their crime, nothing more than making a meager living in a mill that General Sherman had believed to have been abandoned. As the Union troops blazed a trail of destruction on Roswell, the city was occupied by 36,000 troops. Soldiers were told to protect private properties, but to destroy the mills along the creek. The retreating Confederates burned the covered bridge at the Chattahoochee River, hoping to slow the advancement of Union troops. But Union troops crossed the waist deep waters at Shallow Ford. It is said that this was the first time in history that a rifle was fired successfully under water. The mill manager, a French citizen, took desperate measures to save the Ivy Woolen Mill by hoisting a French flag above the mill. This worked for two days, until the letters CSA were discovered on each piece of cloth. General Garrard then burned the mill, charging the workers with treason as he did so. In Louisville the women were held prisoner until such time as transportation could carry them across the Ohio River, some 60 feet deep, where they were deposited on Indiana soil. All newspaper accounts are factually listed, including references from the following: The New Albany Daily Ledger, Cincinnati Daily, Richmond Sentinel, Evansville Daily, and The Louisville Daily Journal.

The Floating Hospitals on the river, and all 11 hospitals mentioned in New Albany, were real. The town itself was at a loss as to how to deal with such a large number of impoverished women and children. Their loyalty was to the Union, and they were committed to aiding their cause in any way they could. General Sherman's order number 22 was offered as a solution to the problem, and entailed transporting any and all refugees from the Roswell Mills as far as 100 miles, so long as those miles were northward bound.

The female prison and Dr. Mary Walker are factual. Dr. Mary Walker won a medal of honor for her work at First Bull Run, as well as her work throughout the duration of the war, including the Battle of Atlanta. She was a prisoner of war of the Confederate forces from April 10th to August 12th, 1864. She was in service to the government of the United States, and an assistant surgeon in charge of the prisoners in Louisville, Kentucky, upon recommendation of Generals Sherman and Thomas. She was the first and only female to win a medal of honor.

The Sisters of Nazareth in Bardstown, Kentucky, found homes for many of the children who were sadly separated from their mothers. These children began new lives, never to see their families again.

The plight of the Cherokee people is historical fact. Roswell was known to the Cherokee as The Enchanted Land, just as the Chattahoochee was called the River of Painted Rock. Warsaw ran a ferry across the Chattahoochee for a time, until eventually the state of Georgia declared the Cherokee Nation illegal. Roswell's original settlers would join thousands of others on what would become known as The Trail of Tears. One of the white men who moved in was Roswell King, a former slave taskmaster from the notorious Butler Plantation on the Georgia coast. He saw prosperity in the rushing waters of Vickery Creek and formed a community. His son, Barrington King, founded a mill along the creek. By 1839, Roswell Manufacturing Company was in full swing making cotton and cotton supplies, and Roswell earned a name as one of the most important manufacturing towns in Georgia. The city grew up round the mill, and Georgia seceded from the Union in 1861.

I tried to capture the changes in New Albany from the 1860's through 1970, including such landmarks as the Pepin Mansion, an 1851 Italianate villa, and the Culbertson Mansion, a Second Empire-style mansion, built in 1867. Both are accurately depicted. The Yesterday House was open in the 1980's, but I altered that for the sake of my story. Mary was real, and she did serve dinner on samples of the china she sold from the shop in her basement. The Old Pike Inn was a tavern built in 1840, and owned by the Kreutzner family. It had a full-scale restoration returning the building to its pre-civil War appearance in the 1990's.

Yountsville, Indiana is my childhood home, and was lovingly depicted. It is, to date, an extremely special place to me. The land in 1970 was exactly as written, from the glorious falls to the surrounding woodlands, and the meadow beyond. Off the meandering stream, the pond was deep and murky to the bottom of its mysterious depths. The sacred mound rose high above Flat Rock, where the falls poured over the horseshoe-shaped walls of shale. My grandfather truthfully did find a petrified papoose in the tree tops when he purchased the land in the 1930's. I have always wondered what happened to it, as it is deserving of prayer. The original barns were painted red, but I chose to make them white on a whim. The vast gardens were realistically described, as was the farm house. The mill could be glimpsed through the trees from across the creek, and the Sleeping Place was tucked nearby. The school was scarcely more than a memory by that time, and while the church was still standing, it truly was devoid of its stained glass. I was there when the last window was removed. The little bridge that crossed the stream in the back woods was true to form, as was the large concrete arch that spanned the highway in front of the property. I never saw the original bridge with the double tunnels except in photographs, but in 1970 the concrete arch had open apertures so that passengers could look out the car windows and view the waters below. That structure was later replaced with fully enclosed walls that blocked the view of the river. All of the animals in The Calling of Crows were, or are real, and will be forever cherished. The banshee stemmed from an old family tale passed down over the generations, and as all stories go could contain a grain of truth. Or was that my imagination?

ACKNOWLEDGEMENTS

I wish to grant a special thank you to my Muse, and Great-Great Grandmother Eliza Blackerby Stroube, whose portrait hangs in a place of honor above my desk. It would seem she has gifted me in so many creative ways over the past years! The daguerreotype on the back cover was taken at a younger age.

Many Blessings and significant gratitude to my tribe; the beta readers who held my hand throughout the editing process, making it possible for me to bring you, my readers, the best work I could produce. A personal thank you goes out to each one of you: Cynthia Galloway, currently of California, Mimi Powers, Indiana, and Sheryl Starnes, Indiana. I cannot begin to express how grateful I am to these three magnificent women and their endless patience! Additional thanks and photo credits to Carla Dowell Bottorff, and her new business, Jill of all Trades, LLC, for the fabulous shot of the Yountsville Mill despite the cold Indiana weather and the freezing river waters! And a gigantic Thank You to Kelly O'Dell Stanley, Graphic Designer and Cover Artist, for sharing her creative expertise and magical touch to bring everything together in a way that only she could!

Additional thanks to Mary Buchanan for shared recipes used throughout the book, and to Alan and Barbara White, owners of the Yountsville Inn and Mill for their kindnesses, tours and assistance. And last, but not least, a loving thanks to gal pals everywhere, but especially those who inspired the roles in my story. You know who you are!

THE CALLING OF CROWS

TESTIMONIALS

"The Calling of crows is full of finite details that allow the reader to paint a vivid picture of the harrowing lives of the native women and children in 1864, and how their footsteps paved the path forward for future generations. The author allows you to travel from the past through time with historical accuracy and a paranormal twist. The need to know more will keep you reading! I felt like I knew the characters, Awinita and Amara, as their strengths infused me. This is a great read that gives history and insight to a period and people."

-Mimi Powers
SUPPLY CHAIN AND RISK SPECIALIST

"Julie Jones has written an intriguing plot of interesting, but little known factual history, along with ancient mystical events, and a murder mystery that threatens our heroine, Amara, an independent young woman living on her own on a Midwest American farm. All three themes present a world of confusion and awe for young Amara, whose strength and intelligence will surprise and delight the reader, who will undoubtedly, like myself be motivated to read more whenever possible."

-Cynthia Galloway
PROOFREADER AND EXECUTIVE DIRECTOR OF TWO NONPROFITS

"I love the way the author intertwined the lives of two very interesting girls from different centuries with such passion and enthusiasm! The history of both 1864 and 1970 was factual and well researched. I found the mythical parts of the story so thrilling that I read it in record time! It is a real page-turner!"

-Sheryl Gatliff Starnes
ELEMENTARY EDUCATION TEACHER AND PURDUE UNIVERSITY
STUDENT TEACHER SUPERVISOR

THE CALLING OF CROWS

Thank you...

for taking the journey through time with Amara in 'The Calling of Crows.' If the blend of paranormal mystery, historical twists, and the bonds that transcend centuries captivated your imagination, I would be honored if you could share your thoughts in a review!

As an independent author, every review truly is a beacon that guides fellow readers to the heart of this story. I appreciate your support in unraveling the mysteries of the past, present, and future. Thank you for being a cherished part of this literary journey!

Until next time,

Julie Jones

ABOUT THE AUTHOR
Julie Jones

Julie is an established Reiki Master-Holistic Healer, versed in both hands-on and remote work on animals as well as humans. She is a singer-songwriter for the rock band, *Remote View*, where she is one of two guitarists. Julie has worked independently in French and Antebellum antiques as well as in Photography and Design.

The Calling of Crows is her second novel, preceded by *The Plantation*, her first endeavor at historical paranormal fiction. Julie is a nature-lover, and lifelong vegetarian, who grew up in the woods and waters of Indiana.

You can connect with Julie on Facebook or visit her website, **juliejonesbookstore.com** to learn more!

Thank you for reading!